PHUL
OF
SURPRISES

PHUL OF SURPRISES

The adventures of Harvey Johnson, Book VI
(second edition)

BY

TOM ASHWELL

Copyright © 2012, 2015 by Tom Ashwell

Printed by: The Pymander Press LLC.
St. Paul Minnesota USA
Submissions and inquirers: pymander.press@gmail.com

Cover Art by: Garrett W. Vance

For
Pam "Pogo" Poggiani,
Derek Benner
AND
Traci Scroggins
You are missed at 'The Bar'.

Acknowledgments:

I can't count how many times I'd like to thank all of those who contributed to this work by suggesting a change or addition, inspiring a character, trait of a character or even offering moral support. Please forgive me if I forgot to thank someone here, as there have been so many over the years, it was difficult to keep track of everybody.

In no particular order:

Michelle "Stryder" Fisher, Dayna Thomas, Alan Groesbeck, Eric Putkonen, Mike Busha, Ken Netzel, Joan Richards, Katrina Swanson, Karen Konzak, Kim Caruefel, Dominic Ertelt, Harvey Johnson, Debbie Klose, Julie Canny, Jeffrey Nisen, René Holly, Derek Benner, Brian S. Anderson, Rachael Kloss, Susan Tellers, Cynthia Curtis, Joe Kessel, Jody Schroeder, Tabitha Tighe, Athenais Snaza, Krista Linkletter, Manish Dewan and Smudge the hacker kitty.

Table of Contents

A note from the author.

In the previous book, the final copy edit was done to make the book more readable. The idea was to reduce eyestrain and promote a better flow. The opinions of readers were mixed, but since the majority preferred the more traditional, paper-saving formatting, we have gone back to it. This is a longer book but on fewer pages. The text has been crammed together, with smaller margins and a smaller font. For those that liked the other format, I apologize. I will take the "blame" only for the higher quality paper in the previous book, as I have found that the near newsprint quality of paper in many paperbacks have deteriorated over the years to where they simply crumble when I try to turn the page. Yes, I tend to hold onto a copy of a book I like, and some of my oldest are simply falling apart. Due to multiple requests, the second edition of book V will have this format, (resulting in fewer pages) and lower quality paper to make it more affordable. I hope this makes people happy.

E-book readers should be happy that the e-book version is to be released at more or less the same time. Last time it took "too long". Additionally, I have done away with footnotes in this book to make it more like the e-book and therefore translate better. Although I am committed to putting this entire series on paper, I am not ignoring e-books. I would prefer that no matter the medium, the readers get the same experience out of it. However, there are things that don't, as yet, translate to e-book format or so I am told. One such thing is the way I sometimes do fun things with page numbers and since page numbers do not apply to e-books, the e-book readers are left out of the joke. I know I am talking about small differences, but those little additions were put there for a reason, and I think they enhance the story. Call them "in-jokes" if you like. Some even accused me of claiming that the story would fall apart without a small thing like a special page number. I never said that, but it goes to show how people can misinterpret what is right in front of them in black and white. I have no doubt that my books get misinterpreted, but that goes with the territory. Reviewers have already done that. In fact one, in particular, refused to finish reading the story because there were two kinds of emphasis on words, such as italicized and call capitol letters. One was for emphasis and then other for raised voices, but he wasn't interested. I can only imagine how he talks. Another point of contention I would like to address is that I was criticized on having the various threads beginning of the story too brief. Again, they were edited to be shorter in order to make the story a faster read. Some said I changed the "point of view" in the story over and over. Nothing is further from the truth, unless they were reading it as a script. The whole series is "fly on the ceiling" or as some call it "fly on the wall". In either case, that is the point of view and it never changes. What they were really talking about was that it changed locations, going from one thread to another as one has to when a bunch of them come together to make the fun stuff happen. Obviously, they were lacking in understanding of how a story is constructed and the proper terms to express their concerns. As my editor put it, I am "too educated to say: 'Meanwhile, back at the ranch.'" Last but not least, I was criticized for the text on the cover being pixilated. While that is true, the answer is two fold. Firstly, the text had to be applied to the photo and then blown up to be printed on the cover by the printers, causing the pixelation but it also serves the story. In the original, illustrated version, the computer displays of the Forcas were pixilated because they used low-resolution raster graphics to display things. Hence the cover lettering. The Butator displays on the other hand, were supposed to be vector graphics displays and had unlimited resolution. I look upon this 'happy little accident' as a way of preserving that idea. The images I speak of, indeed all of them, were cut from the story to save on printing costs. Yes, cost cutting was done.

While I was writing this book, a young lady at a sci-fi convention asked me if my degree helped me with my writing. I had too little time to answer her adequately, as I only had a total of five minutes for all questions and answers put top me by her group. In this rare case, I do not believe there is a short answer. A degree will certainly help someone *get* published, and if your intent is to write 'hard' science fiction then a science degree can help quite a bit there too. However, a degree alone will not guarantee you creativity enough to write. It is my belief that most higher education teaches the student limitations rather than possibilities. At least that was my experience at all three colleges I attended. That being said, I'd like to think that it is my inability to think inside the proverbial box that allows me to be creative. You know the type: The one that cannot understand the fun in playing a board game, for example. The few exceptions to the rule are the ones that get the most attention, like someone I know that has five science degrees and is so brilliant his books practically glow with it. Enough said.

The best advice I can give an aspiring writer is the advice that helped me. I was told to do one thing: Write for one person - YOU, the reader.

A 'Johnson's Journal' entry to summarize the situation for those that have not read the previous books in the series.

It has been some months now since I have been given control of this star ship, the Ezrael. The flagship of the Adityas fleet. It is an enforcement vessel of untold power and capability. We've had nothing but trouble ever since. I am taking advantage of this little respite from all the craziness that has been going on in order to keep notes. I'm not sure if I will ever review this log, but I have been reading the log of the previous captain, Callicrates Plantagenet, and it has been very helpful and enlightening.

My story in a nutshell:

I have been privy to a lot of weirdness in my life. At a young age, my father disappeared, and it was thought he was abducted by aliens. Because of that, I studies science a logic all of my life in hopes of finding out. In college, I got hired as a consultant to the government's most secret agency and I can't even make notes to myself about what happened there, but this one takes the cake! A radio signal came from deep space, and I was the only one that managed to discern the meaning. The signal was trying to tell us to look at the south pole. An expedition was launched and they found something BIG. I was sent there to join some scientists to investigate and it turned out to be a star ship of unspeakable power, but before we could study it a madman showed up from "Black Ops" with a platoon of crack troops, and tried to take the project over. He murdered Bob, my long time boss and friend and caused the ice cave to collapse and the soldiers to switch sides. Forced into the star ship we were separated from everyone else, and there was no sign of the madman Dr. Cornelius Morax. Once we located the bridge and gained some knowledge of the systems, the Major, the commander of the troops, known as S*I*P*Es launched the ship in such a way as to cause the planet to wobble and collapse the magnetic field. The result was a devastated world. We managed to find a walking-talking owner's manual in the form of an android named Pymander who, although helpful, seems to be holding back certain information as if we cannot handle it. He got us to take the ship to the center of the galaxy where I met the emperor of the largest galactic empire, that is being eroded away at the edges by less than benevolent forces. The job I was chosen for seems to be to thwart those forces and restore peace and order, while I try to find some missing ship from the original colonizing fleet that left the mother world in the distant past. He claims we need to find a planet called Earth. I tried to tell him that is where we are from, but he insists our planet is called Urantia, and that many planets call themselves Earth. He wants us to find the original one. In return, the emperor has promised to return my planet to pre-disaster status, as if nothing had ever happened. This is of little comfort as people are suffering back home. Knowledge seems to come from little pills. One kind is temporary, used for visiting a world. They include the language and culture as well as immunity factors to keep us from getting ill. The other kind, impart permanent knowledge. The ones containing all the information I am missing, seem to have disappeared off the ship, and I am stuck with asking the android and the Butator a lot of questions. One man, a janitor, found and took the pills that made him the ship's doctor or Azubuga, which is apparently a doctor with all medical knowledge. He thought they were vitamins, and now I suspect he is regretting the sudden importance he is experiencing. It is true, he can fix anything and I do mean *anything*. Mind you, we brought a doctor with us, a xenobiologist, and they argue like cats and dogs. Still, it makes visits to the infirmary a real treat. Also, some of us, well Linda and myself so far, are protected by a molecule-thick form of body armor, which has a lot of capabilities, and has saved my life many times already. It seems to only work with people who think in 'brain language' rather than words. People that have a running narrative in their heads, cannot use it. This excludes most of the crew sadly, as they do not have 'quiet minds'. Much of the ship is operated by telepathic means, and with a lack of a more conventional owner's manul, we have to ask the android and the Butator a lot of questions.

Along the way, we managed to revive a nine-foot tall harry monster with six inch fangs from some kind of cryogenic chamber, who turns out to be nice but not very bright, and silicon based life of all things!

His name is Mongo, and it suits him. Three more were added to the crew: A genetically engineered angle, (for want of a better term) named Gladrina Urim of the planet Thummim, who has an astonishing array of mental and physical abilities that I cannot even guess at, including the ability to clone herself - which happened, by accident of course! Now we have two of them, only Aniyel, as Gladrina named her, does not have wings - at least for now. Last but not least, a famed scientist from the planet Alberion, Raphael Elroy Mergatroid, (going by 'Elroy' to avoid recognition) that looks like he is from the village of the damned. We rescued him from a rioting group of environmentalists that were bent on killing all scientists on his world. We rescued him so that he might repair our android, since it was shot in the head. Funny thing though, most of the aliens we encounter are as human as I am, but many have some sort of immortality. We have managed to make enemies of at least one star empire and I really don't want any more trouble. The android has told me now that we are not working for the galactic emperor but some energy being that claims to be the creator and has us actually thwarting someone know only as the adversary. To make matters worse, when said energy being, name of Joth Malkuth Parzupheim of Aziluth, or just 'Joth' for short, gives me my assignments, it is done in a special room where a spokesman for Joth takes over the android in an form of technological 'possession'. That entity's name is Metatron, which sounds familiar to me. The ship turns out to be organic, yet it does not look like it at all. It has several very advanced systems including a brain in a box known as a 'Butator'. The adversary's forces have a similar system called a 'Forcas'. I am told it is just that a Butator is benevolent and a Forcas is malevolent, as are the forces that use them. I can't argue with that because so far in my travels, we have fried a world by pulsing its star, freed another world from mass suicide, stopped a world war, blown-up a planet that was full of the worst people I can imagine, and sent yet another, civilized, population to paradise (hopefully) and even got to see human souls being hunted and devoured by a servant of the mysterious adversary. After all that, my head is spinning.

I was told I have the power and authority to do whatever I want, and I haven't a clue as to what to do with it. And if that were not enough, everyone looks to *me* for the answers.

Survivors of the original expedition include some 30 scientists, technicians, medical and support staff and a full platoon of S*I*P*Es.

Apparently, after a captain retires, he is replaced with another, that is chosen for certain character traits. They keep telling me I am such a man, but I am full of doubts. They call me Simkiel, which the language banks tell me means 'Chosen one' I really don't want to be caught-up in a far eastern kung-fu movie. But there you are.

I am very glad that things have now slowed down to a crawl. I think everybody needed to catch their breath and their bearings. But now, it seems that we are getting edgy with near boredom approaching. But do we dare make a move of any kind? Every time we have done so in the past, we have wound up in one emergency situation after another. Perhaps that *would* be better... oh, and I still can't find any orange juice.

PHUL OF SURPRISES
By
Tom Ashwell

1
GIRK
"There's one born *every minute!*"

Somewhere in the Antarctic ocean...

Wet, WET, *WET!* All there was here, was water. The little robotic
probe was waterproof to be sure, but it wasn't used to so much water.
First the gravity had increased greatly, then there was a period of micro-
gravity when it had to grab hold of the glacier to avoid flying off into
the air, followed by another, measurably smaller, burst of intense
gravity. Now, to make matters worse, the gravity seemed to be in flux.
This did not make sense. Attempts to contact the main computer were
sporadic at best, and all it could tell the poor little robot to do was to
wait. Wait? Again! No way!
Waiting seemed to be in opposition to it's self-preservation protocol,
as it was beginning to sink. So it began to displace water below it with
a sweeping motion of it's articulated wheels. In effect, it began doing
the breast-stroke. We'll see who sinks and who doesn't.
What it didn't know was that it was still on a chunk of glacier turned
iceberg, swimming in circles around a pool of water - getting nowhere
fast - as the whole thing pitched in the rough Antarctic seas. The
iceberg was headed north, and was beginning to melt.
What happened earlier, was that it had been the unlucky probe that
found a large, spherical space ship buried in the Antarctic ice. Once the
central computer had been informed of this, it called in the gods. Those
wonderfully unpredictable gods! The little probe had been personally
made by one of them and that made it feel special. It was called
"Prototype" - the first word it had ever heard - by it's creator. Indeed,
special care had been taking in it's construction and that is why the little
robotic probe had survived this long; it had instincts, and the one of the
strongest ones it had was for survival. If it ever got to meet it's creator
again, it planned on thanking him.

What the robotic probe hadn't expected was the gods launching the ship by generating a magnetic pulse in opposition to the planet's magnetic field, causing it to collapse and knock the planet's axis off kilter and making the oceans slosh over the land masses. Not a pretty sight. The glacier the robotic probe was on, was broken up and cast into the ocean. However, when it came to this little predicament, the robotic probe was not alone. There were a few people, two men and two women in fact, on a scientific installation that was not far from ground zero, and they were floating out on the ocean as well, inside what was left of an Antarctic research station.

* * *

Not quite on the far side of the galaxy from Earth, on the bridge of the Ezrael...

"I just had a thought." said Harvey.

"Did it hurt?" asked Lt. Argent.

"Funny guy! You S*I*P*Es have a Corporal, a Lieutenant, and a Major. I was wondering why you don't have any more, uh 'brass'."

"That's easy, the Major left the captain behind on the outpost, and Dr. Morax killed Sgt. Moloch as an example, just before we entered the ice cave, according to the men that witnessed it."

"Oh *my!*"

"That's okay, the Sargent was almost as evil as Morax. The two women, one S*I*P*E and one scientist were left behind at the research station."

"You mean..."

"Yes, back on Antarctica."

"Whoa boy!"

"You said it."

"I've been wondering, how guys like you S*I*P*Es starting working for a jerk like Dr. Morax."

"Well, we're just a special unit that just gets assignments like that, you know."

"Yeah, but the likes of *Morax?*"

"Hey, we didn't know what to expect either. He told us you were a

bunch of radical scientists. There was some sniggering on the way here,
I can tell you."

"I don't know if I like that." said Harvey, wondering what was
wrong with the concept of radical scientists...

"Well, you have to admit, that radical Professors just don't merit
calling in a unit like ours."

"And why *not?*"

"No disrespect intended, but it's not like you were going to shoot at
us or something! Brainiacs are known for their rational acts, not their
irrational acts. Besides, I figured it was a smokescreen and they'd tell us
what was really going down, once we got there."

"What about when Morax shot Bob?"

"That's when we knew this guy more than earned his reputation."

"The Major didn't seem to switch sides too readily."

"He's a tough one to figure. The 'by the book' type more or less.
Just when you think he's more about shooting first and not asking
questions at all, he does something fantastically cool."

"I'll say. Like he did on Loam."

Loam was a planet that was committing suicide over the propaganda
in a book: 'Loam in the Lurch' in which it makes the case that carbon
dioxide was destroying their planet.

"Yeah, just like that. A soldier is to follow orders as long as they
are *legal.* What Dr. Morax did to Bob was just plain murder. I mean,
the guy had legal authorization to take over, and I now know we were
there just to make for a smooth transition and to defend against any little
green men if you got into the ship. What bothers me, is that the Major
could even *think* about turning a blind eye to what Morax was doing."

"Do you think that may be the cause of your nightmares? Your
conscience?"

"Doc told ya, did he?"

"Well, when my main helmsman and "all round right-hand man" has
nightmares that keep him from getting enough sleep, I get concerned."

"Sorry. Can't help it."

"Why'd you go to the Xenobiologist about this and not the Azbuga?"

"The Xeno is from Earth, I mean Urantia, and, well, that Azbuga
guy is a janitor, you know? I don't know if I can trust my heath and well

3

being to a guy that was here just to mop the floors. It'll take me a while, because I don't care if he did take those pills."

"Understood. But have you talked to anyone else about those bad dreams?"

"No. As you know, I'm not afraid to die, but in my nightmare I die in cave or tunnel somewhere, and I'm terrified. It seems so real you know? It's like I can feel the big-ass rock crushing my chest and I can't breathe. It's as if I'm getting squashed like a bug, only in slow motion."

The Lt. thought better of telling him that his last vision in the dream was Linda crying over him. He knew that Harvey was in love with her and was a tad jealous of his friendship with the lady scientist. Harvey had nothing to worry about, but the Lt. didn't want to open that can of worms if he could possibly avoid it. Besides, she had a decade on him at least, as did Harvey. They were not his generation. Dating Linda would almost be like dating his mother, aunt or worse yet, his older sister.

"I think we've all had dreams like that at one time or another." said Harvey, thinking of his own prophetic dreams. Then he began to worry.

"Yeah, you're right. Doc gave me some pills, and they have stopped."

"Good. No more nightmares."

"No dreams at all."

"That...can't be healthy."

"That's what he said. It's only temporary, and soon I'll have to stop taking them."

There was an awkward moment of silence.

"So, what do you think things are like back home?" asked the Lt. in an attempt to change the subject.

"I try not to think about it. All that devastation from launching the ship. I mean, who knew that it would cause tidal waves across every continent?"

"Yeah, but the Major is the one that did it."

"But, like I said, nobody knew that would happen."

"*You* seemed to. As I recall, *you* wanted us to hold off."

"I was merely being cautions."

"Turns out you were right."

4

"Yeah, well, it was just luck. I tend to be cautious whenever I don't know what I am doing. The only time I dash headlong into trouble is when I know exactly what I am doing."

"I'll remember that."

"Yes, I expect you will."

They both had a chuckle.

"I'm going to check on the research being done in the folklore lab." said Harvey, his voice trailing off as he thought about the plight of the people they had left behind on Antarctica.

Argent just nodded, glad that Harvey was leaving. He felt embarrassed that at his age, he had been having nightmares, and they had disturbed him. That was not a way for a good soldier to be. But there was another problem hanging over his head and he was determined to take that secret to the grave.

* * *

On the arctic ocean, there was another large chunk of glacier that was supporting a surprisingly intact research complex.

Benjamin Schmidt A.K.A. "Schmitty"Albert Stark A.K.A. "Stork", Captain Belinda Bothwell and Marjorie McCormick were all playing poker.

"How about you *Boff*-well?" asked Stork.

"Call me that again and *you'll* be the main course for dinner!" she snapped.

"Are you ladies sure you don't want to play *strip* poker?" asked Stork, undeterred. He glanced over at Schmitty and whispered "She *wants* me."

Marjorie scoffed and Belinda, having had quite enough from him pointed her pistol at the human slug, and pulled back the hammer with her thumb, causing him to wipe the smile off his face and swallow hard. They were playing for granola bars and MREs, nothing more. Captain Bothwell had a losing hand and she knew it. She didn't know what would be worse - letting that lard ball see her in her skivvies or her seeing *him* disrobe. Both thoughts made her shudder.

What she didn't know was that Stork was good at stacking the deck.

5

He thought he might have faired better by giving her winning hands before he asked that question, but he couldn't help himself...they were playing for *food!*

* * *

Linda was in her bathroom, brushing her hair in front of the mirror, when she noticed one of her hairs had come out with the brush, but that wasn't unusual, of course. What was unusual was that the hair was part golden blonde and part grey.

She sighed and said to herself. "Father time catching up..." she stopped as she noticed that the colored end had a follicle on it. "What the?" she looked at it closely, and sure enough it was as if that strand of hair had gone from grey to blonde.

Quickly, she went over to her desk and looked at the transition point under her microscope. There was a definite, abrupt change from grey to golden blonde near the follicle. She rumpled her brow and turned to her bathroom mirror, looking along her scalp, and sure enough, there was a line of color close to the scalp where some of her individual hairs had been turning grey. She smiled slyly. Next, having formed a theory, she looked at her left ankle for the scar that had been there since childhood. It *was* still there, but noticeably reduced in appearance. The *lump* was gone! She didn't know for sure what was happening, but she liked it. She was going to have to get to the bottom of this! But not *too* soon...she smiled to herself. This was something she really liked.

* * *

Harvey was looking over the shoulder of the head researcher. They were in the room they'd set up as the linguistics and folklore lab, hoping for some progress in their search for the original Earth.

"Are you sure there isn't *something* we can use? Any kind of lead?" he asked anxiously.

"We're doing the best that we can sir." came the dry reply. "These Butator terminals are fantastic and they supply lots of information about so many worlds, it's just sifting through it all takes a while. It's almost as though it were purposely trying to keep us from finding what we need."

"What about the Demiurge system? Doesn't that have every star, planet and rock listed?"

"Yes, but you've got to know what it's called or where it is. You can't just ask for the planet we're looking, for without more to go on."

"Ah. that *would* be too easy."

The researcher hoped that Harvey would stop hovering and just leave him alone to do his job. This looking over the shoulder business and asking the same questions over and over again was a distraction and was actually slowing progress. Well, there wasn't any to speak of, but he thought that there might be if Harvey would just leave them to it. He had a small team but they were research scientists after all, and they knew their jobs well. It's not as if they weren't *motivated* after all!

As if sensing the tension, Harvey patted the man on his shoulder and said "I know what you mean. Alright, I'll leave you alone now. I'm sorry if I've been a little too pushy. Relax, and the answers will come."

"That's quite all right sir, I understand." 'That was *spooky*, but at least he's leaving'. he thought to himself. He could understand the captain's Anxiety. After all the sooner they solved this age-old puzzle, the sooner things would be put to rights back home. Though the Butator system was usually forthcoming with information, on this particular subject, it was not. It was almost as if it wanted to hinder the search, but the real reason was that the subtlety of the clues were beyond it - being a 'copy' of the mind of an alien - an Angel, if you will. Only a human mind could intuitively find and follow the clues, by design. Too bad they didn't have a human brain in a box instead.

Harvey returned to the bridge with the hope that something would happen there. The research was taking longer than he liked. Still, this little respite had given the whole crew time to settle-in with the ship. Now that everyone seemed comfortable with the way things worked, he had the sneaking suspicion that things were about to get immensely busy, and would not slow down for some time afterward. Good thing too, he was feeling a bit superfluous with no crisis to overcome. He couldn't believe he *missed having* emergencies!

It had been weeks since the Keel, a truly civilized race of telepaths, had gone and the euphoria from meeting them had long since worn off. Now they were getting a little stir crazy. If they didn't get some relief soon, most of the crew might just explode.

He arrived on a quiet bridge, with a few people milling about, taking the odd stab or look at the equipment panels as if they were bored. Once things got hopping again, he feared that they might look back fondly at this 'bout with boredom'. What he had failed to realize is that Humans tend to get upset when things slow down too much, rather than when things move rapidly. Just look at the reactions of drivers in 'rush hour' traffic and the corresponding 'road rage' if you want an example!

He approached the multidimensional display which was showing the galaxy slowly turning and forming majestic spirals. This of course was a rendition of billions of years compressed into a few minutes, and set to loop over and over again making the impressive display. Seeing what only an eternal being could see over a staggeringly long span of time; and from a vantage point that must be several tens of thousands of light years into the intergalactic void, made them all feel privileged. The majestic yet delicate ballet of all those stars, swirling together held in association by invisible threads of gravity was ever so fascinating. Seeing it sped up like this gave him a new understanding of the interactions of heavenly bodies. He never tired of it, so he had set it as a sort of 'screen saver' for the unit.

Out of curiosity or possibly something else, he decided to follow the lead of the crew by fiddling with some of the controls. Over the short time they had been on the ship, he had become quite adept at scanning the immediate area for small objects. He looked around for an asteroid, or other small body. Instead, he found something which surprised him. It was metallic, and moving steadily towards the ship. Not at a particularly fast clip mind you, but a nice steady almost leisurely pace. He zoomed in on it to discover it to be a another craft. Relatively small in comparison to the Ezrael, at approximately nine hundred thousand tons. He zoomed-in to the front of it and found a window. Closing in even more, he saw a man sitting at the controls. It was surprising that this man was not taking such a long voyage on autopilot. They were in the interstellar void after all and only interstellar class ships were capable of reaching this area. The ship was not going fast enough for interstellar flight and there was nothing of interest in the immediate area, with the exception of the Ezrael.

With that thought, the communications display lit up. A call was coming in. It was the pilot of the approaching vessel...

"Hello? Is anybody home?" the male voice asked in a somewhat whimsical tone.

This alerted everyone on the bridge. Something was happening! There was a scramble, but Harvey answered the call. A holographic representation of the man's head and shoulders appeared in mid-air over the 3-D display. It was a nice-looking man with long 'salt and pepper' hair.

He looked at Harvey and smiled warmly. "*There* you are!"

There was an exchange of looks on the Ezrael's bridge. Did the captain *know* this man?

"May I come aboard for a visit?" he asked almost excitedly.

"Who are you?" asked Harvey.

"Mivon MaGirkon is the name, Captain of the Baskabas. Most people call me 'Girk' for short."

Harvey glanced at his Butator screen:

Mivon MaGirkon: Captain of the Baskabas.
Benevolent trader with many resources. Often stocks items that are hard to come by.
Known far and wide as a source of material and information. Friend and ally to all mankind.
Trustworthy in any and *all* endeavors.

There was more detailed information on the screen but that much was good enough for Harvey for now.

"You may come aboard. Frankly, we'd welcome a visitor."

"Great! Running into you was just what I needed too! Perhaps we can make a trade!"

The hologram vanished.

The Major approached Harvey. "I don't like it. I suggest that he be placed under guard while he's onboard."

"It's always prudent to be careful, my friend, but this man is our guest. Do you think you can just have your men watch him closely, rather than follow him around like a pair of bookends?"

He was trying his best to cater to the Major's paranoia, and frankly he shared some of it. Still not 100% certain of the Butator information, he thought it might not be a bad idea to err on the side of caution; but if he could get the Major's men to be subtle about it, so much the better. 'Butator', what a funny name for a ship's computer system. Still, it was named for the genius that made it, and it was much more than a mere computer. It was a copy of his very mind and brain.

"You mean, *covertly?*" he asked with a slightly excited tone to his voice and a twinkle in his eye.

"That'll do." Harvey answered, glad that a satisfactory middle ground had been found, and so quickly at that!

"Very good, and may I suggest that you at least take Cpl. Swanson and Lt. Argent with you down to the shuttle bay? They are the best hand-to-hand men I have - should there be any trouble."

"As long as they're not carrying bazookas, that'll do. I don't want to make our visitor unduly nervous."

The Major nodded, and visibly caught himself - they didn't *have* any bazookas...they had a few M72 LAW rockets and a few FIM-92 Stinger missiles but no bazookas...

* * *

Girk's ship was guided to the area on the ship that had been dubbed 'the equator'. So named because it corresponded to the same area as it would have been on a planet. The equator contained doors that spanned the entire circumference of the ship, which served as a docking bay. It was so vast that it had several decks to it, that could easily accommodate the Baskabas.

The massive hanger that lay behind the opening was practically full of ships and shuttles of almost every possible description. Harvey and the Lt. had spent a week going over them and still didn't so much as glance at all of them. Nonetheless, there seemed to be a sufficient 'parking spots' left so deciding on a bay for Girk to dock at was not a difficult choice even though the Baskabas was a fairly sizeable ship in

10

it's own right. It was like a very large tanker or even an aircraft carrier from back home. In fact, it could conceivably hold a large number of passengers and crew, or a considerable quantity of cargo. This made Harvey wonder if it was a cargo ship or a pleasure liner, or perhaps something else.

After Girk disembarked, he smiled as the sequence of decontamination waves: standing waves of ultrasound at the resonant frequency of pathogens - to shatter them - passed over his body. These guys were not taking any chances! Then he walked right up to Harvey who was there waiting to meet him.

"Fine ship you have here." stated Girk as he looked around the bay, and saw the size of the it and noticed that there were enough of the right kinds of vessels aboard to make an invasion of any system quite simple; provided, of course, you had adequate pilots and troops. This made him raise an eyebrow. He happened to be on the same deck as the military vessels. Harvey and crew had no clue as to what the various crafts were for, so this little detail was unintentional. They might as well have placed the Baskabas on the 'go cart' deck for all they known. This deck just happened to have a large percentage of vessels in the same size range as the Baskabas and they thought it was appropriate to dock it there.

"You seem well stocked on other ships as well." he said indicating a nearby planetary attack vessel, somewhat comparable in appearance to one of one of our B-2's.

"We don't have any other visitors onboard if that's what you mean."

"Indeed. So you mean to tell me you have all these ships and nobody to pilot them?" he asked.

"Well, uh, something like that, I guess; though, we do have a *small* crew."

"In any event, it's quite the collection." he replied dryly. "What flash!"

Indeed, this was just the sort of collection a trillionaire might have if he were in space much; like the inevitable collection of expensive cars a proportionally wealthy individual might have on Earth. Some classic, some brand new. All beautiful and much sought-after.

He gave one more lingering look of admiration at a few of the more sleek-looking craft within sight then said: "Now if you don't mind I'd like to talk to you about a trade."

"Yes, you mentioned that earlier. So what kind of trade do you propose?" asked Harvey, as they began to slowly walk away from Girk's ship. "Surely you don't want..." asked Harvey as he indicated one of the military ships.

"No, no, don't worry. I won't ask you to part with any of your fine collection. I have no need for such things, though they are real beauties! You have *something else* I need; and I have something you need. I am talking about a swap, trade or equitable bargain. You know, *commerce.*"

Girk was a bit of a 'fast talker' sometimes, vaguely reminiscent of a used car salesman, but there was something in his eyes that said he knew a lot more than he was letting on. Harvey had noticed that many people he had dealt with lately; including Pymander and Metatron - though they were largely the same person - yet another mystery to be resolved; knew far more than they let on; and he didn't like not being in on things. It was like being deceived as far as he was concerned. Or was it something *else?*

"I see, and what is it that we have, that you need?" Harvey was starting to get a little puzzled.

"Fuel. Frankly, I'm almost out and I need to get to the citadel, probably gotta make a pickup or something, and I'm uh, running on *fumes.*" He looked at Harvey with a playful 'innocent' look, then continued. "I knew I should have put more than five bucks worth in!"

This struck Harvey as one of the funniest things he had heard in a long while, and he laughed heartily until a few tears trickled down his cheeks. Girk was quite amused too, but waited for Harvey to laugh before he laughed too. They became friends almost at once. There was something very likable about this whimsical man, and he would have a positive and lasting effect on the rest of the crew as well. Well...*almost* everybody.

"What kind of fuel does your ship require?" asked Harvey, not knowing if he could help, and wiping a tear from his cheek.

"It'll run on almost anything; deuterium, tritium, Helium-3...but I'm willing to bet that a ship this size runs on EA. Though you probably have all kinds with a hangar deck like this, at least to keep your collection going if nothing else."

"EA?" asked Harvey puzzled. He did not have a Butator display handy to tell him what it was. He must remember to start carrying one of the portable ones! Then, just as Girk gave the answer, his armor showed him the same information in the heads-up display.

EA, stands for Encapsulated Antimatter, the ship's main form of fuel. A buckminsterfullerene filled with equivalent mass of antimatter - in perfect balance until a single molecular bond is broken.

Although he used this feature on Asbeel, a planet that had gone irretrievably wrong; the armor hadn't needed to tell him anything in a while so this would take some getting used to again. Although it was in communication with the ship's Butator, it waited for him to ask before displaying information. He had to remember to think the questions at the armor rather than ask aloud. He had instructed the armor to never interject because it had become annoying at one point.

"You know, 'Encapsulated Antimatter'. I would imagine that you need fuel with that kind of kick for something this big, if I could have an ounce or two of that stuff I might not have to refuel for some time!"

"Yes, sure, we can spare some of that. How much can your tanks hold?"

"Well, my maximum for that type of fuel is about two quarts, it's pretty hot stuff, as you well know, so a little goes a long way."

"Good. That's no problem then. So, what is it that you have to trade?" asked Harvey, who was perfectly willing to part with the fuel for the asking. Half a gallon? HA! No problem at all! He was told that the pod contained roughly forty *thousand* gallons at the moment, so who'd miss a couple of quarts? Then he wondered how much it might cost 'at the pump'. Then the armor told him: The stuff was worth more than he thought! Then again, it *did* a lot!

"In exchange, I have a lead for you." said Girk flatly.

"Beg pardon?" A lead was just what they needed at this point! But how did *he* know?

"I can help you find the next world in your search." came the answer.

13

"Whoa! Does *everybody* out there know what we are up to?"

Indeed it had often seemed that whomever they had contacted knew more about what was going on than he did. Curious...and slightly annoying at times.

"Mostly, you have been on the news a lot after all."

"Good one!" he said as he chuckled.

"No, *really*." He paused as Harvey gave him a puzzled look. "I'm serious." he added, puzzled himself that Harvey seemed to be oblivious of his own notoriety.

"We're...on...the...*news*? What news?" said Harvey rather seriously, with a hint of panic in his voice.

"Don't you guys watch *any* television?"

Harvey gave him a blank look.

"There's a galactic television network and you guys are all over the news. You're *famous*!"

Harvey's armor relayed Butator information again:

All reporters are "Karoz", transmission is inter-dimensional; in other words, the signal is sent into another dimension, where the signals go everywhere instantly. A form of "quantum tunneling" in the very fabric of space itself for want of a better explanation in terms you currently understand.

The adversary's supporters have a newspaper called "Kolazonta" or "The Chastiser" and all it does is bash the truth about people like you, much like your local paper did back home. Their news network on televison is called "The Kolazonta News Network or KNN." Anchor/founder: Amaliel Amalek is a major player in the spread of propaganda. However, most of the people are as aware of this, as your people were aware of the propaganda of 'Tokyo Rose'.

The network that reports things fairly and accurately is the "Amitiel News Network or ANN". This is where most of the people find the truth. KNN is but one news network among many that distort the truth, if not replace it with complete falsehoods.

"You gotta be kidding me!" Shocked at the fact that their exploits were public knowledge, Harvey was appalled, even mortified. It was one thing to be scrutinized by the public, but it was yet another *knowing* about it. The weight of that was starting to show in his eyes.

Noticing this, Girk slapped Harvey on the back. "Not to worry though, because everyone is behind you!" Then, as he began to walk with him, he muttered under his breath so Harvey could not hear: "Well, everyone that *counts* anyway."

This made Harvey feel a little bit better, but he was wondering how he was going to break it to the crew. Girk playfully elbowed Harvey and said; "If you ask me, it's about time someone stood up to that nasty Kurzi empire; but I wouldn't want to be in your shoes when they finally catch-up with you!"

Harvey looked quite worried by the news, so Girk tried to change the subject.

"What you need to do to start looking is drawn from your own dogma. Emphasis on DOG."

"Huh?"

"Go to what your people call the 'DOG star', and look for Humans from your world there."

"There are such people?"

"*You* know!"

He thought about it for a moment then exclaimed "The DOGONS!"

"Yes. Not only are they there, but the Dogons have a lead for you."

"Thanks, I needed that!"

"Worth some fuel is it?"

"All your ship can hold."

"Wow! Thanks! I didn't know you wanted a lead that badly, but I can't take advantage of you like that, so how about half? And...I'd still owe you."

"Suit yourself."

"One more thing."

"Yes?"

"I know your people are probably bored stiff, so may I suggest you give them some shore leave now, so that they can blow off some steam *before* you proceed? *Trust me*, things are really going to get hopping once you visit the Dogons. Who knows when you'll get another chance to relax."

"Thanks again."

15

"Thank *you*..." he said grinning "...for the *fuel!*" almost under his breath, with raised eyebrows. Apparently his need was great. "Now I won't have to refuel for *months*!" he added gratefully.

This made Harvey raise an eyebrow of his own, and re-check on how much energy there was per unit volume of the stuff. Then he let out a low whistle. It was a good thing it didn't like to go off like a bomb.

* * *

Girk took a few hours to leave, and in that time he got acquainted with all the members of the crew. His somewhat large bag, somehow had anything and everything that was wanted by each one of them. When they asked 'how much?' he would smile and just answer they owed him a *small* favor in the future.

When approached by Girk, the chief asked: "You wouldn't have any...naw! What am I thinking?"

"Go ahead, ask me for *anything*." answered Girk, in a concerned tone of voice.

"Okay, I ran out of cigarettes some time ago, as did some of the soldiers."

Girk looked at the soldiers that were gathering around. They were all nodding.

"Okay, but you really should quit though." he said as he rummaged around in his bag.

"Funny, I haven't craved them as much as I thought I would." said the chief under his breath.

The S*I*P*Es exchanged looks. That was right! They had actually missed the *activity* more than the nicotine.

"Here." he said as he pulled out carton after carton of cigarettes. "These ought to do. *One* carton to a customer."

The cigarettes were labeled: "Pax Smokes: No tar or nicotine, but curiously satisfying!"

They all accepted the cigarettes, but were almost feeling guilty over it and Girk not wanting anything concrete in return.

"Smoke all you want, I guarantee that you won't finish those

16

cartons." said Girk.

"Whaddya mean by that?" asked the chief engineer. "Are they *that bad?*" he asked, wondering of they were poisonous.

"Try one."

"Okay." said the chief as he cautiously lit one up and took a puff.

"Mmmmm! That's great!" he said as he exhaled.

"Good?"

"The best!"

"Before you finish that carton, your urge to smoke will be gone. They are designed for quitting."

"If this is quitting, I can live with it." said the chief as he took another puff and looked at the cigarette. "Thanks Santa!"

"Ho, ho, ho!" said Girk.

"How did you....never mind, I don't *want* to know!" said the Chief. He laughed and patted Girk on the back as the trader left the area grinning.

This whole business with Girk made Linda nervous. She didn't trust the man because he smiled like he knew something that the rest of them didn't - which he actually *did*. It also bothered her that he seemed to want everyone to owe him a favor. It gave her a sense of foreboding. So, she watched him closely. She didn't know which bothered her more; Girk's behavior or the fact that she and the Major were in agreement. In reality, Girk was trying in his small way to make up for the generous amount of fuel the captain had given him. He was planning on conveniently 'forgetting' that anyone on this ship had owed him a favor, but Linda didn't know that. The whole 'you owe me a favor' thing was just to let the crew feel better about accepting what he had to give. However, it reminded Linda of a godfather from back home.

In the soldier's mess, Girk noticed Linda watching him and he seemed a little nervous. This made her watch him even more closely. Finally finished with the S*I*P*Es, he turned and looked Linda straight in the eye from across the room. She almost panicked as he began to approach and backed herself into a corner.

"Miss Linda, glad I caught you!" said Girk, cheerfully. He had that twinkle in his eye revealing that he knew she was avoiding, as well as

17

observing him.

"That's 'Dr. Kowalski' to you. Look, you're not going to get a favor out of me so just forget about it. You can't possibly have anything I want anyway."

"Suit yourself, I wouldn't ask *you* for a favor anyway, but if you don't want this..." he said, as he started to turn around, holding up a small faceted crystal vial containing a small quantity of strangely golden fluid. It had a reflective quality to it she had never seen before, and the facets of the vial seemed to enhance the effect. She couldn't take her eyes off it.

"What's *that?*" she asked, in as cool a tone as she could muster, hoping to sound disinterested.

"Oh nothing, just a fragrance that never existed on your world..." his voice trailing off as if he were giving up on her.

Linda grabbed at it playfully as he attempted to pocket the vial.

"Well, let me *see!*" said Linda, this time anxiously.

Girk smiled, and placed it neatly in her now outstretched palm.

"Go on, it won't bite you." said Girk.

She smiled then sighed nervously. This is the first perfume she had seen in months. She had been on an expedition to the south pole for heaven's sake! Surrounded by scientists in parkas, who would think that she would need any perfume! So, she had not brought any with her. A decision she regretted now having met Harvey.

As she opened the vial, to test it on her wrist then Girk explained: "It's like Gladrina's little trick..." Linda's eyes went wide with that, and she hesitated. She didn't want the entire male population of the ship going nuts around her, as they had done with Gladrina, that is, until they had made an antidote for her particular pheromone trick. "...but it attracts only one man at a time. The one *you* are most attracted to." added Girk, which had the desired effect. It reassured her to the point of resuming her activity.

"It is triggered by that first nervous flush you get when you are near him."

Linda's face lit up into an 'evil smile', and thought about Harvey, as she tried the perfume on her wrist. She took a whiff, and looked puzzled. "I don't smell *anything*." she said.

18

"Only men can smell it, and trust me, it smells *wonderful!*"

"I don't know..." said Linda doubtfully, thinking of 'The Emperor's New Clothes'. "What do you want for it?"

"I already told you; absolutely nothing, in your case." said Girk. "Take it as a small token of my esteem, dear lady." he said while bowing.

With that, Harvey approached, which made Linda smile mischievously and give Girk a side-glance. This was the test!

"*There* you are Girk! I hope I can steal you away from Linda here for a moment." he said.

As Harvey smiled at Linda, she noticed him blush, ever so slightly, just like the moment they first met. That made her think that perhaps this fragrance was working.

"Certainly, what can I do for you?" said Girk.

"*Fantastic perfume!*" Harvey said to Linda, almost under his breath as they moved away, which convinced her it *did* work. Harvey added "You smell good enough to *eat!*" and immediately turned beet red after he realized that it could be taken in a 'naughty' way. "Uh...not that you don't normally smell nice, but I...um, I'm going over there now." as he conducted Girk away from where he had been standing.

As the two men talked, Harvey found himself looking over at Linda, even more often than he used to - before he decided to make an effort to stop. He didn't want to look like a lost puppy, but something made his eyes keep wandering over to her. The whole time she was watching him their eyes met several times. This time Harvey did not look away as quickly. In fact, they exchanged several warm smiles. This both re-assured her and made her feel like she was cheating at the same time, but in the end, she thought she could live with this 'edge'. What she didn't know was that *she* didn't need this, *Harvey* did. Sometimes a man needs a nudge in the right direction and sometimes he needs a good, swift kick! Harvey, in fact, needed a good long hard push with a bulldozer! As many non-jaded men often do.

"I tell you, there is only one thing I miss so far, and that's orange juice." said Harvey. Girk checked his portable Butator, and scratched his head. "Says here, that oranges are toxic. Are you Urantians as tough as they say? As in you like poisoning yourselves?" He was of course referring to the propensity of people from Urantia to consume fermented beverages, and jump out of perfectly good aircraft or off of bridges and cliffs.

"What?" said Harvey as he moved to Girk's side to see what was on the display. "Rats!" he thought to himself. "The display is in that weird alien language!" Which was Enochian, just like the ships controls were labeled when they had first arrived onboard. Due to the telepathic nature of the ship's systems, all of the control's labeling had changed to English in short order. Harvey's armor translated for him and not only let him know what language it was, but the history as well. 'Too much information.' he thought to himself and the armor dropped the subject.

As if knowing what was going through Harvey's mind Girk said "Says here that the Urantians are unique in that they managed to genetically change oranges so that they were safe to eat." He looked Harvey right in the yes and said "It pains me to say, that I don't have what you want, and what's worse, there probably isn't any supply off your home world, *anywhere* in the galaxy." then he added, almost under his breath "Maybe even the universe."

Harvey gave him a look like that of a lost puppy.

"However..." said Girk, raising a finger. "...I just *might* have a good substitute here." as he reached into his bag while still looking at his display.

"Ah! Here it is, and the Butator says it is very similar, if not...well...*better*."

With that, Girk pulled out a beautiful glass bottle of what appeared to be orange juice, only the color was more intense somehow.

"Oh! What is it?" asked Harvey as Girk handed it over.

"It's the closest thing I could find to Orange juice. It stimulates the same taste buds as oranges *and* honey combined." said Girk as he carefully handed it to the captain. "Try a sip."

Harvey shrugged and removed the stopper, hesitated a moment, than took a doubtful sip. His eyes went wide as he felt the flavor light-up his mouth. It was the tastiest thing he had tried since Eth - the immortality potion he was given in what he thought was a dream. Comparing this stuff to freshly squeezed Valencia orange juice - and I mean FRESH as in just picked off the tree - to the cheap blended orange juice at home after it had been sitting in a can for 18 months, and had turned brown and tasted acidic, doesn't cover it. Add the sweetest honey he had ever tasted, and it was fantastic!

"Wow! What is it made from? It's even better than the best orange juice I ever had back home!"

"Honeyfruit." said Girk flatly.

Indeed, it had a distinct, refreshing flavor to it.

"At least now I know what to ask for!" said Harvey, taking another satisfying sip. He was going to relish this!

"Uh, what do you want for it?" he asked, wrinkling his brow, full well expecting Girk to ask for a hotrod ship from the hangar, and at the same time hoping he wouldn't because that would make the juice prohibitively expensive.

"For something like this, I wouldn't ever ask for anything. Besides, this is more like information as your ship has large supplies of this onboard."

"Really?" said Harvey, as he looked at the bottle for any kind of label.

"Really. You just needed someone to identify it for you."

"Well then...*Thanks!*" said Harvey sincerely as he took another sip.

"No, thank *you*. I really needed the fuel and you have been so *generous!*"

The rest of Girk's visit went without incident, and he promised to make himself available when he was needed most. This puzzled Harvey so, after Girk left the Ezrael, Harvey went to the 'phone booth' to ask Metatron about this 'Girk' character. Just to be sure.

"So, what can you tell me about Mivon MaGirkon?" Harvey asked Metatron.

"What do you want to know?"

"You know, is he 'trustworthy'?" asked Harvey almost mystified. Metatron knew literally everything, and it bothered Harvey a bit that he actually *had* to *ask* questions. He also learned from experience, that if he didn't ask the *right* questions, he would get cryptic answers that sometimes left out the information he really needed. In fact, it seemed that Metatron had used that as an excuse to be less than clear to him on more than one occasion. This was beginning to give him have doubts about *everything*.

Metatron, knowing what Harvey was thinking, looked up for a moment and said "Girk, is a dear friend of mine. You can trust him as fully as you trust *me*."

"Anything else you want to add to that?" asked Harvey, hoping to find out more. There was a strange tone in Metatron's voice just then, like he was holding something back, such as some sort of 'in joke'.

"No. Nothing you need know just *yet*."

That was the kind of answer that almost infuriated Harvey. He knew that meant that Girk was yet another being that was more than met the eye. All these demons and angels out here in space were getting to him. He did understand that this was an advantage in that the others assumed that there was also more to him than met the eye. Sadly, the truth was that he was merely human. What he didn't know was that being 'merely human' was his saving grace. Angels and demons, although good fighters, are poor strategists.

"You're not going to tell me any more about him now, are you?"

"That's right."

"Why?"

"It's best you don't know for now, but don't worry, it's a good thing."

"Try me."

"Really, it is best you don't know *just yet*."

"What about the galactic news? Why didn't you tell me we were being watched?" he demanded.

Seeming amused by the captain's new found boldness, Metatron simply said "It's like 'cameras in a courtroom'. If you know they are there, they may adversely affect your decisions or actions."

"Now that I know..."

"There are no reports from *inside* the Ezrael. Only your general actions are known. You know, only what the Karoz actually see. It's really not that different than news coverage by reporters back on your home world, in other words, many of them put a 'spin' on it."

Harvey just glared at him for a moment as if to say 'Why didn't you tell me this before now?'

"It was best you didn't know until you were ready to handle it. Now you are, so now you know."

"What else haven't you told me?"

"Volumes."

"Will I ever get to know those 'volumes' of things?" he asked tersely, using his fingers to indicate quotation marks.

"Eventually. Each when the timing is right - unless you force the issue."

"I may just do that some day, because this is frustrating." said Harvey, half under his breath.

"Knowing too much too soon is what made Callicrates retire."

"Did it *really?*"

"Yes."

"You said he was the captain for thousands of years!"

"Because he was from a primitive culture, he was slower to adjust than you are."

"How much faster?"

"Thousands of times faster." he said with a wink.

"We shall have to talk about that someday."

"You'll find out for yourself soon enough."

"There you go, being *cryptic* again!"

"I think you'd best return to the bridge. There's another visitor on the horizon." said Metatron as he looked over to the side, in the dark, featureless room.

"I wish I could see the things that you do." said Harvey with a little longing in his voice.

"You will...very soon now."

"Really?"

"Yes, really. Over time, your knowledge will grow, allowing you to do amazing things. Very soon now, you will gain a 'second sight' and see what I see. Soon after that, you'll be able to do even more, and you won't ask me for reassurance so much."

That made him feel more confident, so he cracked a little smile, and left for the bridge. Yet again, leaving the android to fend for himself as he exited the room immediately after.

"I really *hate* it when they do that!" muttered Pymander as he headed down the long hallway toward the bridge.

23

2
SANCTUARY!
"Is that a bell rope?"

As Harvey appeared on the bridge, the Lt. looked up at him.

"Sir, I was about to send for you. I think you should look at this."

"I know." answered Harvey calmly. "What is it?" he added as if to contradict himself. The Lt. just shrugged it off as another Harvey Johnson witticism.

"A small ship, running at 110% power, is about to burn out it's engines." said Lt. Argent calmly.

"*Running?*" said Harvey, facetiously.

"Yes." answered the Lt. with a smirk.

"To or from?"

"Can't tell."

"Hail them."

The image of a frightened looking man appeared in the 3-D viewer. He looked at the captain and panicked.

"Who are *you?*" he demanded in a shaky voice.

"Oh, just an interested bystander. Did you know your engines are about to go?" he said calmly.

"They'll hang in there." he said with a glimmer of hope in his voice.

Harvey looked over to Elroy who was monitoring the status of the engines on that man's ship. He shook his head solemnly.

"How do you know they *will?*" Harvey asked.

"Because they *have to!*" The man's voice cracked as if he were about to cry.

Harvey and the Lt. exchanged concerned looks.

"Why are you in such a hurry?" asked Harvey.

"Frankly, I'd rather not say - just in case."

"Well, if you'd talk to us, maybe we could be of some assistance."

The man looked at him with 'puppy dog eyes'. "You'd *do* that for a total stranger?"

"Sure. Why not?" he shrugged, looking around at the bridge crew who were in complete, if not puzzled agreement.

The man seemed deep in thought for a moment, than asked. "What if..." then he was interrupted by his engines failing.

"Is there anything we can do?" Harvey asked Elroy.

"We can pick him up and offer transport. He's not going *anywhere* on his own now."

Harvey nodded at the Lt. who began guiding the ship into the equatorial landing bay.

"Looks like we're going to help you, after all." said Harvey cheerfully.

The man was panicking. "What are you doing?"

"We're rescuing you." answered the Lt. with a big grin. This was the kind of thing he loved.

A cloud of steam was engulfing the pilot of the small vessel as he said "Look, I don't want to get you into trouble too..." then his image faded out.

Harvey gave the Lt. a worried look.

"He's okay sir, his engines went critical, but somehow *our* ship was able to keep them from blowing up."

"Well, that's something at least." said Harvey clasping his hands together, "Looks like we have another visitor!" Harvey thought for a moment, then said to himself "Now I suppose I have to rescue the android from his long walk."

* * *

In the landing bay, the visitor's ship was looking the worse for wear. It had pock marks all over it's aft section as if it had been through one too many asteroid showers - backwards.

"Looks like he's been fired upon." said the Lt. as he examined the marks closely. He may have been unfamiliar with the weapons used, but a good soldier can tell weapons fire.

Elroy concurred. "Yes, that's exactly what that is; mass driver pellets." as he examined the remains of one, as the others exchanged looks, "Somebody has been shooting at him and quite recently at that."

"Well, now we know he was running *from* someone. Does his ship have any weapons?" asked Harvey.

"No." said the Lt. and Elroy in chorus. Then they exchanged smiles.

25

"Who'd fire on an unarmed vessel?" asked Harvey rather absentmindedly. "I hope it isn't Satrina again." Captain Satrina Batna had fired on an unarmed vessel, resulting in their rescuing an angelic creature named Gladrina, who subsequently joined the crew. She was currently using the ship's star charts and database in an attempt to find more of her own kind.

"Well, maybe our guest has the answer." said Pymander as he finally figured out how to open the door.

The man stumbled out of the door, and collapsed on the deck, a small quantity of blood drained out of his mouth and nose. They all exchanged worried looks, except the Azbuga. He went right to work scanning the visitor with a handheld device.

"Radiation poisoning. Like *that's* a surprise."

They all exchanged even more worried looks.

"There's no danger to us, our ship is absorbing the radiation, but he needs immediate treatment or he's done for." explained the Azbuga.

"Take good care of him Doc." said Harvey, as doctor and patient were absorbed into the floor. A curious way to get to the infirmary, but it made sense as an automatic ticket to a place where one could get medical help. Fall down and wake up in the infirmary all patched up. Yes, there was practically nothing the Azbuga, could not fix...including this.

"That still takes some getting used to." said Harvey, then he eyed the frazzled space frame, and wrinkled his brow in consternation.

"Can you *fix* it?" he asked Elroy.

"I'd *love* to! I haven't see any of these good old atomic-powered babies in a long time!" In fact, he had been drooling over the ship since it had shown up. He looked like a motor-head that was about to rebuild an old gas-powered 'muscle car' in the age of electric go-carts.

To that Harvey shrugged, and seemed satisfied. "Two birds." he said to himself.

Elroy, who had been studying the history and culture of Urantia, explained. "This is like finding a Hemi, or something like that. It's a beaut!"

'What's so great about a spacecraft that leaves behind hard radiation?' he thought to himself. Indeed, he preferred electric cars back home. "Oh." he said to satisfy the excited alien scientist.

"You see, it lacks a perfect inertial dampening system; so you can feel the acceleration and banking. It's a joy to ride in one of these." he explained further, sensing the captain's puzzlement. "So you can fly 'by the seat of your pants'." he added slyly.

They both stood there for a few moments, imagining flying it that way.

"I'd love to upgrade it to fusion, then there would be no hard radiation trail and it could run on helium-3." said Elroy. "That would make it safer at least."

"Just fix it up to how it's is *supposed* to be. Okay? *Factory new.* Got it?" said Harvey. Truly *Harvey* did not 'get it'. He appreciated a good sports car back home but he was far from a grease monkey or motor-head.

"Alright." said Elroy sounding almost disappointed. How could he be expected to resist the urge to hop it up it somehow? It was a *classic hot-rod*, after all!

"Let's get back to the bridge." he said to the others. "There's not much more we can do here."

* * *

On the bridge, they found the crew scanning the area and backtracking the small vessel's trajectory. A radiation trail was relatively easy to follow. Under the gaze of certain instruments, it actually glowed and resembled the contrail a jet might leave behind in the atmosphere, growing larger as it stretched back to its point of origin.

"Well, it looks like it was leaving that system over there, and there is another one-man ship on a pursuit course."

"How long?"

"That one is about two hours behind. It's approximately 9% slower than the other ship, which explains why our new pal was running his engines so hot. The safe money says he's the pursuer."

"Well, if that's the ship that fired on our new friend, let's find out why."

"Will do. Shall we approach them or wait here."

"Just give the doc enough time to properly patch-up our guest."

27

"Suits me." said the Lt. who then sat back, folded his arms, and waited.

* * *

Almost an hour and a half later, the man in the infirmary finally woke-up.

"Well, that was a nasty bit of business, but you'll pull through." said the Azbuga.

"Come again?" he asked, unconcerned that his doctor was wearing a black hat, or *Kirtabus,* which served as an intelligent translator.

"You had radiation poisoning but you'll be alright now."

"Thank you for patching me up doc." then he sighed. "So I made it?"

"Yes, you'll be fine."

"Oh good, for a while there I thought he'd catch-up with me before I got here."

"Um...where *exactly* do you *think* you are?" asked the Azbuga, realizing that the man might not know where he actually was.

The man looked panicked, and tried to sit bolt upright, but the Azbuga caught him on the shoulder. "Take it easy, your cells need time to knit."

"What *is* this place? Are you telling me that this isn't Golan!"

"You're in the infirmary onboard the Ezrael, you're *safe*." assured the Azbuga firmly.

"You don't understand, he'll come and he'll kill us all!"

"He *who?*"

"We're wasting time! How long have I been out? I have to get going before he gets here!" Then he looked the Azbuga right in the eye and said "He'll come for you too!" with a conviction that got to him.

The man then tried to get up, but now the bed wouldn't let him. He kept squirming anyway. The Azbuga was tempted to sedate him, but eventually decided against it, as his patient gave up struggling in exasperation, if not exhaustion.

* * *

The relatively tiny attack vessel approached the Ezrael in an aggressive manner, well, as aggressively as a bee could approach a Kodiak bear and stopped just short of the larger ship's surface.

"What's he doing? Is he playing chicken or something?" asked the Lt. rhetorically.

Harvey shrugged. This had him puzzled, and he was determined to find out what was going on.

The one-man attack vessel maintained its position, as if drawing a line in the plenum, meaning the aether, space, quantum foam - anything but sand!

"Hail him." Harvey said finally.

The face of a ferocious looking man appeared on the main 2-D display. "Who are you?" he demanded angrily.

"My name is Harvey, captain of the Ezrael and you *are?*" his voice rising politely.

"Matthew, and I'm no captain. I'm just an angry construction worker!"

"May I ask what you're doing this far out?" Indeed, his vessel was nuclear powered as well and was not well suited for interstellar travel, though it was just about as capable as a speedboat was of crossing the Atlantic ocean.

"If you must know, I'm in pursuit of a murderer, and I seem to have lost his trail." he said, almost as if he were only half paying attention to Harvey and his ship as he double checked his readings.

"A *murderer* you say?" said Harvey, raising an eyebrow, and exchanging a look with the Lt.

"Yes, he murdered my brother, and I claim the *right of retaliation!*"

Harvey glanced at the Butator display:

This is indeed a legitimate and common practice.

The pursuit vessel used by Matthew was provided by his governing body. The capitol city of most worlds maintain a fleet of similar vessels for just such a purpose. Also, an equivalent inventory of escape vessels are maintained to be used by those who will be running.

The route they are taking is locally referred to as: 'Skidaddle Ridge' and is generally avoided by most space-faring civilizations. Indeed, most, if not all known routes to the Rishi planets are so

29

avoided. The reason being that interference is strictly prohibited, unless in the rendering of humanitarian assistance, equal to both parties.

Gazdeen, the world Logan and Matthew are from is somewhat isolationist, and pays little attention to galactic news broadcasts, making them particularly unaware of you and your ship's activities.

There was more detailed information that looked long-winded to him so he ignored it. A habit he was forming that was not the best.

He looked at the Lt. and muttered, "Learn something new every day."

Argent smiled at him knowingly. Then Harvey turned his attention back to the monitor. "Would you care to elaborate?" he asked.

"Not especially. I just want to find the bastard and kill him. His radiation trail ends here. You haven't seen him have you?"

"Possibly..." Harvey answered, drawing the word out.

"What's *that* supposed to mean?" he demanded. "Harboring a fugitive in a case like this makes you fair game too!"

"Who's he trying to kid?" Harvey asked the Lt. who shrugged. The Butator display showed that it was indeed forbidden to hide a runner in this case, and anyone who did, was considered 'fair game' as well. Limited assistance, provided humanitarian and fair to both parties was sanctioned. True, they could just shield the man successfully as long as they wanted because they had the might. But might does not make right.

As if finally realizing, through his rage, that he was greatly outclassed, he added; "This is just between him and me! I have my rights and you should *not interfere!*"

"I'm sorry, I seem to have misunderstood the situation." said Harvey with raised eyebrows. "I thought he just had engine trouble."

"What did you *do?*" Matthew demanded.

"I brought his ship onboard and repairs are underway."

"Then this is your last chance! Release him to me or I'll attack!" He was not sounding very confident.

Harvey glanced a questioning look at the Lt.

"Are you *kidding?* His ship only has nuclear warheads. They can't hurt us at all. The most he could wind up doing is hurting or killing *himself.*"

Harvey nodded.

"Look, the last thing we want here is a fight. Perhaps if you came aboard we could discuss this..." his voice was interrupted by a bright flash.

"He's gone and detonated a nuclear warhead." said the Lt. calmly.

"Is he alright?" The captain asked with genuine concern in his voice.

"Now *his* ship is crippled too, and he got a nasty dose of neutron radiation to boot. I guess he thought a neutron warhead might have done us some harm, and he was too close for his shields to block all of the radiation."

sigh "Better bring him onboard too, and see if we can help him."

"Sir?"

"If we hadn't helped what's-his-name, this guy wouldn't have hurt himself with his own weapons, which makes me feel somewhat responsible. So let's see if we can save him from himself and sort out the disposition of both of them later - *after* they've recovered."

The Lt. nodded, cracked a sly smile and guided the crippled attack vessel into the equatorial docking bay. He had a good idea what Harvey was thinking.

* * *

His radiation poisoning cured, Matthew awoke the infirmary in a bed opposite to that of his quarry. Upon noticing this, he tried to get up, but somehow the bed would not let him. He could not see how. Obviously this technology was much more advanced than what he was accustomed to.

"Damn you Logan! What did you tell them?" demanded Matthew.

"I didn't tell them anything. Talk to the doctor, he's the one who restrained you."

"Oh, I see, so you can kill me at your leisure, I suppose! You'd better succeed because I'll take this to the emperor himself!"

"Do you even know where we are? This is the infirmary of the *Ezrael*." said Logan.

"I thought that ship was a only myth." said Matthew as he looked around in disbelief. "The *real* Ezrael? I thought he named this ship after

31

the legend."

"The *real* thing." Logan said reassuringly.

"Well, it explains things anyway. So what are your plans now that you have me at your mercy?"

"*Relax!* I can't get out of bed either. Besides, I don't want to kill you." he said calmly.

"Don't you? I'm the only thing between you and freedom! Or do you expect me to believe that killing my brother was enough for you?"

"Look, your brother was an accident."

"You'll never get me to believe that!"

"No, it really was! I *liked* Frank! You know that! I never would have killed him *on purpose!*"

"If that were true, why did you run?"

"I know your temper, and you never listen to reason when you're angry. That's why."

"A likely story! The foreman saw you taking careful aim with those bricks!"

"I was making sure they landed in the right place! Besides, why was he in the red zone? He knew that scrap was being dropped from above!"

Matthew looked as if he were considering this for a brief moment. "During *lunch*? Nobody works through lunch!"

Harvey and Linda were watching over the monitor on the bridge.

"So tell me again *why* you thought it was a good idea to put them both in the same room?" she asked innocently.

"I thought that if they could do nothing but talk, that they could resolve their differences."

"Looks like they're making *loads* of progress." she said facetiously.

"Give it time." he said reassuringly. He had noticed Matthew's hesitation a moment earlier and was certain that it was a good sign.

"Hmmmm. What if they *don't* resolve their differences?" Linda asked Harvey, skeptical of results.

"Then we'll just have to restore things to the way they were before we interfered."

"You're not going to take more direct action?"

"*sigh* Ever have a cat?"

"Yes, why?"

"Did you try to teach it to stay off the kitchen counter?"

"Yes, but she just learned to stay off it only when I was home." then the thought hit her. "You don't mean?"

He just raised and eyebrow and smiled knowingly.

* * *

Days later, the two men hadn't resolved their differences, much to Harvey's dismay. He was certain that reasonable people, given no other option but to talk, could work out their differences in less time. Unfortunately, it hadn't worked. Now it seemed he had to try another approach.

The two men were glaring at each other and would not speak further on the subject.

"I wanted to be around when one of your plans failed. Now I'm sorry." said Linda

"It was *you?*" said Harvey surprised. "Please don't do that again."

"What do you mean?" asked Linda indignantly, placing her hands on he hips.

"The ship tries to please everybody, especially the 'higher-ups' like you and me. As you know it can read minds and influence people when they are sleeping. Since you wanted to see one of my plans fail, and this being not that important to succeed..."

"Oh! I get it. It's *MY* fault?" she said indignantly. How could he blame *her* for *his failure?* She thought about it for a moment, checked her Butator link and realized he was right. "It *IS* my fault!" she said out loud to herself as she placed her hand over her astonished mouth.

"Just be careful what you wish for onboard this ship. Best try plan 'B' now." said Harvey as he left the room, hoping she would not be too upset with him. This was the closest they had ever had to an argument, and he didn't like it.

"Plan 'B'?" said Linda, puzzled after Harvey had already left. Her IQ was over 160 but nevertheless she was having a 'Blonde Moment'. It was not something to write home about. "Oh yes." she said to herself, "There's *always* a plan 'B'."

* * *

Harvey and Lt. Argent appeared in the infirmary. Harvey addressed Matthew since he was the most difficult of the two.

"Let me see now, in order to be fair, your ship must be put into comparable shape to his, so we repaired them *both* to factory condition, and in order to negate our interference further, we'll give Logan the same lead he had on you when we first met. Is that satisfactory to both of you?"

"Perfect! No one could ever accuse you of being unfair." said Logan hopefully.

Matthew nodded in approval too, itching to resume the chase.

"Well, since you are both recovered sufficiently, all there is left to do is send you on your way."

He nodded at Matthew and motioned for Lt. Argent to leave with him.

"Where will you go?" asked Harvey as they approached Logan's ship, in the landing bay. "Don't worry, I won't tell Matthew."

Logan looked surprised. "Why, *Golan*, of course, and Matthew knows full well."

"What's there that can help you with Matthew?"

He stopped and gave Harvey a surprised look. "You don't mean to tell me that *you* don't know about the seven Rishi worlds?" Logan scoffed.

Harvey was getting better at operating the information systems available to him, and his armor almost immediately informed him about the Rishi, or refuge worlds. If only he had been able to obtain a general knowledge pill, he wouldn't feel so lost sometimes. Funny how he hadn't bothered to look it up in all this time that Logan and Matthew were onboard.

The seven refuge worlds, A.K.A.: "Rishi" worlds, are evenly spaced throughout the galaxy, one being in the center near NOD.

The other six are evenly spaced between spiral arms, each covering two arms in a 'territory' and each territory overlapping. True, anyone could go to any refuge planet, but it was usually a race against time, so they almost always headed for the nearest one.

List Rishi worlds and corresponding territories:

34

1. **Hebron - Aries/Taurus**
2. **Shechem - Gemini/Cancer**
3. **Golan - Leo/Virgo**
4. **Kadesh - Libra/Scorpio**
5. **Gilead - Sagittarius/Capricorn**
6. **Bezer - Aquarius/Pisces**
7. **Ramoth - in the center, very near NOD, hence the 'accidental' murder rate there like in your nation's capitol city.**

Once a fugitive touches ground on one of these worlds, he is free from further prosecution. Typically, if a person accidentally kills another, they feel that they should not be prosecuted, so they run to a Rishi world. Because of this, it is said that only the innocent run to these worlds. However, it has become all too common that a murder is carried out and then the guilty party takes advantage of this system.

The closest relation to the deceased is permitted to pursue and kill the runner. This is the 'right of retribution'. Anyone helping such a fugitive is fair game as well; however, fair, equal and humanitarian assistance to both parties is permitted.

Harvey wanted an example because had already read this part before, so the system complied:

For example: Suppose that both parties are in a desert, and both are unconscious due to dehydration. If you give one water, to avoid prosecution, you must give the other water also.

He had good instincts as he had already decided to be fair and equal in his assistance to them. Well, more or less...since all of this happened in his head at the speed of thought, there was hardly any delay.

"Oh! *Golan*, I see, yes, uh, so you think you can beat him there then?"

"Well, if I can keep running my engines at 110% most of the way, I can make it."

"Isn't that a little risky?" his voice rising, in an attempt to remind Logan of the incident that landed him in their lap in the first place.

"Yes, but since you've restored my engines to factory condition they should be able to take it more easily now. The only thing is that since his ship is restored the same way, he'll also be able to run at over 100% as well which he couldn't before - all the more reason for me to run extra hot. Still, with a little luck..." his voice trailing off as he choked up. Obviously, this had him very worried, and who wouldn't be? He was literally running for his life, over the accidental death of a friend no less. The stress was showing in his eyes and taking its toll on the poor man.

"Good luck." was all Harvey said as Logan began boarding his small, sleek vessel.

"Um...thanks." he said almost under his breath. He paused like a condemned man entering a gas chamber, then he closed the hatch behind him.

* * *

Matthew was 'chomping at the bit' to continue the chase. When the two hour wait was almost up, it was the Lt. that escorted him to the bay.

"Here's your ship." said the Lt. condescendingly.

"What's *your* beef?" demanded Matthew.

"You're going to kill that guy."

"So?"

"He's innocent of wrongdoing. He hurts as much as you do about it, maybe more."

"Why are you people all so certain of that?" Matthew was getting a bit annoyed at their attitude.

The Lt. sighed and said "My captain told me *not* to show you this." as he activated a screen on the wall. "But it seems you *need* to see it."

The Amitiel system then began to relay the truth to him.

Matthew stood there quietly watching the video, apparently unconcerned with how it was obtained, and saw the truth of the situation. He saw the accident unfold, and the massive grief felt by Logan. Then he saw how he had misunderstood the circumstances, and was blinded by grief himself, only for it to be followed by rage. The screen also showed him how Logan had almost wished that Matthew would catch him, because of his own grief over Frank's untimely death and his own desire to be released from the emotional pain.

Visibly shaken by the detailed depiction of what had happened back home, his attitude was softened. "I see." he said as he glanced at his boots with a sigh. "Actually, I suspected as much." he muttered quietly.

36

"One thing I can say about Logan is that he has never been caught in a lie - no matter the consequences."

The Lt. just looked at him sternly as he deactivated the screen.

After a brief, uncomfortable pause, he said "Well...I suppose I should get to it - can't let him have too much of a lead after all."

"You're still pursuing him?" asked the Lt. in disbelief as Matthew started to board his vessel.

Matthew turned around in the threshold and said "I have to make it look good to save face, but I think I can manage some engine trouble or weapons malfunction just before I overtake him. No offence to your mechanic, of course!" with a wink as the hatch closed.

The Lt. cracked a sly smile and said: "I'm sure Elroy won't mind." knowing full-well that nobody would hear him say that. He nodded as the attack craft launched into space. He wasn't planning on telling the Captain...well maybe not *right away.*

* * *

After Matthew had disembarked, Elroy approached the concerned captain on the bridge "I wouldn't worry too much about Logan, sir."

"Why is that?" he asked, sitting up in his chair.

"Well, you know how I told you that his ship was like an old hot-rod?"

"Yes..." he answered apprehensively.

"Well, I simply couldn't resist." said Elroy, rather mousily.

"Resist *what?*"

The Captain's patience were running thin just about then, and it showed.

Elroy looked even more nervous. "Every hot-rod has one, so since his was missing as if broken from abuse, it was only appropriate to add it on." he said defensively.

"WHAT DID YOU DO?" bellowed the Captain.

Elroy clasped his hands together and hunched his back as he asked "Promise you won't be angry?"

Harvey glared at him and struck an even more aggressive stance.

After a moment, Elroy let it out in a quiet voice. "I...uh...added a super boost mode... it's kind of like the nitrous oxide injectors on your

37

internal combustion engines or the afterburners on your fighter jets." he finished very quickly as if this would be his only chance to defend himself, and he wanted to say it all before the proverbial axe fell.

Harvey looked ambivalent. Here was a possible violation, but he knew nothing about it at the time, but he was still responsible for the actions of his crew. Now the deck was *blatantly* stacked in the favor of the runner. What to do?

"Will he find it?" he asked eventually, in a low, unemotional voice.

"Oh YES! It's control is located in the standard spot on the dashboard. He couldn't miss it for the world!"

"So he'll make it then?"

"There's not much chance of Matthew catching him now. Logan's ship is about twice as fast as soon as he throws that switch." Elroy looked at Harvey for approval, only to see a blank expression. So he added "Don't worry though, unlike nitrous oxide, this won't harm his engines at all, so he can run it for extended periods."

"Will Matthew suspect anything?"

"No, in fact, he'd expect it to have something like that. Like I said, it's standard on hot-rods - especially that model: the Avery 884. A good formula for such a vessel, and a swift one at that!"

"If that's standard equipment...it's almost as if..." The captain muttered to himself trying to figure it out, shaking his head.

After a few moments of suspenseful contemplation he laughed, slapped Elroy on the back, put his arm around the little guy's neck as if he was about to put him in a headlock; but rubbed his head with the knuckles of his fist instead, let him go and said "Come on...I'll buy you a drink!"

As they left the room, Elroy protested "But...but...*I don't drink!*"

The Lt. gave Elroy a 'thumbs up' and a grin as they left. At least *he* was off the hook!

As they stepped through the threshold, Harvey thought about the bar called 'The Right Place' where a bartender named Zeth once gave him the immortality drink in a dream...or *was* it? Now it was Elroy's turn to drink a glass of sky.

* * *

Later, after he verified that Logan was safe and sound on Golan, Harvey entered the phone booth to have a little talk.

"Well done!" said Metatron.

"So you're not angry?" Harvey asked rather quietly.

"Why should I be? You facilitated justice - *as usual*."

"So it was okay then?" he asked cautiously.

"You have the authority to intervene in situations like that. In fact, you have absolute authority over all you encounter. What's more..." he waved his hand at this point revealing a veritable snowstorm of white dots in a three-dimensional flurry all around them, "...all of these worlds are yours to do with as you will."

"Whoa." he said, almost under his breath.

"In fact, *you're* the boss." added Metatron.

"So my little 'adjustment'..." he started asking, indicating quotation marks with his fingers.

"...is no big deal. I must admit, it was brilliant of you to release Logan at the exact point where he could just make it. Bravo!"

"So that sort of *sneakiness* is allowed?"

"It is, but you don't have to resort to it if you don't want to."

"But this way, Matthew saves face, and an innocent man gets to live."

"That's what I like about many of your solutions. They're symmetrical."

"You like symmetry?"

"If I didn't, many life forms, including mankind, might have turned out quite differently." said Metatron with a wink.

Harvey didn't know what to make of that one, and thought it best not to ask as images of lopsided faces and other things flashed in his minds eye - to his horror.

3
MALEK-I-TAUS
"What happens on Taus, *stays* on Taus!"

Back on the bridge, Harvey was trying to figure out where to take the crew for R&R before they resumed their main mission and headed for the dog star. Their latest little adventure convinced him that things were going to get hopping, and soon! Besides, they had spent what seemed a long time, just twiddling their thumbs, getting used to the ship and it's technology, and they were bored stiff. He hoped that they could have some fun before anything drastic happened again and they lost any chance at blowing off some steam. He realized Girk was right that they could handle the coming problems much better afterwards. He approached Pymander with the problem.

"Let me see now, if you want to give your people some R&R with a measure of anonymity, you might want to try one of the frontiers." said the android.

"Uh, *frontiers*?" inquired Harvey.

"Basically, since the most common forms of travel require gravity from closely packed stars, and the density of stars dwindles considerably in the threads between galaxies, those areas tend not to be claimed by anyone, though they are often used as intergalactic highways."

"Something like the wagon trails of the 'old west?'" he asked hopefully.

"A bit like that but more of the trade winds and the high seas, with outlaws, pirates, highwaymen and such. Things can and sometimes do get a little 'out of hand' in those areas. When you show the proper discretion though, there usually isn't much trouble."

"Wow, that sounds like it could be fun! Tell me *more*."

The android gave him a slightly worried look and continued. "There are many worlds in these frontiers whose business it is to provide rest and relaxation. They are much like the resorts you had on your home world, only much larger with very few rules, as these are entire planets organized as such. It's an 'adventure at your own risk' attitude since there is little or no law enforcement there."

"Like an entire planet of tropical beaches?"

40

"Close, but there are usually many themes on each planet - depending on climate and terrain - which are organized as 'nations'. There is one such world near here, that is quite outstanding if I do say so myself. It is in fact one of the most popular places for shore leave, since it has lots of *everything*. Captain Callicrates and his crew preferred it, by the way."

"That sounds like just the ticket. Let's go there. What's it called?"

"It's full name is 'Malek-I-Taus', but most just call it 'Taus' for short."

"What's it like?"

"Very much like your Las Vegas, with casinos, hotels, shows and, uh, *women*."

Indeed, the bleakness of the immediate area around it was very much like the desert as well, not to mention that most if not all, of the gambling was controlled buy the adversary's forces, not unlike organized crime on Urantia.

"We'll need funds." Harvey said, as if thinking aloud. Of course, he was asking the android how they were about to solve that little dilemma.

"Sir, the ship's coffers are brimming with currency, so that's the least of your worries."

"Well then, that sounds like just the ticket! Lt. set a course!"

"Here we go." the android muttered to a sideways glance from Harvey.

It seemed to Harvey that the android knew more than he was letting on.

4

SHORE LEAVE
"Shouldn't that be '*planet*' leave?"

When they approached the planet they discovered a lot of local traffic. Ships and shuttles of every possible description were scurrying about, and it seemed like a miracle that there were no collisions. It seemed chaotic, and had no rhyme or reason to it. In short, it resembled a cab ride in downtown Paris.

They found a relatively open area in synchronous orbit that the local traffic controllers had no problem with them using. In fact, the local authorities were relieved that the crew had arrived for some R&R and not to arrest them for their 'questionable business practices', so they offered them the 'rock star parking' - right above the main complex, not to mention the best hotel rooms at no extra charge.

They began to scan the local bandwidths and what they saw amazed them. Here, they could indulge in almost any vice openly. Some were so shocking that the Azbuga had to snap one of the technicians out of his trance.

"Sodom and Gomorrah." muttered Harvey.

The android caught that and cracked a sly smile. This one was all right. They had chosen well. Just who 'they' were was the question.

"What about money?" Swanson asked the android.

"Oh, there's plenty of that to be had." he said in a matter-of-fact tone which drew the soldiers to the android's presence.

"*Well?*" asked Swanson, who had a point. They had been on this assignment for a while now, and had seen no pay for it. It was, of course, an unusual situation to be sure, but if they were to blow off some steam planet side, they would need some coin of the realm, and that was not asking too much.

With a raised eyebrow to the captain, and with a nod in return he said: "Come with me."

The android led the soldiers down the corridors of the ship to a room that none of them could find later, much to their dismay. It was a large cavernous vault overflowing with all sorts of currency including precious gems, gold, silver and platinum! For some reason, it had other things like graphite. It is interesting what some civilizations will value.

The android walked in while they stood in the doorway, awestruck and positioned himself behind a counter.

"Single file, one at a time please." he said calmly.

Quietly they complied, all wide-eyed at the size of the drawstring sacks the android dolled out, proportionate to rate of pay for their time on this assignment. He was only being fair.

Noticing this, Harvey said to the android "Perhaps to avoid problems with avarice, we should do this elsewhere next time."

"As you wish. Your men, may have their faults, but dishonesty is not one of them."

"Just the same, I'd prefer not to add temptation."

"Fair enough."

Each in turn, once paid, happily hurried off to spend it planet side.

Owing to the fact that they had so many shuttles and other smaller ships at their disposal, most of the crew went down on their own. Only a few went in groups. Most of them had only one or two things on their minds, and this place catered to just such desires. These soldiers were indeed exceptional, but nobody is perfect.

Linda, however, wanted to go shopping and she wanted to bring Harvey with her, at least at first, but she knew she might not get the chance, so she thought she'd play it subtly.

Elroy decided to upgrade the Pantherion - the ship they had confiscated from Satrina Batna - since Harvey had taken such a liking to it's design. The Pantherion's engines and weapons were so inferior as to be little more than a lifeboat - from the Ezrael's perspective that is. After all, the Simkiel needs to be protected! So he went happily to work, upgrading this and supercharging that. He was as happy as a mechanic with a classic car and a garage full of new parts.

5
DEMIGOD POKER
"All right! Everyone ante-up: One *populated* world."

In the largest and most elaborate building in the capitol city of the planet was the most popular combination hotel, casino and brothel. The Lt. and Harvey spotted a beautiful woman with 4 breasts in the casino. She smiled at them and walked away, in an alluring manner. The android offered: "That's Plesithea. You won't get anywhere with *her*. Best talk to the madam; Eisheth Zenunim. They commonly call her 'Zen' for obvious reasons."

"Tell that to Cpl. Swanson." said Lt. Argent, motioning with his head.

Sure enough, there was Plesithea beckoning Cpl. Swanson away from the group, as he rubbed his hands together and sported a big, lustful grin. He had always dreamed of a woman with double cleavage.

"It looks like he'll find out the hard way." muttered the android as the Cpl. was led out through an arched doorway. "She *doesn't*...uh..." he was apparently at a loss for words. In fact, he was having difficulty saying it at all, let alone putting it delicately. "She's the virgin mother of all the angels. You see, energy beings are not conceived in the same way."

The Lt. and Harvey exchanged a look and shrugged, obviously distracted by a group of unusual looking individuals playing a card game. They stood there and watched to see how it compared to any game that they knew.

That's when Linda came by to 'steal the android' as she put it, to go shopping. She had hoped to bring Harvey, but he seems busy with the boys, so she decided not to disturb him. Besides, men almost never want to go 'shopping'.

"You boys go ahead and play your card game, I need to steal Mr. Roboto here." she said as she ribbed the android. This only made Pymander raise his eyebrows.

The two men shrugged it off and moved closer to the gaming tables.

"All right, everybody ante up!" said the dealer in a loud booming voice.

The respective players, in turn, placed what looked like marbles, with a faint glow to them, into a transparent bowl set into the center of the table.

The players looked similar to normal Human-beings for the most part, each with their own style and attitude. There was a four foot tall, gruff man wielding an over-sized and heavy war hammer; a very tall, leggy woman with long, jet-black hair wearing a very revealing leather outfit; two eight-foot tall, six fingered men, who looked like warlords from mediaeval times, but one of those looked like he was made of shiny metal. The dealer, in this case, appeared to be normal, except that he was somewhat translucent, with a slight glow about him. All of this made Harvey and the Lt. very curious.

The 'chips' were not the only difference from poker as they knew it. The deck they were using was to a tarot deck as a tarot deck is to a regular deck of playing cards - and then some. The cards had not only life-like images on them, but the images moved and what's more, they reacted to outside stimuli and even made faint sounds. Harvey had seen demonstrations of 'moving' ink before, back home. They used 'clock reactions' to produce a stick figure that appeared to move on the paper. If this was a trick of ink, it was very high tech. He moved a little closer to get a better look at the cards. They seemed to actually be alive, with the possible exception of the various 'death' cards which were simply terrifying to behold. In fact, if one stared too long at a death card, one felt like they were actually dying... Some of the other cards seemed to be in a torturous state, but he wasn't about to ask any questions, wishing to keep a low profile.

Harvey was entranced. He had not played poker since his college days, probably because had not much of an interest in the game in general, but there was something about this particular version of the game that held his attention. He didn't know if it was the players, the chips, or the deck itself. More likely it was the combination of all three. There seemed to be an air about the whole thing that made him think it was more symbolic than it appeared - like so many other things they had encountered out here in space.

He looked over his shoulder for the Lt. who was no longer standing next to him. In fact, Lt. Argent was nowhere to be seen. "Huh." he said to himself. Apparently the Lt. had lost interest in this game and had run off in search of something more interesting. So, Harvey turned his attention back to the card game. As the betting, raising and calling came to an end, the hands were laid out on the table in some sort of ritualistic manner and then an amazing thing happened.

It looked as though the characters walked out of the cards and onto the table in some sort of miniature holographic computer display. Harvey could see epic battles being fought in his mind's eye. He heard the clank of the swords and shields, the battle cry of the warriors and could almost smell it! The closer one was to the table, the more real the battle became. He could only imagine that if he were sitting at the table, it would be like being *in* the battle. He looked at the players and indeed, their bodies flinched a little from time to time as if they were experiencing the fight for themselves. A curious card game indeed! Upon closer examination, some of the characters in the battle resembled the players. This made him instinctively back away a little as if he might be pulled into the battle at any moment.

Finally, after what seemed like a whole day of fighting, there was only one 'card' left standing. The owner of the card then collected the pot. Having wandered closer to the table he was able to observe the chips. They looked like blue marbles with white patterns on the surface and looked almost like...*planets.*

Harvey was then hit with an astonishing epiphany; the chips represented *worlds* and one of the players had just won a rather large jackpot! Goodness! The cards actually did represent living beings trapped in the cards...people on various worlds fighting for more than just their lives but their very *worlds!*

He looked at the players again and recognized some of them. They were demi-gods! Actual minor deities playing for keeps! This was 'high-stakes' poker indeed! When this realization hit him, all he could think about was escape. What if they, horror of horrors, *invited* him to play? Forget the ethical considerations; if and when he lost, he could never bear to pay the bill! He was not much of a gambler, so that alone kept it from being tempting to play, but these stakes made it *completely* out of the question!

Slowly, he began to move further away from the table when the translucent one said "Captain Harvie! Leaving us so soon? Why don't you sit in for a hand or two?"

The forces of the adversary or those that are not 'in the loop' were mistakenly informed that Harvey Johnson was Harviel, an angel that was promoted to fleet captain, so they think of his name as Harvie not Harvey. Anyone calling him by that spelling believed him to be that angel. The badge of authority, and energy signature, given to him by Emperor Qayin as a badge of authority made his head appear to glow to anyone that had the third-eye ability to see it. Most that could not see it that way, saw it on a subconscious level. This, halo, for want of a better word, lent credence to the idea that he was an angel. This idea was also spread by KNN. The folks at KNN knew the difference but also know the tactical advantage it gave him, so they never set the record straight - at least in public. Only those who knew first hand, or were well-studied enough to know that an angel cannot captain the Ezrael, would call him Harvey.

The rest made sounds of invitation and approval, a general hubbub of four other voices at once, almost under their breath, and the short one happily thumped the remarkably sturdy table with his war hammer. They looked up and him expectantly. The entire casino went silent. All eyes were on him.

Needless to say, he was very nervous as a result. He tried to keep his composure, and not stammer. He thought of the best response he could. "No thanks...too rich for my blood."

This was met with uproarious laughter which confused him, he didn't know what to think anymore, so he chuckled nervously along with them. Aries got up and slapped him on the back and guided him to a chair that seemed to just appear, as he had not noticed it before. No one else seemed to be surprised by this. The table appeared to be larger as well. He reluctantly started sitting down and said "Really, I can't afford..." the laughter ignited again. He looked around the table and smiled wearily. This was exactly where he did not want to be.

Aries then returned to his own seat directly opposite Harvey. "Stop! You're killing us!" he said has he leaned toward Harvey, then looked at the others side by side while laughing as well. "Unless of course, that's what you want!" he added to more laughter.

Isis, who was sitting next to Harvey elbowed him gently and said "Come on! You've got more worlds than you know what to do with. Give us a chance to win a few from you! You know, 'share the wealth'." She waved her hand around the table indicating the other players. Then

47

she leaned toward him, placed her hand gently on his thigh and said in a pseudo under-her-breath manner, "Besides, you might just win a few back from *us*..." squeezing his thigh as she said the word 'back', making him nervously jump at that moment. This got another round of laughter from the others and the short one began thumping the table with his war hammer again in approval.

As the sounds of amusement began to subside, an inkling began to kindle in his mind. Was what Metatron had said earlier actually true? Were all those worlds not only his responsibility, but *actually his*, in every sense, to do with, what he would? He looked down in the small bin before him and it was by far, the most full of those little marbles! The responsibility hit him like an avalanche. Now all he could think about was how he felt he was failing all the people *on* those worlds. He was also losing hope that he would ever get out of this. There was too much at stake, if it came to being impolite, than that is just what he would have to do. There was no way he could win at this game, not even if the *knew* the rules, and he had no intention of risking entire worlds, let alone a single life.

Just as he was thinking about all of this, he heard all of them say "Girk!" in unison. He looked up to see Mivon Magirkon grinning down at him. "There you are Captain Harvey!" he said "I've been looking all over for you! Did you forget about *our* business?" Turning from the relieved man to the rest of the players. He said: "You simply *must* let me borrow him for a while, we have urgent business to attend to. You understand!"

There was the same general sound of agreement as there was before and a few smiled and waved Harvey off. He wasted no time getting up, bidding them farewell and quickly walked away with his benefactor.

"Boy! Am I glad to see you!" exclaimed Harvey. "Thanks for bailing me out!" he added.

"I turn my back for one minute and you're off playing demigod poker. *Shame* on you!" he said glaring at Harvey who could only avoid eye contact, obviously he *was* ashamed of himself.

"I don't know how you keep doing it but I'm indebted to you again." said Harvey humbly.

"I figured you needed rescuing. That's the highest stakes game of poker there is, and you didn't look like you wanted to play." said Girk, more cheerfully this time.

"You got *that* right!" said Harvey, perking up.

"Besides, you were unwilling to risk even a single life on a gamble like that, so somebody had to bail you out." he said with a broad smile, as if proud of him, mere moments after he had chastised him for getting into the game in the first place. This was a little odd. Girk was reminding Harvey of his father. "I'm proud of you for that!" he added.

"How did you...never mind." Wondering how Girk knew what he was thinking while at the table, but thought better of it. Obviously, he *was* more than met the eye!

Girk just smiled. A moment later, stopped in front of a door. "Here we are." he said as he indicated that Harvey should walk through first.

6
SHOP 'TILL YOU DROP
"How do you make a woman happy?"
"Give her a bag full of money and let her loose at a mall."
(Inscription on a tombstone of the unknown husband's last words.)

"Is there a place I can look for a new outfit?" Linda asked Pymander.

"There's an interesting market near here."

"That'll do." she said with a grin, so the android led the way.

Linda was unprepared for how revealing the outfits were. She had seen other women walking around the lobby in what she assumed to be swim wear or in some cases 'play wear'. Few were in outfits that covered well, except those that were by the pool. She assumed it must be the UV rays or something. The currency she brought with her was what she liked to call triamonds. They were silicon diamonds which were invisible unless a little dirty, so they often had a dye on them, making them visible at the same time as denoting their relative value.

She was in a large market, with a wad of cash in hand. There was no restraining her. She hesitated though, just outside of earshot of the shops. "So, how is this done?" she asked the android.

"I thought you knew how to shop." he said dryly.

"No silly!" she playfully backhanded the puzzled machine. "Is the making of the deal done *differently* here than it is at home?"

"Oh I see." he said, finally grasping her quandary. "No, it's about the same everywhere; you look over the merchandise, and buy what you like. The only thing here is that since most goods for sale are prototypes or new fashions, haggling is *strongly* encouraged to help set the prices for the rest of the galaxy, you see."

Haggling? Had she heard him correctly? She love to haggle! And to help set the prices for the rest of the galaxy? Hold her back! A sly glint appeared in her eyes as she purposefully began to march toward the market. She was going to *enjoy* this!

sigh "Here we go." muttered Pymander as he slung his backpack over his shoulder, and trudged after her.

* * *

50

Harvey looked around the main hold of the Baskabas, which was full of refugees. It was indeed a cargo and transport ship. He stared at the throng, and they quietly stared back at him, their eyes imploring him for help. The image was vaguely reminiscent of photos he had seen of WWII concentrations camps, with the difference being that the people were well fed and cared for. However, they were still very worried. Who wouldn't be?

"They're from a war-torn world called Rahab. Somehow it's star got blown-up last month. If it weren't for Sithriel, *all* of them would have perished."

Harvey almost blushed, because it was his ship, the Ezrael, under the command of the Major that had accidentally pulsed that particular star. The Major was only *testing* the weapons! However, his own feelings of guilt alone made Harvey want to give them all the help they needed, though he would have done anything he could for them in any event. He knew what it was like to be displaced from one's home by mass destruction. The Major had initiated that one as well. He was starting to wonder about the Major, just thinking about this.

Noticing his friend's worried look, Girk added; "Don't worry, he always manages to save everyone that deserves to be saved from such disasters."

This made Harvey feel better, but not much, because he didn't understand.

Girk gave him an imploring look that was almost as intense as the one in the eyes of the refugees. "You wouldn't know of any place I could plant them would you?" his voice rising, almost as if he already knew the answer. Indeed, the Demiurge database on board the Ezrael was the most complete possible and only people like Harvey had access to it. If it wasn't shown by Demiurge, it didn't exist. Harvey's causal mental inquiry was relayed to that system by his body armor. The answer was exactly what he was thinking, so he became confident. Talk about leading questions! Harvey didn't have to think about this one. "As a matter of fact...I *do*." he said, now sporting a sly smile. He had just the place to relocate them, and it would solve another problem as well. He liked 'killing two birds'. Had he lucked out this time or *what?*

The refugees exchanged puzzled looks. These two men in front of them were smiling and even chuckling a bit, but they didn't understand a word that was being said. Was this a good thing or a bad thing?

* * *

"I need a new outfit or two." said Linda as she went from shop to shop with the android reluctantly in tow.

The shops were tents and kiosks that one might think of as temporary. Truthfully, most of those shops had been there and in operation by name since before Humans on her home world had invented the wheel. Tents and kiosks were just what the culture preferred here, and it served to give the place 'atmosphere'. Besides, the valley they were in had been formed by the erosion of visiting traffic over the millennia. It had been a bit of a hill, when the market was first founded. Solid buildings cost more, were less flexible and less mobile.

There were all manner of things for sale. Most had the rustic look of being homemade, but also incorporated high technology; such as a pair of hand-stitched leather shoes that had anti-gravity pads in the soles..."Springer soles" they weren't made to make you fly. What they were for is making it appear that you weighed less than you really did; a vanity thing. Perhaps the hand-done work was a smokescreen. Either way, Linda acted as if she weren't interested. Although she wasn't a stick, as she put it, she wasn't overweight either, and didn't have any vanity in that area. As a matter of fact, she had quite an agreeable figure. Inexplicably, she bought a pair anyway, csiting that she liked the styling, but didn't want them for their stated purpose. "But of course ma'am!" was the response. She had no idea why she had the irresistible impulse to buy them but she went along with it just the same. She had learned to trust her intuition. This time it was literally *screaming* at her. After all, one couldn't go wrong with *shoes!*

There were lamps, that somehow worked without batteries or being plugged in, there were pots and pans that cooked without a range, there were self-cleaning rugs, actual flying carpets, pens that would work on any surface and never needed a refill of ink. There were even keys that worked on any lock; a rather suspect piece of technology until she discovered that keys and locks were a thing of the deep past, like candles might be considered today. Only primitive worlds used mechanical locks and these keys were a nice, convenient way to escape from a jail on a primitive world without too much trouble.

There was even a camera that took moving pictures that it printed itself on ordinary paper, telepathy style walkie talkies, rather dangerous working genie lamps, nicknacks of all descriptions, and clothes of all manner and description. The last thing on this list was what she wanted to see! When she discovered the 'clothing district' amongst the streets in this tent city, she was like the proverbial kid in a candy shop.

Once she discovered the value of the triamonds she brought with her, her eyes seemed to glaze-over. She was shopping for clothes because she almost no idea about what the fashions were like. The shopkeepers assumed that she knew that they mostly had exotic or formal wear for sale, being a vacation spot of course! So, she wound up purchasing several tasteful outfits that were more well-suited for night clubs than anything else. The rule of thumb was that the more revealing the outfit, the more formal it was, and conversely the more it covered and/or left to the imagination, the more casual, and alluring it was. Having a sensible degree of modesty, she invariably picked casual or 'clubbing wear'. A 'mistake' she wouldn't soon discover, but one that would not serve the mission's interests very well in the future. After all, wearing informal outfits was not to covey a feeling of authority, and since she was no exhibitionist, she inadvertently went with what was considered sultry, which meant that what she had purchased was to her the equivalent of blue-jeans and a tee-shirt as well as some proper formal wear. What she was really getting was the equivalent of something more revealing than the 'dental floss' bikini's of Rio! Had she purchased revealing outfits, she would have been taken more seriously in the future. Some cultures seem to be just plain *backward*. She should have known this after designing outfits for Gladrina and Aniyel, but then again, that odd failure and triumph was reason enough to sample what was out there.

Once she got a clue or two from these kinds of outfits, she planned on designing her own and having the ship manufacture them for her as she had before. Only these new outfits would be more in keeping with the styles. If she was going to be seen on the galactic news, she was going to wear something that didn't look like a sugar sack to the public. Sadly, due to her clothes covering so much and so well - leaving so much to the imagination - she would be known far and wide as a sex pot for her troubles. Thus, sadly, adding to her fame. I guess things are not so different out there after all.

Purchase after purchase went straight into Pymander's backpack. At first, she asked if the garments would wrinkle when stuffed into a backpack and could he please use something else. He kept assuring her that it would be all right. When she finally realized that there was 'no way' that all of her purchases could have fit in a simple backpack she confronted him on the subject.

"Do you have everything in that little backpack?" she asked as she looked it over in puzzlement. It didn't even seem to have much in it, as it didn't bulge anywhere.

"Yes, and more." he said dryly.

"How does it all fit inside?" she asked still puzzled - half expecting it to be a technological marvel.

"Simple. It's bigger inside than outside."

"I knew it!" Pleased with herself, she had to ask the next logical question.

"How...does it *work?*" Now more interested in the backpack than the garments she was there to purchase. The scientist in the other hemisphere of her brain was asserting itself once again.

"Essentially, it's a dimensional pocket. It contains a folded portion of space, that is virtually unlimited in size, completely manipulable by the user of the backpack and inaccessible to others. It's standard equipment for expeditions...and - I might add - quite handy on a shopping spree."

"Uh, well that's nice." She felt rather inadequate, as the science it would take to do such a thing is beyond anything she knew, yet this was an everyday utilitarian piece of equipment. It was best to shrug it off for now and go back to shopping, rather than feel like a cave-woman in a supercomputer center.

* * *

"It's called 'Loam'." Harvey said to Girk as they looked over the star charts on the bridge of the Baskabas.

"Loam huh? Sounds like a nice place."

"It is, or rather it *was*, and with their help could be again."

"What happened to it?"

"You mean to tell me that you don't know?" he asked, wondering if the galactic news had reported that story.

Girk just gave him a blank look and said: "It must have been before you caught the attention of the news."

"Well, they got brainwashed by a book, and lost almost all of their people as a result."

"There's a lot of that going around."

"What?"

"Whole societies being brainwashed by a single book. It's happened on your world a few times."

"Indeed. Now that it's all sorted out, there is plenty of room for immigration on Loam, with a ready-made infrastructure that's almost perfectly intact. They're just asking for people!"

"Sounds ideal! Thank you Simkiel, on behalf of all the survivors of Rahab." he said formally while bowing.

Harvey blushed.

"Now, I have something for *you*!" he said in a more serious tone.

Harvey looked at him, and narrowed his eyes. That had the sound of something important!

* * *

Linda tried on lots of outfits, and let the merchants talk her into almost anything. After all, she needed many examples and had lots of cash, and plenty of storage space to haul it all. What was a girl to do?

What fabrics! There was even a 'mood fabric' that changed not only colors but *patterns* with your mood! Whatever you were in the mood for, it duplicated. Sometimes you didn't know until you looked in the mirror then presto! Yes! That was it! She got three styles of those, since the cut couldn't change.

Self-repairing fabric, texture changing, and oh so many varieties, until she found a salesman that had just what the doctor ordered. It was so perfect that she almost returned everything else she had bought that day...it was an outfit that could do *everything*! Despite spirited haggling, it also cost as much as everything else combined, and then some! It changed color and pattern, it changed style and it even repaired itself! It could also become exactly like the background rendering you almost invisible wherever it covered. It was self-cleaning, cooling and warming - so you were always comfortable when wearing it! The variability and durability of the fabric was astonishing. It could even change it's texture and cut, so it covered more, less or just differently. They were rare outfits, and billed as the last outfit she would ever have to buy. Boy! Were they right about that!

"Every nano-strand is made up of molecule-sized robots, that can change color, shape, texture and configuration at your whim. All hand assembled by the finest robotics engineers, this is one of only three garments like it in existence." explained the merchant.

"I hope this is worth it." she muttered to herself, while looking over the final, firm price. For something this expensive and unique, there was little wiggle room to haggle.

"If I may..." began Pymander as he pulled her to the side. That price is much is more than you brought with you, so even if you returned *everything*..." his voice trailed off as she gave him the puppy-dog eyes. "*sigh* Oh, alright!" he said as he unbuttoned his shirt.

"What are you doing?" she asked, wondering what he could possibly be up to.

"This is for emergencies only, so I hope you appreciate this." he answered as he took out a knife and sliced his chest open. The red, blood-like coolant ran from the edges of the wound on his pseudo-flesh and he reached inside. Fascinated, Linda watched intently as he reached around for something, then pulled out a bag the size and shape of an American football. Pymander smiled, and wiped the coolant off of the bag, and handed it to her.

"Is that what I think it is?" she asked.

"A king's ransom." he answered triumphantly as he began re-sealing his chest with a tool he produced from the repair kit on his belt. "*Literally.*"

"Let me get this straight: you keep *this* in your *chest cavity?*"

"No, I have a teleporter in my chest cavity, so as long as it will fit, I can retrieve anything that might be needed from the ship."

She let out a low whistle. "We could have gone to the ship for this you know."

"I was simply trying to save time." he said, now finished re-sealing his chest.

56

She gave him a peck on the cheek, said" You're so sweet!" walked over to the merchant and handed him the bag. He reluctantly opened the bag and his eyes lit up! He smiled as he turned away and waved her on to the garment. It was hers now. He and his descendants would never have to work! He was retired as of now. That made her wonder about the profit margin.

* * *

"There is a spy in your ranks." said Girk rather pointedly. Usually he was a little round-about, but this time he was as direct as he could get.

"What?" was all Harvey could say at first, then he regained his composure and said "None of my people..."

Girk cut him off, "One of your trusted people has been, or very soon *will be* replaced." He stared directly into Harvey's eyes with a seriousness that could not be ignored.

Harvey looked very confused. How could someone be mistaken for one of his crew? Someone *had* to be able to tell the difference!

"This information comes directly from the master spy Zophiel, so it's accurate."

Harvey didn't know the name so his armor showed him that Zophiel was indeed a master spy and his information could be trusted. So he just nodded 'knowingly'.

"The infiltrator's name is Nergal, who is an *expert* at disguise. In fact, he's the very best. What he usually does is kidnap a trusted individual and replace them by disguising himself as that person, being sure to keep his hostage alive for their knowledge. So anyone he has replaced in this manner is relatively safe."

"Relatively?"

"Safe, until he's caught, then they're a bargaining chip. Also, due to who you work for, he'll try to get his hostage to commit all seven deadly sins in the meantime."

"All seven?" asked Harvey, rather amused.

"Yes, all seven DEADLY sins!"

They both chuckled at this.

"Well, I'd best find out who it is and rescue them then!" said Harvey jovially.

Girk looked serious again. "I don't know who it is, neither does Zophiel, but I can tell you it is *not* someone you know well *personally*, but it *is* someone who has your confidence. A male that has your complete trust. He has already been chosen, that much is certain."

"Can a scanner..."

"Yes, but if you do that, you'll tip him off. Nergal has destructive capabilities and sensors of his own, so he'll know if you scan him."

"He's a machine?"

"It appears so, though I think he is really using a telepresence robot."

"What do you mean by 'destructive capabilities?'"

"Typically, once he is found out he somehow manages to destroy the ship he's in. No matter how he is detained."

"Somehow?"

"No one has ever survived to tell how, but it is known that the ship is typically blown-up from the *inside* with some degree of malice, I might add. So watch out! It has been theorized that he has a body cavity bomb like the Cheriour, but how he could survive such a thing is a mystery."

"I have heard of the Cheriour, extremely strict galactic cops and all but...'body cavity bomb'?"

"They have some anti-matter inside a body cavity and the containment field is powered by their bio-electricity. The idea being that if *they* die, so do *you* and a lot of your friends. That is one reason nobody dares even *try* to kill one, tough as they are."

"OUCH! That would do the trick! Okay...so how can I ferret him out?

"Ferret?"

"It is a small animal that was used to chase snakes out of boroughs and such."

"Oh I see! Well, details are sketchy, but what we do know is that in casual conversation, Nergal will by necessity be a little slow to answer in detail to personal questions, as he'll have to put the question to his hostage through a communications device, and then get the answer the same way before answering you. Look for such delays, that's the best way to find him out, but beware not to tip him off, or he'll blow up the ship."

Harvey nodded thoughtfully. "That puts a new spin on the expression: 'blowing it'."

"Indeed. I'd advise you that once you identify him, do your best to nab him before he gets a chance to detonate anything." added Girk with a worried tone.

"Do *you* think it may have a bomb inside him?" asked Harvey, worried.

"Personally, I think it is not likely, since Nergal has passed scans for such material - that much we do know. It's more likely that he rigs something up at the time. Somehow, he managed to destroy ships before even when he had been placed in restrained custody, so he's pretty resourceful."

"Thank you. At least that's a start." said Harvey.

"I wish that there was more I could do, but that's all I have right now." he said dryly.

The look in Girk's eyes made Harvey worry.

"Don't worry, since this of such importance, I would have told you even if you couldn't have helped me. In fact it is the main reason I sought you out this time." said Girk as he patted Harvey reassuringly on the back. That was not what Harvey was worried about.

"Thanks." he said, with a puzzled look. Girk was a strange fellow. But then again, so was everyone else out here!

7

"What goes 'Woof, Woof, Splash?'"
"I give up."
"A Dogfish"
BUT SIRIUSLY FOLKS...

Johnson's Journal:

There are no complete Penemue pills, as such, for Dogon since it is so far off the beaten path. Well, that's the excuse the Butator is giving me. Sometimes I think the ship's systems are just not telling me the whole story. I also get the feeling that Metatron and Joth are holding things back. It is like there is some kind of terrible secret they are afraid I will discover. I'll have to get to the bottom of this some day, but the more that goes on with it the more I feel as if I am being mislead. I don't have to say how much I dislike the idea.

I've instructed the ship to make Penemue pills for Dogon anyway, based on all known information from the previous visits, including the Dogon language from back home, in hopes that we'll be at least able to communicate. Curiously, this is the only ship that has any records about any visits to that world. With our database being the most comprehensive one possible, I wonder how Girk even knew about that world.

The body armor Linda and I have also incorporates a real-time translator like used in the Kirtibus hats and glasses, and it can also alter my speech, if I let it, to be understood by the natives. Sometimes I think Linda hasn't got the hang of using it as she frequently wears the hats and glasses, but I hope what we have suffices. We have virtually no cultural information to go on and extrapolating from scarce data worries me. Something just isn't right about this whole picture, I can feel it. Still, a few S*I*P*Es will be along for security reasons. Elroy has been working on fitting the working parts of the Kirtabus hats into the S*I*P*E helmets and the lenses of the glasses into the video systems for a few weeks. This might be a good field test. The major insisted and this time I agree with him. In fact, I find myself trusting his judgement

a little more all the time. Why does that worry me?

* * *

The shuttles returned more or less randomly and some were less skillfully piloted than others. In most cases, the men were simply tired from lack of sleep, inebriated or in a few cases - worse. It is a good thing that not only were the shuttles somewhat more simple to fly than a car is to drive, but they had automatic collision avoidance systems. If they hadn't, things might have gotten 'messy'. As it is, the ship helped guide many of them back into the docking bay to avoid accidents. Given this, it is not surprising that both Swanson and Argent were in no shape to pilot the ship. The third best at piloting the ship, and indeed the man that helped guide the wayward remaining shuttles, was named Taggert. He was not much for 'partying' so he elected to stay behind and get some practice in. Good thing too, because he was going to be needed for more than just the docking of wayward shuttles.

"Swanson, wanna take the helm?" asked Lt. Argent when they got back on board.

"What's wrong with *that* guy?" he asked, pointing at Taggert, already at the helm. "I'm a pit too bolluted to take the wheel."

"Yeah, I think we bophare." admitted the Lt.

Taggert didn't mind. His skill was measurably less than either of the other two, but he thought that with more practice, he could improve considerably. People able to pilot the ship without developing vertigo were few and far between. After all, it is not everyone can handle the panoramic view - and I do mean completely around the ship, up down, sideways and all ways all at once. All the S*I*P*Es turned out to be better at it, in general, than the scientists, and the working theory was that it had to do with the S*I*P*Es using video monitors with a view from behind. It took getting used to, most of the people that tried to help just got sick, or a headache or both after too long in the chair. It seems not *everything* on the ship was immediately easy to use. Perhaps this was to prevent the ship being hijacked should the enemy ever make it that far. Harvey found that he could sit in the chair long enough to choose a destination and time of arrival and then let the ship run on autopilot without any problems. Soon, he would learn he didn't even

61

need the chair.

It was two weeks to the day, and the last of the stragglers were coming up from the planet on the last shuttle. Once they were on board, Harvey wasted no more time.

"Set course for the Dog Star." said Harvey.

"Sir?"

"Sirius."

"What do you expect to find there, sir?" asked Taggert.

"I have a been given a tip that the Dogons really do exist."

The helmsman gave him a blank look.

"The Dogon tribe in Africa claimed to have been visited by aliens from Sirius, and accurately drew a map of that system a full fifty years before we were able to confirm it. I think that makes it a good place to look for clues."

Taggert smiled as he plotted a course. Play time was over, and it was back to business. That suited him just fine. For him, this was as good as any shore leave.

8

DOGMA

"My Karma ran over your Dogma..."

In the early evening, a lone dolphin swam up to a waiting figure at a point. The Human was a man in his forties, in good physical condition and dressed in traditional ancient African robes of state. He was a king, proud, intelligent, strong and above all, *wise*.

The Dolphin, rolled over onto it's back and the human stooped down to rub it's stomach. It was an affectionate act like that between human and pet. The dolphin then rolled back over, and started speaking to the man, in a squeaky voice that only dolphins can make with their blow holes.

"The servants of the creator will arrive in the morning." it squeaked.

"Really? I shall have to make preparations. Thank you."

"You are welcome my friend." squeaked the dolphin.

He bowed to the dolphin, which acknowledged his respect, and they both went their separate ways.

* * *

High in the night sky, a third moon seemed to fade into existence. It shone brightly as if to announce it's arrival. A few hours later, a shuttle left the 'moon'. Some time later, several figures slowly approached the quiet encampment from the south - the correct direction to approach to indicate that you had good intentions, but that wasn't all that important as the people that they were approaching, being civilized, appreciated that aliens most likely would not know their customs.

As that part of the planet rotated into the view of the dog star, the long shadows of the visitors stretched across the compound, and began to shrink. The king still sat quietly on his throne, as if waiting for something. Finally, as the light began to permeate the primitive-looking village, the inhabitants began to emerge from their huts, and one by one they were struck with the realization that they were not alone. One by one they gathered to stare back at the strangers. It had been a few generations since Caucasians had been seen on this planet, and as a result, they were quite a curiosity.

Finally, one of them spoke to the visitors.

"Hi." said a rather precocious young girl, as she grinned and ran to hide behind her mother, only to peek around her to look at the strangers again with a smile.

The king watched their reaction intently. One of the strangers smiled at the little girl and even went down on one knee as to be less menacing. He reached into his pocket and produced a piece of candy, and held it out to the little girl, with a sideways glace at the mother for permission. The little girl gingerly accepted the candy and smiled after trying it. This told the King enough. They were friendly indeed, as he had been informed.

"Welcome to Dogon!" he said as he stepped off of his throne.

"You know we're from another world?" asked the man that had knelt before the girl.

"There is no one like you on this planet, and the arrival of your ship..." he pointed at the Ezrael in conspicuous stationary orbit, without looking at it himself "...was far from clandestine."

They exchanged looks, and smiles. So far, the scant information they had was correct.

"We merely wished to show the proper respect." said Harvey humbly.

The king looked at him and smiled. "You must be the leader." he said with a big grin. "Welcome, servants of the creator, to our little nation! I am king Theopolis, you may call me 'Theo'."

"You can call me Harvey." Harvey indicated the individuals in his party one by one introducing them.

At once, young women scurried up to them and presented them with an interesting form of a flowered neckless or garland - not unlike a Hawaiian lei, and stayed by the sides of the men.

"Psst, hey *guys...!*" said Harvey.

Argent and Swanson gave him a puzzled look. Then they realized what the offer was.

"Well?" asked the King.

"Well, meaning no disrespect to the young ladies here..." Harvey began uncomfortably.

"Say no more my friend, it is not only clear we are more open about certain realities of life and that these two have had recent 'shore leave'. I can also see that you, in particular, are already smitten by someone." He clapped his hands and the smiling young ladies scurried cheerfully back to the rest of the crowd. Swanson gave them both a lingering, if not lustful, sly crooked smile as they went.

"Don't worry, no offense is taken. We were merely offering you the highest respect and hospitality. Those young women will find husbands soon enough."

"How..?"

"...do I know so much that seems out of place in this world?"

Harvey just nodded with a cheerful, if not slightly puzzled, look on his face.

"Like so many you have met, we too are more than we seem Captain Harvey!"

* * *

After a breakfast feast in their honor, they finally thought that they could get down to business. It seemed as if the king were attempting to prevent them from even asking the questions they had come to ask. Indeed, he had already been informed as to what they were there for.

"Doubtless you have many questions Simkiel." said the king finally.

Harvey just nodded solemnly.

"Unfortunately, they will have to wait until this evening. For now, it is time for us to do battle with our neighbor to the east."

They exchanged glances. The king was rising and he was getting fitted with what appeared to be very ornate but ineffective-looking, if not primitive armor.

"I'm sorry." said the king as if he had suddenly become aware that he had just offended someone. "Would any of you gentlemen care to join us?" he asked, looking back and forth at the men, making eye contact with each. "I seem to have overlooked that fact that you brought *fighting men* with you!"

"Hell yes!" exclaimed Swanson slamming a fist on the table, eager to get on with some killing. The others ignored him for now.

"What are you fighting over?" asked Lt. Argent intently, to a sharp glance from Harvey, who didn't want to get caught-up in any squabbles they had no stake in.

The cultural information they received from the ship's Penemue pills didn't cover everything. Indeed, this seemed to be the first time that they were not thoroughly informed about a world, which was quite unsettling.

"Ha, ha, ha, ha! I like you! You have the will and gumption to fight but the fighting alone is not enough! You must have a cause! Very well...the neighboring tribe has encroached on our farmland and they refuse to retreat. So, we are fighting this little war over who will have dominion over those fields."

"What if you are killed?" asked Argent.

"Killed? In war? Not much chance of *that!*"

Harvey and Argent looked surprised at this, if not amused. Swanson looked puzzled, if not upset.

* * *

Swanson wound up volunteering to go with them, itching for a fight as he was. Harvey and Argent waited behind at the village in order to learn more about these people.

During their interviews with the villagers, they fond that no one was suffering from any medical problems, and though they lived in quite primitive circumstances, they were not strangers to high technology. After a few pointed questions about the occasional piece of high-tech gear that appeared here and there, they discovered that the villagers used to travel the stars but gave it up for a more laid-back life here on Dogon.

* * *

When they returned, Swanson and the king were holding each other up. At first, Harvey and Argent thought the worst and rushed to their aid. When they realized that they were both intoxicated, they almost let them drop.

"How did it go?" asked Argent.

"We losht, tank goodnehss!" proclaimed the King, as he waived the opposing army into his village.

They swarmed in rapidly as if taking over. This made Argent and Harvey more than a bit nervous. "There has to be a reason that so much was left out of the pills." remarked Harvey, hoping said lack of information was due to some grand design and not just random chance.

Argent nodded knowingly, as he raised his M-29A1, but Harvey motioned for him to hold off. "Best not provoke them until they decide what to do with us."

Argent shrugged nervously.

Clearly, Swanson was having the time of his life. He approached with some difficulty.

"Do you mind telling me what happened?" said Harvey, looking around at the conquering army nervously.

"They don't fight a war like we do, sir." he said.

"Tell me something I don't know!"

"To them a fight is, well, a *fight*." He held up his fists. They still looked puzzled.

"Don't you get it? Fisticuffs!" He looked puzzled in more ways than one. Almost as if the term he had just used was foreign to him.

Swanson then struck the pose of a Victorian boxer about to fight using the Marquis of Queensberry rules.

The light came on.

"It was the biggesh, besh, brawul I was ever inn..." he suddenly began to slur his speech as if he had just *remembered* that he was drunk. With that he appeared to lose his balance and almost fell over. Correcting his stance, he continued. "The looshers buy the beer! He, he!" With that he staggered off to join the 'after war party'.

"That explains a lot." said Harvey.

"Yeah, but what a *civilized* way to fight over something." said Lt. Argent with a far-off look in his eyes. "Funny thing though."

"What?"

"Swanson isn't much of a drinker, yet he's soaking it up like a sponge."

Harvey stared at him for a moment until he shook it off. Then he said "That's probably why he's so smashed!"

The Lt. moved closer to Harvey in order to talk without being overhead. "Sure, he spars to hone his combat skills, but he's not much of a brawler either, and when was the last time you heard anybody use the term 'Fisticuffs'?"

He raised an eyebrow at that one, as the King approached. "Come!

Join in the festivities!"

"But you said you lost. Why are you so upbeat?" asked Harvey.

"Because we didn't *want* to win!"

"Come again?"

"They only farmed our land because they couldn't feed their people, and we weren't farming it because we didn't need it. You see, they are not very good farmers and we are!"

"So why go to all that trouble? Why didn't you just give them the use of your land then?"

"That, would have been charity, and men are too proud to accept that. This way, they win the right to the land fair and square, and I might add, they get the assistance of our farmers for a whole growing season as well. Now, will you stop asking so many questions and join the party?"

Harvey and Argent exchanged a smile as they joined in. These people might not be the Keel, but they were close enough! Civilized folks were few and far between it seemed.

* * *

As dawn broke, and a shaft of light came into the hut through the carefully placed skylight, waking the visitors.

"Owwwww, is it just me? Or is that ant breathing too loudly?" asked Argent.

"It's *you*. Ants don't have lungs." said Swanson flatly.

"On this planet do." offered Harvey.

"Oh yeah, I forgot." said Swanson.

"Is it just me or does that one have asthma?" asked Argent.

"Give it a rest hangover boy!" said Harvey playfully.

"Did you guys have enough to drink last night?" asked Harvey.

"I should hope so Shimke-el. That stuff was really good." slurred Swanson.

"Why didn't you have any?" asked Argent.

"Two reasons. First, I'm not much of a drinker, and the other is the way that stuff is made."

"Fermentation is fermentation." said Swanson, taking a large gulp of some more drink that was leftover in a cup by his bunk. "Ahhh, 'hair of the dog!'" he added as he swilled the last of it.

Argent knew enough from experience to listen to the captain.

"That may be so. Call me a wuss if you like, but I just don't relish the thought of drinking something that was fermented with human saliva." he said with a twinkle in his eye.

Swanson made eye contact with Harvey, then immediately headed out the door with his hand over his mouth.

The Lt. sat there smiling.

"Don't you feel ill at the thought?" asked Harvey.

"I might have if you told me beforehand, but I figure, 'what the heck? What's done is done'."

"Good man." he said, slapped him on the back and helped him up to the sounds of Swanson retching nearby. "Besides, I was just kidding!"

Swanson didn't hear that through his own retching sounds.

They chuckled, and headed toward the town square to find the others.

"Why didn't you guys tell me last night?" Swanson asked the king, as he began sitting down at the breakfast table.

"Tell you what?" asked the king, truly puzzled.

"How your libations are made."

"Grain, fermented in vats?" he said in a puzzled tone. "How else does one make beer?"

"What about the saliva thing?" he almost demanded.

The king chuckled softly. "If I thought you might want some of *that* stuff, I'd have offered it to you! I know it's not for everyone!"

Swanson glared at his now grinning crew mates, and proclaimed "I'll get you guys!" to the chuckles of all.

For the rest of breakfast, from time to time, Swanson kept shaking his head, and every time he did, laughter erupted all over again.

At one point, a young lady approached with a bowl of small leaves. "Here, eat some of these, they will help with your hangover."

Argent eyed her suspiciously until the king leaned forward and said "You don't have to marry her if you don't want to. She's just trying to help."

This, of course, caused even more laughter and Argent finally laughed out loud as well. Beaming at the young lady, he thanked her and ate some of the mint-like leaves. Swanson begrudgingly had some too. With breakfast finished, it was finally time to get down to business.

"Now that you understand us better Captain, it is time for you to understand the answers to your questions." said the King.

Harvey was beaming. He saw the wisdom of what might look like delay tactics, and no longer wondered why certain information was missing from the knowledge pills. In this case, it was better to learn this way, when one was not in immediate peril, that is.

"So Captain...what is it that brings you to our world?" asked the king.

"Curiosity mainly...and information. We were told to come here."

"What information do you need?" he asked, with a concerned tone of voice. "And who sent you?"

He and his people were keepers of a more than a few secrets, and some were not to be revealed lightly.

"I was told by Girk that you could tell us something of the world where the thirteenth Adityas ship wound up."

He looked puzzled, and exchanged looks with his lieutenants. None of them seemed to know what he was talking about either.

"Of course I know of the trader you mention, but not of the ship you mentioned."

"Does the number thirteen not mean anything to you?"

They all gave him blank expressions.

"A *lost* thirteenth *anything?*"

"We have no knowledge of this. Perhaps you should speak to the Dogons."

"Aren't *you* the *Dogons?*" blurted the Lt. in utter disbelief.

The King smiled. "We are humans from Urantia, just like you. It was the Dogons who brought us here, many generations ago."

This time it was their turn to exchange puzzled looks.

"Do we have to start all over again with someone else?" asked Argent.

Theo smiled broadly and asked "Have you not seen disk-shaped craft that travel under the water?"

"Yes! We call them Unidentified Submerged Objects, or USO's! I've seen some myself!" said the Lt.

Harvey had a glint in his eye, he was hoping that he suspected the truth.

"The Dogons are a very intelligent and benevolent race, and they have been looking after us on Urantia for thousands of years. They have given us a great many things subtly, but have also been known to take direct action, such as saving sailors from sharks."

"Wait, are you talking about some sort of intelligent fish?" asked Argent.

Harvey gave Theo a knowing look.

"No...no they are air-breathing mammals, and they have brains that are almost identical to yours and mine, they are just a little more *intelligent*, that's all."

"Not Mermaids!" exclaimed Argent.

"No, not Mermaids, but you are thinking in the right direction." By this time King Theo was grinning from ear to ear. "Come, let me *show* you."

He led them to a point at the edge of the ocean, picked up some sort of megaphone from a nearby pole and used it to amplify a squeaking sound he made that can only come from quite a lot of practice.

"They'll be coming soon. We just need to wait."

They didn't have long to wait as a school of dolphins swam up almost immediately, and three of them poked their heads out of the water, looking up at the Humans, while the others milled about behind them.

After what seemed like a long pause, Argent exclaimed: "You've got to be kidding me!"

"Actually, it makes sense." said Harvey with a twinkle in his eye.

"What? You can't be serious!"

"Why not?"

"Well, they're...they're...*fish!*"

"Mammals, actually." said Harvey, in a quiet, reassuring tone. "Just like our new friend here said."

The Lt. still looked puzzled.

The King tilted his head, and almost put his hands on his hips, but Harvey beat him to it.

"As the King also pointed out, they have the same kind of brains that we do, so it only follows that they have a comparable *form* of intelligence."

71

Argent gave them a blank stare of disbelief.

"What's more, as their brains are larger in proportion to their bodies, it stands to reason that they are more proportionately intelligent than we are. Again, just as he told us."

"I might not say that. We have our share of idiots." squeaked the dolphin in the middle, startling the Lt. In fact, he jumped so profoundly it caused the other dolphins to laugh, causing him to blush.

"Now I'm being laughed at by flipper and friends!" he complained, which only caused the others to laugh. "They'll never believe this back home." he moaned.

"Like they'd believe the rest of it?" Harvey asked rhetorically.

Argent stood there, staring at the dolphins. One waved a flipper at him.

"Oh.....kay." he started. "So you're telling me that you understand what I'm saying?"

"Yes, we do." squeaked the middle one.

Argent shook his head, because he really didn't know what to think about this.

"Greetings Captain." the middle dolphin said in it's squeaky voice as it looked at Harvey.

"Hello." replied Harvey with a twinkle in his eye. He had often marveled at the intelligence of dolphins, and now he was conversing with one! Marvelous!

"We are honored to be in your presence." it said as the three of them appeared to bow, as much as a dolphin with it's head out of the water can appear to bow.

This puzzled him. *He* was the one who was honored - to speak to dolphins from another planet! Wow!

"I can't believe this. Talking dolphins." said Argent, half to himself. "What's next? Singing microbes?" he asked rhetorically.

"Actually, yes, if you like." answered the android.

Argent rolled his eyes at that one, and threw his head back, as he took a step back and turned around, much to the android's delight.

Harvey smirked at the two of them and addressed the middle dolphin. "The honor is mine." he said humbly.

The dolphins seemed to be pleased with that.

"We have a lead for you." squeaked the middle one.

"Yes?"

"Seek the Gordian tunnels."

"That's it?"

The Dolphin on the right squeaked "There are sacred documents there, that will help you. Specifically, a map."

Harvey gave the dolphin a blank look.

"Sorry. That's all we have." it squeaked, and by it's body language seemed to shrug as it exchanged looks with the others.

Harvey and Argent exchanged a puzzled look as Theo shrugged as well.

9

THE TUNNELS OF MEHUMAN
"What is the sound of one hand clapping?"

On the bridge of the Ezrael, they quickly located the Gordian tunnels. They were called 'The tunnels of Mehuman' by the natives. It seems that some things are not translated as well as others, but the ships Butator was able to understand what they were looking for and locate it quickly. If only it could locate clues to their overall mission as easily!

Harvey approached Argent. "Are those...?"

"I don't know." he said almost under his breath, not wanting others to hear.

"Stiff upper lip." said Harvey as he gave the Lt. a light tap on the shoulder before returning to his chair.

The Major then appeared at the bridge door and immediately sought-out the Captain, with the Chief engineer in tow.

"I think it is safe to assume that you'll be traversing tunnels, so I wish to equip my men appropriately." started the Major.

"Of course." answered Harvey. "But why tell me?"

"I want to try out some of the ship-made supplies, and I thought you would like to know."

"Such as?"

"These." said the Lt. as he help up a small electrical cell.

"A *cell?*" asked Harvey.

"We ran out of cells for our tactical lights a week ago."

"I see, and why is it important for me to know that you'll be trying out ship-made replacements?"

"The lithium cells only last about twenty minutes in our tactical lights as it is, but the Butator claims these will last perpetually." answered the Chief engineer.

"Neat!" said Harvey as he accepted the cell from the Chief to get a closer look. "How do they do it?"

"I am told it is like a solar cell, inside the cell casing that use neutrinos instead of photons." said the Major.

"NEUTRINOS!" exclaimed Harvey.

"YES! Amazing isn't it?" said the chief.

"How do they get it to work?" asked the Captain.

74

"I have no idea, but you can be sure I am researching it as fast as I can." said the Chief.

Harvey hefted it in his hand. It had some weight to it - more than a lithium cell - but still not too heavy.

"I don't know what all the fuss is about." muttered the Major. "The computer states that it works like solar cells."

The scientists all exchanged puzzled looks.

"You just have to know how to ask the right questions, I should think." said the Major. "Besides, I don't want any kind of solar power running anything essential. Darned unreliable 'green' tech!"

Just what material neutrino-sensitive 'solar-cells' could be composed of, was what the scientists were pondering, but they all thought it best not to rain on the Major's parade. Not only was he a stick in the mud that wouldn't use the term Butator for the ship's intelligence system, sure, it worked *like* a computer, though it was to a computer what a super-computer was to a simple 4-function calculator. Obviously, his understanding of science was far less than that of his soldiers and it seemed pointless to say anything.

"Now, back to business!" said the Major triumphantly. "I suggest that all S*I*P*Es carry at least two sets of regular cells as a secure backup until such time that the ship-made power cells have proven themselves without a doubt in a field test."

"I thought you ran out." said Harvey.

"We still have a few with some life left in them, to use in a pinch. I want a backup plan. Always a backup plan."

"Suit yourself." said Harvey as the Chief shrugged.

"No problem here." added Linda.

"I just don't want them to fail and have you lot complaining that I didn't inform you about what was going on, that's all." said the Major.

"Fair enough." said Harvey, and he set his attention on the task before them. "Now to the task at hand?" he added, indicating the ship's main display.

There it was - an underground labyrinth that made The Gordian knot look simple by comparison. Not only was it three-dimensional but ever-changing too, and talk about traps! However, this was the only route to the Emperor of the Ahasuerus Empire that was open to visitors. Once they made it through the maze, they would have the choice of an audience with him or to meet him in mortal combat - but not both.

"Looks like spaghetti junction." commented Linda, her voice trailing off as she contemplated the complexity of the maze.

"How 'bout The Gordian knot?" asked DeSoto, in an attempt to join the conversation.

"How the hell are we supposed to plot a path through this mess? It'll take years!" exclaimed the chief. "It keeps changing! We'd have to analyze patterns and everything!"

"You got something better to do?" asked Harvey rhetorically.

"No, not really." answered the chief in a defeatist tone.

"Wait. There's a better way." said Harvey after examining the image on the screen for a moment.

"What are you talking about? This is impossible!" exclaimed the chief.

"The natives deal with it, so it must be possible...but I don't see how just yet." offered Linda while she attempted to use a Butator terminal to analyze the maze.

"Got it! Take a look at *that*." said Harvey calmly, pointing at the main Butator screen as he sent the image from his terminal.

The entire bridge crew looked closely at the display. Then the chief noticed something.

"Ghost images like with a multi-layer board!"

"Precisely!" said Harvey.

"Okay, what are those?" asked Linda.

"When you x-ray a circuit board, sometimes there are ghost images of hidden foil patterns from inside the board, and some are deliberately put there to confuse any would-be copiers. Unless you've seen something like it before and know what it means, they're easy to dismiss."

"You mean...?"

"Yes, there are stable tunnels deep underneath the changing streets!"

"The locals must use them to get around." said the chief.

"Oh! That's low!"

"Literally!" said Harvey and the chief in chorus.

* * *

Dr. Morax had learned very well how to tap into the ship's systems and stay out of sight. The latter was simple due to the way the ship operated, but for some reason he was getting more powerful as a psychic. The longer he was onboard the ship, the better he felt as well. He even found he could navigate without the need for his cane. Still, he kept it out of habit if nothing else. Well...there were the 'goodies' built into it after all!

He learned that Harvey was leaving the ship and would therefore be vulnerable. This prolonged visit to a remote planet made for a perfect opportunity to ambush him. So, Dr. Morax set out to find a shuttle that was capable of the flight and long distance communication so he could call Captain Batna for help. He made his way to the hangar bay and started examining ships, looking for high tech, and all the while keeping an ear to the floor, metaphorically speaking. He could force one, perhaps two, weak-minded individuals to not 'see' him, but he didn't want to be caught in that situation. As it was, he was mentally instructing the ship to ignore his presence and it took a lot of effort. Normally that would drain him in no time, but since he had arrived on the ship, he had felt stronger every day.

One small ship caught his notice right away. It was as if it were calling him to it. He passed several ships with the proper equipment to approach this one. It was beautiful to him. Absolutely seamless in constructions like the Ezrael. Shaped roughly like the classic representation of the human heart, he recognized it as having belonged to what he called the kludge, named Gladrina. There were no apparent windows and he could not find a door. There was a curious depression in the side of the hull that looked like a shallow six-fingered hand print. He slowly, hesitantly reached out an touched it. In his mind, it spoke to him in happy greetings, so he asked it to let him in.

At that moment Gladrina, felt the attempt to enter her ship. She smiled to herself, knowing that if she told Harvey, he would drop everything and waste more time trying to capture Dr. Morax. Instead, she thought she'd teach that bad man a little lesson. "DANGER: DO NOT *ALLOW!*" she said to herself as she contacted her ship telepathically. Morax dropped to his knees, "You naughty little..." was all he could say before he collapsed on the deck. He was just conscious enough to trigger morphing into the floor and off to his hideout to recover. He was going to be out for some time. Gladrina simply smiled knowingly. At least he had been bitten, in a manner of speaking, and that momentary telepathic contact told her much.

* * *

There was little or no reaction to the approach and subsequent landing of the craft. The ramp opened up and several soldiers spilled out - bull pups at the ready. Still, very little if any notice was taken of the visitors. Harvey and Linda had elected to dress as locals, and carry only edged weapons. Well, Linda had a small energy weapon in her cloak - just in case - as she had not as yet learned how to throw energy bolts using her body armor. She really wanted to ask how Harvey had managed to do that, and all of the other tricks, for that matter.

The Penemue pills had little cultural information this time as well, not by design, but due to the fact that the locals simply wanted to keep their most closely guarded secret, so it was not because the place was far off the beaten path this time.

Linda was the first to make a move. She held up her scanner and used it to lead her to a tunnel entrance. Again, the locals took very little notice of this. The entrance was hidden, though not well, and only one person raised her eyes for a moment. A woman who was sweeping her doorstep and seemed slightly amused rather than curious.

"Well, they don't seem to want to stop us." said Linda.

"That's what worries me." said Harvey. He looked around at the few faces that glanced his way, smiled slightly and then looked away, then he added "They seem *amused* if nothing else." Then he muttered under his breath "I hope it isn't a trap."

Famous last words.

Argent and Swanson opted to enter first, pointing their weapons this way and that, shining their bright tactical lights on the walls, ceiling and floors.

Swanson, was itching for a fight and the Lt. could see it, so he let him take point.

After getting an "All clear!" from the S*I*P*Es, Harvey smiled at Linda, shrugged and said; "Ladies first!" as he motioned for her to take the lead.

She smiled, and added "Except into danger." as she strolled past him into the darkness.

"But it's *clear*..." Harvey muttered, his attempt at chivalry shattered, yet again.

Linda heard him and smiled out of the side of her mouth. She, being more experienced at this, wanted him to try harder, but he was simply confused if anything, and discouraged as well.

She simply shrugged it off, not knowing the damage she had done to Harvey's fragile confidence in that area and headed into the darkness ahead. The short tunnel led to what looked like a long slide. Even the bright tactical lights on the soldier's weapons could not reach the end. Linda shrugged and made a move to jump onto the slide. The Lt. reached out and stopped her.

"Where are you going?" he asked.

"Wherever I wind up." answered Linda, cheerfully.

"Perhaps you should let me go first." the Lt. interjected as he almost pushed her aside, in search of another passageway that seemed to lead perpendicular to the slide.

"Be my guest." she muttered just before the Lt. walked right into an optical illusion.

If he had been running, the wall might have knocked him out. As it was, he got a good smack on the nose for his trouble, even through his visor. He fell backwards onto the floor.

"Or not!" he said, dazed as he held his nose, and tried to get up.

As Linda and the Xenobiologist scurried up to examine him, Harvey walked slowly up to the wall.

"Amazing paint job." he marveled.

"You're telling me!" said the Lt. in a muffled voice as he held his nose away from the doctor.

Harvey shone his light on the wall over and over again. "Somehow the absorption pattern is different from a wall...it must be very sophisticated paint."

"It would help if it were a little softer." said Argent in a muffled tone as he held his hand over his nose.

"Hold still!" snapped the Xenobiologist, who was trying to treat the Lt. for a broken nose.

Harvey cracked a sly smile, and scanned the wall with his body armor. Sure enough, it was a very sophisticated paint job indeed, from a technological level appreciably ahead of the state of the art back home.

"Amazing." he said under his breath. "We'll have to watch out for more of these."

Lt. Argent gave him a look as if to say 'Ya think?'

They adopted a policy of walking with their swords extend in front of them, sheathed of course. Indeed, in the course of things they would find a total of fifteen such optical illusions in this way, and would soon find their way to more interesting traps.

"Well, there seems to be no other place to go...but down the slide." said Linda as she held her scanner this way and that, and settling on the slide. "Gentlemen?" she asked, indicating that direction. "There's nothing down there but the bottom and a few tunnels leading away from it."

Swanson took the initiative this time.

"Down is where we want to go and down is where this leads. See you in hell!" he said as he dived onto the slide, head first!

Argent and Harvey exchanged a look and then the Lt. shrugged and followed, but feet first, and sitting up, rather than prone. The rest waited behind for a report. They didn't have to wait as long.

"Come on down, the water's fine." came Swanson's voice over the radio.

"Water?" said Linda. She was holding her scanner and could not see any water indicated.

"He's joking!" said the Lt. "It's all clear, and dry." he added moments later.

This time Harvey decided to go ahead of Linda, almost cutting her off. She had expected him to offer the chance to go first, and it confused her a little that he didn't. In fact, it put her off as he blazed past her on his way to the slide, as if ignoring her.

When they all in turn reached the bottom of the slide, they were happy to find that the slide terminated some three feet above the floor, so all they had to do was stand up naturally. Neat!

By this time, they had reconnoitered, as the Lt. had put it, enough to know that there was only one promising way to go from there.

Harvey took point, much to the chagrin of Lt. Argent and Cpl.

Swanson. In truth, the Captain wanted to avoid Linda because of his earlier mistake. Like most 'nice guys' he didn't understand enough about women to know he was making things worse, not better.

"Really sir, *we're* here to protect *you*, and point, is well...THE most dangerous position." Lt. Argent said earnestly, indicating his broken nose.

"I appreciate that, but my body armor will protect me."

"Mine's no slouch either."

Linda looked at the Lt.'s nose when he said that and it made him roll his eyes.

"Just relax, you've more than earned a break from trail-blazing." he said looking over his shoulder.

Now, at that moment, a few things happened at once, which taught Harvey a little lesson.

First, he had told his armor to be more specific about warnings, which lowered his awareness to danger in general. He liked it that way because he was getting a little tired of it warning him of so many vague dangers, hence the setting. In any event, the armor knew it's job well, and optical traps fooled it almost as easily as they fool the eye. After all, the armor is not all knowing. Due in part to this, and the fact that Harvey was not paying attention; not to mention his quicker than normal pace, all combined to make it almost impossible for him to react in time to avoid the trap. Just as he finished talking to the Lt., he was warned not to take another step, indeed, the armor stiffened up to prevent it, and at a normal pace it might have worked, but momentum being what it is, Harvey tumbled head-first into the floor, and vanished!

That got Argent to stop abruptly. He was more able to do this because of all of his experience. He motioned the others to stop. "Where'd he go?" asked Swanson.

The Lt. kneeled down and began feeling the floor. He found the edge of the drop off. Almost immediately, Harvey's hand appeared out of the floor, almost a foot to the left side of the Lt.'s hand. He grabbed it and helped Harvey out of the hole.

"What's it like down there?" he asked after helping the captain out of the floor.

Harvey grinned and winced at the same time, and lifted his shirt, showing a few evenly-spaced marks. "It's a classic Burmese tiger pit."

81

"Ouch! Are you alright?"

"The punctures are small and the armor is keeping the flesh together of course, but it still *smarts*."

"Now you know what I go through every time I get shot." Argent said flatly.

Harvey looked distinctly puzzled for a moment, then realized that he was a veteran of many conflicts. S*I*P*E armor was as good as it got back home, but it couldn't ignore physics any more than his armor could.

"Let me see that." said the doctor.

Harvey reluctantly removed his shirt, embarrassed at being checked out by Linda, who was at first concerned for his well-being; more then she was amused at his blushing at being shirtless!

The doctor examined Harvey very closely, and decided his patient was alright.

"Amazing the way the molecular armor keeps the flesh together, it is better than anything I could do, even with super glue."

"You're kidding about the glue, right?"

"No, that stuff is great. We've been using it on animals for decades, and it works fine instead of sutures or staples. In fact, in most cases it is *better*."

The idea of having a wound glued shut was not that appealing to the Captain.

"All right. Show's over." he said as he put his shirt back on, making eye contact with Linda.

"Nothing I haven't see before." said Linda softly.

"Alright you two, I'd say 'get a room' but hand holding isn't exactly something that needs privacy." said the doctor.

To that Linda chuckled and Harvey looked as confused as ever.

They began to map out the outer limits of the hole and soon discovered that in order to cross it they either had to erect a bridge or crawl into the hole and cross it from inside.

"How 'bout that sir?" asked the Lt.

"I wouldn't recommend it." he replied to a raised eyebrow. "In order to get out, I had to stand on some of the spikes, they're quite sharp and there isn't much space in between them." as he indicated the punctures in his shirt.

82

"I see, that's where your armor and ours differ; yours will not allow a point to penetrate at all, and with ours it's the slow blade that gets through." he thought for a moment. "Could we *run* across?"

"No, you'd be likely to miss a spike, not being able to see them, and you have areas that aren't protected." he said indicating Argent's face. True, he had a visor for protection, enhanced vision and a heads-up display, but was not wearing his full helmet gear due to the heat from being underground, his mouth and jaw were a great place for a spike to enter his cranium.

Argent just rubbed his exposed chin and muttered something about having to get some of the ships armor to work for him some day. Then he retrieved a rope and tubing from his backpack and smiled at Harvey. He put together two tripod-like mechanisms out of the lightweight tubing and smiled at Harvey again.

The captain, using the telekinetic features of his armor, managed to levitate one of the mechanisms across to the other side, rope in tow. Argent then detonated a remote charge that fired securing bolts into the stone floor. He did the same with the other where he stood. Within moments, they were taking turns pulling themselves across on a pulley supported harness that each one sent back for the next.

"The resourcefulness of the military never ceases to amaze me." said Harvey flatly.

"Thanks!" said Argent as he smiled to himself. He didn't tell Harvey that Linda had told him about the 'space pack' and he had used one to pack literally a ton of supplies. He had everything they could possibly need.

* * *

A good twelve hours later, they emerged at the far end of the tunnels where the walls were dripping with some sort of green goo.

"Well, that was sticky." said Lt. Argent as they emerged, and pulled what looked like a bamboo skewer out of a seam in the back of his helmet. Indeed, a lot of them had many a skewer stuck in their backs.

"Oh! You're gonna have to pay for that one buster!" said Harvey.

As they were talking, a guard, who had his back to them almost jumped out of his skin.

"Where did you people come from?" he demanded.

"The tunnels of course." answered Harvey flatly.

"But...but...NOBODY..." he exclaimed, completely baffled.

"You mean to tell me that no one has ever found the lower tunnels before?" asked Harvey in disbelief.

"Well, uh, others have *found* them before, but only after months of camping out and watching the locals to see if they slip-up. But they never manage to get past the static maze, traps and illusions. You really are the first to make it through in my lifetime." explained the guard. "Congratulations! So are you here for an audience or a challenge?"

"Audience." said Harvey.

"It figures! Nobody would be crazy enough to engage the emperor in single combat! C'mon, I'll take you to him."

They shrugged and followed. They had presumed that they had to find a way to get past the guard, and instead he was taking him right to the person they were there to see.

Sure enough, the emperor of this world was formidable indeed. It seemed that only Mongo would stand a chance in a fight with him. He stood a full nine feet tall, and was stocky to boot. Sure, the gravity was noticeably less than Urantia's, but not enough to explain the man's size. In truth, the largest and strongest were chosen to wed, so that after hundreds of generations, the royal line consisted entirely of massive brutes by design.

When they entered the throne room, the Lt. could not hold his tongue.

"He looks like a shaved Sasquatch crossed with a Gorilla!" he exclaimed.

"Please! Don't antagonize him!" snapped Harvey, with a hint of fear in his voice.

"Oops! Sorry!" he said under his breath, as he sported a big grin, knowing that if there was a fight, it was Harvey that would have to meet the challenge.

"He does, at that." said Harvey under his breath, rather amused by the thought.

As they approached the throne, the emperor stood to greet them.

"Captain Harvie!" he bellowed.

"Does everyone in the whole gosh-darn universe have to know who

I am?" Harvey rhetorically asked his companions out of the corner of his mouth.

He smiled nervously as the emperor lumbered forward, with a determined look on his face.

Not knowing what to make of it, Harvey braced himself. Sure enough, the emperor drew his rather formidable battle axe. Without skipping a beat, Harvey drew his sword and the fight was on.

"I thought he said 'audience'." muttered the Lt. calmly.

"He *did*." answered Linda firmly.

"Then why are they fighting?" asked the Lt. unconcerned, yet genuinely puzzled.

"Emperor's prerogative." said the guard who had escorted them to the throne room.

Linda and Lt. Argent looked surprised.

"Then why ask?" asked Lt. Argent.

"For most, it would be their decision; but since your friend here is a pubic figure, he has to prove he is who and what he claims to be." answered the guard calmly.

"First of all he doesn't 'claim to be' anybody in particular. Secondly, how's he supposed to prove his identity by fighting a brute like him?" demanded Linda.

"Well, if he truly *is* the Simkiel, then he will not only win, but the emperor won't even be able to even cut him either." answered the guard with a matter-of-fact tone.

A sly smile crept across her face. Surely Harvey's molecular body armor could protect him against almost all cuts. This part should prove interesting.

"Of course, if he loses..." began the guard.

"He won't." said the Lt. cutting him off with a smile of his own.

Pymander then stepped in and said "Excuse us." as he whisked them away from the guard's earshot. Satisfied that they were not going to be overheard, he said "I don't want to worry you too much, but that axe IS big enough to not only breach his armor, but decapitate him as well."

Linda turned pale. Both she and Argent slowly looked over at the giant brute that was energetically pursuing Harvey's head. He noticed their gaze, and grinned slyly at the tiny little people. They waved nervously and returned to their "huddle".

"*NOW*, you tell us?" demanded Linda, almost in a panic.

As Pymander spoke, Linda relayed it through the body armor's communications "If he simply hits you and knocks you back, that won't harm you, because the force is more than enough to move you away...but don't let him back you up against a wall, or swing the blade down on you from above. And...your armor was breached by the spikes in the pit, so it is a little vulnerable in those places."

"Got it." replied Harvey, although this was not news to him.

"We've got to get him out of this!" said Argent.

"Agreed." said Pymander. "But *how?*"

They all turned to watch the fight.

The Emperor bellowed "Have at you!" and lunged at Harvey.

Sparks flew from the clashing blades as Harvey expertly deflected blow after blow. How such a heavy weapon could be diverted by a mere sword was a little bit of a mystery, but this was a high-tech sword with abilities of its own. It had been specially selected for this purpose.

As the fight continued, it was obvious that the Emperor was giving no quarter. Harvey may have managed to divert the blows, but was showing signs of weakening under the onslaught. He gave a slightly worried look to Linda, and then focused. He cut the Emperor across the abdomen, just enough to draw blood, in hope that would end the fight.

A gong rang out and a man announced "First blood!" to cheers from the court.

The Emperor paused. Looked down at his stomach, grinned and said "At last! A worthy adversary!" He laughed heartily then lunged at Harvey, redoubling the attack. This had the effect of driving Harvey back to the far wall, and he was none too thrilled at the prospect of having no retreat, especially against a solid surface. He knew of the danger all too well.

Although he found himself unable to disarm his opponent, Harvey was able to cut the Emperor two more times, once on each arm. Obviously, he was trying to dissuade his opponent, but to no avail. Each cut, and corresponding sounding of the gong, spurred him on with that much more vim and vigor.

"Doesn't this guy ever get tired?" Harvey asked rhetorically.

The Emperor went for a death blow, to the gasps of his crew, only to throw him violently against the wall. Seeing that his shirt had been sliced open but there was not a mark on the man himself, the Emperor should have been satisfied with this, but instead he was astonished by, it even though it was what he wanted to see! Taking advantage of his momentary distraction, Harvey struck a devastating blow to the emperor's axe handle, cutting it in half, and the emperor fell to his knees from being thrown off balance. Harvey quickly placed his blade against the emperor's throat. The Emperor kneeled there, not knowing what to think. Bewildered, he finally said: "I yield!" to the cheers of all but Harvey.

The Emperor slowly looked at Harvey then lowered his head in defeat, as if present it for decapitation.

Harvey got a maniacal look in his face, lifted his blade and, to the horror of his companions, roared loudly as he swung his sword like an axe toward his opponent's neck...

10
DON'T SHOOT THAT WEASEL...
...HAND ME THE FLAME THROWER!
(With profuse apologies to "V".)

Harvey's blow stopped just short of the Emperor's neck, as if it had struck a piece of wood and wedged itself in the grain. He had very good control of his blade. He looked over at Linda, winked and said "Just kidding!" Then he sported a big grin while extending his hand to help the big brute back onto his feet - as if a he had the strength or stature to do so.

The Emperor had the look of true awe on his face. "You...you're *sparing* my life?"

"OF COURSE!" said Harvey in a loud voice for all to hear as he deftly sheathed his sword.

Climbing to his feet, the Emperor said "It is said that the Simkiel is not bloodthirsty." Now on his feet he added "I admit I had my doubts, because servants of the adversary can and often do the same things that you did, but none of them would spare a life given the chance to take one. I doubt you no more, you must be the servant of Apharoph!" He then knelt down before the Captain again, who in turn looked up and rolled his eyes.

"Get up! No *good* man should kneel before me!" insisted Harvey in an annoyed tone. It was true that he did not wish this sort of thing from anyone.

"Again a sign of your true colors! The Simkiel is not one to demand this kind of respect." he said, rising to his towering height. "My kingdom is yours to command, chosen one of the almighty Apharoph!"

Linda beamed at Harvey, as he again rolled his eyes to the cheers of the court.

"All I need from you is information." said Harvey flatly.

This made the Emperor give him a puzzled look.

"We need to analyze your ancient folklore, the old stories of how your people first came here, and any corresponding star charts."

"You speak of the sacred scrolls. Even I have never seen them with mine own eyes." said the Emperor from the head of his great table. They had retired to his private chambers to further discuss what Harvey and crew needed.

"Then how do you know that they exist?" blurted Argent.

Harvey gave him a sharp look, but Argent just shrugged back.

"There are monks that have tended them for two thousand generations. That's why." the emperor answered, almost cheerfully.

"So how do *we* get to see them?" asked Harvey.

"I'm afraid that you'll have to navigate the oldest and most treacherous of the tunnels, under the sacred mountain."

"Not *more* tunnels!" exclaimed Lt. Argent. Harvey gave him another look, and Argent just sulked. He was beginning to hate tunnels, especially since he had been having nightmares about them. The less time he spent in a tunnel the better. The last stint underground had been enough for him. He thought about this as he rubbed his nose a bit.

"Which way?" asked Harvey with a grin. The Emperor pointed at an archway on the far side of the room. "You see, the great hall is the only entrance to 'The Labyrinth Of The Ages'. Hence the fact, that to enter them, you have to get past the likes of me."

Harvey said "We thank you, but we must get going."

"Of course...your need must be pressing indeed, to have come this far."

The Emperor motioned for them to enter the tunnel system the through the old doors that were behind him.

Harvey, tried the door and it would not budge. The emperor, seeing the need, pulled on the door as well, it took effort from both of them and the soldiers, but it finally swung open, creaking as it went, of course, to reveal thick cobwebs across the entire doorway.

"I thought you said monks were in there." said Harvey, puzzled.

"They only come and go once a year for supplies, and they are about due." replied the emperor.

"That's a lot of cobwebs for only one year." muttered Harvey forgetting that the year on that world was much longer than the one he was used to, due to the size and power of the local star, the 'Goldilocks' zone was much further out.

"I don't want to go in there." said Argent nervously, as he saw what lay behind the doors to be right out of his nightmares.

"Why not?" asked Harvey, giving him a surprised look, like he were suddenly a coward. Even now, this was not the impression one wanted to give the Emperor of this world!

Argent approached Harvey to speak without others hearing them "You know those nightmares I've been having?"

"Yes." he answered apprehensively. "I thought we got past that with the last set of tunnels..."

"Well...*That's* the tunnel!" He said, visibly upset.

Harvey had never seen the Lt. like this. The bravest man he had ever known was almost cowering at entering an old tunnel.

"Wuss!" said Swanson as he walked through the cobwebs into the dark archway. "See you in HELL!" he said loudly over his shoulder as he disappeared into the depths of the passageways.

Not to be outdone, Argent took a deep breath, rolled his eyes and followed. He hesitated just past the threshold and asked Harvey and Linda with a sheepish grin "Whatever happened to: 'last one there is a rotten egg'?" before disappearing into the tunnels.

Harvey gave the Emperor a worried look, and a goodbye salute. Then followed the soldiers.

Linda curtsied, and scurried after them with a big grin on her face. She loved quest-like adventures!

The Emperor just sat there shaking his head as they left. "Heaven help them." he muttered. "They're going to need it."

* * *

Argent was constantly trading 'point' with Swanson. They criscrossed back and forth as if they were sneaking up on a fortified enemy position. Swanson was grinning ear to ear because Argent kept looking at the ceiling and crouching as if it were going to cave in. Each would pass the other, then take cover as best they could by leaning against the wall. Over and over they leapfrogged down the passageway, as if they were under heavy enemy fire.

"Kids these days!" said Linda.

"Ye**p**" said Harvey, with great emphases on the 'P'.

They smiled at each other and followed the pair of soldiers, by calmly walking down the middle of the passageway.

They navigated the entire labyrinth without much incident, it seems that the worst part of the tunnel system was a real old-fashioned maze, not to mention the fact that some of the ceilings really *were* about to cave-in due to their age, but they held. This, of course made Argent all the more nervous. Eventually, after many wrong turns, they found their way to the library.

"Look." whispered Argent, pointing at some monks with their backs to the party.

Swanson began creeping up on them, with his bull-pup set to flamethrower as if he hated libraries. Argent slowly pushed the barrel of Swanson's weapon downward, and gave the Corporal a look who shrugged, and grinned sheepishly.

The monks, upon spotting them, undisturbed, motioned for them to enter.

"Welcome wise ones." they said in unison.

This made the crew exchange puzzled looks.

One monk, wearing more elaborate robes than the others, approached the group.

"What is the distance that cannot be traveled?" he asked, with an expressionless face.

"Sheesh! We come all this way, and they ask flaky questions!" exclaimed Lt. Argent, who had just about had it.

Harvey gave him a puzzled look, so much so, he cocked his head.

"Why can't they come out and say what they mean? Next thing you know they're going to ask you what the sound of one hand clapping is!" complained Argent.

The monks got excited at this and huddled together to write it down and discuss it.

"Jeez! They're writing it down!" exclaimed Argent.

"Okay, okay, you've made your point." said Harvey calmly, waving the man off.

He approached the monk that had asked the question and asked "What does this have to do with looking at the scrolls?"

"Nothing. We were told that wise men would come and we thought you might be able to enlighten us. Instead, you give us another mystery." He thought for a moment, cocking his head to the side and said "Perhaps that new mystery is the road to the enlightenment we seek."

"While you're pondering this..." Linda said, as she held up one hand opening and closing it rapidly as to clap, " ...may we examine your scrolls?"

The monks for the most part were fascinated with Linda's hand, as it had indeed made a clapping sound.

"By all means." said the head monk as he stepped aside and motioned for the visitors to enter.

"Might as well ask what happens when an irresistible force meets an immovable object." commented Argent. The monk's eyes went predictably wide. "I'll save you the trouble...the object is destroyed." The monks again huddled, taking notes.

"Sheesh!" said Argent as he walked past them into the library, deliberately trying to bump into the monk with his shoulder. Luckily, the monk was watching and quickly, yet respectfully, dodged the irate soldier.

With the Android's help, they quickly located the scroll they were looking for. Linda took photos of it with her body armor and send them to the ship's Butator. To the monks, it looked as though she were simply scrutinizing the scrolls. Then she said "Thank you!".

"That's IT?" asked the head monk, now visibly taken aback.

"That's it. We're done." answered Linda.

"I am very glad you are not taking them with you." he said with great relief.

"We don't want the scrolls themselves, we only want the information they contain." explained Linda.

All of the monks breathed a collective sigh of relief, as the head monk motioned the visitors toward the exit.

"Let's get back to the ship." said Harvey, triumphantly. "This may only be a small piece to the puzzle, but it is still a piece none the less."

"Is the way we came in, the only way back out?" asked Harvey.

"No, not at all." answered the head monk. "Those doors over there can only be opened from this side, so it is an exit only. The tunnels behind it will take you to a secret cave entrance to the mountain. That's the fastest way out of here."

"Someone ought to tell the Emperor that. He seems to think the tunnels we came in by, were the only way in." Harvey said.

"They are. But to exit, one must go this way." answered the head monk as he indicated the exit doors.

"Well let's not waste any more time and get going. I don't like hanging around here for so long." he looked at the head monk "No offense." he said

"None taken, wise one."

"Something is nagging at me. I think we ought to get going and soon." said Harvey to the rest.

There was a mutter of agreement and they all headed into the exit tunnels. This was a lot of bother for a relatively small amount of information.

Argent mumbled something about "All that trouble and a broken nose; just for a photograph" before taking point.

Often, things are not as easy as they seem. In this case, the comparatively simple task of exiting the mountain was about to become deadly. Perhaps this was meant to teach Lt. Argent a lesson about patience, but then again maybe not. It could be just 'one of those things'.

* * *

Over the horizon, silently gliding in with the rising sun, casting a giant shadow that looked like a scorpion, came a star ship. It was large, powerful and malevolent. The flagship Zebuleon, captained by none other than Satrina Batna herself. She was generally bloodthirsty, but today she was ravenously out for *revenge.*

"They're under the mountain, in the catacombs." said the navigation officer as she monitored at the scanner.

Captain Batna chuckled softly, narrowed her eyes and said rather coldly "Rattle their cage."

The weapons officer correctly took it to mean a carpet bombing. So she proceeded to pepper the area with what they considered to be sufficient - small bombs the size of a baseball with destructive power equal to one of our own 'Bunker busters'.

Needless to say, there was more than a little shaking going on in the tunnels.

"What the *hell* is going on?" demanded Harvey.

"Unless I miss my guess, it's an aerial bombardment!" replied the Lt. over the growing noise.

93

"I know that! Who is doing it and why?"

"Beats the heck out of me!" he replied with a sheepish grin. This was his worst nightmare literally coming to life. He had never told anyone that he was claustrophobic, to boot! The real test of a soldier is not how well he faces death, but how well he faces his worst fears. For Argent, this was that test.

"You're a lot of help!" Harvey shouted over the growing roar.

Rocks and other debris fell all around them. They had to get out of there fast!

"The cascades are unstoppable now." said the Zebulon's weapons officer, after the second sweep.

"Excellent! You may discontinue. Helmsman, and get us the heaven out of here!" The order came none too soon, as 'company' had just arrived.

The Ezrael, under the command of the Major, noticed the bombardment and had arrived to investigate, just in time to see the Zebuleon take off at full speed, leaving only a tiny spy satellite behind. This of course didn't fool the Ezrael's sensors, but they left it alone for a plethora of reasons.

"Shall we pursue?" asked Taggert, at the controls.

"No, let them think they got away, we can deal with them later. We should do what we can to rescue *our* people first."

"Aye, aye, sir!" said Taggert.

"You're in the army soldier, not the navy."

"Yes sir. It's just that I've always wanted to say that."

"You've missed your calling, do you *know* that?" he said in uncharacteristically good humor.

"Yes sir."

"Bloody lack of discipline! I ought to keel-haul you for that. Would too, if it weren't for one thing." said the Major in his best 'pirate voice'.

"Lack of air out there, sir?"

"BLOODY LACK OF BARNACLES!" he bellowed.

There was now a distinct glint in the major's eyes. Secretly, he had always wanted to be a high-seas pirate. What was happening to them or why did not even occur to him, but they were both in good spirits, as if they knew somehow, everything would be fine. In fact, it was the ship that was telepathically assuring them on a sub-conscious level, because of what was about to happen.

The soldier swallowed hard with a worried look on his face.

"Now! Unless you have other plans, can we get on with rescuing our people?"

Taggert shook his head and said "Aye- I mean, YES, *SIR!*"

The Major gave him a sharp glare, then a smile. Despite the situation, he really was in a good mood!

* * *

In the catacombs, Harvey & company were having a grand old time dodging the cascading cave-in. They ran down the largest tunnel, as it collapsed behind them. It was almost as if the collapse were chasing them, perhaps playing with them in a way. Harvey even thought at one point he could hear the echo of a woman chuckling, but he shook it off. He had no way of knowing that a woman *was* watching, by some means and his armor had somehow allowed him to faintly hear her laughter, but he was to discover more about that much later.

As they had their escape cut off one way, another wall would open up and lead to another tunnel. This continued for several minutes, but it seemed like hours to them. Finally, the rumbling slowed, almost to a stop. It appeared as if the worst was over. Good thing too because the tunnels were getting smaller, fewer and further apart.

"Looks like we're getting a break!" said Harvey over his shoulder, as he led the way. His body armor showing him the best route out of the mountain, and constantly warning him of impending doom. What had him the most worried is that the Adad - or prognostication - system had told him that someone was about to die, and the only way to save that person, at this point, was to let more than one die instead. He didn't dare ask who it was, or inform the others as that would ensure that all of them would die, as they would be delayed by asking too many questions and squabbling about it. All he could do was follow the advice that would lead to only a single fatality. He found himself hoping that it would be the android again, since he was 'easily' repaired the last time when he was shot in the head and all they really had to do was replace his brain. Attempting to repair him was how they had wound up with Elroy on the crew. Alas, the system sensed his questions and informed him that Pymander would escape with minimal damage. His heart sank at the news. He didn't dare inquire further. He just didn't have the heart. If it was going to be Linda, he would gladly offer his life up instead. Things do not work that way, however, and the Adad system told him it wasn't going to be Linda, unless he tried to stop it. That was something, anyway...or was it?

11
MORT
"They'll have to kill me before I die!"

Their luck finally ran out as the wall of the tunnel gave way under the enormous weight of the sliding slabs of rock, and caught Lt. Argent under just enough of a slide to pin him with malice. It was as if the slab of granite were swatting him like a fly. His armor protected him somewhat from the initial impact, but the continuing force crushed him in short order. He didn't have the time or strength to let out a cry, but nonetheless, the android found him, and exclaimed "The Lieutenant!" Which brought Linda running back despite the obvious danger.

Frantically, the android tried to lift the slab off of the ill-fated soldier to absolutely no effect. He was no stronger than the average man, but that didn't stop him from trying so hard that he actually began snapping muscle fibers - his 'minimal damage'. As Linda arrived and appraised the situation, she momentarily paused, realizing that the Lt. was finished. When her armor's Butator confirmed it, she calmly sighed, placed her hand on the android's shoulder and said "There's *nothing* we can do for him now."

Surprisingly, the rumbles from the bowels of the mountain got louder and the ground began to shake more vigorously. She quickly looked around and shouted "We have to get out of here NOW!" Then she looked down at the Lt., to see him look up at her. His stiff, slow movements were reminiscent of that of an animal that had just been run over by a car and had only moments left to live. He smiled weakly at her and gave her the 'thumbs up' with his free arm. She went down on one knee, held his hand with both of hers, pressing it to her forehead for a moment, until it went limp. She said "Goodbye Stephen." as she lowered his hand just in time to observe the life force fade from his eyes - something no one should ever have to see.

The android put his hand on her shoulder as if to comfort her, and she slowly rose to her feet, a single tear slowly wandering down her cheek, leaving a path of clean skin on her dusty face. She acknowledged the android, then started slowly down the tunnel, apparently unconcerned for her own safety. The android, turned back, and Linda watched as he drew his sword then grabbed the Lt.'s hair with one hand and sliced the head off with a single blow. Then he calmly sheathed the blade, dropped the severed head in his space pack and continued on his way. Horrified at this, it snapped Linda out of it and she called to the others "The android's gone NUTS!"

Harvey replied with his armor's communications from some distance further on, "We've got more important things to worry about right now!" Now that he knew who it was that wasn't going to make it, he had to focus on getting the rest of them out alive. Though Lt. Stephen Christopher Argent was a friend, he felt relieved that it wasn't Linda, and further, he felt disappointed with himself for feeling a way that he thought of as selfish.

If only he had listened to Argent's concerns about his prophetic nightmares, the poor guy might be alive now. His own dreams had been prophetic too, but at least when they repeated, he could try other scenarios until he found a way to succeed. That was one of the ways he always seemed to know what to do. Now he knew for sure that it happened to other members of the crew. Food for thought.

* * *

Onboard the Zebuleon, they monitored the signal from the spy satellite they had left behind. It was so small that they believed it to be undetectable by the enemy. The truth was that due to the size of the satellite, it had limitations and had been left unmolested for that very reason. It could only sense generalities at low resolution at best. Tactically, it made sense to allow them to continue to rely on such things, because it also made it child's play to feed them dis-information. In this case, they fed it to themselves.

"One of the life signs has just ceased!" said the tactical officer with glee.

"Can you tell which one?" asked Satrina with a glimmer of hope in her voice.

"The sensors show it was a male, and the female is mourning. Nothing more."

"Excellent! Take *that,* Simkiel!"

She grinned inanely and rubbed her hands together, obviously thinking she had killed Harvey.

98

* * *

Linda eyed the android warily as they made their way out of the
tunnel system and eventually back to the ship. She had never had a
reason to doubt the android's sanity before, but now she wasn't about to
let him out of her sight. He had definitely gone nuts and nobody would
believe her. He had to get rid of the head sometime and when he did,
she was going to be right there to catch him, literally, red-handed.

The android calmly made his way to the infirmary as soon as they
got back to the ship. When he arrived, with Linda in tow, he handed the
space pack to the Azbuga.

"What's this?" he asked.

"Lt. Argent's *head* is in there." said Linda, as she glared accusingly
at the android.

The Azbuga raised his eyebrows at the nodding android.

Linda was sporting a big frown with her arms crossed. "What are
you going to do about it?"

The ship's doctor simply raised an index finger at her, to ask her to
hold that thought for a moment, as the android whispered something in
his ear. She thought she heard him repeat the word 'Aputel'. He looked
surprised gave the space pack back and sent him into another room,
with a light pat on the back. Then he approached Linda. "I'll take care
of everything."

"But..."

"There's nothing to worry about, I assure you. Everything will be
just fine. *I'll take care of it.*"

She was exasperated at this point, let out a big sigh and glared at
him shaking her head as she left the room. Someone had better put that
machine to rights, and soon.

12
PHUL
"All I ask is a tall ship and a star to steer her by."

As the Ezrael was surfing star winds down the Pisces valley next to the Aquarius arm of the galaxy, it's Butator alerted Taggert and he in turn, informed the Major immediately, and he went to Harvey with the news.

"Captain."

"What is it Major?"

"The Butator has detected a large asteroid headed for a populated world."

"How big is the asteroid?"

"Wow! It's over five parasangs in diameter!" he said as he read the data of his Butator terminal.

Harvey just gave the Major a blank look, then he looked at his own Butator display.

A parasang = approx. 3½ miles it told him.

"It's a 'planet-killer' sir - almost 18 miles across!"

"How long before impact?"

"Butator says, over two years for us, sir, or third of an orbit for that world."

"Isn't that outside the 'goldilocks zone'?"

"Binary system sir, making for an even larger orbit than we've yet encountered."

"Of course, a binary system would have a goldilocks zone further out...does every system in the galaxy have one further out for one reason or another?" he asked rhetorically. "Well at least we've got time to investigate the planet I suppose." he said, almost as if speaking to himself. "What's it called?"

"Phul." came the answer.

Butator display:

Phul is a rogue planet that was captured by a binary star system, and has three moons in different orbits and as they line up, they can cause massive tide surges. The planet orbits along the

plane of the two starts, so it has no polar ice caps, making for a mostly oceanic world and a very hot region along both equators. The stars are known as the northern sun and the southern sun, always parallel in the sky. The circular orbit without any tilt or variation makes for no seasons, just continuous summer weather. It had an elliptical orbit with seasons, until it was changed, which resulted in the polar ice caps melting.

Again, there was a lot more information but this was enough for him.

"Phul, huh? Hmmmmm...."

He went deep into thought and said finally "I have an idea."

* * *

Johnson's Journal:

A large asteroid was discovered, heading toward a populated world called Phul. Records show that it had been visited by Callicrates, who then encouraged the population to overthrow an oppressive Merman demigod named Dagon. They killed him and as a result, removed the ring from around the planet, serving as a warning to other demigods. Logic would dictate that since all planets start with a ring, Urantia must have had something similar happen on it. I wonder what demigod may have been slain by *my* ancestors? I'll have to investigate that some day when I have the time.

The very fact that such beings exist, let alone angels and demons, almost gives me the willies. However, I am assured by Joth that they are bound by certain rules that are designed to preserve free will. I am also told that I am not only able to interact with such beings on their level, but I am also capable of getting the better of them. Is there any end to all of this? I wonder...

However, centuries ago Phul plunged into civil war that has raged ever since. Also, the asteroid we discovered that was headed for this world was sent there by a malevolent star empire as a means of 'testing' a civilization. The idea is that if they manage to survive the ordeal, they are worth fighting, if not, it was considered to be 'no great loss'.

We have two Urantian years before the asteroid will hit, so there is time to see what is what down there. If this world turns out to be like Asbeel, a world that I recently found to be irretrievable, then I won't lift a finger to save them; but if they are at all salvageable, I will do my level best to make the Empire of Barbiel pay for this mistake AND salvage the civilization of Phul. After all, these people are at a very low-tech level - about my home planet's seventeenth century or so; and therefore have no means of stopping the asteroid let alone detecting it in time. This should prove to be an interesting visit in any case.

It should be noted that the Major agreed that we visit this world before deciding wheather to save it or not. I think Asbeel was on his mind as well.

After some thought, Harvey named the asteroid "Loki", and announced elaborate plans to observe the cultures on Phul in a clandestine manner in order to get honest information. Callicrates had deliberately omitted the pertinent information from the Butator banks. All they had was language and immunization. It was almost as if he had designed it so that a visit would be mandatory to glean the needed information. In truth, it was partially for that reason, and the fact that their culture was going through so much change, that it was omitted. Surely, future expeditions would be misinformed by any information he could have left for them.

So, each of them went off to research how they wanted to blend in to the population.

As Linda read the original, outdated information about the Mermaids of Phul on her Butator monitor, she sighed and said to herself "I wish I could go undercover as one of *them*."

The ship's doctor or Azbuga who was just within earshot approached her, looked at the image of a Mermaid and said "You *can*."

She turned to him with a sly smile. She had always had a thing for Mermaids and now she could actually *be* one, if only for a while. It was too good to be true!

The Azbuga led Linda to yet another medical laboratory. "This is the transmogrification lab."

"Of course it is." said Linda sarcastically. "What else would it be? Does your tongue get tied into a pretzel knot when you say that?"

He shrugged as he walked over to a Butator monitor, which brought up images of Mermaids.

"Here, pick one." he said as he indicated the monitor and stepped aside for her to see.

She walked over to the monitor and noticed that many of the images showed Mermaids with dark hair.

"I can change my hair color?" she asked, cradling her soft golden blond locks.

"Indeed. You can change almost anything about your body, but the effect is only temporary."

"How temporary?"

"That depends on the change. You will revert to your normal self between two months and seven years, without being changed back in the lab sooner, of course."

"That's quite the range!"

"I did say it depended on what was changed."

"Any ill effects?" she asked, now wondering if she really wanted to go through with it.

The Azbuga tilted his head and gave her a look. Indeed, the medical systems aboard this ship and the knowledge that Azbuga possessed all came directly from the designer of life itself.

"Okay! I was just asking!"

She looked over the images for a moment or two and picked one.

"This one." she said decisively.

"Alright, but you'll have to remove your body armor first."

She gave him a worried look. Her body armor had been her 'security blanket' for some time now.

"You can put it back on again afterwards, it just stops the implementation process, that's all." he added reassuringly.

She thought about it for a moment, and asked. "What about reverting?"

"The armor has no effect on that process, as it is internal, at that point." he said reassuringly.

She grinned slyly. There were definitely advantages to working here. The rest of them made their plans and went down to the planet separately. This was going to be a long one. So much for the snap decisions of the past. She liked the idea of taking time to decide what to do.

* * *

In the aftermath of a fierce sea battle, there was a lot of wreckage floating around. The only survivor was a man who was lying unconscious on a large section of a hull. The commercial salvage ship, Raven, was busily retrieving any serviceable materials, as it came upon the survivor.

He was on his back, in scorched clothes, as if he had been caught in an explosion. The captain leaned over the side of his ship as a longboat came up beside the wreckage, and one of he sailors examined the man.

"Does he live?" asked the Captain.

"He breathes." answered the Bosun.

"Well, best bring him onboard then."

"What if he's a pirate?" asked one of the crew.

"We can lock him up in the brig. If he's a freeman we can let him out."

"Aye-aye cap'n!"

The man groaned slightly as two sailors lifted him off of the wreckage, and into the longboat.

"Are there any others?" asked the captain as he surveyed the horizon.

"No." answered the Bosun flatly.

The Captain just looked over the extensive wreckage and muttered "Pity."

In the infirmary, the ship's physician examined the stranger.

"I can't find anything much wrong with him. I think it's just a little exposure and dehydration." said the ship's doctor to the Chief Officer.

"Put him in the brig to be on the safe side." With that he gestured to two sailors who were standing by the door. They looked at each other and shrugged before taking the half conscious patient to the brig.

Hours later, after a long sleep, the stranger awoke fully and the guard sent for the captain immediately.

"Ohhh my *head!* What happened?" he asked the guard as he sat up and saw the man watching him.

"You don't know?" asked the guard.

"I think I remember a big explosion." he said flatly as the captain came into the room with Bosun Chandler in tow.

"Do you remember anything else?"

"Water...floating...*here.*" he said thoughtfully as he counted them off on his fingers.

"Well, you haven't got the pirate's brogue..." said the Captain thoughtfully. "...which is not easily lost." After a long pause and a shrug, he added to the crewmen "You can let him out now."

"Thanks!"

As the cell door was being unlocked, the captain asked the man "By what name are you known, sailor?"

"Harvey." he answered with a big grin on his way out of the cell.

* * *

Linda jumped out of the hovering shuttle craft into the vast ocean, and waved as Taggert piloted it away.

She looked up at the shuttle craft as her legs started to meld together over the next few minutes.

"That feels pretty weird." she said to herself.

"What does?" asked Harvey over her armor's communication system.

"Never *MIND!* It's okay. I'm just *starting* my part." she almost snapped, but she could feel that he was genuinely concerned about her, and not being nosey. Then she mentally instructed her armor not to transmit any more thoughts unless she specifically told it to, for the duration of this assignment. No more stray thoughts were finding their way to Harvey!

Harvey felt her emotional state, and rightly kept silent. Then he returned his attention to the task at hand.

"Well...Harvey..." the captain was at a bit of a loss with only a single name to go by for this new man. "I'm Jeremy Remy, Captain of the salvage Terra Firma ship, Raven." said the captain. "What can you tell me about yourself?"

"Not much."

"Don't tell me you're a cook..."

"I'm pretty sure I'm not very skilled in the galley."

"Good. We have an overabundance of cooks."

The captain was, of course, referring to the only way out of being inducted into he navy. The war had been raging on for so long that it was normal practice for everyone to serve. Needless to say, a lot of them didn't make it. So many were reluctant to be put into harms way. The galley being the most protected part of the ship, was the safest place to be short of dry land. So, in order to have the best chance of survival, many opted for the culinary arts rather than the art of war. Hence, an over abundance of cooks, and only the best actually got to cook, making for very good food indeed. Besides, there were only so many ways on can prepare fish.

"I never was one to sit-out a battle. You'll find no cowardice in me."

"Good. We're delivering our cargo to the main Terra Firma port, but first we're going to rendezvous with the Dagiel and deliver some supplies. The fleet admiral can decide what to do with you.

"Fair enough! I can't wait to get back into the fray." said Harvey with a smile.

Most men that seemed to want battle, were trouble. Somehow, he felt that this one was different. Still, this was going on his report to the admiral.

"Indeed. Bosun Chandler here will show you to your quarters. Get some rest, and in the morning report on deck for your assigned duties."

"Very good sir." said Harvey and followed the Bosun.

* * *

It didn't take Linda long to find the Mers. In fact, her landing in the water and sounding like a Terra Firma dweller, was what attracted a whole school of them.

"Well, hello!" she said as the first curious Merman swam up to her.

"What's a nice girl like you, doing in a place like this?" he said with a conceited smile and a faked deep voice.

Linda gave him a look. 'Did he really just say that, AND sound like a lounge lizard?' she thought to herself. Here she was halfway across

106

the galaxy from home and self-centered men were still using the same old lame pickup lines! Sure, he was handsome, but it was already evident that he had very little active gray matter behind his piercing blue eyes...

"What is wrong with this area?" she asked.

A mermaid swam up and asked "Did you just fall out of the sky or something?"

"Yes. Something like that." answered Linda.

The Merman smiled at her, made a gesture that was reminiscent of what a lounge lizard from home might have done, pointed his finger, tilted his head an winked at the same time, as he made the sound of a click. Oh yeah, this was her definition of a total loser. Besides, she was not here for what the soldiers so quaintly put as 'R and R'.

"Wow! Are you an angel?" she asked.

"An angel with my name on her!" said the Merman, in his faux manly voice.

"My name is Linda." she said to the Mermaid, ignoring the Merman.

"Hello, I'm Nervidia. That self-absorbed jerk over there calls himself Lance."

"As in, I have a *lance* for you!" he said smiling at Linda, as he approached even closer to her.

"Linda, angel or not, I think we need to get to shallower waters. It isn't safe out here."

"Safe from what? You still haven't told me."

"Forneus, the eater of Mers."

"Forneus?!? Where?" said Lance, almost in a panic.

By this time the circle of Mermaids was closing in and they all took a turn introducing themselves to Linda. They felt her hair as some sort of greeting, and seemed impressed with it. Indeed, her hair was much more fine than that of the average Mermaid. Their hair had grown almost coarse with the harshness of the sea, but Linda's was fine and free flowing in the water.

"Take it easy Lance, us girls can protect you." she smiled at Linda as she spoke, then added, just below Lance's ability to hear "Though we don't know why we'd want to." The Mermaids within earshot all giggled and Lance smiled nervously at them as they all began following Nervidia's lead toward safer depths.

107

Linda swam next to her new friend. After a while, she started asking a few questions.

"So what is the story here, anyway?" she asked, not knowing how to be subtle in her information-gathering.

"You really *did* drop out of the sky, didn't you?" asked Nervidia.

"You got me. I'm from another world and I just want to get to know this one a little better before I return." said Linda, hoping the truth would help.

"Oh, okay." said Nervidia, completely unfazed. "We suspected as much."

Linda gave her a puzzled look.

"It has happened before."

"Recently?"

"Not in a long time, but we know there are other worlds and strange beings with powers beyond our own."

"Tell me more..."

"There's not much to tell. A long time ago, the Kurzi empire came, and gave us the Mergod Dagon, and another sun, melted the polar ice caps and the water grew. Soon we had more ocean, but the Humans lost most of their land. Then came the wars, and Dagon led us into battles and conjured Forneus - a sea monster that ate ships at Dagon's command and would also make enemies lose the will to fight. But the Mermen mostly died out in the battles anyway, leaving us with jerkweeds like Lance over there."

Then Linda looked over at Lance who then smiled broadly at her. She scowled and looked back at Nervidia.

"Then, some time later, we got a fourth moon for a while." Said Nervidia.

"A fourth moon, you say."

"Yes, it appeared in the sky, things happened and then the moon disappeared."

"What kind of things happened?"

"The Humans managed to kill Dagon and the planetary ring went away. That's when things got really warm here."

"Ring?"

"There used to be a ring around the sky, it was said to be the crown of Dagon."

Linda checked her Butator link, and it confirmed that almost all planets start out with a ring, until a demigod is killed on that world, then the ring is removed, thus serving as a warning to demigods everywhere. The forces of the adversary tend to avoid direct intervention on such worlds. Urantia is one such world. Unlike Harvey though, she was not curious about what demigod had been killed back home.

"Then what happened?"

"The fourth moon disappeared and there has been relative peace between the Humans and Mers ever since. However, the Humans fight amongst themselves. The bad ones are trying to conquer the good ones. So sometimes, when we can, we help the good ones."

"How do they differ?"

"The bad ones would kill us for food, and the good ones, well, let's just say they are friendly and sometimes we can get one of their men to become one of us."

"You can do that?"

"Oh yes, we can turn a Human into a Mer but they can never go back. It's the only way we've been able to maintain our species without forming harems. We are like Humans as we select a single mate for life."

"That's not necessarily a Human trait." Linda muttered.

Leaving dry land, and losing one's legs in favor of a tail, and thus taking all the fun out of the reproductive act, was not the easiest thing to convince a land dweller to do. However, that never stopped them from trying! The high death rate in the war also helped.

Everything Linda was being told was being relayed back to the Ezrael and put into the mission file. The same was being done by the others. Since the natives seemed to know all about extraterrestrials, it appeared that there was no need for covert operations. But Harvey wouldn't have it, citing that the planet had been overtly meddled with before and it wasn't very effective. So she continued for months, and so did the others. Swanson and Aniyel had joined the Pirates. Swanson to be a regular marauder and Aniyel managed to obtain work as a governess for the Pirate leader's daughter. The pirate leader, Commodore Malik, was a brash and evil man, but he would not have anything spoil his daughter. When Aniyel demonstrated not only an uncanny ability to bond with Droxina, but to heal and sooth her when

109

she was taken ill, the Commodore insisted she take the job. You see, he had put Aniyel's predecessor to death for failing to prevent a crewman from seeing Droxina in her bathtub. The sailor was blinded for his trouble, as a lesson to any that might try to get a glance of the beautiful young girl's form. Aniyel proved to be most effective at insulating Droxina from anything the Commodore thought might upset her. Aniyel used her telepathic abilities to be one step ahead of everything. Swanson, well, he didn't file much of a report. In fact, he got into his role as a marauder a little too enthusiastically. A fact that worried Harvey.

Linda's new physiology allowed her to stay submerged indefinitely, and manage the pressure of the depths. It was a strange feeling having a tail in the water and legs on land. The transition felt good though it took a while to complete. She worked in concert with Harvey, and kept in contact with him. She even sank several pirate ships, and saved more than a few sailors from drowning. Of course, that didn't hurt with the attempts to recruit men to become Mers. They wanted to get out of harm's way and a watery life sounded preferable to a watery grave!

The slick, skin-tight clothes the Mermaids wore, coupled with the endorphin release whenever she changed from legs to tail and back again, started to arouse her. When this was over, she would find herself wearing more provocative attire, in hopes of finally getting Harvey over *his* inhibitions and into her arms where he belonged! Girk's perfume aside, she wasn't making much progress toward snaring him! Or was that attitude just rubbing off from the Mermaids? However, inducing desire in him was not the answer. Harvey was so afraid of rejection and the subsequent awkwardness that would then ensue, that he didn't dare confess his feelings for her. In other words, he didn't want it to get 'weird'.

She practiced the transformation and it became faster and easier with each change, though it took a lot of energy. She found herself eating like an athlete. 'This is going to be a hard habit to break when I get back!' she thought to herself.

She became deft at sinking and disabling pirate ships, even steering them into reefs. Skills, she taught her fellow Mermaids, to great effect.

Eventually, in her travels with the schools of Mermaids, she made a discovery that would change *everything*.

* * *

Admiral Var Adar Bahram of the Terra Firma fleet was no ordinary man, and he instantly saw that Harvey had something special about him. Indeed, his subconscious mind was able to see the metaphysical badge of authority that the Emperor of the Galaxy had given him, but his conscious mind couldn't quite grasp what it was. All he knew was that Harvey was extraordinary, and could be trusted completely. So, the two men got on like the proverbial house on fire. The admiral took Harvey under his wing, and groomed him as a possible eventual replacement. He found Harvey's tactics to be effective and his advice sound. In no time, he had promoted Harvey to Chief officer.

Of course, Harvey was able to get tactical information from *his* ship, cloaked in orbit, as well as tactical planning from the Major, who remained on the Ezrael to co-ordinate the entire mission.

When the Admiral decided to look for the pirates at the north pole, Harvey learned a valuable lesson about this world.

The pole, such as it was, consisted of small, rocky islands loaded with mean, vicious killer penguins. The ice caps had melted leaving only the rocky mountain peaks. The extra fresh water made the sea lose salt concentration and the shorelines all but disappear.

After all the fish in the area had gone, the penguins turned on the polar bears, because they were better swimmers. The tuxedoed terrors attacked like piranhas and wiped them all out. Now they attack anything that comes by, including killer wales and walruses and so on.

"Sometimes the pirates hide out at the pole and even eat some of the penguins." explained the admiral. "Their body fat is a main component in some explosives, so they all harvest a few from time to time. The penguins number in the millions there. Bloody plague."

"Pilot, sent course for the south pole." said the captain, then he turned to Harvey. "We check the northern pole every now and then to see if the pirates have anchored offshore - as they occasionally do, to hide from us and regroup - despite the danger."

"Danger?" asked Harvey.

"Your amnesia must be complete. The penguins, of course!"

He didn't know what to think, so he gave the captain a blank look. "Aren't we safe on the ship?"

"You don't know about them eating hulls?"

Harvey shook his head.

"You MUST be from another planet!"

Harvey practically blushed.

"The veracious little blighters can chew though a ship's hull, and perhaps because of it the pirates like to hide here sometimes. But, yes, we're relatively safe because our wood is harder, but we're not invulnerable."

Harvey gave him a worried look.

"Don't worry so much. We're fine as long as we don't stay too long."

After they arrived at the pole, they soon saw that the pirates were nowhere to be found. The penguins took immediate interest and headed towards them like an oil slick on the water.

"Well, that costs us a wildebeest at least." muttered the Admiral.

"What?" asked Harvey.

"Just wait...you'll see" said the ship's captain.

Sure enough, the men brought the carcass of a wildebeest up from the hold and placed it on a sort of trebuchet. Before he knew what was happening, they launched the carcass out over the ocean toward the approaching mass of penguins.

"Hard about!" shouted the captain, and the ship made it's best speed away from the tuxedoed terrors.

Harvey watched as the penguins made short work of the wildebeest before they were out of view. "Wow!" he said. "I take it, that was to keep their attention while we escaped."

"Exactly." said the Admiral.

Harvey thought long and hard about this. Perhaps restoring the planet was the thing to do, as well as save them from Loki. This was obviously nature out of balance.

After nearly two months of fighting the pirates side by side, the Admiral decided it was high time to bring Harvey onboard with the main purpose of the vessel.

"Harvey, the time has come to let you know about our mission." said the admiral. "The cannon under the tarps over there, are really a new weapon that can bring about a swift end to this age-old war."

"Really?" said Harvey as he gave the tarps a sideways glance as he raised an eyebrow. Why hadn't he noticed them before?

112

* * *

Following her best Mermaid friend, Nervidia on her playful swims along the continental shelf, Linda was finally led to the underwater ruins of a large city.

Delighted, Linda examined the ruins for a while. She noted advanced construction techniques, and incredibly accurate masonry. Massive stones that had been cut to tiny tolerances and moved, at least to their positions on the walls, and placed in an interlocking fashion - not requiring any mortar.

"Are there more like this?" she eventually asked Nervidia.

"Oh yes, many, but none so large as this."

"This is not Mer architecture." she said as she looked closely at the structures.

"You remember, I told you the story about when the Kurzy empire came they evoked Dagon and he melted the polar ice caps and flooded most of the lands, so the Mers could dominate Phul."

"You mean the land masses used to extend to this continental shelf?"

"Of course! But the original continental shelf is further out. We don't go there because of the sea monster that likes to feed on us."

"Oh yes. Forneus." This didn't make any sense. If Dagon had changed the world to make it more friendly to Mers, why was there a sea monster in the depths, that liked to eat them? That should have occurred to her almost two months earlier, but she chalked it up to the information overload of a whole new world without the Penemue pills.

* * *

A pivotal sea battle was about to begin, and Captain Sedo Hostel of the lone Terra Firma ship Dagiel wasn't happy about it.

"Four of 'em. The scurvy dogs!" he muttered to himself. "Battle stations! They're rounding on us!" bellowed the Captain.

The four Piscine Pirate ships were gathering in an attack formation. Two were headed for either side of the Dagiel, apparently planning on taking her on by crossfire, a technique that had worked well for them in the past. The captain was ready for this, but had only expected the usual

113

pair of ships. Four, might prove more than a challenge. Although the flagship was the most powerful ship in the world, he was a little concerned about trying to defeat four enemy vessels at once. It was too late to run now, either they were to be triumphant or sunk. This was exactly what was expected of the Pirates, and the design of the Dagiel had taken this into account. Still, the captain didn't like the odds much.

The Pirate ships approached at about 100 yards, the maximum effective range of the torpedoes in common use. They were usually powered by chemical reactions with the water, and therefore would not go off until wet. They fired them from short gun barrels by first breaking the clay cover on the back, or letting it break on the nail inside in the case of shelling, and pouring water into the "flash hole". Then the torpedo would shoot out of the barrel into the water and travel in a straight line. Once it struck the hull of the opposing vessel, it shattered the nose cone, exposing more water reactive chemicals which then exploded, hopefully causing a hull breach.

There were many devices and tactics in place to avoid these detonations. The Pirates favored lowering a chain mail skirt into the water, detonating the torpedoes at a safe distance out from the hull, but the skirt could only take one shot in any spot before it was breached, so a rapid second shot, aimed proportionally ahead usually penetrated this defense. However, the drag factor also slowed their vessels making them an easier target.

Also, they liked to use a shallow and glancing angled hull. The response to that was to put protruding spikes on the torpedo nose cones to catch the hull and redirect the torpedo straight into the bottom of the hull. Another reason for the shallow hulls was for the narrow and shallow channel to the small pirate sea. These hulls had the marked disadvantage of allowing for much less sail, so this was abandoned somewhat in favor of speed, which was all important. Kites and more recently airfoils, were used to make up for the lack of sail, and a catamaran hull design helped considerably. Speed meant survival.

The size of the Dagiel, afforded it five gun decks and each fired a torpedo at once, sending a diagonal row of torpedoes, that would hit right after each other, giving a rapid fire on each breach. Hopefully an effective strategy since the Pirates had started using two skirts, and mobile inner guards. It might take three direct hits to clear a path for a fourth to reach their hulls. Sea battles frequently took a great deal of time, wearing down the defenses over time, it was an exercise of endurance, but this may make short work of the enemy vessels, thus minimizing damage on this vessel.

Another curious piece of equipment they used, was a pair of water skates. ,They were curved blades that dug into the water like an inverted shark fin, with hinged flaps on the sides. When one makes the classic skating motion, the flaps stick out the sides, pressing against the water and act as mini hydrofoils. As one moves feet forward, they close, allowing for little resistance. In this way, a water skater can stay above the water and travel at a respectable clip. The problem is that they cannot stop without sinking into the water, and are also not very useful on choppy seas. A skilled water skater with strong legs can then rise out of the water, and continue on. Most cannot master that technique and require launch off of a moving craft. Since ships did not get very close to each other, the skates were devised as a way of getting troops over to the other craft. In practice, it just added the surface of the sea as a battlefield. The sailors fought in the water between the ships, with swords.

This time things were different. This time, they were fresh out of dock with the most powerful ship in the world in tip top condition. It would be a pity to lose her so soon. He worried that the pirates had learned of the Dagiel and were determined to discredit the entire project.

"So, they plan on wearing us down rather than concentrate on one side. Good." he said. Amateur battle tactics increased his chances of a clear victory. His confidence swelled.

They thought that they would be able to damage the Dagiel and avoid destruction due to the reload time and the smaller target two ships made rather than all four. What they didn't know was that this was a more advanced ship, as well as a larger one.

"Odd numbered decks fire on the first ship!" was the order from the captain of the Dagiel.

The pirate ships lowered their chain mail skirts, just in time to be surprised by one of the innovations that were incorporated into the Dagiel. Sure, they fired the classic torpedoes but they were larger, faster and much more powerful. The surprise came when they fired their upper deck guns. You see, torpedoes were the weapon of choice, because no one had ever managed to get large guns to work because they had not managed to invent gunpowder - until now. Using the same water-reactive chemicals they used for their torpedoes, powdered finely and a new mechanism had been devised for sufficiently rapid mixing in order to build up the necessary pressures to fire a projectile. A difficult proposition but they had finally managed it. Now they had something new. It's called artillery.

The unexpected aerial bombardment made short work of three of the ships, with the forth burning out of control. They managed to pick up the survivors of the other three ships, and board the fourth. This, is where their captain was, and he turned over his saber but refused to talk. They were limited in what they were allowed to do, since he had rights under the world government, even though he was a pirate and a follower of Dagon. So, he kept refusing to talk, that is until he met Harvey. Then he spilled his guts like a suicidal samurai.

At the sight of Harvey, he almost panicked. He may have been a sociopath, but he could see Harvey's aura of authority, and he was terrified by the prospect of facing what he thought of as an angel in disguise. You see, though Harvey had not worn wings for some time, their phantom image remained for even the slightly psychic to see. So, he confessed to all of the activities of the pirates, that the legitimate government had suspected and feared. Their crimes went further than was dared to be believed. He also gave them the location of their port, and the secret to entering the hidden sea. None of which was on any chart because they had built their port on a shoal and beyond a particularly stormy and treacherous channel, aptly known as Hell's Gate.

The captain had often felt something special in Harvey's presence, not to mention that he admired the man's integrity, insight, bravery and work ethic. Now, largely thanks to this man, the long conflict was about to end. Soon, they would be able to invade the Pirate stronghold, and end this conflict once and for all. Besides, a prophecy stated that once the pirates were put down, there would be a global change that would facilitate an unending period of prosperity that had never been seen before. It seemed that this new age was about to be upon them. He firmly believed that.

Having been long enough, and it was high time to rendezvous

onboard the Ezrael, which had been cloaked all this time. Now, Harvey was convinced that this world was well worth saving, and if he didn't act soon, the asteroid would be very difficult to stop. In fact, deflection was not quite what he had in mind. Despite Swanson's arguments to the contrary, it was determined that even though the Pirates were bad, they had potential. Perhaps they were just mislead. The current government was benevolent and the people were bright - an argument for fish being brain food!

At Harveys' urging, the Admiral and the fleet captain listened to what Linda and the other mermaids had to say. Afterwards, they could not help contemplating an attack on the secret port.

"Do you think we should go Harvey?" asked Admiral Bahram. "You've never been wrong before."

"Hit them with everything you've got." said Harvey.

"That's just my problem. If it is a deception, then all other ports would be defenseless, and I haven't time to send scouts to find out."

"Don't you believe *me?*" asked Linda.

"Being the female of your species, yes." replied the Admiral as he looked into Linda's earnest eyes, Nervidia and the dozen other Mermaids that had accompanied them.

"Good, then take it from us, we've already scouted it out for you. The pirate port is *there.*" she answered soberly.

As the captain looked into their eyes collectively, they nodded solemnly.

He stood there for a moment, pondering the very existence of life as he knew it. Eventually, called his fleet captains to his office.

* * *

The armada had trouble with the weather in the strait, but the instructions from the mermaids were accurate. They made it without losing a single ship. That took some doing because the entire free fleet was huge. It was simply the D-day of their planet: despite the shortage of ships overall, this was the largest invasion in the history of their world.

When they rounded the point to the inner harbor, they discovered what was left of the Pirate fleet, massing just as the Mermaids had reported.

The Admiral sounded the attack and shouted "SHOW NO MERCY!"

Chapter 13
DEBT PROTECTION
"I don't need my debt protected, I need it eliminated!"

The bombardment caught the pirates by surprise.

They had no sentries or lookouts. Why should they have any? Their secret port had been undiscovered for literally centuries.

The new aerial bombardment was such a shock as to cause mass panic both on the ships and on shore.

The Pirate leader, Commodore Malik stood there watching the chaos. "So they've perfected it." he muttered as he watched the Dagiel's gun's fire salvo after salvo, leveling his port city.

"You are beaten."said the conjurer.

"It's *not* over." he said, half to himself, as he turned away from his sinking fleet. He was determined to win at *any* cost. Evil typically accommodated such people.

His men were surrendering in droves. All seemed lost.

He turned to the conjurer, who said: "Only Forneus himself can help you now."

"Then I have no choice." he said, deep in thought. He knew the greater the evil, the higher the price. Not wishing to lose after all he had invested in this entire campaign, 'in for a penny, in for a pound' as the expression goes.

"What does he demand in sacrifice?" he asked the conjurer, hoping he could pay the price.

The conjurer rolled the teeth and consulted his charts as he said "The greater the need and the greater the conjuring, the greater the sacrifice..." he stopped as he saw what had to be done. He looked as though he had seen a ghost. He knew that shooting the messenger was not out of the question with this one.

"What is it?" Malik demanded.

"You're not going to like this..." he said unsteadily, cringing in anticipation of a physical attack.

"Tell me."

"You're *really* not going to like this..." he said shrinking away.

"TELL ME!" he bellowed, moving forward with his weapon raised.

119

"Your...*daughter.*" he swallowed hard, as if he thought he were going to be killed just for saying it.

Malik was silent in thought for a moment then simply said "Prepare the altar. I'll fetch her."

After he left the room, the conjurer said "*Pure* evil." under his breath, grinned broadly, and headed for the upper deck.

Commodore Malik went to his stronghold and removed a small chest from his most secure strongbox. It contained what resembled a desiccated devil fish crossed with a stingray. He carefully removed it and headed for a point, far above the water. He spoke the ancient words, even though they did not matter. What mattered, was what happened next. He tossed the desiccated fish into the water. That is what got the attention of Forneus. Slumbering for a month, after having gorged himself on half a dozen blue whales, he awoke suddenly to the presence of his child's body rejoining the ocean. Without hesitation, he made fantastic speed to the shallows, leaving a massive wake behind him.

The next stop for the pirate captain was his daughter's quarters onboard the flagship.

"Come with me sweetheart." he said quietly.

"Okay Daddy!"

He led her by the hand to the stone sacrificial slab on the deck. She looked at it then up at him and smiled innocently. She really did not understand what was going on, not having any knowledge of such things. She really *was* that sheltered.

"Go ahead, climb up there and lie down on the big table sweetheart." he said with a hint of sadness in his voice. He did his best to hide his grief from her.

"Okay!" she said cheerfully and climbed onto the sacrificial slab, and assumed the supine position. "Will this do?"

"That's will do just fine, precious."

The conjurer tried not to grin as he began reciting the arcane words as the sky grew dark; the Commodore accepted the knife from the conjurer and slowly approached his daughter as the words of summoning were recited and lightning struck all around as he raised both arms.

"This is what I am willing to sacrifice to serve my god Dagon!" his

120

said as a glimmer of realization and fear appeared in Droxina's eyes. She saw the utter sense of loss and surrender in his eyes, and felt a twinge as if something had taken a small bite out of her insides a split second before he plunged the dagger through her heart, pinning her writhing body to the alter. Her last breath was a gurgling horrified scream, that coincided with the culmination of the storm into a large, dark shape beneath the waves. It would seem that there is no birth without pain.

A single tear fell from his eye and landed on his daughter's face, and took the appearance of being hers.

While he stood there, Anyiel approached the body, placing her hands on either side of the girl's head, and wept. "She's gone." she said sadly.

"Cheap, at twice the price." he spat at her. "Obviously, your services are no longer required. You may leave now, unless you wish to be sacrificed as well."

Anyiel just glared at him. Anyone evil enough to sacrifice their own child was beyond redemption in her book. Actually, he was as sad as he could be, but didn't dare show his emotions to his crew for fear of seeming weak. The soothsayer was impressed, glad of the level of evil that the Commodore had just demonstrated. They were certain to win!

The dark spot in the ocean moved rapidly toward the vessel and then surfaced with malice. The head and upper torso of Forneus, the sea monster was a fearsome sight, to say the least.

Commodore Malik stepped forward and glared unflinchingly at the hideous creature.

"What is thy bidding, oh my master?" growled the beast in a guttural tone that can only come from a throat designed to swallow whole ships.

Commodore Malik smiled evilly, and said "Win me this war and with it, this *world*."

With the semblance of a nod, the sea monstrosity sank into the depths and swam away at high velocity toward the enemy fleet.

On the Dagiel's bridge, Harvey and the Admiral were directing the battle, using a system not unlike semaphore flags.

They were winning quite handily and were becoming pleased with themselves. Then the proverbial other shoe fell.

One after another in a line, the ships began sinking beneath the waves with an abruptness that was not to be believed. They looked at each other and said "Oh no!" in chorus.

After a few more ships were swallowed without a chance to fight back, Harvey finally said "That's enough of THAT!"

With his signal, One of the S*I*P*Es, inside a submarine fired a torpedo into the sea monster.

"That's enough of *what?*" asked the Admiral.

There was no time for a response, as there was a large underwater explosion, and an eruption of bubbly water and green blood plasma. Then silence.

Harvey, without looking at the Admiral, said "Wait for it........THERE!" he pointed.

The mutilated carcass of the sea monster floated to the surface, causing some sizeable waves.

"What? I don't understand. What just happened?" demanded the Admiral.

"They *cheated*, so I took the gloves off." answered Harvey.

"*What?*"

"I think it is about time I told you *who* and *what* I am."

"Indeed!" He crossed his arms, as he glared at Harvey. He had long suspected something hidden about this man and was glad to get an explanation at last.

"Well, I didn't say anything before because I though you might not believe me."

"After what I have just seen, I'll believe *anything!* So let's have it!"

"All right, try this: I was sent here by the creator, to help your world."

The Admiral's eyes narrowed, and he nodded thoughtfully.

* * *

Sailing out as a conquering hero, the Pirate Commodore did not realize his mistake until he was being boarded.

They flowed onto the ship like a swarm of locusts. This was to be their final skirmish. It didn't take long for the surprise to wear off, but by then the pirates had lost. They were helpless and their commander was in the enemy's hands.

Beaten and on his knees before the altar, sobbing as he saw the floating remains of Forneus, he demanded to know how they had won.

"The one I serve is *all* powerful." said Harvey flatly.

"I have heard that boast before." muttered Commodore Malik. Then he looked over at the mutilated corpse floating in the wake, pointed at it and added "Despite *that*...you'll have to *prove* it to me."

"What would you accept as proof?" asked Harvey cautiously.

Malik didn't hesitate. "Restore my daughter and you have my loyalty to the end." He was looking at her body, tears welling up in his eyes. That sacrifice was bearable if it meant winning, but to lose the war *and* his daughter was completely unacceptable.

They all looked over at the young girl's body and Harvey consulted with his people in a small huddle.

Malik could not hear what was being said, but thought he knew that he had them. *Nobody* could restore the dead without trade, a sacrifice of another and even then, the result was a demon possessing the body - not a good result. Now that he had lost this war he wanted his daughter back, and that was not going to happen. He was certain of it.

After getting the nod from Pymander, Harvey approached the corpse.

"Clearly..." said Harvey, standing at the alter in front of her lifeless body, "if the one I serve, were to restore her to you, that would secure your loyalty."

"It cannot be done!" he interjected. By this time, he had been allowed to stand, and he approached the altar himself.

"And if it *could?*" asked Harvey.

"I would serve the one you serve for the rest of my days." he said solemnly. Deep down, he hoped it would be done. He didn't care who or how, just as long as he got his daughter back.

"Just so *everyone* is clear on this - by restoring her, you would be convinced you are on the wrong side, and join with us?"

"That is correct."

"I *will* hold you to that." said Harvey sternly.

"Stop stalling! You...you can't do it, *can you?*"

"Oh, I wouldn't be so sure about that..." Harvey's voice trailed off as he whispered something, grasped the knife handle firmly with both hands and yanked it out.

She arched her chest to follow the retreating blade as the wound vanished in a small flash of light around the edges. Restored, Droxine inhaled as if startled, and sat bolt upright, her eyes wide as if she had just been surprised almost to the point of a heart attack.

This startled everyone, including Harvey, and they all took a step back, except Malik, who stared, in stunned disbelief. "No one can restore the dead without trading - a life for a life." he said to himself. This power was completely unknown to him.

Droxine looked over at him and smiled. "That didn't hurt at all daddy!" she said. "Apharoph gives you his blessing." she said to her father, now in tears.

"It...*can't*...be!" he said as he slowly approached her. "It just...*can't*...be..."

She held out her arms for him and he embraced his precious daughter.

He turned to Harvey. "Is it... *really* her?"

Harvey simply nodded.

"No trickery?"

He shook his head solemnly.

"With the true power of life and death, the one you serve *must* be the almighty!"

After a prolonged embrace with his daughter he turned to Harvey. "I am a man of my word. I swear to serve this Apharoph of yours."

"All you need do is make an effort to do the right thing." he replied, almost under his breath, as he put his hand on the man's arm reassuringly. "He is all about free will. He is not making demands of you...this is a gift....as is *all* life."

He didn't know how to reply to that. "What must I do to repay *you* then?" he asked eventually.

"The gift was hers. You extinguished her life but the one I serve restored it to *her*. She is innocent in all of this. One day you will still have to answer for that and everything else you have done."

"Is there no *hope*...for me?" asked Malik, humbled.

"If there weren't, we wouldn't be talking." said Harvey as he raised his eyebrows.

With that Malik embraced his daughter again.

"This thing called *good*? It is what you are?"

"It is what we aspire to be."

"Ah, so achieving pure good is as difficult and elusive as achieving pure evil?"

"Something like that."

"So how does this *good* thing work?"

"Follow your conscience, for starters."

"He hasn't got one. He's a classic sociopath." Pymander interjected softly.

"*That's* a problem... and it explains everything." said Harvey, stroking his bearded chin as if pondering the problem. He had no idea how to cure a sociopath and was certain the Azbuga didn't either. "We can't ask you-know-who to fix him can we?" he asked Pymander.

"That is against the rules. He has been made a sociopath, and this is his personal 'cross to bear' as it were." he said almost coldly.

"Can he be advised?"

"Of *course*. But that would take 24/7 supervision. You see, his type has no clue about right or wrong. He'll have to learn and it will be slow, arduous progress."

"Is there nothing we can do for him?"

"Well, we could supply him with an artificial conscience. *That's* allowed." suggested the android.

"There *is* such a thing?" asked Harvey, surprised and delighted.

"Oh yes, it is usually small and robotic and sits on his shoulder. Let me see, in his case a parrot model would be appropriate..." Pymander's voice trailed off as he checked the Ezrael's inventory of such devices. "Darn it!" he said as he made a discovery. "We're fresh out of parrots!"

"Can't the ship *make* one?"

"In this case, no. It is a specialty item." Meaning that Joth doles them out.

"What *is* available then?"

"You're not going to like this." said Pymander cautiously.

"What is it?"

"You're *really* not going to like this."

Harvey glared at him. "TELL ME!"

"We only have the penguin model left."

"Well that's going to look stupid on his shoulder, besides, penguins are *evil!*" said Malik.

"That's why we have that kind left over. Nobody wants a penguin on their shoulder. Parrots are preferred."

"I don't mind a gizmo whispering in my ear, telling me what is what, but I have to admit, a penguin would not be my first choice. Those little buggers are *vicious!* Besides, the men would think me *mad!*" said Malik, genuinely concerned.

"Can you alter its appearance?" asked Harvey, hopefully.

"No, well at least not enough...but we could make it invisible." suggested Pyander.

Malik cracked a sly smile, nodded and chuckled softly. This would definitely do.

"Alright then, that's what we'll do."

"Very well sir." said Pymander as he produced a life-sized penguin from within his tunic.

"How did you...never mind!" whispered Harvey.

* * *

"Harvey, why did you let all those people die? Why didn't you just defeat them?" asked Linda.

"Freedom just handed to you is cheap, but when it is hard fought for and won by your own blood, it is a precious commodity indeed. In the end, our own nation somehow forgot that." answered Harvey.

"Yes. We *did* seem to forget. But, I simply must ask you about the girl."

"Bringing her back?"

"Yes, isn't that kind of, well...*blasphemous*." she said as if she were searching for the right word. Clearly, she was uncomfortable with the concept. She thought about it and said "You know...you and Pymander often go to this phone booth thingie to talk to this Joth character. Can I go there and ask him about this?"

"I don't see why not." answered Harvey. "But be ready for weirdness."

She just gave him a puzzled look as they headed out the door, looking for Pymander.

They appeared in the ship's galley, where the android was preparing a feast for the S*I*P*Es. They had done a good job and he decided to

126

treat them to a meat dish they had never had before. He was busily grilling large Mastodon steaks and had not noticed Harvey and Linda entering. He would have made a good short order cook at any greasy spoon. Roughly one-third of the men were standing around, eagerly awaiting their turn. The others were at the tables, happily eating and chattering about how good the food was.

"Everyone whose name starts with an 'S'...your steaks are ready!" he bellowed, without turning around.

Several men scurried forth, plates at the ready. Pymander obliged by placing a large, thick steak, cooked to order, on each man's plate. They thanked him in turn and went off to the buffet to get the rest of the meal.

Harvey cleared his throat. To this, Pymander turned around, and smiled broadly. "You missed the 'J's' and 'K's'" he said jokingly.

"Glad to see you've found a hobby you like." said Harvey. "I'm not going to ask where those steaks came from."

"A mastodon, of course! What can I do for you sir?" asked Pymander soberly.

"It can wait." said Harvey as he got a quick jab to the ribs from Linda. "Until you're done treating the men to a decent meal."

"HEY!" shouted the regular cook, somewhere at the tables. True, he was just one of the platoon that happened to have spent more time on KP than the rest of them. That *didn't* mean he was any good at preparing food.

"NO OFFENSE!" he shouted over his shoulder.

There were only a few men left to serve and all of their steaks were on the grill, and cooking. It didn't take long to lure Pymander away. The men were happy and didn't mind his leaving, though they all waved a thank-you to him.

As they were left, Harvey motioned Pymander to walk through the door first, activating access to the internal hallways of the ship. Usually, Harvey only did this when he wanted to talk to Joth, and Linda being in tow, made the android suspect the truth.

"Okay, as I see it, Linda wants to talk to Joth?" he postulated, breaking the silence.

"I knew I kept you around for more than your cooking skills." said Harvey with a glint in his eye.

127

Pymander turned to Linda as they were walking to the phone booth "Well, m'lady, are you sure you want to do this?"

"Yes. There's something I *have to* know." she replied flatly.

"You two are so much alike." he muttered.

Harvey and Linda glanced at each other and blushed, then looked away quickly so that the other wouldn't see. To this, the android simply shook his head and muttered "Kids these days!"

After a long hike, during which, Linda had thankfully refrained from the 'Are we there yet?' question; they arrived at an intersection around what appeared to be a column that was actually the outside wall of a round room. It seemed to be about twenty-five feet in diameter. On one side were large closed doors with no knobs or handles with a sign above it which simply read 'Metatron', and nothing else.

"This is *it?*" she asked.

"Yep." answered Harvey.

"Okay." she said, looking it up and down. "Hardly fancy. Like everything else here."

"'Functional' is the word. He's not much for pomp and circumstance." answered Pymander.

"How do you...open them?" she asked, indicating the doors.

"You need to say the 'magic' words." replied the android indicating quotation marks with his fingers when he said "magic".

"Like, 'open sesame'?"

"No, you need to say 'Pihon Metatron'." Nothing happened.

"How come nothing happened?"

"I'm not organic, so I can't operate certain things...this is one of them."

"That's cute. How do you close them?"

At this point, the conversation was striking Harvey as very familiar, and he had a puzzled look on his face. A look that was not wasted, I might add, as Pymander gave him a look, with a twinkle in his eye, as if to acknowledge it and say "See? I said you two were a lot alike!"

"Just say 'Sigron Metatron'."

"Great!" she paused and said: "PIHON METATRON!"

Her voice echoed down the hallways as the doors opened.

Only darkness awaited inside. This was a different kind of darkness than was usually found in the doorways of the ship. This was the

128

normal darkness of an unlit room.

"Pymander has to go in there with you." said Harvey.

"Aren't you coming?" she asked, wondering if he wanted to take control of the conversation, and secretly hoping he didn't.

"I didn't think you wanted my company, in this case."

"Quite right, if you think I can handle it from here."

"I have confidence, you can." answered Harvey, a little hurt that she didn't seem to want his company, and wondering what he was going to miss-out on. This worried him only a little.

She smiled like a little girl, motioned for the android to follow here and entered the room. When they were inside, Harvey heard Linda say "SIGRON METATRON!" and the doors closed, leaving him alone and feeling left out. It was quite some time before the doors opened again and they came out. Linda had a distant look on her face.

"Well?" he asked, in anticipation.

"Joth is the creator. I have no doubts now." she said flatly.

"And?"

"And what?"

"You were in there for some time."

"No we weren't."

"Check your watch. I was seriously in danger of getting bored."

Sure enough, more than forty minutes had gone by.

"Well, time *does* fly!"

"Grrrrr..."

She leaned over and pecked him on the cheek and said "You sweet, sweet man!"

Harvey, taken completely aback, put his hand on his cheek, blushed a bit and asked "What was *that* all about?"

"Joth told me *everything!*" she said as she winked with a twinkle in her eye. Apparently, her doubts about him were completely gone.

"I wish he'd tell *me* everything." Harvey muttered under his breath.

"Come on, let's get to the bridge, everybody needs to know this."

"Needs to know *what?*" asked Harvey, worried she was about to reveal something to the crew that could change things.

She didn't reply as they entered a doorway that just appeared in the wall, and vanished after they walked through it, leaving the android alone.

"The amnesia is bad enough, but I really I hate it when they do that!" he griped as he began to trudge down the long corridor back to the bridge.

* * *

Johnson's journal
Now that the people of Phul are sorted out, it is time to get back to deflecting the asteroid that has been aimed at the planet. It has taken two months but I managed to find a clue for out overall mission. Parasiel is the word. I don't know if it's a planet or a ship or a person but I will find out. As for the people that sent the asteroid Loki toward Phul, I have a surprise planned for them. Indeed, I have had time to formulate a plan.

14
A TASTE OF THEIR OWN MEDICINE
"A spoon full of sugar wouldn't help with this!"

"Now that they're all sorted out down there, I think we should take care of that pesky asteroid." said Harvey to the crew. "We have a 'tractor beam', don't we?" indicating quotation marks with his fingers. He knew that they had something like it because they've used it before, but he couldn't remember what it was called. He also knew that it was more than powerful enough for what he was planning.

"Yes, of course we do." said Linda, then a sly smiled came across her face. "What are you up to?" she asked playfully.

Harvey just gave her a wily look, then asked the android "Is there a way we can *reshape* it?"

"Of course. We can even bring it into the cargo bay, and you can carve it up at your leisure." came the surprising answer.

"How? It's bigger than we are!"

"The ship can change it's size to accommodate the cargo." said Taggert.

This surprised everyone. The ship had many surprising capabilities, and some bordered on magic, but this was fantastic!

"Wonderful! Better than I had hoped! Bring it onboard then, and get me a jackhammer - a very large one." he said, leaning forward.

"Sir?"

"You know, whatever equipment it takes to physically alter the asteroid's appearance." he said dryly.

He got a curt nod, as he headed to the cargo bay's observation deck.

After the asteroid had been captured and she thought she had waited long enough for Harvey to have his plans for it underway, Linda paid him a little visit. To her surprise, he was wearing a headset and was guiding a thermal beam to alter the asteroid's surface. Indeed, the ship had been enlarged so much as to dwarf the asteroid. He was busy carving some sort of arrangement of weird symbols into the surface of the asteroid when she arrived.

"You didn't waste any time." she said, still not understanding what he was up to.

"The sooner the better now."

"Wouldn't it be easier to use an asteroid from *their* system?" Linda asked, correctly guessing where he was going to send it.

"I want them to know where it came from, besides it's only fitting to use their own weapon against them."

"Uh, just how do you expect them to recognize this asteroid over all the other rocks out there?"

"Simple. Asteroid composition is unique to each system. This system has cobalt and strontium in their asteroids like our home system's asteroids have iron and iridium in them."

"Okay, so what's that you're writing on it?"

"You can use your body armor to translate it."

"Oh yeah..." she sais as she mentally instructed it to translate the lettering.

"I only found that out recently myself." he said to reassure her.

"You're *not*...!" she exclaimed, almost laughing and wishing that she had thought of it first.

"Would you ask the helmsman to set a course for the Barbielian home world for me? I have a little art work to finish before we release this thing."

"I hope you know what you're doing." she said. Amused as she was, this was going to stir up a real hornet's nest.

Harvey smiled and returned to his 'carving' of the surface of the asteroid as Linda headed for the bridge.

When he finished, Harvey returned to the bridge just long enough to give the Major an assignment that made him grin.

* * *

On the home world of the empire, Barbiel itself, a soldier manning a deep space scanner, spotted something.

"SIR!" said the scanner operator to his commander.

"What is it?" snapped general Nisroc.

"There's an asteroid approaching at C8!"

"What? That's impossible!"

"Well, it's doing it and it's a *big* one sir!"

"Activate the guns!"

"Already did, but it's moving too fast sir!"

132

"Asteroid deflector?"

"It came on automatically, but only slowed it down *to* C8, sir!"

"Let me see!" said the general as he pushed the operator away from the scanner.

"Right for the capitol..." he muttered as the Forcas showed him a trajectory. Then he focused in on the asteroid itself, to get a close-up view of it. His face went white. Not only was it going to impact in seconds, but it had a large smiling face carved in the leading edge, with the words "Hi there!" carved in it. His last act in this life was to press a button that transmitted the information to the flagship of the massive Barbelian fleet in deep space.

Seconds later, their world exploded like an egg that had been shot by a rifle bullet. This may have been a fitting end for so many tyrants, but unfortunately, many more of them were busy off world, spreading and administering their malice.

Harvey turned in the stunned silence to the Major. "I want to see you in my office. I have a job for your, 'special talents'."

"With you." he replied and they both left the bridge.

Nobody on the bridge was talking. Deliberately destroying a populated planet, and with malice, was hard to swallow even if it was a planet of Nazis; but, it had Joth's approval, so there was no real argument.

* * *

"What it is?" demanded general Uvall of the ship's captain on the monitor. Long range communications were buzzing with the news. Uvall was on the far end of the galaxy, visiting one of the heads of the allied Kurzi empire when he heard the news.

"The home world has been obliterated, sir. Everyone that was on the planet, including General Nisroc are now gone." came the repeated message.

"How?" he demanded.

"An asteroid hit it, sir."

"We have defenses for that! It's our favorite means to test the mettle of other worlds, you idiot! Do you mean to say that we failed our own test?"

133

"It was traveling at eight times the speed of light, *after* the asteroid deflector had slowed it down, sir. They didn't stand a chance."

"No natural..." the epiphany struck him. This was deliberate, a slap in the face, a challenge. True, they had destroyed countless worlds in this way, but it hardly seemed fair that this be done to *them!*

It's funny how evil people have no sense of fair play. Murders may kill indiscriminately, but if one of their own gets killed, they seem to think it is the greatest crime in history.

"General Nisroc, dead? No matter, he'll be back. Until then, I want to deal with this *personally*."

"Yes sir!"

Officers of the empire had been known to kill a subordinate for relaying bad news, but since this came from the other end of the galaxy, and they had suffered such a devastating blow, he thought it better to preserve what remaining forces they had, for now.

"Uh, sir..."

"What it is captain?"

"There's a Forcas file that was sent, just before the impact. It shows the asteroid, composition analysis and an estimated point of origin."

"Show me."

He observed the happy face, the 'Hi there!' and the other information. Obviously, *someone* had a death wish and he was more than happy to help them out.

"What's left of the fleet?" he asked soberly.

"An entire globular cluster class invasion force."

"Excellent! Contact them. We converge on Phul!"

"Right away sir!"

The screen winked out. The captain was glad to have 'gotten off' with his life and limbs intact!

General Uvall rolled over in bed "Satrina, my dear?"

"Yes general?" she said, as she stretched, as if just waking up. A ploy of course, he knew that she was well aware of the situation.

"How long before Nisroc is reconstituted?"

She yawned again as she checked a crystal ball on the bedside. "Not long... the Shekinah made it a priority...so any time now."

"Excellent!"

She raised a cautionary finger. "But...I can't quite tell what, but he

134

will not come back as a human this time. It will be something closer to his true nature."

"Even better." he said, sporting an sly smile.

15
ONAYPHETON

"I'll be BACK!"

The bridge lights were dimmed to increase the enjoyment of a light show. They were enjoying some 'down time', as the captain had put it. The main viewer was displaying the formation and rotation of galaxies, including a few galactic collisions. As the crew watched this, a male figure, clad only in a bathrobe, wandered in. He looked up and noticed the light show, and took a bite from the apple he had in his hand. He wandered to a position behind Linda, and chewed for a moment. No one noticed his arrival until he commented on what they were watching. "Wow! That's COOL!"

Everyone, shocked at hearing his voice, turned and looked at him as the lights automatically brightened.

"B-but I saw you DIE!" Linda stammered in astonishment, as she rose from her chair.

"I WHAT?" Argent asked, puzzled at such an assertion, and looking around wildly.

"You *DIED*...over two MONTHS AGO!"

He looked around the room and they were all nodding vigorously.

"You look different somehow..." she said as she stepped toward him. She looked closely at his puzzled face and noticed his chin scar was missing as well as the few gray hairs that had been on his sideburns. "What the..." she said as she picked at him with her fingers. "You're *younger*...?" She looked at the Azbuga who had just appeared in the doorway, smiling broadly at her puzzled look. "He looks like he could be his own son!"

"Physically, he's twenty-five again." he said with a twinkle in his eye.

"So this isn't an android body." said Linda.

The Azbuga smiled and nodded.

The puzzled Lt. looked at his hands and noticed that there were no signs of age or scars of any kind. Then he quickly looked at his right arm by the shoulder, his tattoo was missing. Wide-eyed now, he looked up at the doctor like a child would when they are faced with the seemingly impossible. But in light of what had happened on the pirate flagship, they knew it *was* possible.

"Doc! What kind of miracle did you pull out of your little black bag this time?" asked Harvey as he appeared in the doorway and walked over to the puzzled Lt. "Glad to have you back!" he exclaimed as he shook the puzzled Lt.'s hand and patted him on the back.

"Actually, I can't take all the credit for this one. Thank the android in this case."

"The HEAD!" exclaimed Linda, finally starting to understand as coherent thought began to overwhelm emotional reaction.

The others looked almost embarrassed. Was she really going to obsess about the Lt.'s head again?

"Precisely." replied the Azbuga with a nod.

The rest of the bridge crew looked surprised. There really *was* a head?

"I suppose you couldn't tell us because we wouldn't have believed you." Linda postulated.

"You've got it!"

"*And,* you thought I wouldn't approve, like with Droxina."

"Right again!"

"WHAT head? And why don't I have any scars anymore?" asked the Lt. finally as he stared at his hands and kept turning them over and over and started looking at his abdomen and arms. "Where'd my tattoo go?" he muttered under his voice. "That was expensive... and it *hurt* too."

The doctor took on a serious look, as he looked right into the Lt.'s eyes and said "Don't tell me you *miss* them!"

"Maybe the tattoo." he said almost childishly.

"I wouldn't recommend getting it back, because the boss does not like them." said Pymander.

"But...?" he replied still puzzled and his eyes imploring for an explanation. "Why don't I have a belly-button either?"

"I think you'll need to sit down for this."

The Lt. turned white and quietly complied.

"The android did remove the Lt.'s head as Linda here witnessed."

"I thought he couldn't harm anyone." she interjected. "That's why I was so upset about it - and probably why nobody would listen to me."

she added; glaring at a few of the bridge crew who were nodding solemnly now, as if ashamed that they hadn't believed her. One or two of them were actually looking at their shoes, hanging their heads in shame.

"That is true, but that only applies to *living* humans. The android had to wait until he was actually dead before he decapitated the good Lt. here."

To this, the Lt. looked very puzzled, as he reached up and felt around his neck and swallowed hard. All this talk about him being dead, even though he seemed very much alive, especially to himself, was making him feel very nervous indeed. He wished that they would stop talking like he wasn't there, but he was dying to find out more.

The doctor continued his explanation "He then took the head to me, and explained that the process was permitted to be used. It involves cloning and the transfer of memory and engrams from the dead brain."

"What? Am I a...a *zombie*?!? Do I still have a *soul?*" asked the Lt. in a mild panic.

"I said it was a *permitted* technique - remember who we work for - so the soul is preserved also."

"I see." he said as he sighed in relief. Then he thought about it for a moment and looked puzzled. 'The emperor can capture someone's soul?' he thought to himself, as he hadn't been in on Linda's briefing.

"The clone took the customary eight weeks to grow and the technique is relatively simple." he turned to the Lt. "That's why there are no scars, and you have the appearance of being about twenty-five, because that's where the body matures properly, but the cells in this case are brand new. In short, you're going to have an even longer life than normal."

"I'm a *clone?*" said Argent in disbelief, but the others ignored him for the time being.

"Uh, what about the telomere problem with clones? He may look twenty-five but he'll start aging faster in short order, and not live as long as he had left anyways." said DeSoto.

Argent gave the Azbuga a worried look that caught his eye.

"That isn't actually true in this case. We didn't just rip old, specialized DNA out of a cell before we ran the electricity through it and expect it to not only reset but generate new telomeres, that's bassakwards. You see, these clones are made from an electrical process of generating new, unspecialized or *stem cells* from a tissue sample, which then have full, new, telomeres because the material and nutrients are available to a cell, to build them as they reproduce while under the electrical current, so he actually will have a full life span that starts *now*. In fact, he's got at least 400 years to live from this point. Also, the cloning process I used has a near 100% success rate, not like the haphazard stumbling-in-the-dark cloning techniques of your favorite sheep experiment."

"*Huh?* Well, where'd you get the *egg cell?*" demanded DeSoto, knowing full well there were very few women on board and any egg cell - no matter how well preserved - could not have lasted the thousands of years the ship had been 'on ice'.

"That isn't needed with this process. We grew the clone in it's entirety in a tank, just like we did with Aniyel - straight to adult. I know, in her case it was more or less 'natural' for the cells to grow like that, but with normal, un-modified Humans, we just give them a little help in the lab. Just like her, he doesn't have a belly-button since he never developed in a womb this time."

"Oh." DeSoto looked at his toes as he often did, when he stood up for 'conventional wisdom' as he saw it. One of these days he was going to learn to keep his big mouth shut, or even better, get the best of that smarmy overgrown toaster!

"Wait a second! Why I don't remember actually *dying*?" interjected the Lt. as he felt around for a belly-button, turned white again and buried his face in his hands for a moment. He took a deep breath to regain his composure. He was starting to believe what they were saying, and it was a little difficult to take.

"Put simply, the brain has two kinds of memory; temporary and permanent. Much like in a computer's corresponding RAM and ROM. During the time we are awake, we are recording everything we experience with our temporary memory or RAM; and as we sleep, that temporary memory is converted into permanent memory, or ROM. As this happens, related areas of the brain are stimulated and we experience the fallout as dreams."

"With you." said the Lt. uneasily.

"In this process, the only memory that is transferred is the permanent kind. Since you hadn't 'slept on it', you wouldn't remember any of the events of the entire *day* of your death. Call it a beneficial side-effect, by design."

The Lt. looked like he was thinking deeply, then he said "So, this really is ME, even though this body is a copy, it is really, actually...ME?"

"Yes, absolutely, besides, your body copies itself roughly every seven years anyway, so it's really you through and through."

"And I'm *younger* than I was?"

"Yes, you're not going to age, like anyone onboard this ship, and that's saying something. If you get off the ship and stay off, I'd say you have at least 450 years to go."

"Four *hundred* and fifty *years?*" he muttered in disbelief.

"That's correct. You see, your cells divide so many times for you to grow up that they take away seven eights of your telomeres. Your cells now contain full telomeres. They are actually eight times as long as they were when you were twenty-five, and depending on your normal rate of aging, you are looking at almost four centuries before old age catches up to you; but don't worry, you'll simply start aging normally at that point. That's all."

"What if I get killed again?"

"We'll clone you a new body. Just like we did this time."

He thought about it for a moment, then he grinned inanely. "You mean we can't actually stay *dead?*"

"Well, let's just say that you can be metaphysically inconvenienced. As long as the brain and a viable tissue sample are preserved, you can be brought back like this."

He jumped to his feet and exclaimed "COOL! This is totally *weird*...but it's cool!"

"I must say that you're taking it rather well." said the Azbuga. "Most people are freaked out by it at first."

"You can say that again!" said Linda.

There was a general feeling of relief on the bridge. Having a form of immortality was both reassuring and 'creepy' at the same time.

"Wait a minute, is that how a crew can serve on this ship for thousands of years?" asked DeSoto.

"Well, that's part of it."

"Come on, what's the other part?" demanded DeSoto.

"Didn't you hear me say that people on this ship do not age? Haven't *any* of you noticed the effects yet?"

"What effects?"

"As you sleep, the ship's beds encourage a slightly larger than normal production of stem cells, and lets them into your bloodstream. They start replacing missing cells, damaged cells and older cells, in that order of priority."

"Wait! *Stem cells?*"

"Yes. Your body generates them anyway for things like making blood and muscle tissue. The ship just slightly increases your production, and inhibits their immediate specialization which allows them to replace other tissues, in addition to the normal applications of course."

"Whoa! you mean..." she thought of the hair she had noticed that went from gray back to blond!

"For example, if you lose some tissue it'll grow back, and, like I said: you won't age on this ship either. Those replacement cells have *full* telomeres, like the good Lieutenant here. He just took a shortcut and got there before the rest of you." He realized that most of them didn't have the medical knowledge to completely understand but he was getting a little tired of repeating himself.

The chief let out a low whistle. "You know what all this means don't you?" he asked of he crew.

There was a dead silence on the bridge. Most of them had a hard time swallowing the idea, even knowing who they really worked for. Now there was less doubt.

"If you will come with me to the infirmary, I'll demonstrate the process on another project."

"Project?" asked Linda.

* * *

Harvey, Linda, the Chief engineer, Elroy and Lt. Argent all joined the Azbuga and the Xenobiologist in the infirmary. In the middle of the room was the vat that they had used to grow Gladrina's clone Anyiel, and more recently Lt. Argent.

141

"Now, we have been asked to clone Droxina."

"What?!?" exclaimed Linda, *who asked?*

"Uh, *who* is *Droxina?*" interjected the Lt., holding up his hand.

"You did." he said firmly to Linda.

"The daughter of the pirate leader Malik. It's all sorted out now, even though we haven't done this part yet." he said to the Lt.

"I most certainly did NOT!" protested Linda.

"Well, actually, since we are also dealing with time travel, you might not have done so yet, but as far as I am concerned, you have already."

"We can do that?" asked the Lt.

"Yes." said Pymander. "In fact, you will probably go on a few time travel assignments before too long."

"This just keeps getting cooler and cooler!" he said, hardly containing his enthusiasm. He liked serving on this ship.

"Well, given who our boss is, I can believe that time travel is not beyond him either." added Linda.

"So, as I was saying, that little stunt with Droxina was done by us, using the ship's equipment for a little slight of hand. First we removed a tissue sample, a split second before she was killed, using the quantum teleporter..." began the Azbuga.

"How did you *know* to do that?" asked the Lt.

"Like I have been saying, Linda paid us a visit from the future, and told us what we already did - from her perspective."

They all looked at Linda, who shrugged and shook her head.

"Um, why didn't we use the quantum teleporter to escape the tunnels that killed the Lt. here?" she asked.

"Nobody knew how to properly use the quantum teleporter at that time, but now we do. Then chief spent most of the last two months studying how to use it and more for just such occasions."

"Oh. Cool Chief."

The chief nodded.

"What about Linda time traveling?" asked the Lt., keen to hear the story.

"She said that we took a sample from her natural stem cells, since we could pick and choose, and of course a tiny bit off the end of her nose."

"Her *nose?*" asked the Lt.

"That's for a later step."

"Oh."

"You took adult stem cells because you can't actually generate them like you said, didn't you?" said DeSoto.

"Actually, to generate stem cells from normal cells, you just need to reverse the bio-electric flow. Now are you going to let me explain this or are we going to play '20 questions' all day?"

They made the 'it is zipped' motion, and the Azbuga continued.

"So, we stimulated the cells to grow and put the sample in this tank over here. Once there was a sufficient mass of cells, we placed the sample from the nose in the vat, at approximately the point where her nose would be, causing the stem cells to specialize. As you can see, bones and a circulation system are forming."

"Huh?" said the Lt.

"Stem cells are unspecialized cells. Once they come in contact with specialized cells, they specialize as the tissue they are touching, according to the DNA map."

"Wow. Straight to adult." said DeSoto under his breath.

"I am glad you are paying attention." said the Azbuga. "Now, after Droxina was killed, we also removed her brain, also using the quantum teleport. The next step was to liquify the tissue and separate out the memories."

"Like the Penemue pills?" asked the Lt.

"Yes, exactly like the Penemue pills only this is not synthesized and there is a lot more volume involved since it is literally everything in the brain and not just some specialist knowledge like a language or cultural information."

"Okay, so far so good." said Linda.

"At the correct stage in her clone's development, I shall inject the memory proteins into her developing brain's bloodstream, and they will plug into the corresponding places they occupied before, not only anchoring permanently but generating the corresponding engrams as well. Two months after it has begun, she wakes up thinking it was day before she died."

"Okay, that's what you did with me, but are you saying she'll live four hundred years too?"

"Good question. Normally we'd do that, but we can control telomere production with our equipment, so we limited her telomeres to what they would have been anyway."

"So she'll live a normal life span from this point on?"

"Exactly."

"You have that much control over the process?"

"Of course."

She let out a low whistle. "So what was all that jazz about Apharoph she spouted?"

"When we restore someone this way, their soul is preserved as well. So, in her case, she had a visit with the creator while we grew her a new body."

"Um. Why don't I have any memories like that?" asked the Lt.

"You were kept in limbo instead."

"Oh."

"Droxina has a purpose and she was getting the knowledge she needs. You didn't need to meet Apharoph, so you were just 'put on ice' so to speak."

"Okay. I can deal with that I guess. The big guy has no special instructions for me." said the Lt.

"Well, if you want to talk to him..." offered Linda.

"NO! I mean, maybe later." said the Lt.

It was at this point that Harvey was overcome by curiosity on a related point so he pulled the Azbuga aside, and summoned Gladrina with the ship's communications system. "I want to have a word with you and Gladrina." said Harvey.

She entered without delay.

"I have been avoiding this, but I'd like something cleared up." he said to her.

"Yes captain?"

"You once told me that you thought my form of immortality was better than yours."

"Yes, I remember that." she said reassuringly.

"At the time, I didn't know what you were talking about. But now I think I do. Do you care to explain what you meant? What is your form of immortality?"

"We partially re-programmed two genes. One to ignore telomeres

144

and the other to not allow cells to die - *at all.*"

"So *that's* how you do it." said the Azbuga. "Can your cells reproduce should the need arise?"

"Yes. If an arm were cut off and it is not re-attached within a certain period of time, a new one will begin growing."

"Wow! That sounds pretty good to me! So what makes my form of immortality better...in your opinion?" Harvey asked, not actually knowing what had been done to him.

"Well, for starters, yours needs repeat application from time to time to maintain."

"And that's better? How?"

She leaned forward to speak frankly. "Think about it. If you *cannot* die, ever...unless of course every last living cell is destroyed."

Harvey's eyes went wide.

"So that is one of the reasons my race has decided to revert to human form."

Harvey silently smiled at her. He could only imagine what it would be like to live forever. In a way it had to be torture.

"We've got a few options here. One...simply lengthen the telomeres. I'd use an IV and stem cells in the proper saline solution. Over a number of infusions, enough of your cells would be replaced that you'd live as long as the Lt. here." offered the Azbuga.

"Then what happens?" asked DeSoto. "Isn't there a drawback?"

"Weren't you listening? After a time, say 400 years or so, you grow old again but it can be re-done. Also, bone layers build up, but they get thinner."

"Okay, what are some other options?"

"I can modify P53 to ignore telomeres, as it was done with Gladrina. It still has the bone layer problem, in addition, you will have to be killed to die, and your offspring might also have the same form of immortality. If two of you with the same modification have a child together..." he said eyeing Linda and Harvey, "...your offspring *definitely* would inherit it."

"Ooo." said Linda. The idea appealed to her.

"Next, up is something I think Gladrina has done in addition, now this is the spooky one. You activate what our people have dubbed the 'vampire gene'."

145

"That's the 'cannot die' thing?" asked the Lt.

"Exactly. Your cells cannot die, unless physically damaged beyond the ability to function. Chop your head off and let it sit for a year, add blood and it will spring to life. No bone layer problem and no new cells - only for replacement of missing cells. Severed limbs re-attach once in contact, and blood needs to be replaced about every 180 days. Also, children will have the same problems. Sunlight may permanently destroy cells, so they avoid the light to avoid long term degradation. In Gladrina's case, those drawbacks have been addressed."

"No wonder they call it that. Sounds like a vampire to me."

They all nodded.

"Actually there are vampires, and we might have to go against some of them before too long."said Pymander.

"Sounds gruesome, no natural way to die. What happens if you get bored?" asked the LT.

"You have no idea." said Gladrina.

"In order to be able to die naturally, she needs to have her DNA re-programmed to be normal again - something her entire race wants to do."

"Oh yeah!" said Gladrina.

It was a bit unsettling to have someone so enthusiastic about becoming mortal.

"So, let me get this straight. Those are the only forms of immortality? Not that they seem like limited options..." said Harvey.

"Well, there are more forms of it."

"Like what? Humor me, I'm curious. I want to know what we're up against."

"Well, people like Satrina have a really scary form. After death, they can possess a body for example."

"Doesn't that make the possessed body go all mushy?" asked the Lt.

The others glared at him.

"What? I saw it in a movie!"

He got more cold stares.

"Actually he's *close.*" said Pymander.

All eyes went to the android.

"That only happens when there is a mismatch."

Stares.

"If a soul invades a body of the opposite gender, the body rejects it."

"More than just because it's being invaded in the first place?" asked the Lt.

"Yes. There is some rejection at first, but the people we are dealing with are very old and powerful. Once they invade they can stay unless ousted, or the body gets sick enough from gender rejection."

"Ousted? You mean exorcized?"

"Close enough."

"Ahhh..."

"But sometimes the body dies and then you have an un-dead."

"Ewwww..."

"Hold the phone! *Souls* have *gender?*" interjected Linda.

"Yes." said Pymander painfully. "This always happens. It's the whole 'soul-mate' thing."

Linda looked deep in thought.

"How's that work?" asked DeSoto.

"*sigh* In the beginning, souls were whole. Then after an incident I don't want to get into, they were all split, into masculine and feminine. Men get masculine souls and women get feminine souls. Got it?"

"Go on."

"That's it."

"What about..."

He cut DeSoto off. "Don't go there! I know what you're about to say and you're wrong. That's something else."

"Oh." Desoto looked at his shoes again.

"So what's the point of it all?" asked Linda.

"Isn't it obvious?"

"I want to hear you say it."

"You are supposed to try to find the other half of your soul."

"Then what?" asked the Lt.

"Then, over the course of your lives together, you get a taste of heaven."

That was enough. She grinned broadly and eyed Harvey who turned beet red.

At that point the Lt. approached the Azbuga and whispered in his ear.

"You don't have to worry about that little problem anymore." the

Azbuga said reassuringly.

Argent was relieved. It would seem that he really did take his medical problem to the grave after all.

16
AOD
"HERE'S...JOHNNY!"

Nisroc wasn't killed once and for all, he was only 'metaphysically inconvenienced'. An immortal being such as Nisroc cannot be permanently put down by simply killing his physical form. One had to defeat him by other means, which will be explored much later.

In a dark cave in a distant world, the sorcerer Aod, was preparing to perform his favorite task. He chuckled softly as he skillfully rallied the necessary dark forces. Nisroc would be brought back across the veil all right, but this time he was going to be something even more menacing than mere *human* form! This time Nisroc was going to be a creature so large and powerful that it would take entire armies to defeat him. He was going to be something closer to his nature as a fallen one - a being composed mostly of fire. Something so terrible that it had to be relegated to myth in most worlds. In short, the largest most powerful being the dark forces could muster. Something as close to invulnerable as was permitted in the physical realm, and it was something Harvey would face in the coming months. Heaven help him then!

A Sorcerer is one who traps a demon to drain it's energy for personal use. Sometimes the demon is trapped by the devil in animal form and sent to serve the Sorcerer. Such demons are allowed to run more or less 'free'. They protect the Sorcerer because if anything should happen to said Sorcerer, the demon would die. However, a demon trapped in an energy field by the Sorcerer *can* be released and in such case, the demon is allowed to seek revenge on the Sorcerer that trapped the demon in the first place. Some Sorcerers trap more than one demon. These are the cobalt Sorcerers and are very uncommon, as well as frighteningly powerful and consequently much more dangerous. Aod was the most powerful of all the cobalt Sorcerers. He had trapped many demons to do his bidding. If they ever got out of their confinement, there would literally be hell to pay! That's the way he liked it. Total evil.

17
PAYBACK TIME!
"Where's that twenty bucks you owe me?"

"Did you know that little stunt of yours cost us a lot of fuel?" complained the Lt. resuming his post as helmsman the following morning. "We're dangerously low on resources now. I hope you realize the EA pod is practically empty. Didn't you guys fill up?"

Harvey just smiled at him and then carefully fiddled with some controls on a Butator console.

"So why *did* we come back to Phul without recharging the ship first?" asked Linda.

"Oh...you'll find out." said Harvey, as he continued to check on a few things on the console. Finally satisfied, he looked up at Linda and smiled knowingly.

"Well, I hope you know what you're doing, because HERE THEY COME!" said the Lt. which got the whole crew to look at the main 3-D display.

Just over a quarter million ships flowed into the system, looking like a giant swarm of gnats. As this was happening, they crew could hear the intro to Kashmir by Led Zeppelin playing. Harvey threw a look at the Lt. and cleared his throat.

"Uh, sorry. Stray thoughts you know." said the Lt. nervously as he stopped the strangely appropriate music, much to the amusement of the bridge crew. A little levity often helps in such tense moments after all. The crew did not know at this point how low the ship was on fuel, had they known, the reaction might have been very different.

As they were silently surrounded, the Ezrael's systems kept tracking them and updating the Butator display with tactical information about the approaching ships. Given the positions they were taking and the combined fire power, the fleet could dissolve a planet.

"No way, no friggin' way!" the Major kept muttering as he looked at his display. He gave Harvey a truly worried look "We don't have enough juice to stop them all, we just *don't*."

Harvey smiled. "Let's hope *they* know that too."

Everyone looked puzzled and alarmed. Not enough 'juice' to stop them?

After everything they had been through together, they wanted to trust their captain, but this seemed like suicide. Still, he did plan this, and he had always had an ace up his sleeve before. In the end, everyone was assured by the fact that Harvey didn't seem the least bit worried. In fact, he seemed almost giddy.

As the fleet closed in, general Uvall had them scanning for anything that could account for the asteroid. When they detected the Ezrael, and the Forcas identified it, he then realized that he might be in trouble.

The problem was twofold; first he didn't believe in the legends of the Hyperachii fleet, and second he had confidence in the firepower of his own fleet. Over a *quarter million* heavy attack vessels? No one could withstand their combined firepower. *No one!* He kept telling himself that, and outwardly scoffed at the warnings that were on the Forcas display.

Forcas display:

Target ship IDENTIFIED: "Ezrael" Flagship of the Hyperachii fleet.

WARNING!
* EXTREMELY DANGEROUS *
* DO NOT ENGAGE *
* AVOID CONTACT AT ALL COSTS *
* MOST DECEPTIVE AND POWERFUL OF THE
CREATOR'S FLEET *
* MOST INTENSE DANGER *
* TO STAND AND FIGHT MEANS DEATH *
* RUN AWAY AND LIVE *
>>> DIRECT CONFRONTATION IS FORBIDDEN <<<

This ship has been observed destroying planets and even *stars* with a *single shot* from its main guns.

Last known to be captained by: Simkiel Callicrates Plantagenet.

Crafty and dangerous but, still merely Human. However, he has repeatedly proven personally immune to directed energy weapons and attempts at mind control.

Ship has invisibility capability but is detectable if Harchiel filter is utilized.

Limits of power, range and abilities of this vessel have not been ascertained. The Admiralty suspects that such limits are nonexistent!

No one has ever damaged this class of ship, let alone breached it's shields.

Ship and corresponding fleet are all categorized as invulnerable.

Related standing orders:

1) AVOID AT ALL COSTS!
2) DO NOT ENGAGE!
3) FLEE ON SIGHT!
4) DON'T THINK, RUN!

"Stuff and nonsense!" he boomed in his traditional manner, to waves of renewed confidence from his crew.

General Uvall, although apparently having the upper hand in this situation (can you say 'overkill'?) still did not want to accuse, since it would be better for morale to get a confession before firing. If this was indeed the 'guilty' party, he would be able to avenge his home world's destruction - and for that he had to be sure he had the right ones. Besides, he was worried that the Forcas was correct, and he didn't want to engage this ship unless he had to. But, he didn't let on, as his men might lose confidence. The last thing he needed was a repeat of that nasty business at the Crab's Head nebula mutiny due to a lack of confidence by the crew because their commander faltered in battle. It was a complete disaster involving cannibalism, so it's best not mentioned really.

He hailed the Ezrael, and his image appeared on the bridge in front of Harvey.

"I am general Uvall, of the empire of Barbiel." he said. "I take it that I am addressing Simkiel Callicrates Plantagenet?" he continued in a matter-of-fact tone, as if he were not at all upset. He was hoping to impress them with his knowledge of the Ezrael, when in fact Harvey full-well expected Uvall to know he was the captain now. Then he thought it might be some sort of put down, but he was in a generous mood, so he let the feeling pass.

"Callicrates went on to bigger and better things. My name is Harvey."

Harvey was intentionally using the fact that the phrase 'bigger and better things' meant something different to both cultures, and it worked.

The Forcas display in front of General Uvall changed to read:

"Previous captain Callicrates was promoted, current captain 'Harvie'. Presumed to be 'Harviel', angel guard previously stationed at 2nd heavenly hall, promoted to captain of the Ezrael. WARNING: Angel; strong sense of justice, suspicious of everyone, and due to angelic status, is very tough, powerful, intelligent, knowledgeable AND TELEPATHIC. USE TELEPATHIC PROTOCOLS WHEN DEALING WITH SAID ENTITY *HANDLE WITH CARE*"

Upon seeing this, General Uvall swallowed hard, then simply said "Acknowledged."

"What can I do for you General?" asked Harvey rather innocently.

"Well..." he was very nervous. How could this be? He had to have the upper hand...didn't he? Then why couldn't he lose the sinking feeling in his gut? He continued "One of our worlds was destroyed, and we traced the attack back to this system." he said dryly.

"My congratulations on your deductive skills General, in identifying the asteroid's point-of-origin so swiftly." He had hoped to have had lunch before they arrived, now he was going to have to dispatch them on and empty stomach. Oh *well!*

"We have our means." said the general, attempting to sound humble. But completely oblivious to the fact that Harvey was demonstrating knowledge of the nature of the attack - or was he?

"So I take it that you are here to investigate?" asked Harvey.

"Just as I take it the you are here to punish the guilty party." came the reply.

Uvall had seen through this little song and dance - just as Harvey had expected. Still, it was a way of making their relative positions known without shooting at each other.

"'Been there, done that." said Harvey as he waived his hand, which upset Uvall. His temper took over. The Forcas warnings be blessed! He had the upper hand and this little punk was not going to get away with this! No matter *who* or *what* he was! THE GLOVES WERE OFF!

"I demand *REVENGE!*" he bellowed red-faced, smacking a fist into his other hand for emphases.

"When an instigator is slapped in the face for his trouble, he can't yell; 'revenge' because there is nothing *to* avenge." said Harvey. "Vengeance *has* been had. Or should I call it...*justice*?"

The Barbielian fleet was beginning to completely surround the Ezrael, giving them no avenue of escape.

"You dare call what you did to our world a simple 'slap in the face'?" he demanded.

"It's no more than you wished on Phul, and those people had done you no harm..." said Harvey, as spitefully as he had before. Several of the bridge crew were nervous. They didn't much like Harvey provoking the Barbielian general. The Major gave Harvey an imploring look, others on the bridge were wide-eyed as if to say: "Are you *CRAZY?*". The only calm people were Harvey and the Lt.

Uvall, scarcely able to contain his rage simply fumed, at a loss for words.

Harvey continued "...so you had no *legitimate* reason for attacking them. How many worlds have *you* and yours destroyed in this way general? Hmmm? I think you got off *lucky!*" Harvey's tone sounded like a disgusted parent disciplining a wayward teenager at the police department after a drunken car chase through the zoo at 3AM.

Uvall looked like he was about to explode, his mouth trying to form words. He had never met with such utter defiance before and he *hated* it! If only Harvie could be *turned!* Oh what an ally he would make!

"Now don't try to give me that lame story about *testing* civilizations either. You're just a bloodthirsty tyrant and it's high time someone put you back in your place." said Harvey jabbing his finger in the air at Uvall's image, to punctuate the remarks. One could feel the tension. It was as if Harvey desperately *wanted* them to fire on the Ezrael.

A quiet calm came over Uvall's face. "It has been a very long time since anyone *dared* to talk to me that way." He was impressed with this man's iron. It was a pity he had to be killed, as he might have made a good servant of the empire. Once he was *broken* and *turned,* of course.

Harvey looked the hologram right in the eye. "Well I say it's about time someone *did!*" he said firmly, with fire in his eyes as if he were losing his temper.

General Uvall's blood boiled. What daring! What arrogance! Still, he couldn't have that sort of misguided defiance go unpunished.

His ships had finished surrounding the Ezrael, and had locked their weapons on the target by this time. "Might I remind you that you are in no position..."

Harvey cut him off. "It is *you* who are in no position to say *what* is *what*!"

"Sir!" whispered one of the bridge officers to the General. He raised an eyebrow, indicating to continue. "It looks like they're dead in the plenum! He must be bluffing!"

"Sir! I agree. He's bluffing!" said Uvall's first officer.

"These guys *never* bluff!" he snapped.

"Why not?"

"Because they don't *have* to!" he spat. Being outclassed, was never a fun thing. Although he had a vast numerical superiority, he still had nagging doubts, if not due to the identity of Harvie's employer, not to mention the history of clashes with the Hyperachii fleet.

"The power emissions off that ship are several orders of magnitude *lower* than ever recorded. It's surprising that they can even maintain life support."

The General looked at the readout, and what he saw filled him with the confidence he needed. A sly smile crept across his face as he chuckled softly. He wasn't about to be bluffed by anyone. He assumed that Harvie was betting on the reputation of the Ezrael to bail him out of this. Of course! The energy needed to move an asteroid at that velocity over that distance would drain any *fleet* let alone a single ship! It had to be a bluff! He had to have caught them before they could refuel. Wonderful! His luck had not deserted him after all!

By this time, Harvey had his arms folded and his head cocked slightly. "If you are *foolish* enough to fire on this vessel, I promise you a quick and decisive battle."

"Oh...on that point at least, we agree." said Uvall coldly. Confidant that he was to be victorious and convinced that Harvie was ready to die a warrior's death. "See you in hell." He said as he terminated communication.

"Not today." muttered Harvey under his breath.

The bridges of the Ezrael and the Kunospaston both sprang to life.

"Great! He bought it! He he!" said Harvey gleefully, rubbing his hands together, almost jumping up and down.

"How can you be glad when we're running on fumes and they're about to fire on us?" asked the Major rhetorically.

Harvey just looked at him and raised an eyebrow, as if to remind him of a previous "Major" incident.

The Major's eyes went wide and he raised his index finger and shook it at the captain; "Oh *yeah!*" he said with a sly, gleeful look on his face. "You *sly* DOG!"

Meanwhile on the bridge of the Kunospaston "Signal all ships to fire on my command!" barked the General. He waited a moment then spat "Goodbye and good riddance; *SIMKIEL!*... FIRE!"

The combined firepower of over a quarter million heavy attack vessels converged on the spherical ship. It looked small in comparison to the attacking fleet. At first the shields appeared to stop the assault, but Uvall ordered them to maintain fire. After a few moments, it appeared that the Ezrael was shrinking, apparently being destroyed under the barrage.

"It's *working!*" exclaimed the helmsman.

Now beginning to laugh maniacally, he said "Of course it is! I just remembered! It has been proclaimed that an angel cannot subdue us! MAINTAIN FIRE! HA, HA, HA, HA, HA!"

The crews were getting excited too. No one had ever lasted this long in a confrontation with one of these ships before, and now it seemed as though they were about to destroy one, and it was the *flagship* to boot! Sure enough, there was a sudden collapse, and the beams passed each other as if there were nothing left to shoot at, and almost hit the ships that were opposite. Before anyone could cheer, a sudden jolt rocked the Kunospaston, and it began to list out of control as the emergency klaxons began sounding.

"Cease fire! Stop!" commanded Uvall in a near panic. The firing stopped just as his ship almost drifted into the beam from the ship that was opposite them.

"That was *close!* What the heaven just happened?" he demanded of this crew as the helmsman desperately worked to stabilize the ship.

The tactical officer brought up an aft view, which showed that the drive section of the ship had been neatly removed.

As they stood there with their jaws dropping, an image of Harvey appeared on the bridge. "Playtime is over General. I now have every one of your ships targeted." he said dryly.

Uvall's jaw dropped. "HOW?!?" he demanded.

"Sir! There are other damaged ships, and there's a...*pattern* to it." said the tactical officer.

"Let me see...PLOT IT OUT!"

The officer manipulated a few controls and the Forcas constructed a three-dimensional display of the fleet. The pattern of damaged ships was the same as the markings on the asteroid that had destroyed their home world, complete with the "Hi there!" in their own native script. The Kunospaston was located at the center of the nose of the grinning image.

Uvall was astonished. The Ezrael was now positioned between Phul and the Barbielian fleet. They had the ability to detect it if it had gone invisible, which it hadn't. The only explanation would be if it had teleported, but that was impossible! There were no mechanisms at either location and nobody but nobody could build a teleporter large enough to do the job either.

General Uvall had not survived this long without knowing when to retreat and regroup. This was one of those times. He slowly turned to Harvey's patiently waiting hologram and calmly asked "What are your terms?"

His crew did not react visibly to this, due to the draconian discipline of their fleet. This was a little different than wavering in battle - they were soundly *defeated!*

"Basically, I want you to leave, and never bother any less technically advanced worlds again." he said dryly.

"May we at least defend ourselves?" Uvall asked almost hopefully.

"Anyone who attacks you without just cause is 'fair game'."

Uvall raised an eyebrow at that.

"In such a case, I might even consider assisting you." Harvey added.

"Fair enough! As far as my authority goes I agree, however, you will hear from my superiors about this." cautioned Uvall.

"Of that, I have absolutely no doubt." said Harvey as his hologram faded from view.

The Butator and Forcas systems linked and exchanged the details of the agreement, so there would be no misunderstanding. It was the very same document that the major had been 'drafted' to write. The Major was quite proud of how it had worked out. Being a military man himself, he knew what Uvall might have wanted and respected.

In an impressive display of efficiency, the Barbielian fleet put it's damaged ships into tow, and headed for the nearest 'friendly' port for repairs. Uvall had wanted more information, so he left behind some stealth probes. That didn't fool the crew of the Ezrael, but they left them intact as a means of feeding the Barbielians with false information both now and in the future.

As the fleet faded into the interstellar void, DeSoto asked "Okay, now that they're gone, can somebody please tell me what just happened?"

"Well, as you know, we were low on power." began Harvey.

"*Low?* Didn't the helmsman say were running on *fumes?*"

"Okay, and do you remember when the Major here blew up the star at Rahab?"

"Hey! I refuse to take the rap for that! He that said that nothing could harm a star!" exclaimed the Major, pointing at DeSoto, as if afraid of another attempted lynching.

"That's ancient history." said Harvey reassuringly. "The point is that not only did the shields protect us, but they absorbed the energy and stored it in the pod."

There was a collective "Oh!"

"So you figured that we'd not only be safe from their energy weapons, but we'd get the energy we needed *from* them to boot!" said DeSoto.

"Precisely. Besides, I let them detect our diminished power levels, which helped egg them into attacking."

"Brilliant! But how did we get behind their flagship and fire on all of those ships at once?"

"Pymander informed me that they could still sense us if we turned invisible, in fact, anyone that has invisibility technology can, so as with the case of the asteroid, we changed size instead."

DeSoto looked puzzled. As was typical for him, he was thinking about making the ship larger...

"We got so small that they couldn't detect us." offered the Lt.

sensing DeSoto's puzzlement.

"Ah! I see!" the light finally coming on.

"Then all we had to do was to kick it down to 'warp 97', and let the pre-programmed weapons take over. The whole thing took about 2 seconds."

"*That's* why they didn't know what hit them!"

"Now, they're stuck with a mystery to ponder." added Harvey with a sly smile.

"You *do* realize that they'll be back and with *everything* they've got." cautioned the Major.

"In fact, I'm *counting* on it."

The major gave him a puzzled look.

"Whatever they throw at us next, we have to trounce utterly and completely as well. Then, they'll truly accept our terms."

"They'd have to." said the Major thoughtfully. "Brilliant strategy if I may say so. Are you sure you didn't go to West point?"

"I picked up a few tactics down on Phul."

"Yes, I see. Well done!"

Harvey gave the Major an acknowledging nod and continued "In any event, it'll be some time before they return, so might I suggest we use that time to get our act together?"

"Agreed." said the Major, partially under his breath. He was beginning to have a lot of respect for this civilian.

"I have a few things to attend to, so if you will excuse me? Pymander, you're with me."

The two made their way to the phone booth without a word. Harvey wondered why the android seemed to be holding back a grin, and felt even more nervous about what he was planning. Upon entering the room, he had the distinct sensation that the android knew what really went on in there because he grinned at him just before the change.

"You know why I am here."

"Sometimes you're worse than Joan De Arc."

"What's that supposed to mean?"

"Every time you do something you come to me for approval."

"Well, I did destroy a populated planet."

"And saved countless others in the process."

"Is that really how this goes? It boils down to simple math?"

"You know, there is just such an asteroid headed for your world." said Joth changing the subject just a little.

"What?!?" exclaimed Harvey.

"Relax, it isn't going to hit for almost *fifteen years*."

"Good, there's *time*."

"Besides, if you miss it, I'll let you go there in force and fix-up the planet."

He let out a low whistle. They had best not miss it in any event. Then the look in the android's eyes faded.

"Time to leave." he said to himself as he instinctively headed for the door.

18

A SHIP FOR ALL SEASONS
"Pass the two million sun block!"

"Now for phase four" said the captain to the bridge crew.

He got puzzled looks from the bridge crew.

Counting on his fingers he went over his plans.

"One: Study the people of Phul and see if they are worth saving. Two: If they are, then return the asteroid to the Barbielians. Three: Soundly defeat their fleet to make them think twice. Four: Fix Phul's other little problem."

They still looked as if they had no idea what he was talking about.

"What? I posted it on the Butator system? What do you people use it for all day? Playing that 'Monsters and Mayhem' game?"

Most of them hung their heads in shame.

"Oh." was all he said about it. But he did shake his head slightly while he closed his eyes.

"Now Linda here reports there is more to this planet than meets the casual eye." he continued.

They all looked at Linda, who smiled modestly.

"So, before we do anything about it, I propose we take a look and see how feasible the proposed solution is."

"So what's the deal?" asked Swanson.

"This world had two polar ice caps that melted with the 'arrival' of the second sun, flooding most of the land mass."

"We all *know* that." said Swanson condescendingly.

"There are apparently a few surviving structures and geographical features that would be quite useful to the population if the water levels were lowered. So I propose we go down there and assess the situation before we take action."

"What action?" asked Swanson.

* * *

Harvey stood on the hangar deck scratching his head.

"What's your boggle?" asked Gladrina, who had arrived to check on her ship. She hadn't looked it over since Morax had put his filthy hands

161

on it and thought she ought to, for that very reason.

"Well, I'm trying to find a ship that can be submerged, so we can check out the underwater ruins."

"Some of the ships are submersible." she said. "How deep are the ruins?"

"Some are a about a hundred feet down, but most are at about a thousand feet. The few ships I have found that are submersible can't go down that far." he said frowning. There were deep sea submersibles, to be sure, but there did not seem to be a *ship* that could reach those depths. Most ships were designed for the vacuum of space, not the pressures of the deep ocean.

"That's no problem. My ship can navigate to those depths...and more." said Gladrina with a twinkle in her eye. Ever since she had arrived, everyone had been curious about her strange vessel. Now it looked like she was offering a ride in it.

"Really?" asked Harvey with a glimmer of hope in his voice.e

"Oh *yes*. It is designed to work in *any* environment." she answered, still with a twinkle in her eye.

"So...that means we can go there in your ship?" hoping that was what she was getting at.

"Of course, silly! Let's go!" she cupped his cheek as she walked by on her way to her ship.

This made Harvey blush and Linda surge with jealousy. She playfully eyed him suspiciously, as they made their way to the ship as well. They met with Elroy and the Chief engineer, who had been watching from the bridge and showed up without being summoned. It seemed they were more interested in the workings of Gladrina's ship than visiting underwater cities.

They all stood there admiring it for a moment before the Chief finally asked "How does it open?"

"Molecular dissolution door, I should think." answered Elroy, in awe of the technology. He had heard of such a thing before but never witnessed it.

"That's absolutely right!" said Gladrina cheerfully. She reached out her hand and placed it in the six-fingered hand print beside where the hatch should logically be, entered an entry code of sorts, by a combination of changing her finger positions and rapidly tapping. Part of the hull seemed to dissolve away revealing a set of steps that led inside. The ship and Gladrina herself being telepathic, did not need such things, but this made it possible for others to operate it, under the right conditions and was exactly why Morax had tried.

"Follow." Gladrina said simply as she entered.

Harvey motioned for Linda to enter. "Ladies *first*." he said sweetly.

"Except into danger." she said cooly as she accepted his hand to steady her first step into the ship.

The other two, anxious to see what was inside, yet not wanting to betray that feeling, kept trying to be the gentleman by saying "After you." and "No, after *you!*" back and forth until Gladrina put a stop to it.

"Hurry up, Alphonse! You don't want to be fused into the hull when the door closes!" she said, like a mother attempting to get two of her children to stop fooling around.

Harvey gave her a worried look, and she gave him a reassuring smile back. Just as she planned, the two scientists panicked, and scurried in shoulder to shoulder. Once inside, they stopped suddenly and regained composure as if knowing how comical they looked. Linda did her best to stifle a snigger, which made them both blush and Harvey just smiled broadly. Curiously, there were exactly as many seats as there were people, which was noticed by everyone, but no one commented on it.

Gladrina just shook her head and sat down in the pilot's seat, and placed her arms on the armrests and her hands in hand-shaped depressions. The doorway then vanished as the ship came to life.

"How does that work actually?" asked the Chief, glancing over to Elroy who shrugged. "It's just that Laghima class ships are the stuff of legend."

"Really?" asked Gladrina, rhetorically.

As a point of fact, in ancient times, she and many others of her kind had used such ships to defend both Urantia and Alberion from enslavement by malevolent aliens that lusted after gold. But that is a long story in and of itself.

"I know you two have been studying it." she said to them.

"I only found it to be free of energy and completely inert." offered Elroy.

Indeed, he had conducted every test they could on her ship and

163

could not even determine its' composition.

"Well, it is probably non-energetic at times, but we've seen that it is far from inert!" offered the Chief.

"It's one sweet machine, no doubt about that!" said Elroy.

"It is not a machine or a life form. It is comprised of what my people commonly refer to as intelligent matter." offered Gladrina.

"How's that?" asked the Chief.

"It is a kind of artificially intelligent, psychic matter. It seems inert but it will react if sufficiently acted upon either psychically or physically."

"What powers it?" asked the Chief.

"My *personal* energy." answered Gladrina as she focused on piloting her ship out of the Ezrael.

"That must be one helluva drain...." remarked the Chief. "Where do *you* get the energy from...ultimately?"

"From eating *food*. My cells can generate certain energies like your electric eel can generate electricity, only much more efficiently, I might add."

"Still, the drain must be *enormous!*" he exclaimed.

"True, it would kill one of you, provided you could even get the ship's attention, but it's not so bad for me."

"What about interstellar travel? *That's* gotta be a drain!"

"It's like what running a marathon would be to you."

"So I guess you gotta keep in shape, huh?"

"My people don't atrophy - by *design*." she answered with a twinkle in her eye. Indeed, a great deal of tweaking had gone on with their DNA.

"So what are the limitations?" asked Elroy.

"There really aren't any. Provided I can supply the required energy, it can do anything I understand how to do."

"So you mean to tell me that ship can even change shape, form and function?" asked Elroy.

"Yes, as a matter of fact, it's a lot like the Ezrael, in that respect, but in general we tend to keep such ships looking pretty like this one, so it's recognizable."

"Can it go invisible?" asked the Chief.

"Yes, of course."

"Wait just a shucky darn minute here, you mean to tell us that when we found you, you could have had weapons?" insisted the Chief.

"Frankly, it has been a long time since I have had to configure weapons, and by the time I realized that Batna was trying to kill me rather than subdue me, I had already been drained of energy past the point where I could have formed them, much less *fired* them." She turned to look him in the eye. "Had I tried, I would have surely died."

There was a sobering moment of silence.

"Smooth ride." said Harvey in an attempt to change the subject.

"I'm using gravity propulsion, like most ships. There is a gravity bladder in the ship's heart." she answered casually. "Here we go. Hang on!" she said as the ship hit the water. There was no jolt and the Chief engineer, being the only one that braced himself, relaxed as inconspicuously as he could, hoping that nobody had noticed. Gladrina smiled silently to herself as she piloted her vessel into the depths of the ocean.

19
ARK
Wife - "Noah invited us over to see his new boat."
Husband - "Let's wait until it stops raining before we go."

Gladrina expertly piloted her craft to the area Linda had indicated while back on the Ezrael. It wasn't very deep, but the extent of the ruins surprised everyone. Pyramids and other stone structures abounded, with aqueducts, streets and arenas all more or less intact.

"Now for the deeper ones." said Gladrina once everyone had seen enough.

"I never saw those. They were, not only, too deep for a mermaid, but it is dark down there." said Linda.

"Don't worry, my scanners are locked on." said Gladrina.

The light from above faded as they dived ever deeper down the slope of the under-water mountain. The outside of the hull began to glow brighter and brighter to compensate, and they kept the aqueduct within view. It was a spooky thing to see, even though the slope was not very great. At last the ship slowed as the ruins of a more modern looking city appeared before them.

"Wow." they said quietly in chorus.

They marveled at the extent of the ruins, infrastructure and the degree of preservation.

"I wonder how long has this been underwater?" asked the Chief rhetorically.

They all wondered.

After following a few miles of streets, Harvey had seen enough. "Okay, I think that pretty much proves it." he said. "Let's get back to the Ezrael."

Gladrina sensed the wheels turning in Harvey's head and smiled at him in approval. She liked the way this one thought. Linda caught it and glared at her, who simply shrugged as if to say 'Hey, it's not what you think!'. Linda caught the meaning but eyed Harvey carefully for the rest of the trip back to the mother ship. Gladrina was very beautiful and to make matters worse, automatically gave off pheromones that drove all men crazy. This of course had the whole male population of the crew completely lovesick for days. Of course, a 'Gladrina antidote' had been developed but Linda had lingering doubts about its effectiveness. Now that she knew Harvey's shared feelings for her, she was not about to let him stray. No sir, he was *hers* and nobody was going to turn his head! Now, to get him to take her on a date...

* * *

"Okay helmsman, is the Nathaniel in position?" asked Harvey.

"Yes sir, they are waiting." replied LT. Argent.

"Okay then. Touch down, mid ocean."

"Won't that change the ship's appearance?" asked DeSoto, knowing full well that the ship took on a representation of the planet that it had last touched.

"Only if we let it." answered Argent. "Besides, we're only touching water, not land."

"Oh."

As the Ezrael approached the sea, the water rose up to meet the ship, due to a powerful electric charge. The Ezrael began draining away massive amounts of seawater, sea life and even seaweed into it's surface, which is an event horizon connected another Hyperachii ship, the Nathaniel, which was hovering just above the surface of a desert planet, in a system that the Ezrael had visited not long ago. The Nathaniel spewed forth the water that was being collected by the Ezrael and not only gave the planet an ocean, but one that was already teeming with life. Sure, it would take years to stabilize, but at least this was a start.

A month later, when the oceans of Phul were drained to the point where the edge of the continental shelf became the shoreline, the Ezrael rose further away from the water to halt the flow. What the crew saw from the monitors took their breath away; there were ruins of cities all over the 'new' coastline.

"Those are from the time before Dagon." explained Linda, almost under her breath. "When the mermaids showed me, I *knew*."

"Now, there is plenty of fertile land for the Humans, and still more than enough ocean for the Mers. A good balance once again."

"Where did the water go?" asked DeSoto.

167

"Someplace it was needed." was all the captain said.

20
THE CLUSTER
"What do lizards have to do with it?"

"Helmsman. Set a course to a nice planet - like home - for some well deserved shore leave." Linda had been urging him over the last month or so to let her eat "off-ship" at a nice restaurant. Maybe she wanted a 'date'...? In the end, Harvey decided, wrongly, that she just wanted a fancy meal at a restaurant because that's the sort of thing women like.

There was a cheer from the S*I*P*Es. They liked that fact that Harvey often gave the men R&R after each assignment. This, of course, was Joth's advice through Metatron, but the Major had other ideas. He thought this was spoiling the men.

"The nearest place is a 95% match in fact." said the Lt.

"That'll do nicely."

* * *

They arrived to find a moderately populated world in mid 20th century development. Since they had not as yet achieved space flight, they were not officially aware of space faring civilizations, it was decided that a low profile should be kept. The landing party did not want to wait for the Penemue pills to kick in so they brought Kirtibus hats, the sunglasses and even matching suits with them. ,The suits being made of advanced material that was not only armor, but had other functions, as well. They resembled some sort of gang - all wearing identical hats, sunglasses and suits. Men in black, if you will. Until they had slept sufficiently, they would have to rely on this equipment for communication. Because of that, a few details about this world came as a surprise.

They landed their cloaked shuttle more than a good walk from a sizeable town in order to avoid creating a stir. Landing in a natural clearing in lieu of a farmer's field in case they would be discovered when coming or going; they disembarked only for Harvey to look in wonder at the foliage of the forest.

"Ah! Isn't that amazing?" said Harvey. "Halfway across the galaxy, and the life forms are just like they are back home!"

He pointed at a bird he had spotted on a branch of the nearest tree.

Linda could hear chirping and it sounded like a songbird from home. Then a very curious thing happened, the bird was quickly swallowed by a nearby leaf, but the chirping sound did not stop.

"Well, maybe not *exactly* like back home." replied Linda as she put her hat and sunglasses on and deliberately slunk past a stunned Captain. "Careful... with your mouth open like that you never know *what* might fly in."

"Wow, that five percent difference counts for a lot." he said to himself.

The rest of them followed her as Harvey took up the rear. The hike into town was uneventful, as the clothing they were wearing was typical enough for that time and place. They were just walking down the side of the road, minding their own business. A few steam-powered cars went by, although a few waved at them, nobody stopped or challenged them.

When they arrived at the restaurant, they were greeted at the door.

There was little known about this world, but due to the fact that they had recently developed nuclear power, they were just interesting enough to have Penemue pills handy for some background information and the languages, of course. Other than the fact that the sundry life forms on this world were odd, nay more dangerous than most, such as the man-eating cactus of the southeast, or the bird-eating tree of the north, which we've already seen, not much was known - especially to the landing party.

"Ah! A nice large party! Welcome to Omri Baasha's restaurant! Do you wish to be seated in the splattering or non-splattering section?"

They exchanged puzzled looks, but only for a moment as their attention was attracted by the thud of a medium-sized, wet object impacting with the glass barrier between the two halves of the restaurant. What looked like the mouth of a very large eel, drenched in blood and bile was pressed against the glass, and as it slid downward, squeaking against the glass as it went; without further hesitation, they all said "NON!" in chorus.

"Very good choice! I really should have known because none of you are wearing a JCN."

{Okay, I wanted to leave this as an obscure thing for there to be some discussion and conjecture about, but I am told it is better to

170

explain things. Here goes: Americans call it a raincoat, and the English call it a Mac, but since I don't much like IBM and HAL has been taken (each letter before IBM), I used JCN (each letter AFTER IBM). The JCN is to protect you from the disgusting mess of a meal, so I chose IBM to make fun of and not MAC. Got it? Good. What am I smoking? I only smoke the occasional cigar.}

You see, Linda had suggested that they visit a health food restaurant to see what they had. Well, the inter-cultural differences and the inexact translation had led them to a place where the food was alive. You see, they viewed healthy food as being alive - a healthy state indeed. Unhealthy food has been killed, and frequently cooked as well. A not very healthy state to be in. However, the non-splattering area was for freshly killed food to avoid the mess - an option that was gaining in popularity. After a dish was still twitching (as in still sizzling, for here) when it was delivered to the table.

Finding that much of the food was uncooked - such as something like raw squid, they decided to trust the Butator information that the food was harmless to their systems. They actually had an enjoyable meal.

Linda looked over the menu and the Butator added comments as the questions formed in her mind.

Entrees:
Piske (fish)
Squarnsk (squid)
Mare Snork (sea snake, but not like ours)
Fleeger (eels, like what they saw splatter on the barrier)
Sploonts (popular item, a lot like shrimp, but you drink a glass of them in fresh water, so you have to drink it quickly, as fresh water kills them. They look like fresh water shrimp, all long stringy and hairy looking, but quite good if you don't chew that is...)
Sneerka (even the waiter does not know what that is, and it is very smelly)
Fawna (land animals)
Squrtz (like a squirrel with large fangs - apparently to fend off the killer leaves)
Snorkl (a weird looking grub that is a foot long and quite nutritious)

171

Qatz (Much like a domestic cat, gaining popularity as a pet, so not much call for it lately)

Whuv (much like a dog, quite tasty, again, gaining popularity as a pet, so not much call for it)

Cooked, and processed food for the alternative crowd (popular with the men in this party)

Moobow (picture a cow that looks like it was a white bison, can even get this one cooked as in a steak, but tastes a lot like cow)

Underorn (picture of a unicorn, but the meat is tangy and best served cooked so it appears here on the menu)

Snort Scavenger (pig, eh?)

Snerkoid (don't ask!)

Desserts:

Glazier (ice cream, but a lot richer than they were used to, and kind of crystalline, like sherbert, as well. You don't want to know where they got the milk.)

Gork (like an "almond bark" candy, served in a bowl with a spoon...)

Klopski (don't go there, no really DON'T go there!)

Flappitz (just keep on walking!)

Sorry, no chocolate.

Swanson and Argent kept betting each other what the next splat on the glass barrier will be. Swanson won a lot and Argent is getting only slightly miffed. Other than that, the evening went off without a hitch.

Linda kept looking over the table at Harvey and he kept looking away, but not after smiling politely, of course. Well, it wasn't what she was thinking but maybe it was a start. When she said "we" she meant just the two of them. Sure, it was nice to have an outing with the whole crew, but she was going to have to have a little talk with him, and soon.

When they left the restaurant, everyone was talking loudly and having a good time, with the possible exception of Linda and Harvey. They had avoided making eye contact all night. Harvey might glance at her, she'd look up and try to smile but he would look away before she did. Now, they were walking with the rowdy men, back to the field outside of town where they had left the cloaked shuttle.

"Thanks for taking us out to dinner." she said to him as they walked together, behind the main group. It was quieter and more private that way.

"It was your idea, and the least I could do." he said hardly looking at her.

"What's the matter Harvey?"

"What do you mean? "

"You haven't been yourself, since Phul. Do you want to talk about it?"

"Not really. It's something I need to come to terms with on my own."

She thought to herself about the loneliness of command. The weight on his shoulders. They walked side by side in silence for a little while, enjoying the cool evening air. They were already walking close to each other and they slowly got closer. In an attempt to reach out to him, Linda gently grasped Harvey's hand. He didn't attempt to pull his hand away, instead he held it gently. She smiled softly at this, not knowing what was going through his head, but assuming something else.

The others up ahead were being noisy and a bit rowdy. Running back and forth, checking out every bit of metal or refuse on the road, and commenting on the odd steam-powered automobile that went by making a putting sound. Strangely enough, there was one that looked like a sports car but had the distinctive wine of a turbine engine. Surely these people were quite intelligent and inventive. Wondering about this, Lt. Argent went back to ask Harvey about it. When he saw Harvey and Linda holding hands, and his eyes went a bit wide in surprise (or relief) they suddenly let go.

"You're not fooling anyone you know!" he said with a sly grin.

"What can I do for you." asked Harvey flatly.

"Oh, well, yeah, uh, why doesn't this planet have space flight?"

"They haven't developed that far yet."

"They've got steam-turbine cars and airplanes. Why not rockets?"

"Rockets come later."

"Oh yeah? They have a nuclear power plant. How about that?"

"We developed nuclear power before we went to the moon."

"Yeah, but it's like they know more science than that, but don't use

173

it."

"Okay, it's more like *can't* use it."

"Come again?"

"Every time a world like this manages space flight, the Kurzi empire or the Empire of Barbiel or someone like that bombs them back into the stone age. The knowledge remains but the infrastructure is gone. They know what to do, to go back into space, but it's difficult to do once all your industry is gone. You have to practically start from scratch."

"So, that explains all the steam powered gizmos."

"You got it."

"So that 'sky fish' I saw earlier..."

"Is a dirigible *shaped* like a fish." said Linda

"So the tail movements were propelling it?"

"Exactly."

"Did you take a fast-acting knowledge pill or something?" she asked.

"No, I just did my homework."

"Tell me more." she had a twinkle in her eye.

"Well, the dirigibles are not the only interesting aircraft. For instance, the fixed-wing powered airplanes have the cockpit under the fuselage. For better view."

"That's an interesting idea!"

"Their firearms are even more clever."

"How so?"

"They use a small quantity of water, trapped in a cylinder with a movable slug sealed at the barrel end and the projectile is placed in front of it, when a high-voltage current is sent through the water, it splits the water and detonates it almost simultaneously, and to great effect, throwing the projectile at velocities comparable to our chemically propelled bullets."

"Sounds a lot like your water-explosion based piston engine design, where the little 'hockey-puck' in the top of the cylinder kicks the piston and sounds like a diesel engine."

"I keep forgetting you've studied my career." he said mildly blushing. Many of Harvey's devices were never put to practical use, even when they were proved to be viable.

"That doesn't make their design any less brilliant. It shows me that

174

intelligent people even from different worlds can apply the laws of physics in different ways." she saw him blushing, so she changed the subject back to the locals.

"Yeah. Poor people. Oppressed by a technologically superior empire from space. Every time they manage space flight. PFFFT!"

"That's our job, to beat those empires back so worlds like this can be free to do what they choose to."

"Then why aren't we kicking more ass? With apologies to the lady for my crude language." asked the Lt. as he bowed his head at Linda, who smiled at his manners.

"We're working up to it. I want to assess the whole situation before we go head-to-head. But this is not the time and the place for this conversation."

"Understood, sir." he said then gave a salute and ran up to re-join the others.

Linda looked at Harvey and smiled.

"What?"

"Oh nothing." she said and smiled again.

By this time they had reached the field where they had 'parked' the shuttle. Some of the soldiers were throwing small rocks and things at the shuttle to see how the cloaking handled it. Since it was a shuttle that came from the Ezrael and not an 'acquired' shuttle, the cloaking was very good, if not approaching perfection.

"Hey! The shuttle's *gone!*" said Swanson, after throwing a fist-sized rock into the physical space he knew the shuttle had to be.

"Relax." said Harvey, just arriving within earshot.

"What are we going to do?"

Harvey just walked up to where the shuttle door should be and it opened for him, reveling a warmly lit interior.

"What the..." said Swanson as he approached the shuttle to the side of the door and attempted to feel an invisible shuttle. Instead, he hand went past where the surface *must* have been. "I don't...I don't understand it!"

"Didn't you know our technology is the best in the galaxy?"

"I'll say it is!"

Harvey smirked, then silently stepped aside, motioning for Linda to go first. She smiled at him and walked past, swaying her hips as much as she could without being obvious. It worked, because it did catch Harvey's attention, but not just his.

"My, oh MY!" said Argent to a glare from Harvey. Indeed, although Linda was in her forties, she was looking good from any angle.

"I heard that!" she said from inside the shuttle.

Swanson, still amazed by the technology of the shuttle, walked completely around the open doorway, penetrating the physical space the shuttle had to be occupying. Shaking his head in disbelief, and he entered last.

* * *

Once they were back on the ship and settled, the Major approached Harvey.

"We've got a little problem." started the Major.

"What is it?" asked Harvey.

"We're almost out of ammunition."

"Well, just get some from the ship." said Harvey flatly without looking up from his screen, as if he couldn't be bothered with such a minor detail.

"What do you mean?"

"I should think by now you realize that the ship can manufacture almost anything, and typically make it better to boot, like with the batteries."

"So it can make...*bullets?*"

"Yes, and as I understand it, and they're *intelligent* too."

"*Smart* bullets?" said the Major, wringing his hands together thinking about 'smart bomb' technology. "Have you already looked into this?"

"Yes, actually. I found out that like much of the ship's technology, they are telepathic, and understand the intent of the shooter and comply."

"You don't mean...?"

"Yes, I do. A single round that can do almost any job, and it *never* misses the target...haven't you been reading *any* of the notes I've been sending everybody?"

The Major looked like a child on Christmas morning. He could

176

hardly wait to play with...AHEM...*test*, this new ammunition.

"Well, I'd best get started." he said as he left the room. Harvey simply shook his head. If that was the worst problem to come his way today, he was going to be one 'happy camper'.

* * *

Curious about why the Lt. had seemed to be avoiding her and wishing to renew their friendship, Linda deliberately took lunch at the same time as the soldiers, and approached him.

"Mind if I sit here?" she asked.

"Not at all." he answered without looking up.

She placed her food tray on the table as she sat down slowly near the Lt.

"So, *whatcha doin'?*" she asked in a playful, if not immature way.

He seemed busy going over his body armor with a few things on the table. It looked almost as if he were cleaning his weapons.

"Just touching-up my armor." he said, again without looking up.

"I thought that stuff was maintenance free." she said, still hoping to start a conversation.

"Well, it is more or less, but since the operating technology is fluid, sometimes it dries out a little and I have to replenish it." he answered, still without looking up.

A soldier's armor and his weapon are of paramount importance. If either of them failed in battle, it could mean his death. The whole philosophy with the S*I*P*E concept was to armor the soldier to the point where they survived *every* battle.

"So *that's* the stuff?" she asked, knowing full well what the vial of bluish liquid was.

"Yep. Shear thickening fluid. Armor by the glass. Nano-sized titanium footballs in a zinc emulsion."

"The gray bits." she said, noticing where the Lt. was adding the fluid to his vest.

"Yep. That's where it is starting to weaken."

"I've read about that stuff but never played with it."

"It's not too far removed from wet corn starch." he replied flatly.

This wasn't going too well. Linda and the Lt. had an instant friendship before and she was devastated when he died. She missed their little chats, and now it seemed as if he had changed. Besides, he was close to Harvey and as such could be a sort of 'go between' as well as a source of information about the target of her affections.

"Is there something you wanted to talk about?" he asked, looking up from his work, now that he had finished.

"Um, just that I miss my friend."

"I have missed your company too." he said with a nice smile.

"So what's the problem?"

The Lt. hesitated for a moment, then sighed softly. He was thinking that he had to just 'suck it up' so he did.

"I died, and the android tells me you were there for my last moments. I don't dare ask you what it was like. Looking at you, I feel like you know how I would face death, when I don't know myself. I don't want to know and please don't tell me. I'm almost afraid that you're going to tell me anyway. Does that make sense?"

"I'll promise not to tell you about it, if that helps."

"Well, maybe I'll want to know someday, but not *now*. Okay?"

"Deal!" she was ecstatic!

He stood up and said "Now if you'll excuse me, I have to report to the gym. I still have to build up some muscle. I think the Major put me back on active duty a little too soon."

Suddenly struck with curiosity, Linda asked "What's the Major's name anyway?"

"Just call him 'Major'." the Lt. answered so quickly it was almost as if he had snapped at her. The evasive glint in his eye spurred her on.

"No, really, what is his proper name? I noticed he is not wearing a name tag on his uniform like the rest of you."

He leaned forward and said "We razzed him so much about it that he made us all swear never to reveal it to anyone, and though I'd like to tell you, I am a man of my word, so you'd best ask him yourself." he winked and left the room.

Linda sat there eating her lunch, wondering what the Major's problem with his name could possibly be. What kind of name could get a soldier teased to the point he ordered his men not to reveal it to anyone? She was going to *have* to find out!

* * *

First thing, the next morning, the major made his way to a room they had dubbed the quartermaster's room. It had all manner of devices for producing goods in unlimited quantities. He walked up to the scanner and placed a rifle cartridge and a grenade cartridge side by side inside it, closed the door and pressed the button. It looked a lot like a microwave oven, and sounded like one while it was working. Indeed, a bell rang when it was finished it's analysis.

He retrieved the ammunition and made his way to the indicated machinery and waited. Out popped a ship-made duplicate of each. Pretty as you please. He only wanted one for starters because he wanted to check out the telepathic qualities and fire them before anybody else, just to make sure the ammo was 'good'.

He picked-up the ship-made rifle cartridge, and examined it closely. The bullet itself appeared slightly iridescent. He wondered how smart it was, and he heard a voice inside his head reply "Smart enough to get the job done...SIR!"

Startled, he said out loud "Are you, talking to me?"

Silence.

He tried thinking the question.

Then he heard in his head "Yes sir! Major SIR! Ship's bullet number one ready for action, SIR!"

This turned him for a loop.

He thought at the bullet "So, you're a bullet and you're ready to die at my command?"

"YES, SIR! I can hardly wait! SIR!"

"Why? How can something intelligent be so suicidal?"

"All I know about that, sir, is that we're part lemming, sir!"

The Major dropped the rifle cartridge, and he thought he heard it say "Weee!" as it fell to the floor.

He was not about to have the same conversation with one of the ship-made grenades...

He imagined himself asking the grenade "What's your purpose in life?"

And the grenade answering with what he 'just knew' it would, "To explode, of course."

He shuddered at the thought as he picked up the cartridge for testing at the gun range. This time he was positive he heard it giggle in anticipation.

* * *

Linda had checked all the records she could get her hands on. Even the Butator couldn't help her. She asked each of the S*I*P*Es when she had the chance to talk to them in private. Each, in turn, laughed and told her they were not at liberty to say, and that she should ask the Major himself for his first name. This only deepened her resolve. He wouldn't tell her directly, so she had to find out by other means, so as a last ditch effort she went to Pymander, who chuckled softly at her just like the S*I*P*Es did.

"Do you know what the Major's first name is or not?" she demanded.

"In a word, yes."

"Well?"

"It's really best that *he* tells you."

At this point Linda could have gotten angry or defeated. She took a deep breath and said: "I'll remember this."

* * *

By mid morning, the Major had tested enough of the bullets that he had approved them for a field test by the men. Despite *his* successful tests, he still had his doubts and was going to leave it up to the men. After all, they were the ones that were going to use the ammunition, and they would have to deal with the ramifications themselves. Yes, the Major had a conscience - a big one. He approached the ship's captain for permission to test the ammunition planet-side.

"I've been to the gun range and tested the ammunition the ship made for me, but I'd like the men to test it planet-side in more realistic series of tests."

"Do you think that is necessary? What if the locals see you?"

"Well, we can go to the wilderness areas away from everyone."

"Good...and?..."

"And, frankly, I need to trust this new ammunition, and so do the men."

"And..." said Harvey, knowing full well that the Major was holding something back.

"And they need to blow off some steam, so we'd be killing two birds so-to-speak."

Harvey stared at him blankly.

"Okay, the men were fascinated by your story of a tree that ate birds, and they want to see it for themselves."

"That makes sense."

"Well, there is one other minor thing, not worth mentioning really."

"Go ahead."

180

"I can screen the men's DNA when boarding the shuttle on the return trip, telling them it is a screen for pathogens. That way I can ferret-out your spy."

"Good idea."

"I don't buy into the idea, but after this genetic scan, if my men all pass, I want you to accept that non of my men is your spy. Alright?"

"Fair enough."

"Good, well, we'll get a shuttle and find a suitable location within the hour." He left not knowing whether this would finally satisfy Harvey. He didn't like spies and he liked the idea of one of him men being suspect even less.

* * *

The soldiers literally had a field day with the new ammunition, getting used to it's capabilities. Some of the concepts like turning a corner were not alien to them, as their mini-grenades that the M-29A1's could launch, were capable of similar maneuvers. However, the ship's ammunition proved to be much more versatile and much easier to control. All they had to do was think about what they wanted the bullet or grenade to do and, presto, it did it! Within the limits of physics, of course, but even then, they seemed to have fantastic capabilities. They began showing off by shooting without looking and every bullet hit the mark. When the Major saw this, he realized that the men were completely competent and comfortable with the new ammunition, so he decided it was high time they returned to the ship. Besides, they were having too much fun with the whole exercise. He loathed 'clowning around' with dangerous things like guns. Besides, shooting the snake trees just to see them writhe in pain was disturbing to him, so he had them switch to shooting targets in front of a berm.

The only one that gave the new ammunition a serious side-glance was the Lt. he seemed to be deep in thought about something. Indeed, his concern was that it would soon make them all poor marksmen. He had his own reserve quantity of regular ammunition and he intended to save it for a 'rainy day'.

As planned, in an effort to ferret-out the spy, the Major 'set-up shop' just outside the troop transport and as they were on their way back to the ship, they were genetically checked one by one against the records. As planned, he told them it was a test for pathogens, as to not tip off the spy. Then very idea of checking for pathogens did not alarm anyone as

181

they were getting very comfortable with not only visiting other planets but the Azbuga's ability to cure absolutely anything. The fact that they were all given inoculations against all planetary pathogens should have alerted some of them. But soldiers, being soldiers, they didn't complain, they just followed orders.

In the end, as the Major predicted, everyone checked out. He had been ruthlessly efficient and thorough in identifying his men. He was now completely satisfied that none of his men was the spy and if there was indeed a spy, he would have to be ferreted out by other means. He agreed to 'keep his eyes open' just the same - more to satisfy Harvey than anything else. This news of course left Harvey puzzling over who it could be. He didn't want a witch hunt, but he couldn't have a spy in the ranks either. He hated this kind of problem.

* * *

Linda finally caught up with the Major after his outing.

"So! I finally have you to myself!" she said, causing him to swallow hard. The Major was a plain-looking man with very little experience with women, especially attractive ones. This made him nervous around her as it was. Now it seemed that she had designs on him. So, he jumped nervously.

Linda noticed this and was glad to have this kind of power over him. Now, when he found out what she was *really* after, he would probably be more forthcoming. "Don't worry. I'm just curious about something." she said reassuringly.

He seemed to relax. "Oh? Good."

"I was only curious about your name."

"Major."

"Yes, but Major *what?*"

"Just 'Major' works. I'm the only one with that rank aboard." he said nervously. Was she on to his secret? He wondered if any of the men had talked. "Why do you *ask?*"

"Well, I just suddenly got curious about it because you don't wear a name tag like your troops and, well, none of them would tell me when I asked."

"Not *one* of them?"

"Not a one."

"Good men!"

"Indeed. The only thing anyone would say was to ask you directly."

"I'm glad they kept their word. Well, thanks for bringing this to my attention." he said as he tried to walk past her.

"Just a second. You never told me your name." she insisted, not about to be fooled by such a childish trick. He must be desperate to avoid letting anybody know.

"Sure I did, now if you'll excuse me..." he said as he tried to walk past her again. She smiled broadly and placed her arm against the wall. When he tried to duck, she bent her elbow, putting it in his way. He stopped, looked her in the eye and sighed. "I didn't think that would work on you."

"I'm not as polite today as I am curious." she said grinning from ear to ear.

He sighed. "Do you *have* to know?"

"Yes. I simply *must!*"

He leaned forward and whispered a name into her ear. Her eyes went wide and then she became amused, then she started at him in disbelief. "Do you expect me to believe that one!"

"Spelled with a 'y'."

She thought about it for a moment. "What's your first name?"

Again he leaned forward, paused for a moment then gently whispered a name into her ear. She got a serious look in her eyes. "Like the historical figure?"

"My father was an historian and a true patriot. He claimed we were related, so he named me after that man."

"You poor thing. You poor, poor thing!"

"So you *won't* tell anybody?"

"I won't breathe a word. Now that I know I can see why you keep it a secret."

"Thank you!" he breathed a sigh of relief.

"So, I take it you resisted becoming a Major?"

"Oh yes. Ever since, I've tried like the dickens to make Colonel."

"Makes sense."

"So, may I *go* now?"

"Hmmm. What's your *middle* name?"

"All anyone will ever know is 'A'."

"Fair enough. Angus."

"Nope."

"Arvin?"

"Nope."

"Aaron?"

"Will you please stop guessing!"

"Aardvark?"

"*Please!*"

"Come here *you!*" she said as she hugged him, much to his surprise. "I won't breathe a word of it to anybody. I promise."

That was all he wanted to hear.

"Will you tell me if I guess your middle name?"

"No."

"I didn't think so." she said smiling broadly, now seeing the Major in a new light. She finally let him be on his way, much to his relief.

* * *

Something was bothering Lt. Argent so he brought it to Harvey's attention.

"Corporal Swanson, is acting funny sir. I believe he is your spy."

"Why tell me? Why not tell the major about this?" asked Harvey. Actually, he suspected the reason.

"I did sir, but he just dismissed it as the man being a little overwhelmed by all of this." he said, indicating the ship.

"And?"

"Well, it's just that Swanson was always one of the most accepting of our situation. He had a sense of humor, always kidding about things. Now he keeps to himself, volunteers no conversation and frankly, looks around a lot as if he were being watched. Also, he's also forgetful about a lot of personal details, like the first names of his best friends. Including MINE!"

"You're Lieutenant Stephen Christopher Argent. Everyone should know that."

"Well, *he* didn't. In fact, he called me 'Buddy'."

"That's funny, even *I* know not to call a military man 'buddy'..."

"'Buddy's only half the word, but I get what you mean. He and I were like brothers, but it doesn't seem like that anymore."

"I hate to bring this up, but could all this be due to your being 'brought back'?"

"In a way it is. I hate to admit it but I'm more alert and clear-thinking than I used to be. I might not have noticed the difference as quickly if I hadn't been 'brought back' as you put it. In fact, I probably would have dismissed the whole thing like everyone else has."

"No, I think you misunderstood me. What I meant was could *his* attitude towards *you* be due to a problem he has with your being bought back?"

"Oh I see. No, no way. If anybody would think it was cool, he would. In fact, we used to talk about that very possibility, with the way science is progressing back home and all. That's actually why I was able to handle it myself - I've been thinking about the possibility of this for years."

"I see you're handling it well, it's just that *sometimes*, being faced with something, is harder to handle than you thought it would be."

"True, but I think there is a lot more to this. It doesn't explain how he treats everyone the way he does, not just me."

"Good point. So you are certain there is a problem?"

"Abso-fricken-lutely. He does not know a lot of things he should."

"You told the Major about the 'amnesia'?"

"Yes. He wasn't concerned."

"Why not? That sounds very suspicious to me." asked Harvey. "But then again, Swanson seemed more or less normal on Taus."

"Yes, that's true." he said thinking. "But... when put to the test, he does eventually answer correctly, but with a far off look in his eyes."

"That sounds like what I was told to look for, but then again, it could just be fatigue."

"He used to be so outgoing, now he won't even play cards with the rest of us. Even his body language has changed."

"Hmmmm, that's hardly conclusive, but it does sound fishy to me; who wouldn't want to lose a week's pay to you in a poker game?" The Lt. winced at that one.

"So the Major dismissed this?" asked the captain as Argent was lost in thought.

"He's convinced that since everyone passed the genetic tests, there *is* no spy. Frankly, I believe that he thinks you are a little paranoid."

"Well, that's a switch! But, in any case, I don't suppose it would be a bad idea to interview Swanson. Have him escorted to the infirmary, and we'll have the doctors give him the 'once over', just to make sure he's human since our spy *isn't*."

The Lt. gave Harvey a satisfied look, said: "Thank you." as if to say 'finally!', and left.

This fit the profile that Girk gave him. Come to think of it, Captain Batna had bitten Swanson on the leg. Could this just be some sort of engineered virus causing his strange behavior? They were about to find out.

* * *

They found the Corporal in the mess hall, hunched over a bowl of soup. He was looking around as he ate. As he spotted the two M.P's that entered by two of the doors, he froze. His eyes moved to the other doors, noticing one that was unguarded, he now had an 'escape route'. His eyes returned to the M.P's who had come together and were scanning the room. When one spotted him, he nudged the other and indicated with his head. That was enough for Nergal. He bolted for the unguarded door.

The ship made bullets from the M.P's sidearms never missed a single mark. Each one hitting much harder than the last - as instructed. Despite this, and the fact that all the soldiers in the room had 'played' with the same ammunition earlier that day, they all dived under the tables - perhaps it was in case Swanson fired back, or at any of them, for that matter. He was repeatedly hit, but Nergal would just not go down. He was only slowed, slightly reacting to the impacts, but not as much as expected. He bled from his wounds, but not enough to stop him. He had taken 20 rounds and was going to reach the unguarded door. Just as it seemed that he had enough of a lead to get away, a much louder shot rang out, and one of Nergal's knees bent backward and he finally went down.

They looked over at the door Nergal had been heading for and the Lt. was standing there with a .500 caliber revolver in the spy's face, an act which kept the spy at bay. "I was watching on the monitor, and it looked like you boys could use some help." he said glibly before he began to grin from ear to ear. He had been dying for an excuse to use his new 'hog leg'.

The M.P's quickly grabbed the now compliant spy and bound him with two sets of cuffs - just to be sure. They tried to lift him up but wound-up dragging him on his knees. Two big, burly men had a hard time doing this, that is until the ship reduced the gravity for them. Nergal was heavy, tough and impervious to pain. Isn't that how some races described Humans? If this was typical of how tough Nergal's species was, they were all in very deep trouble.

"Thanks for the assist." said one of the M.P's to the Lt. as they hauled the spy away. They weren't proud. The job was more important than that.

* * *

In the infirmary, Nergal in the guise of Cpl. Swanson had been completely restrained, and a thorough examination was underway. They first examined the broken knee, and soon discovered that the skeletal structure was metal. True to Girk's information, Swanson had been replaced with some sort of cyborg. No wonder Nergal was such a master of disguise; all he had to do was customize the flesh to look like one of the crew and presto, he was 'in'. The unanswered question that was on everyone's mind at that point was 'What had happened to the *real* Cpl. Swanson?'

When Harvey arrived, they had finished removing the flesh. It was apparently grown from Swanson's own DNA, and was determined to be non-essential to the functionality of the machine. In other words, it was entirely for appearance.

The only discernible damage to the machine was the broken knee. It's machine face was still capable of expression and one could tell that it was not-at-all happy to be there. They had kept the Captain out of the room until they were sure that it was safe. Obviously, if this thing had been able, it would kill the Captain at this point since it had nothing else to lose.

"Did you get anything out of him yet?" asked Harvey who was glad to have the enemy agent in custody, but also felt violated in a way, because the enemy agent had been there in the first place.

"Nothing yet. He's been compliant with our examinations but quietly defiant. He hasn't responded to any questions. We've disconnected the control mechanisms, so he can only move his head, which doesn't appear to have any weapons in it, so it's safe."

"I can get him to talk. All I need is a car battery, jumper cables and a couple of knitting needles." offered the Lt.

"Gee... no 'death ray laser' in the eyes?" Harvey muttered as he looked over the mechanism from head to toe, ignoring the Lt.'s remark.

The restraints remained just the same, mostly to keep it from falling off the gurney. The back had been raised so as to place the machine in a reclined, sitting position. It still had some control over it's neck and upper back. That was allowed so it could stabilize it's head.

Harvey gave a nod of acknowledgment to the doctor, and turned to Pymander and Elroy.

Pymander was familiar with this form of technology, and Elroy was fascinated. The cyborg seemed just as alert as Pymander, but he knew that the 'other side' was incapable of such a technological marvel. The scans told them that the cyborg had some internal organic organs - just to keep the flesh coverings alive, and the head had computer circuits and an ounce of water in it. This had to be an extremely well-programmed computer and he wanted to pick-apart the logic used.

Further examination would reveal that it was the product of quantum bi-location. If there were a technological brain behind it, it would have to be the size of a moon and located somewhere very cold, even for space. The system of control was referred to as 'telepresence'. It could be remotely manipulated by a life form or a technological intelligence. Quantum bi-location was often used for instant communication anywhere in the universe. In this case, the remote operator was a non-human life form, named Nergal.

Pymander walked up to the cyborg, grasped it's head with both hands and shouted "WHO'S YOUR OPERATOR? WHO ARE YOU...REALLY? WHAT HAVE YOU DONE WITH CORPORAL SWANSON?" He pushed it's head back with a note of disgust as he let go. Apparently he didn't care much for these things. In fact, he had dealt with them before.

This tactic seemed to actually rattle the remote operator, but it tried not to show it. It finally spoke in a voice that was no longer sounding like Swanson "Isn't that quaint? One telepresence device interrogating another!" it sneered.

"Quite." muttered the android under it's breath. This made Elroy raise an eyebrow. The others understood that the android didn't want to give any information to the cyborg. Letting it continue to believe such incorrect things was advantageous. If the forces of the adversary knew there were sentient machines out there, they might just stop at nothing to obtain an example to duplicate.

The cyborg continued "All right, I'll talk, but only to the *boss!*" It's eyes on Harvey, who stepped forward.

"All right, what do you have to tell me?" he asked.

It leaned forward as far as it could, to get as close as it could to him. Then it said, as if in confidence "The bothersome meddling of you and your kind is coming to an end. Nisroc is coming! Prepare yourself for *your* end!" It seemed to laugh a bit, then suddenly slumped as if it had 'died'.

Harvey looked puzzled at this, and raised an eyebrow to the doctors, who shrugged. At that moment, Elroy's eyes went wide. Obviously he had thought of something that was dreadfully important. "Quick! Tell me again how much matter it uses for telepresence control?" he demanded of the doctors, with more than a hint of panic in his voice.

"About an ounce... of water." came the answer. The sense of urgency was at once contagious. Without hesitating, he started pushing the gurney toward the door and shouted: "IT'S GONNA BLOW!"

Everyone else seemed puzzled, the Azbuga looked at the scan and said "But there's no explosives in..." then HIS eyes went wide and he ran to help push the gurney toward the door. "Where to?" asked the Lt. who was closest to the door. "OUTSIDE!" exclaimed the doctor and Elroy in chorus. He correctly assumed that to mean space, so he placed his hand on the panel and thought about the outside of the ship. The gurney disappeared into the doorway and appeared in space, just outside the hull, and slowly drifted off into the void. The Captain, on the intercom said, "Helm! Get us out of here *fast*! Use 'kick' shields *now*!" Kick shields being a nickname for a technique of starting the shielding at the surface and moving the effect outwards to 'kick' things away from the ship.

"Keep your hair on." came the calm reply from Taggert at the helm.

DeSoto turned to Elroy. "Now tell me why we've just treated a 'dead' cyborg as if it were a nuke."

"I'll explain in a moment, and if I'm wrong, we can just pick it back up, if I'm right, there's gonna be one mother of a blast any moment now." said Elroy, not knowing if he should wish to be right; and thereby being a savior, or wrong so they would be safer, AND able to learn some things about their enemy's technology.

The kick shields moved the gurney quickly away from the ship, and then it moved, directly toward the gurney, then pushed it along at a good clip. Of all the directions the helmsman could have chosen, this was the absolute *worst*. The object finally caught his attention and figuring this was what they wanted to avoid, he quickly reversed direction, then *really* kicked it down - which seemed to be almost too late. The distance between the antimatter blast and the shields was small. In fact, the explosion encompassed the entire ship. Fortunately the shields absorbed the energy, as it was not as much as the nova had hit them with a few months earlier, but it was still considerable. Had that blast occurred inside the ship as planned, he assumed that they would all have been surely killed.

DeSoto looked puzzled. "Okay, now that 'it' HAS gone 'boom', do you mind explaining to me *how* it managed that little trick *without* any explosives *or* fissionable material?"

"Well, you know already how bi-locating matter works, right?"

"Yes. As I understand it, it's the process of locating something in two places in the universe at once, and whatever you do to one instantaneously happens to the other, making it very useful for instantaneous extreme-range communications."

"Exactly. So, instead of using a few molecules, they used an ounce of water. Harmless in and of itself, wouldn't you say?"

"Well, yes of course." he said, wishing that Elroy would get to the point.

"So what do you suppose would happen if they introduced an ounce of antimatter to 'their' ounce of water?"

"Ohhhh myyyy...!" his voice quavering. "Such a method would be undetectable...they could blow anybody up, at any time, just so long as they had already planted some sort of bi-located matter on them. It could even be something they ate or drank! It's positively diabolical! A completely undetectable bomb!" he exclaimed.

"Exactly."

"What impresses me is that you figured all this out that *quickly*." added Harvey.

Elroy blushed a little. "Well, it *was* just a *hunch*."

"Very well done then! You saved us all!" He leaned forward, and added, "Hardly a day goes by when I don't get a new reason to be glad that you're on board. Thank you!"

"I'm glad to be here too, sir, just don't give me too many close calls like that one!" said Elroy.

"Deal!" as if it were in his power to grant. They all had a chuckle over that exchange. "I do have just one question though." asked Harvey.

"G'head." Elroy said confidently, finally feeling as though he had hit his stride.

"If the energy of the explosion was bi-located, and we absorbed a bunch of it with the shields, does that mean that if they were watching their explosion, could they see the missing part and figure out what had happened?"

"I hadn't thought of that. Yes, if they watched, they couldn't have missed that."

"So we can assume that they know we are not destroyed."

"I'm afraid so." realizing the tactical advantage Harvey had wished for.

"What about the energy we absorbed? Could they...?"

"No. Once the energy is expended, as in this case, stored, it no longer exists at the other location. That is one way bi-located matter can get 'normalized'. Otherwise, it would be a great way to get free energy. Quantum entanglement and bi-location only seem to work with physical matter."

"Good." he said under his breath. Another bullet 'dodged.' He went on "Now back to business. For their sakes, I hope that they haven't harmed Corporal Swanson."

That made the Lt. smile. Harvey was not going to leave anyone behind. He knew he liked this civilian for some reason.

"I think that we can assume he is all right for the time being. They needed him alive at first to answer questions and now as a hostage."

"Agreed." said the Major. This made the Lt. smile.

"Now let's go get our man back!"

"Good! We *never* leave a man behind." said the Major.

* * *

"Okay, let's see what we've got." said Harvey to the crew in the briefing room.

The Major piped up first "We think we've determined where and when the switch was made, based on interviews with the rest of the platoon, his behavior seems to have changed abruptly after visiting Taus. Further, since that visit he has found one excuse after another to avoid piloting the ship - a skill he would have lacked - being a cyborg."

"He's had several opportunities to pass on intelligence and material since then." said Harvey thoughtfully.

"In fact, we suspect that he had passed something to someone on Taus. You see, he visited the ship during his leave. He wouldn't have done that if he was really on leave, and we suspect he was bagged as soon as he arrived."

"So he came here and brought something back?"

"Yes. We know he came back here but we can only *guess* he brought something back with him. But what else would he be doing?"

"I wonder..."

"Just hope that it wasn't a DNA sample of the ship." said the android.

Harvey turned pale. "Clone?" he said under his voice.

"Theoretically, but I doubt that they have the resources. At best, they might produce a greatly inferior ship, like they did last time. Even

191

malformed, it still might be able to do us some damage."

"How does *that* work?" asked Argent.

"It's like it is with bees; if you give royal jelly to a normal developing larva, you get a queen who can sting over and over, otherwise, you get a drone, a far inferior result that can only sting once and then it dies, but it can still sting a queen - and enough of them can kill her. They just might have the ship's DNA but they have no idea how to properly grow a new ship to full potential."

"So you're saying this ship is a Queen Bee?" asked the Lt.

There was a faint tremor on the ship when he asked that question. The Lt. looked up with his eyes as it happened.

"Yes and no. The ship we are on is male." answered the android. "In fact, the only male in the fleet, so it is more like a lion. That's why he objected just then."

"Huh?"

"The tremor, he was upset at being called a queen."

"Wait, one male ship and twelve supporting ships? I bet the others are female! That *is* a lot like a pride of lions." said the Lt with a sheepish grin.

"Indeed." said the android. "More than you know."

"You say it has happened *before?*" interjected Harvey, who had been deep in thought about how to defeat an evil version of the ship.

"Yes. They managed to clone the ship just well enough to constitute a threat."

"Are you telling me that this ship has a doppelganger out there somewhere?" asked Harvey, visibly worried.

"A dopple-*what?*" asked Argent.

"An 'evil twin'." explained Linda.

Argent turned white. "An evil twin of this ship, could be out there right now...gunning for us?"

"Well no, I don't think so. That was a long time ago and I am almost certain it was destroyed."

"*Almost* certain?"

"Well...*sigh* we never did find all the wreckage." Pymander said almost under he breath.

"Gotcha. Well, I have no doubt that whatever it was that Nergal might have snuck out of here will come to our attention when they use it against us, so we'll have to remain on our toes. In the meantime, the task at hand?" said Harvey as the Lt. nodded.

The original Doppelganger, though malformed, was powerful and could restore itself, but more like a cancer than a proper repair. So after losing a battle with the Hyperachii fleet, it limped off and licked it's wounds. The forces of evil studied it and built a better facility to grow a new ship in. This time, it would be whole, and the cancer would be controlled. Twisted and evil, it would be more powerful than the Ezrael...they could not use a DNA sample from the first Doppelganger because it had been damaged throughout. A new DNA sample was required and they were willing to wait for it- now that the better cloning facility was in place. It would take years to generate, but would be well worth it.

They all looked at the 3D Mithras display. Mithras is the title name for Demiurge, the architect of the universe. Elroy was next to speak. "You see how Taus is situated on a galactic thread?"

There was a thin line of stars and rogue planets that resembled a thread, that lead like a path to the next galaxy. "Almost all galaxies have thin lines of stars connecting them, and they are commonly called 'threads'. Since most ships are propelled by gravity effects, these threads are a convenient way to travel from galaxy to galaxy."

"Like the 'trade winds' back home or the tides of Phul?" suggested Linda.

"Indeed." he said with a smile, reminiscent of a teacher whose students were beginning to catch on.

There usually is a natural way to travel great distances and the 'infrastructure' usually seemed to be in place...almost as if the universe had been 'designed' that way, as indeed it was: by Mithras Demiurge!

"Since we can travel by kinetic energy conversion, gravity shear is not necessary, but it is the principal means of long distance travel by the adversary's forces since they lack higher tech. It's unusual for there to be a thread coming off a valley, but there it is: leading right to a void."

"Uh, 'void'?" asked the Lt. raising his hand.

"A void, is essentially a hole in the universe, devoid of light or dark matter, or least it looks that way."

The Lt. seemed satisfied with this answer but he probably didn't understand it.

"I see where you're going with this. Nergal and his accomplices probably caught up with us there, and since Swanson was abducted rather than, uh, 'eliminated', they might have conducted him back over the same route, out of the galaxy." said Linda

"Exactly my thinking." said Elroy, smiling at her. "I think he was quite probably subdued when he was being distracted by Plesithea."

193

"Not much to go on, is it?" asked Harvey rhetorically "Well, let's give that a try, unless there are any better suggestions?" He was hoping that someone, anyone, with better detective abilities than his own, would have some insight.

Everyone was silent. There were no other suggestions, and they all knew it was a 'long shot' indeed. Whatever had happened to Cpl. Swanson could very well had happened to any of them - and it still could - unless they destroyed the enemy's *capability* to do this. They had to succeed. Swanson was well-liked, and nobody was happy to think about what might happen to him, should they fail in his rescue. He would certainly be killed, which meant one shot at this.

* * *

Harvey was a little unsure of the direction that they were taking in the investigation. He may have been good at solving other kinds of puzzles; but the others were figuring things out before he was lately, and to make matters worse, he had never thought of himself as a sleuth in any way, shape or form. It was for this reason that he entered the 'phone booth' to obtain some answers, if not some guidance. He was more nervous than usual this time.

"I thought I told you not to be so uptight." said Metatron.

"Well, it's just..."

"Whom I speak for?"

"Yes."

"Think of him as your *best friend*. The only being that knows you better than you know yourself, and *trusts* you because of it."

"You've said so before...it's just so *difficult*."

"Look, every time he has manifested, it has been under humble circumstances, right?"

Harvey thought about it. "Come to think of it, that's right!"

"Those things; pomp and circumstance, ceremony, fancy clothes all of that stuffy nonsense that others indulge in, do you really think for one moment that he *values* any of that?"

"I suppose not."

"Well?"

"Well, what about showing reverence and respect? For who and what he is?"

"When you meet someone you care about do you smile, and say hello or do you bend knee and compliment them until they are sick of

194

it?"

Harvey thought for a brief moment then said "Point taken."

"Great! Now what seems to be the problem?"

"Don't you know?"

"Yes, but since you came here to ask, I thought I'd do you the courtesy of *letting* you ask."

"Okay, 'please tell me about what I'm going up against here, because I think I'm out of my depth.'"

Metatron smiled warmly "Well, at this point, you will go head to head against the Adversary."

"So, will I finally get to see what I am up against in all of this?"

"Something like that but it would be better if you two didn't meet in person so soon."

Harvey gave him a puzzled look.

"First things first. What you're looking for now is called 'the cluster'. It is a group of artificial brains in that dark zone you're headed for."

"*Dark zone?*"

"Your astronomers sometimes might call it a hole in space, what Elroy called a void, but the region's official name is Abadon. It lies beyond the galaxy, where the light has not yet penetrated due to a lack of photons - a form of desert if you will - and it is very cold, even for space. It is one of the few places where my presence isn't felt, because I am not there. The artificial brains the adversary designed require great cold in order to operate properly, and they are of great size as well. Your man Swanson is there, and as yet, is more or less unharmed. You *can* rescue him and destroy the cluster, thereby freeing an entire world of enslaved cyborgs in the process."

"Enslaved?"

"They have had tele-presence devices implanted, and have been controlled from afar for a long time. The cluster is mostly made up of these artificial brains. Once it is destroyed, the cyborgs will again be permitted free will."

"Are they like Nergal?"

"No, that was a construct, they are mostly humans that tried to improve themselves with prosthetics, but all they achieved was becoming more susceptible to the direct control of the adversary's forces. That led to many more being mutilated, and parts replaced with technology to obtain control over them. Throw a few Gynoids into the mix and you'll see what you have there. Sure, there are a small number of true machines there, but they'll flee before you get there."

Harvey thought about it for a moment. "How do I find the cluster in this 'dark zone'?"

"Like any other road trip. Follow the path before you to the dark zone, then stop and ask for directions." he said flatly.

"And what of the world of cyborgs?"

"It's called Camaysar."

"Thank you."

"No, thank YOU...for taking on this assignment."

"But I don't really have a choice, do I?"

"You could refuse, and abandon Swanson to his fate."

"I *can't* do that!" said Harvey indignantly.

"Exactly! You feel compelled to help your crewman, and in doing so, you will free an entire world."

"If I had known that world was enslaved..."

"I know, you would have willingly freed them anyway. There are many enslaved worlds, and you will free a good number of them in your time. This is just a method of showing you what needs to be done. Follow your conscience and you will do well."

"I have so many questions, and so will the crew."

"Here." he handed Harvey a pill.

"A Penemue pill?" he asked holding it up.

"Yes, it will fill in many of the rest of the blanks. The crew is already turning to you for answers, and this will give you the ones you need for this assignment...and a few more."

"But do I have time for this pill to take effect?" he asked, knowing full well it normally took a night or two's sleep to process all the knowledge that a penemue pill imparted.

"This is a special formulation. It will work almost instantly."

"Wow! How..."

"Don't ask. I'm bending the rules of the physical universe for you this time. Pray I don't bend them any further." he said in a deep voice with a twinkle in his eye and a wink.

"Thanks!"

Finally! Some real progress!

The light faded from the android's eyes and the door opened. The audience with the creator was over. Harvey felt...validated. Unfortunately, with all the other influences out there, it was a feeling that always faded over time as it invariably does for everyone. It's just part of the human condition. The zealots that are always certain, are the ones that are deluding themselves.

He hurried to the bridge by passing through a doorway that presented itself to him in the middle of the wall.

Pymander just sighed and trudged down the long hallway muttering "One of these days..."

* * *

When they reached the dark zone, they found the planet Tuphon just inside, orbiting a dark star. The planet was relatively warm, with a breathable atmosphere. The heat of the planet itself kept the surface warm, if not hot, and the inhabitants were allergic to sunlight much in the same way Humans are allergic to molten metal.

"Prepare to enter the Dark Zone." said the Lt.

"What's to prepare for? Just do it." said Linda.

The Lt. grinned. "I know, I just thought it should be announced."

"Big deal." she muttered under her breath, with a scoff. She didn't like all the fancy labels for things. 'Dark Zone', sheesh!

Indeed, it was a big deal, after all. The bridge crew began taking all sorts of measurements. This was a fascinating phenomenon. They were about to enter the dark universe and thought that they were about to observe dark matter first hand. The intriguing part was that in the dark zone, there was alleged to be a total lack of photons.

Upon hearing that, DeSoto blurted "Now that's something I *have* to see!" as usual, oblivious of the howling error in his logic.

21
TUPHON
"Abandon all hope, ye who enter **ABADON!**"

In a way, DeSoto had his wish.

When they 'saw' the edge of the photon sea, they were amazed. It looked like an expanding boundary, that ebbed and flowed like water on the seashore, but on a grand scale. To them it looked like they were inside a weird balloon animal. The only way they could observe the situation correctly was to look at the tactical displays that showed the photon flows from 'the outside'.

"Ladies and gentlemen, there it is, The area known as Abadon." announced the android.

"Shall we pass the boundary?" asked the Lt. who was at the helm.

"Let 'er rip." said the captain calmly.

"This is fascinating!" exclaimed Linda while examining her Butator screen "It's *not* expanding at the speed of light!"

"Air does not expand at the speed of sound." explained Pymander.

"So, you're telling me that the sea of photons theory is correct?" asked DeSoto.

"The surface isn't smooth either, it looks like there are a few shafts of photons." observed Linda.

"The fabric of the universe is far from uniform out here." explained Pymander. "Those are like tributaries of a river. Those photons are *leaving* the area, not *arriving* like the light is."

"I can't help feel like we're fish that are about to fly over the land." said the Lt.

"That, is not far from the truth." answered the android as they entered one of the photon tributaries.

This got a raised eyebrow from Harvey, just as they passed the major threshold.

The viewers all changed at once, but still showed tactical views of the immediate area.

"Hey! How are the scanners still working?" asked DeSoto. "I thought vision would be impossible in here."

"Just be glad the ship can process other forms of imaging data, or else we'd be flying *totally* blind!" said the Lt. who was having a bit of trouble getting used to the new, eerie images he was now seeing in his head.

"So why can *we* see in here?" asked DeSoto, still trying to disprove everything, anything the android told them.

"This ship has a supply of photons inside it, like a fish bowl has water in it. If it didn't, we could not see anything inside the ship when we travel faster than light." said Pymander.

"You still haven't convinced me of that one." he muttered.

They were interrupted by the Lt. "WHOA!" he blurted as the ship stopped dead, just short of a planet.

"I thought you could navigate in here." said Harvey.

"Yeah, but those two were distracting me, besides, the images I am getting are less reliable."

Harvey raised and eyebrow at the android.

"As I said, the fabric of space is not uniform here. The means of viewing this area are not reliable because of it."

"Dead spots?"

"Worse."

"Great! Now what do we do?"

"Hope for the best?"

"I hate to interrupt, but this is the place." said the helmsman "To ask for directions. What's this planet called?"

"That would be Tuphon." said Harvey.

Pymander gave him a sly look. Harvey was coming along nicely!

* * *

When they stepped out of the shuttle, a curious thing happened. They lost the light inside it as the photons leaked out and several of the scientists that had come along to witness the phenomenon 'up close and personal' buckled up into the fetal position the moment they were no longer shrouded in photons. There was a force field holding in the majority of the photons, but some were leaking out with each crewman as they crossed the threshold.

The Azbuga leapt to their aide.

"What's the matter with them?" asked Harvey.

"I was afraid of that." he muttered. "Best get them back to the ship ASAP." he turned to Harvey "They can't handle being away from *his* presence."

"Whose?" asked Linda.

"Joth."

"How come some of us can?"

"It ain't easy!" said the Lt., sounding as distressed as he might be in

199

the heat of battle.

"Brave men like the S*I*P*Es can handle it for a while, but you and Harvey have a part of him covering you."

"The body armor?"

"They are of him, made by him personally, so you can still feel his presence."

"So, photons are 'his presence'?" asked Linda.

"Not entirely, but in the lack of neutrinos, they suffice. His energy is in them and in the light, that is why it destroys evil so effectively."

"Wow!"

Harvey turned to the Lt. "How's it feel?"

"Like I was a child and I just got deliberately abandoned by my parents at the mall."

"Ouch!"

"Only much, much worse."

"Ouch again! How are those sunglasses working?"

"Okay, I guess. This is weird, wearing sunglasses to see in the dark."

The translator sunglasses could use a form of sonar for seeing in just this situation.

"Good." He turned to the Azbuga. "Get them back onboard, and come back for us."

"Gotcha."

"I wonder how Swanson's taking it?" asked Harvey idly.

"Oh, he'll be fine. They obviously brought some photons with them or he would have known something was wrong." said the android.

"So, once we get onboard the ship he's in, we'll feel alright again?" asked the Lt. hopefully.

"Instantly."

"Okay, we'll try to find out what we can, and meet you back here." said Harvey.

They parted ways, and Harvey could see that the S*I*P*Es were on the edge of panic, but to their credit - none of them lost their heads. They found that if they held the ship-made ammunition in their hands, it took some of the edge off. It was somewhat amusing to see soldiers holding ammunition tightly, but that was what they did. It made a lot of sense to them on many levels, but they looked like a child holding a piece of a security blanket.

Although the ammunition, could navigate without light, but it was more difficult for them, as well, so they were a little less accurate.

200

Marksmanship now came into play. Nothing but trouble in this zone.

They hadn't gone far when the first shafts of light caught up with them. They found it difficult to search outside these shafts of light, but they managed. It was simply very difficult to step out of them, especially knowing how lonely and abandoned they would feel once they did.

"It's like you don't know what you have until it's gone." muttered the Lt. as he slowly and with great effort stepped out of a dim shaft of light. "It's almost as if the area in the dark does not even exist...like stepping off a cliff!"

It wasn't long before they found a creature hiding in a tiny alcove, cowering from the dim light that shined across the entrance, blocking it.

"What is this?" asked the Lt. as he approached it.

"Looks like a Vampire." said Linda, noticing the teeth.

"What if I *am?*" it snapped in a deep raspy voice.

"Well, that would make you evil, wouldn't it?"

"That is correct. I serve the Shekinah, and if it weren't for that blessed shaft of pain, I would drain all of you!"

"The light?" she asked, unafraid.

"Is that what you call it?" he said as he extended his hand into the dim shaft of light, only to burn his hand and retract it quickly. He held his hand in pain. "How is it that you can survive this 'light'?"

"We're from the light zone." offered Harvey.

"No! You're here to destroy our *world!*" he was in a panic. What one might expect if met on the edge of a lava flow by beings that climbed out of it that said they were from the inferno.

"Not really, we just stopped for directions."

"That is *all?*"

"Yes. We just want someone to point us in the right direction. That's it."

"Mmmm. Let me out from behind this light and I'll try to help you."

"How can we trust you? You just said you'd drain us all!" exclaimed the Lt.

"I keep my word. Just don't tell anyone I helped you. As none of you are pure good, none if us are pure evil. The difference is, here you can get torn apart for being the slightest bit...*nice.*"

Both Harvey and Linda's Amitiel systems told them that the Vampire was being truthful, and it was indeed a being of it's word.

"Well, best get you out of that alcove then." said Harvey as he unfolded an emergency blanket and held it up to block the light.

"That could be quite useful here. I don't suppose you could spare one of those?" said the Vampire as he cautiously crawled out of the alcove, noticing the strange tingle of being bathed in non-energized photons, and stood up next to Argent who was made even more nervous by this. The blood sucker was horrific in appearance. Ugly, like a bat, but had more human-like features. It looked like death to him.

"Um, sure. Here you go." said Harvey as he unceremoniously hung the emergency blanket to the Vampire's outstretched claw.

"Now that photons and light are penetrating, this will come in handy." he said as he folded it up and tucked it away. "Alright, you did more than your part, and I'll do mine. What directions do you need?"

"We're looking for the cluster." said Linda.

"Ahhhh! You *do* come to destroy!"

"Just the cluster. You and yours can keep this world." offered Harvey.

The Vampire's eyes narrowed, and it cracked a sly smile. He pointed one of his horrific claws toward a mountain range. "Go there, follow the signs. If you are not torn apart by my kindred, then you may be worthy to visit the dark overlord, Botulus Alacritas. He can tell you how to find the cluster. That is, if he doesn't kill you on sight. That, is *all* I can do for you."

They looked in the direction the Vampire was pointing and then looked back and he was gone.

Harvey indicated with his arm for Linda to move in that direction and said "Lady's first."

"Except into *danger!*" she corrected flatly, without taking a step this time.

"Oh, I keep forgetting." he said defensively, and followed the S*I*P*Es that had already started on their way. They really wanted to get back to the ship, ASAP!

Linda shook her head slightly and rolled her eyes, hoping that Harvey would learn to 'get it right'.

* * *

The planet wasn't entirely devoid of photons, they were just not very dense in their distribution and, to put it mildly, there were few, if any, sources of light. There was, in fact, enough light to just barely make out the existence of things. Think of humidity at the seashore. The photons themselves did not harm the dark beings there, but light did. It seems

202

the energy level of light was far too high. Radios hardly worked, and when there were enough photons around to allow them to work, the radios acted like weapons of mass destruction and flashlights were like 'death ray weapons' from old movies back home, so they decided to stay together and not use the radios unless they needed them as weapons. Good thing too, as they were being observed by a small army of Orcs, Imps and Ghouls. When they attacked, they got a surprise.

"Try not to use the guns, if you can." said Harvey.

"Why not? We've got lots of ammunition." answered the Lt.

"It's not that, they're just so loud."

"But doesn't your armor protect your ears?"

"I don't want anybody to know we're coming!"

"Ohhh...."

Just then, a few imps jumped out at them and the Lt. instinctively fired a round at the closest one. T he muzzle flash seemed to singe the others. In a moment of inspiration, he switched on his barely effective tactical light and pointed it at the affected monsters. The light seemed to act like a flame thrower. Noticing this, the Lt. turned on his targeting laser and used it to cut the remaining monsters in half like a sword.

"This is gonna be *good!*" he said excitedly with an evil grin as he cut the last imp in half. "Is *this* quiet enough for ya?" he asked Harvey.

"Steady. Don't get too worked up." Harvey was worried about the Lt. causing too much of a ruckus and attracting an entire imp army. He was worried about the single gunshot attracting even more monsters, as there were far worse things lurking in the darkness on this world.

The Lt. just gave him a look as he took point. If there were a few imps hiding in the woodwork, there were bound to be more. Sure enough, he managed to flush them out. Time and again, he found he could simply use his tactical light or targeting laser to mow them down. Funny, the lack of photons in the local space made light rare, but highly effective as a weapon. It made no sense to him. It was like a species living on the ocean shore when they were allergic to water. The truth was that photons were invading and this was like a fog, and the tactical laser was like a hydraulic cutter.

Then the main force attacked. They came over a hill, all yelling and growling, waving primitive-edged weapons at them as the line approached.

"We're going to have to go full-auto!" said the Lt. as he cut down as many as he could with his targeting laser and tactical flashlight. The other S*I*P*Es were doing the same in an overlapping fashion but they were coming in too fast for the soldiers to handle. There were just too many of them.

Harvey didn't panic, he had his radio set on full power and simply keyed it up. The entire first wave fell like they had been shut off. The leaders that were watching from the hill, decided that if they had weapons like that, and they couldn't even lay a claw on even one of them, it was best to retreat. Why lose the entire army over a handful of men?

"Nice job." said the Lt. to Harvey as they continued. "I was afraid I was going to have to use a flair." he added with a grin.

* * *

They made it to the citadel, surprisingly, without further incident. Everything they met cowered from that point on. Word must have gotten around about them and their powers of mass destruction! To their surprise, the guards did not attempt to dissuade them.

"You come to challenge the Dark Overloard 'Botulus Alacritas'?" Here, let me show you to him." One would think they would get used to this kind of thing. Perhaps Pymander was correct when they had first met and he called *their* world 'backward'.

When they were conducted to the throne room, they could not believe their eyes. There was not only enough light to see by, but there, on the throne sat a dark, *creature,* for want of a better term, that had some sort of arrangement of antennae on it's head. The antennas were constantly spewing red electrical-looking arcs between them. The creature had a maw that looked like it could not only rip a man's head off with a single bite, but it could also rip the arms off, as well, with the additional sideways moving jaws. It's stare made anyone freeze with fear as it seemed to be sizing-up one's soul and deciding what seasonings to use when eating it. Worst of all, it had to be a full twenty-five feet tall. Not even Mongo could hope to do battle with it.

The beast glared at each of them in turn. Then his eyes met Harvey's, who uncharacteristically didn't even flinch. Without skipping a beat, the monstrosity threw a red lightning bolt at the Captain, hitting him in the center of his chest!

22
DEVIL TOUPEE
"Nope. I am NOT going there!"

The red lightning had no effect on Harvey, thanks to his body armor, and taking advantage at the dark overlord's moment of hesitation from his surprise at this, Harvey threw a blinding blue lightning bolt right back at *it!*

Needless to say, the guards in the hall all fell, and some, the closest without cover, vaporized on the spot simply due to the brightness of the bolt, but the full intensity was directed at the ruling dark overlord, who subsequently slumped forward and fell out of his throne onto his knees before Harvey. Not dead, but wishing he was, he slowly got up, smouldering hole in his chest, and all. He greeted the visitors: "Wonderful! I haven't had such a rousing exchange in aeons!" his booming voice echoed in the gigantic hall.

"You're not angry?" asked the Lt. who was expecting more of a fight.

"Not in the slightest! I have finally met a creature *worth* fighting!" With a wave of his hand, the room lit up brightly. This of course made it more comfortable for the crew, but the rest of the dark overlord began to smoulder, ever so slightly. For a being from the Dark Zone, he was tough to be sure, and could take normal levels of light, but bright lights would slowly erode his physical existence. However, he was attempting to show off. It was also a test of his new found adversaries.

"Hmmmm, you handle the light so well, you *must* be from the light zone..." he almost muttered in a disappointed tone. He was full well expecting the light to do them some damage and soften them up a little, to make his battle that much easier. "What do you want?" he said as humbly as he could. Apparently anything that could handle light better than he could was worthy of respect!

"The cluster." answered Harvey firmly, wishing to waste no more time. Indeed, he had struck a somewhat arrogant stance, like the conquering hero in a B-movie.

The dark overlord's eyes narrowed, and glowed bright red as if they were about to spew death rays. Then he chuckled softly. "What's in it for *me?*""What do you have in mind?" asked Harvey, knowing not to ask what he *wanted,* thanks to the Penemue pill from Joth. Asking what he wanted, would have been no different from saying 'Anything you want.'

With that the dark overlord, looked around as if afraid that someone was listening in. Satisfied that they were alone - another reason for the lights...he summoned a smaller version of himself. This one stood about nine feet tall, and hadn't seemed to get the hang of arcing in his head yet, though he was attempting it with vigor, apparently trying to impress them, but only managing the odd spark or two.

"This is my son, *Myron*." He almost spat the name with contempt.

"What does he have to do with anything?" blurted the Lt.

"Is this man one of your Lieutenants?"

"Yes actually. Answer him as you would answer *me*." Harvey answered flatly.

"As you wish. Take my son with you and I'll tell you everything about the cluster, including how to utterly destroy it."

"What?" said Linda.

Harvey raised a cautionary finger, as women are often thought to be the highest authorities by the adversary's forces, and he didn't want to have any hiccoughs. "Why would you want to do that?"

"He's defective." answered the overlord.

"What do you mean? He looks...uh...'all right' to me."

Indeed, the younger dark overlord seemed to be a healthy specimen. Well, as best as they could tell for a hideous monster.

"It's just that he's got a...well...*nice* streak." Botulus looked embarrassed!

"Oh!" said a puzzled group in chorus.

"I caught him actually *healing* small animals that someone else had maimed. Can you imagine? I can't have that!"

Myron looked down at his feet, as if ashamed.

"Yes, I understand." said Harvey flatly.

"Of course, the official story will be that I sent him with you to show him how weak you light dwellers are."

"I see." said Harvey as he gave Linda a worried look.

"Don't worry, I'm only asking this to get rid of him, since his weakness reflects on *me*." He leaned downward toward Harvey as if to speak to him privately "I can't bring myself to kill him, being so pathetic and my own flesh you understand."

"Of course." agreed Harvey with understanding in his voice. He knew enough not to insult him by saying that there was a streak of kindness inside him!

"And I certainly don't expect him to return to take my life." the dark overlord added in a matter-of-fact tone. "His older brothers all failed in

206

that respect."

"WHAT?" said Linda.

"That's their rite of succession here." said Harvey flatly.

She looked at Botulus, who did his best to shrug. "I got the red rage," he said pointing at his arching head "the day I killed *my* father. Ah, I can remember the sound of his flesh being torn apart by my claws as if it were yesterday!" he said nostalgically.

"Talk about EVIL!" exclaimed Linda.

Harvey leaned over to Linda as if to speak to her privately. "That, is what we are always up against. This one's just honest about it. I think it's called 'lawful evil'."

Harvey turned to Myron, and asked "Myron, what do *you* think?"

Myron smiled at Linda and said quietly, with a steely, almost screeching voice that made shivers run up and down everyone's spine; "I *want* to go with you!"

Linda looked mortified.

Harvey then turned to the dark overlord, and said "Fine, he is welcome to come with us."

Botulus let out a deep, low, satisfied growl of approval and nodded. Then he whispered to Linda "Don't worry, angel of light, his voice will change soon."

"That's not what's bugging me." she muttered as she glared at Harvey.

23
THE DEVIL'S OWN
"I suppose I could stay a *bit* longer!"

They made their way back to the evacuation point with their new crewman. Every time they were challenged by any kind of creature, they retreated in fear at the sight of Myron.

Fortunately, the shuttle had landed much closer to the citadel, as there was not chance of being shot at. Botulus had granted them 'safe passage', an insult on this world but one the Ezrael crew didn't mind one bit. Getting out of there was what they all wanted.

"Why are they so afraid of you?" Linda asked him after a rather large group of monsters ran in fear at the sight of Myron.

"Are you kidding?" interjected the Lt.

"To me, they are food, and they know it." said Myron, in a voice that sent shivers down her spine.

"Uh, yes, I see. Try not to talk too much dear." she said as she patted him on the arm, as far away from the claws as she could reach.

Myron had a crush on her. "She called me 'dear'!" he thought to himself. This was going great!

When they arrived at the now waiting shuttle, even though they had been told about Myron, the crewmen jumped back in fear at the sight of him. This only made him laugh - if you could call it that. He rhythmically hissed. It was a disturbing sound that ran shivers down their spines. What had Harvey gotten them into?

"Watch, your, uh, *head,* I suppose." said the Lt. as the young Dark Overlord attempted to enter the relatively tiny shuttle. He bumped his head a few times on the ceiling, until he got hang of it. When he sat down in one of the chairs, the metal in it flexed under the stress, and his head still almost hit the ceiling. At least this way he wasn't hunched over. He sat there and appeared to smile.

"What's he made of?"asked the Chief engineer at the sound of creaking metal.

"Don't ask." said Linda as she walked past.

"Let's get back to the ship." said Harvey once the last of their party had hastily entered. It felt good to be surround by photons again.

Linda looked over at Myron, and despite it being bright inside the shuttle, he was not smouldering as his father had been. Perhaps this one was actually 'nice'.

The shuttle ride back to the ship was relatively quiet. Nobody knew what to say, especially Myron. They all just sat there quietly.

When they arrived, Linda asked Harvey "What are you going to do with him?"

"Are you kidding? I don't know what to do with Mongo most of the time."

"Why not introduce the two. Maybe they'll be friends." offered the Lt. "Just might get both of them out of your hair long enough to figure something out."

Harvey gave a thoughtful smile.

"Oh boy..." said Linda apprehensively.

"Myron, come with us." said Harvey.

"Yes, chosen one." said Myron in his monotone.

"Just call me Harvey, okay?"

"Yes, Harvey."

"He's your pet, you have to clean up after him." said Linda, playing the scolding mother.

He rolled his eyes and led them all through a doorway. They arrived in an open field, where they had set-up living quarters for Mongo in a nearby cave.

"How?" asked Myron.

"This ship can teleport you anywhere we left behind a teleportation gate, just look behind you."

Sure enough, there was a twenty-foot diameter black sphere behind them.

"Any time you want to visit the ship, just walk through that thing. Okay?"

"Yes Harvey."

"Also, from time to time, we'll want to either visit you or bring you with us on a mission. Got it?"

"A *mission?*" it almost managed expression.

"Yes. If you're going to learn from us, it's best you came along on the odd mission where you might be helpful."

Myron grinned as he eyed Linda.

"I'll go anywhere with nice lady!"

Linda just buried her face in her hands for a moment and Harvey gleefully asked her "*Whose* pet?"

Just then they were distracted by a loud thud. Mongo had arrived by jumping off the ledge on the cliff. His kind, being impervious, never thought much of jumping out of shuttles in orbit as a way of arriving on a planet.

209

He had seen them arrive and was wanting to play.

"HI!" he said cheerfully.

"Mongo, I'd like you to meet Myron. If you don't mind, he will be staying with you for a while."

Slurdrahk and the Dark Overlord's eyes met and they were at once wrestling.

"Now you've done it, they'll kill each other." said Linda mockingly. "Oh! Please, no!" she said in as unemotional tone she could muster.

"I think they are fast friends." offered the Lt. as the two figures smashed against the cliff face, dislodging some rocks. "They're just wrestling."

"I hope you're right." she said in a worried tone.

By then the two titans had completed their greeting, and Mongo was the first to approach.

"Thank you for bringing me a friend."

"Fiend is more like it." said Linda, under her breath.

Mongo laughed. "Oh! ho, ho, ho! He like me, he look bad but he have choosies too!" 'Choosies' was Mongo's term for free will.

"So he can *choose* to do good." she asked.

"Yes. He wants to be good."

"Can you teach him?" asked Harvey.

"Oh yes! I teach him how to be good."

"Very well. We'll leave you to it."

"Thank you! Bye-bye!"

Myron waved goodbye to Linda, looking a little sad. She noticed this and hoped he would grow out of his 'puppy love' very soon!

They entered the sphere and found themselves on the bridge of the Ezrael.

"That door thing still gets me." said the Lt. "I tried to map the interior of the sphere when we first got here, and all those teleporters muck things up a lot."

"What do you mean? The doorways are event horizons, just like the spheres." said the Chief.

"Well, how can that plateau and mountain be *on* the ship? I mean, where is it *really,* anyway? You can't tell me, where we've just been, is *inside* the sphere!"

"It's an unpopulated world, far off the beaten path. The ship really isn't here anyway."

"Isn't *here?* Where is it then?" This was much worse!

"The ship is technically comprised of many places that are nowhere near each other. In other words, the ship has no exact location."

"Oh that's clear. Then what's the sphere?"

"The whole thing is an event horizon."

"I get that. So, everything we see, is elsewhere, and when we go out of the ship on a shuttle, we're being teleported to that location from some place far from it?"

"Close enough."

The Lt. grinned. "So, even if someone breached the shields, they couldn't harm us, in here, wherever we are."

"Exactly! In fact, the best they could ever do is reach the event horizon of a hull we have, and we could teleport them at will to anyplace we have a receiver."

"Oh, that's cool!"

"I thought you'd like it." said the chief with a wink and a smile. He was learning a lot about this technology from Elroy and together they were having a grand old time.

"So we were never really in any danger when the Barbielians attacked?"

"Nope!"

"COOL!"

"Okay, now that, that's sorted out, can we get on with things?" asked Harvey.

"Oh, yes of course!" said the Lt. as he relieved Taggert at the helm. "Let's rescue Swanson!"

"Glad you approve." said Harvey dryly, with a twinkle in his eye.

They followed the directions from Botulus Alacritas, and found a blinding flash of energy in the area they were headed for.

"Are we too late?" asked the Major.

"It's the bi-located antimatter explosion they threw at us." explained the Lt. "They must have sent their ounce of water out into deep space, detonating it at a safe distance from the artificial brains, that's why we had time to react, so my guess is that we're close to the cluster now."

"Good, let's sneak up on them." said Harvey.

"You do realize that when we travel faster than light, we're invisible anyway?"

"Yes, I know it's part of the photodynamic design of the ship, but I'm saying keep it invisible when you go sub-light."

"Ohhhh..."

Photodynamics are a lot like aerodynamics. When traveling faster than light, the snowplow effect builds up, light waves in front of the

211

ship that, due to the Doppler effect, shift into the gamma range. When one arrives at one's destination, the resulting gamma ray burst usually sterilizes the planet. So, if one goes invisible while traveling at such velocities, this is no longer a problem.

When they finally saw the cluster, it seemed that it kept getting larger as they approached but they were not getting any closer.

"It's HUGE!" gasped Linda, once they were close enough to make out what she thought were portholes.

"That's what we're looking for; the docking ports." said Harvey as the Lt. nodded and maneuvered the ship into the massive docking bay. The Butator confirmed that they were in the right place to save Cpl. Swanson.

"What's that? Oh my...is that a ship?" asked Linda in surprise.

"That's the Mephistopheles, one of only seven Maskim class cruisers ever built." explained Pymander.

"Jeez, they're larger than the Ezrael." muttered the chief.

"Actually, *this* ship is as big as it needs to be, even as large as the universe itself. Besides, do you really think that size *matters?*"

Linda rolled her eyes.

"More riddles!" said the chief as he slapped the android on the back and chuckled.

"*Can* they take us?" asked the Major marveling at the gun ports so large one could sail an aircraft carrier into them.

"No, even though that is precisely what they were designed for. Once they were found to be ineffective against a ship like this, they wound up only being used for mass invasions - quite effectively, in their heyday, I might add."

"Then why make so few of them?" asked Linda.

"Well, two reasons really. ,One is that they had to dissemble three planets to make the fleet and the other is that the shipyards making them were destroyed by Callicrates so they can't make them anymore. ,That ship is very old and likely is docked here because she's no longer in working condition."

They silently docked the invisible Ezrael, next to the Maskin flagship. Now it was time to get on with the rescue mission.

Linda was coming too, and despite the danger, there was no leaving her behind. Harvey didn't mind so much, as long as she was wearing her body armor. She decided to take her favorite outfit, the one that could change itself at her whim *and* self-repair. Thinking it was just the thing, she told it to change into something appropriate for such a mission, yet something alluring to make Harvey look twice. She found herself wearing what looked like a leather body suit, complete with a stylized face mask. "Ohhhh, that's hot!" she said to herself as she looked at it in the mirror, making multiple poses. "That'll drive him *crazy!*" she sported an alluring grin as she headed for the shuttle bay.

When Harvey saw Linda in her new outfit, he blushed. She looked like she was ready for some spy-type burglary work in a cold-war era film.

"Mrs. Peel." he said with a big grin, as he tipped an imaginary hat.

"Just keep your hands to yourself buster!" she said playfully as she slunk past him as seductively and cat-like as she could on her way up the ramp to the shuttle. She loved torturing that poor man!

Lt. Argent let out a low wolf whistle after she disappeared inside.

"I *heard* that!" came Linda's voice from inside the shuttle. Evidently, the Lt. had forgotten that the S*I*P*Es were not the only ones with augmented hearing.

"*Thanks* a *lot!*" snapped Harvey in a loud whisper, obviously concerned that Linda thought he was the one who had whistled.

"Anytime." chuckled the Lt. with a big grin as they began to walk up the ramp. 'But I'm not the one she is after.' he thought to himself.

Harvey's face was beet red by this time. He kept shaking his head, and smiling wearily. This was going to be a long day.

* * *

They had never been discovered here, so they had grown complacent over the millennia. Not even Captain Callicrates had been able to find this place, so it was assumed that no one ever would. That is why they had minimal security. If you could even call it that.

Harvey and co. knew that they were not expected, but wanted to keep the element of surprise as long as possible, so they approached quietly in a small craft that was cloaked.

"Is it just me, or is this too easy?" asked Linda as they approached. She was beginning to question the wisdom of coming along.

"Don't jinx it." cautioned the Lt. quietly who was piloting the shuttle the ten miles down the long docking bay.

"They don't even know we're coming." said Harvey reassuringly.

The major nodded with a glint in his eye. He loved the fact that the enemy had no idea they were there. Their confidence worried Linda. She could not shake her sense of foreboding. She didn't tell him that she had been having nightmares about being eaten by a monster, but she was not going to let that keep her away from all the 'fun'. Besides, she was the type that always had dreams about being eaten by a monster. It's just that the recent ones were always the same.

"*There.*" said Harvey to the Lt., pointing at a suitable landing pad near the entrance to the cluster's innards.

They landed quietly without incident and managed to disembark into the entry port with relative ease. Maybe this *was* too easy after all...

* * *

Mastema, had a fleet of seven Maskim-class ships under him; the old 'command fleet' as it was called. His flagship is the Mephistopheles was undergoing a re-fit to make her more space-worthy and battle ready. He is also the editor of the Kolazonta. The Kolazonta News Network, A.K.A.: KNN, and therefore, knew what a threat the Ezrael was. He was not timid and knew it would eventually escalate into a head-to-head fight some day. Just like last time. He was on the bridge, overseeing the re-fit when he got a call from the Shekinah, known to Harvey and company as simply 'The Adversary' for now.

"Mastema, when you capture them, I want the woman, Linda, to be tortured for some time before you kill her, then send me her head on a *platinum platter*."

"Of course, Shekinah, it will be done."

"But leave the Simkiel to me. I will deal with him *personally*."

"As you command." He bowed and the communications screen went blank.

He turned to his minions and said; "The Mephistopheles must be ready for launch within four hours! MOVE!"

* * *

As Linda was looking in a dark doorway, she shrugged at not seeing anything, turned her back and a clawed hand appeared out of the darkness to cover her mouth, another gripped her around her waist and she was abruptly pulled into the darkness with such force that her arms and legs stuck out in front of her.

The humanoid beings of unspeakable ugliness dragged her literally kicking and screaming onto the Mephistopheles.

214

The imps that had grabbed her, threw her to her knees before Mastema. That didn't stop her from quickly leaping to her feet with what she thought of as the cat-like nimbleness of a kung-fu master. Despite that, she still had to crane her neck to look up at his face. He was very tall, as if he were one of the Titans from ancient Greece, but, in fact, he was actually one of the few surviving Nephelium.

"Now my dear, let's see what you have under that!" he bellowed as he lifted her by her throat, grabbed the front of her outfit and tore it off!

As expected her outfit tore along the seams, but to his astonishment, it self-repaired before his eyes. In moments it was whole again. Now, Linda, who was not exactly well covered at that moment, was about to be embarrassed, but her armor anticipated her feeling of modesty, and quickly colored itself over, shall we say - all the *important* places. It also, pinched her skin a little in the right places as to create the appearance of a seam where the undergarments it had just painted on her would begin and end, thus adding to the illusion. Try as he might, Mastema could not remove them. It was common practice to strip prisoners, especially the female ones, before throwing them in a cell, thus humiliating them. Psychologically, forcing a woman to strip was the most humiliating, but he enjoyed doing it himself. He liked the intimidation factor it added, given his size and ferocity. He found himself unable to remove the undergarments on her, even when trying to claw through her flesh to get under the edge. So, he finally gave up in frustration and threw her to the floor. On her hands and knees, with her hair mussed over her face, she tossed it back, and looked up at him with a glint that struck some fear in his heart, because he had only seen that look in the Shekinah's eyes before. 'Hell hath no fury' after all. No one else had ever dared to be so defiant and that worried him.

"I'll deal with you and your glued-on undergarments later, my dear. In the meantime, if you don't mind, I have to kill your friends." he said coldly, masking his apprehension. She was in the service of the Simkiel, and as such was probably a being of incredible power in her own right. Why *else* would she be so defiant? That, was weighing heavily on the minds of his guards as well, as they fidgeted nervously. The fact that the Shekinah specifically wanted her killed, spoke volumes as to how dangerous she was. His claws had left no marks on her skin when he had attempted to remove her undergarments, and they should have cut her flesh to the bone, so he believed that torturing her was going to be difficult. He needed time to think about *how* to manage it. The nagging doubt at the back of his mind was also fueled by his wondering why she had not tried anything...yet. It was almost as if she *wanted* to be captured.

With a wave of his hand, two ghouls came to drag her away to a cell.

"Now to kill Harvie." he said, half to himself.

This simply made Linda narrow her eyes in anger as she was dragged out of the room. He may be able to grab *her* and slap her around a bit, but she'd be darned if she was going to let that oaf hurt her man!

"Sir! The Shekinah forbade you to kill the Simkiel!" blurted one of his lesser minions.

Mastema smiled at the pathetic henchman, lulling him into a false sense of security.

"Yes, of course you're right." he said calmly.

The imp, who was 'dumb as a post' - no offense meant to cellulose-containing plant life - smiled, glad to have been of service for once.

This moment of satisfaction did not last because Mastema took it by the throat, and as he squeezed every last ounce of life out of it, he bellowed "DON'T... YOU...EVER...CORRECT...ME...AGAIN!!!" taking out all of his frustrations on the unfortunate underling. His grip increased exponentially with each word, and with the last word, the imp's head popped neatly off its shoulders and its torso went limp. With that, Mastema dropped the remains on the floor, shaking the fluids off his hand. Then he looked at the remaining cowering imps and ghouls. "GET ON WITH IT!" he commanded, and a flurry of frantic activity ensued.

* * *

Her holding cell had no amenities at all, not even a toilet. It was plain and featureless.

"This is the pits!" she thought to herself.

"What is?" she heard Harvey's voice say.

"Oh yeah, I forgot about the armor's communications system again." she thought at him.

"Where *are* you?" he asked. "You literally disappeared right after we entered the cluster."

"I was grabbed my Mastema, but don't worry...I'll manage." not wanting him to see her this way, and wishing him to stay away and remain relatively safe.

"Are you sure? We can be there in a few minutes." The route to get to her was being plotted before his eyes, by his body armor's Butator.

"Don't worry, I'll catch you up." she told him confidently. "By the way, he knows you're here and is planning to kill all of you. Especially you, my dear."

"Thanks for the heads up! We'll be on our toes!"

Then she instructed the armor to not allow further outgoing communications until she was darn good and ready. Her stray thoughts were *not* to be sent to Harvey! She wondered if he had noticed that she called him 'dear'.

* * *

Joe Buckley, a one-handed, bigoted, Black and White, Asian, Vampire, Eskimo, Elf, mail clerk; was busy sorting mail, on the graveyard shift. Most of the beings on the cluster were sleeping since it was during the 'day'. Just about 2pm by our clocks. The mail room was quiet except for the sounds he was making, as he busily sorted the day's mail. There was not a lot of support staff, but there was enough to populate a small city. After all, each artificial brain in the cluster was as large as a planet in its own right, and no matter how well designed or built, all constructs of man require maintenance and repair. Everything was silent, until the klaxons went off and a half second later, the doors burst open with a small army of heavily armed men.

Buckley just said "Oh no, not again!" and expertly put his hands up. Well, one was a hook.

"I bet they call you 'lefty'." said one of them with a wink.

He just nodded.

"Hurry." the leader said to the other S*I*P*Es, who were busily planting charges on the critical points inside the cluster by sending them off via the mail system. Indeed, the artificial brains were so large, it would have taken them literally years to cover enough ground to plant all the necessary charges, but fortunately they had a mass-driver distribution system, not unlike a pneumatic tube system back home. So, all they had to do was find the mail room, and send off the charges to the every critical point in the cluster from there. Even though they were antimatter mines, they needed a lot of them to destroy that place. Once the charges were planted, then they could rescue Swanson and Linda on the Mephistopheles. The poor mail clerk was tied down to his chair with a very large antimatter charge placed on his lap, and a timer with

217

big numbers turned upwards for him to see a countdown. However, that was just a failsafe. The charges were intended to be detonated by remote-control. Then they headed to the Mephistopheles to rescue Linda.

* * *

When Mastema sensed Harvey and the S*I*P*Es coming, it was too late for his henchmen. They were all gunned down in the outer room before they could react. He barely ducked behind cover before they entered this inner chamber. Mind you, he was impervious to such low-power weaponry, but he wanted to see the look of surprise on the Simkiel's face as he shot him point blank. He pulled out his rifle and waited for them.

The Lt. was the first to cautiously appear in the doorway, pointing his M-29A1 this way and that. He kept his back to the wall, and looked all over the room for more 'hostiles' as he put it. He was unable to discern that Mastema was hiding behind a blind that was an optical illusion. Not even his weapon's sensors could tell. So, he signaled the 'All clear' and the others shuffled in, and started looking around.

The Lt. spotted what looked like Linda's body suit in the middle of the floor. He picked it up and grinned inanely at Harvey.

"Put that down!" hissed Harvey as he stopped and slowly looked around.

"What's the matter?" Lt. Argent asked as he absent-mindedly stuffed the body suit into his space pack. It is was Linda's she might want it back, and if it wasn't, it might be something they could learn from. Either way, he was taking it with him. "This means that Linda is running around here somewhere, stark *nekked!* Don't you want to see that? I know I do!"

Harvey just ignored him. He couldn't understand Argent's cavalier attitude in the face of danger, so he just shook his head and scowled disapprovingly. At least he wasn't saying that he had already seen her that way.

"I don't know for sure, but I have the feeling of impending doom." said Harvey gravely.

"What does your armor say?" asked Argent, suddenly serious again.

"It tells me that I'm right, but it can't quite pinpoint the danger either. Whatever it is, it must be hidden somehow...or *moving.*"

They all solemnly looked around for the danger. Was it a trap? A bomb? A sniper? They had no idea.

Harvey wasn't the only one. The adversary felt something, halfway across creation in purgatory - and almost panicked over it.

Mastema had Harvey in his sights, and was ready to squeeze the trigger on his high-powered mass-driver rifle, which incidentally, could easily penetrate Harvey's armor. No 'mere Human-being' could use such a weapon. It would take something as solid as Mongo to not be thrown a good distance by the recoil, but Mastema was one of the most powerful and solid humanoids there was. Besides, he believed in 'overkill', especially in cases like this. He couldn't kill his enemies with too much malice for his taste.

"Stay your hand!" the adversary telepathically commanded Mastema, shaking a tightly clenched fist in the air for emphasis.

"Why should I? He's the enemy, let me kill him for you." he answered.

"I have plans for this one. *Stay your hand!*" more firmly this time with blood running from wounds in the palm from a fist clenched so tightly that the fingernails broke skin.

"No! He's too dangerous! Enemies like him must die! I *must* disobey!" he insisted as his finger began to squeeze the trigger...

* * *

"Let me see now. What do I have?" Linda asked herself with crossed arms.

Then she remembered the only thing she had was her body armor. "Duh!" she said aloud as she smacked herself on the forehead. The Ghoul watching on the security system suspected that she was referring to her mental powers. What happened next, absolutely convinced him of it.

Linda looked at the armed Imp, guarding her cell, and said "Sleep!" in a firm tone. It collapsed as if it had been shut off. Then she looked at the door, and just as firmly said "Open!" as she waived her hand. It unlocked and swung slightly ajar. She walked out the door and muttered "Almost *too* easy!" as the smile ran away from her face.

She came upon a mirror and realized that she still appeared to be in her underwear. "This is ridiculous!" she said as she changed the armor's configuration to re-create her body suit as accurately as it could. This time it was of course, literally *painted* on. The armor could not reproduce a weapon without material, and it did it's best to give her cat-

219

like claws, that appeared any time she thought of defending herself. At least now she could *shred* an assailant. She didn't know that it was the armor that allowed Harvey to throw lightning at the dark overlord Botulus Alacritas or she might have figured out how to do it herself. As it was, the body armor did not make suggestions, it simply followed instructions as best it could, to bring about the desired outcome. It would automatically protect her in every way it could, but she never asked about energy weapons, so it was not going to tell her. Lasers coming out of her eyes would have been her choice here, had she known it was possible. She liked the psychological effect of such things. For now, cat suit and all, claws would do nicely!

The ghoul watching set off a klaxon to alert everyone to her escape, and it drew her attention to the security camera. She smiled at it, and the image on the screen winked out. The ghoul watching it let out a low whistle. "She must be an angel." he said under his breath. He wasn't going to mess with a being of that level of power, no matter how angry Mastema would be about it. Given that, he took his own sweet time reporting the problem. The delay allowed her to make her escape, and that was just fine with that particular ghoul.

With the klaxon and security system disabled, she quickly made her way toward the space port. It seems that none of the imps or ghouls were brave enough to face her! She could easily stare them down the moment that they appeared in a doorway.

"That's right! Back off or I'll shred you!" she said to the slowly retreating ghouls, as she grew her claws in front of them, and took a swipe in the air that would make them turn tail and run.

"Cowards!" she bellowed as they ran from her. She laughed. Truly, the adversary's forces *ran* from a fair fight! This was wonderful news! Sadly, this was not true of all of their forces, as they would find out soon enough.

Linda was having such a good time, in fact, that she missed the one doorway she went through, that led to a room with a floor that was a lot lower than the hallway. The room was a pit that contained a nasty beastie. Before she knew it, she had landed in it's maw, and it instinctively swallowed her whole. The imps that were watching smiled gleefully. Now they would not have to deal with her or face the wrath of Mastema anymore, things were definitely looking up!

* * *

The Shekinah was furious. Mastema was beginning to squeeze his trigger. Apparently, he had forgotten *why* even the most treacherous obey without question. Just as his finger was at the threshold of setting off the weapon, he had an excruciating aneurysm. He would not die from it, but he found himself wishing that he had. A being so powerful as to be able to claw his way out of the underworld, was now in the fetal position on the floor, quietly whimpering like a wounded child. Fortunately for him, he was not heard by Harvey and company, the sound being deadened by the cover.

"That'll show him!" said the evil one triumphantly. This was the most that could be done from within prison but it was enough. It was also a condition that had been negotiated at the beginning. After all, one had to maintain control of one's minions!

"The feeling has passed." said Harvey with a shrug. "The armor tells me there is no more *mortal* danger...it must have moved on, whatever it was."

"Good, let's go." said the Lt. who didn't like staying too long in one place on missions like this.

They slowly crept along, missing the now unconscious Mastema behind his cover.

They made their way, following their instructions from the bridge. The ship's sensors were able to scan the complex and discern Swanson's whereabouts. He was not alone. There were at least three, sometimes as many as five in close proximity with him at all times. They were afraid of the worst. Now that they had no further use for him, they may be torturing the poor Corporal...or worse!

When the rescue party finally made their way to where Swanson was being held, the Lt. cried out "You gotta be kidding me!"

There was Cpl. Swanson, dressed in Sultan's robes, lying on pillows being fanned by harem girls with some of them feeding him grapes.

When he noticed the rescue party, he looked up and said "Oh, hey guys!" almost unconcerned with their arrival.

"What have you been doing?" demanded the Lt., lowering his weapon and showing jealousy over how much fun Swanson was having.

"Isn't this place great? I love it here! We have *got to* come back here for shore leave next time!" Then he ate another grape. Apparently the harem girls were unconcerned by the arrival of strange, armed men.

"Do you have any idea where you are or how long you've been gone? You're A.W.O.L., SOLDIER!"

"Oh! Did I take too much time?" he asked innocently. "I didn't

221

intend to go A.W.O.L.!" he said, almost panicking as he sat bolt upright. Apparently the best he could do in his current state.

"You were kidnapped and taken halfway across the universe you dolt!"

Harvey raised a cautionary hand. "Explanations later." he said as his armor warned him of impending attack.

"You're right, let's just get out of here while the gettin's good!"

Harvey gave him a puzzled look. He'd not heard that expression in a very long time. Argent shrugged.

"Oh c'mon guys! I'm doing somthin' called 'the seven deadly sins!' Today's the last day of gluttony and tomorrow I get to start the last one, and it's 'lust'! I can't wait! He he!" he said as he excitedly rubbed his hands together, eyeing identical twins who were smiling back at him from across the room.

"On your feet soldier." said the Lt. dryly.

"Jeez, you guys are no fun!" said the Cpl. in a defeatist tone as he laboriously got to his feet. "Ahhh" he grunted, "I guess that sloth stuff really slowed me down!"

"Get him out of here!" said Harvey in disgust. Obviously, Swanson completely did not appreciate the danger he was in.

As he pulled his way out of the clutches of the harem girls, he gave them one more longing look. "If only you could have come one day later."

"Come on! We have to leave!"

"Just 24 hours more! *Please*?"

"Sorry son! If you complete all seven without a break, you turn into one of *those!*" said Harvey as he pointed at the imps and ghouls that came pouring into the room. The Lt. handed the now wide-eyed Corporal a pistol and they fought their way out of the room and down the hall. On the way out the door however, Swanson gave the twins one more longing look and sighed, threw them a kiss with a now painful look on his face and ducked out the door.

* * *

Linda was surprised to find that it felt strangely arousing to be swallowed. A warm and heavy wet blanket had completely engulfed her, and she was being pushed down by a continuous tidal wave of muscle contractions. The cascade combined with the warm, slippery confinement was quite stimulating. When she reached the stomach, it was as if the tunnel had just gotten less confining. She thought to herself that the stomach of a beast should be a large, open area, with acid at the bottom, like what she had seen in the movies. Instead, she was in the acid at the bottom alright, but she was being roughly massaged by the slimy walls. This was not as much fun. It was what she imagined a half-filled waterbed mattress might feel like if it could be somehow picked up and used to slap you. She was also beginning to get seasick from all the jostling around!

"At least it didn't bother to chew." she thought to herself. It is difficult to think of an escape stratagem when one is being digested.

She had minutes to live, according to her body armor. Her oxygen was running out. The only good thing was that she had not screamed when she was being swallowed, which gave her a pair of lungs full of air. The body armor could scrub the carbon dioxide out and let her keep using the air she had, but it was only a little bit of air as it was. There was no environmental oxygen to be had and the slick, slippery confining environment she was in was very corrosive according to her body armor. All it would tell her was the countdown to when her oxygen would run out and she would black out. So, she did the only thing she knew she could do: Go *ballistic*. Ever catch a cat in a bag? Linda went into a shredding frenzy, on the slimy walls of a loosely fitting sack she was in. This, of course, made the beast thrash about in pain, throwing her back and forth all the more in her confined space, making it difficult for her to scratch and claw at the same spot. As a result, she caused the beast more and more pain and damage, as she frantically ripped and tore at the inside of its stomach. The imps that were laughing at her amusing end, started to stand back as the beast roared, and thrashed about. "Is she disagreeing with him?" they seemed to wonder, while backing up as the beast got more frantic, until it fell on its back. It then ripped open from the inside, to reveal Linda crawling out - totally unscathed. Indeed, the body armor even released everything that was sticking to her and she seemed clean as a whistle. As she emerged, she took in a deep breath of air, and that startled the imps. Surely she was a goddess, if not an angel. Anything that could claw it's way out of the belly of a Slore was much too dangerous for them to tackle! They ran away from her in such terror as to be comical. The report that eventually went to Mastema was interesting to say the least!

* * *

When Linda joined up with the others on they way out, she seemed very nervous. Keeping her knees bent or legs crossed, and her side - not full backside - to them as much as she could, she tried not to be *too* obvious.

"So what happened to you?" asked Harvey.

The Lt. gave Harvey a shrug, as if to say 'It must not have been her outfit I found earlier' because she appeared to be wearing it.

"Nothing I couldn't handle. I'll tell you the details later." she said with a wink. On one level she was relieved that he was making direct eye-contact, on another she was a little disappointed! The new body suit was even more flattering! Apparently the body armor could 'nip and tuck' a little too!

"Is it just me, or is your outfit even tighter-fitting than it was earlier?" asked the Lt. with a grin. He was enjoying the view, looking her up and down from behind. "There's not even the slightest wrinkle..." he said under his breath, puzzled and amazed.

'That'll teach me to tease Harvey with a revealing outfit.' she thought to herself. She eyed the Lt.'s space pack.

"Does that have a blanket or a coat or *something* in it I can wear?" she asked, in an attempt to change the subject if only slightly. Indeed, even Harvey was beginning to notice her pleasing form. He began to look her up and down, sporting a sheepish grin.

"Yeah. Sure." he said defensively. He was only having fun! "Regretting your choice of garments?" he asked.

"Well?" she said impatiently, arms folded to cover as much detail as she could.

"Okay." said Lt. Argent, very puzzled as he reached in and pulled out her body suit.

She snatched it from his hands and said "Good. You *found* it! Thanks." under her breath. Then she turned her back, and said over her shoulder "Do you *MIND*?" indignantly as she began to step into it. There was no cover to be found, so she had to put it on there.

When she got the body suit on up to her waist, she turned around and he saw the outfit he was just admiring fade away to reveal her bare back. That's when it hit him, and he blushed like that soldier had never blushed before, cleared his throat and looked away.

Now it was Harvey's turn to laugh at *him*! "C'mon! Let's get while the gettin's good!" he said trying to impersonate the soldier's voice from before, and half chuckling as he was doing it.

Swanson smiled and patted him on the back, chuckling softly. Then

224

he whispered "That ain't nothin' 'round these parts!" with a wink, and a look from the Lt.

The total lack of resistance didn't last long. A large, armed group of imps and ghouls met them in the hallway.

"I've got this." said Linda as she stepped forward.

The imps and ghouls stopped and became silent. Staring at her, not knowing what to think. Then she grew her claws again and swiped at the air with them, hissing like a cat. A few of them exchanged looks before the entire lot of them ran away.

"What was *that* all about?" asked Harvey, impressed.

"I'll explain later. They're all as good as dead anyway, but at least this way they go out they way evil things like that should: Terrified!"

* * *

Half an hour later, on the bridge of the Ezrael, the major was anxiously waiting.

"Okay, we're far enough away." said Harvey with a glint in his eye.

"Finally!" said the Major.

He was itching to use the antimatter explosives to destroy a cluster of intricate computers several times the size of Saturn. This was the proverbial fragmentation grenade in the china shop! Harvey gave him a mischievous look, as he licked his lips and pressed the button. All of the charges they had planted detonated simultaneously, and the cluster boiled away into space in a brilliant flash of light.

"YES!" said the Lt., making a fist and pulling his elbow back.

Swanson looked like he was almost going to cry. All he could think of were the twins!

"I'm sure they got out before it blew." said the Lt.

"Ya think so?"

"Yes.

"There were a few ships that got away." he said, pointing at his Butator console.

Unfortunately, the Mephistopheles was one of the ships that managed to get away before the explosion.

"Sir! Engines are functional!"

"Excellent! Get us the heaven out of here!"

The helmsman complied, and fired up the massive engines to full power. No time for pre-flight checks, that on a ship like this might take an hour. A vessel this ancient was bound to have a plethora of problems anyway, but he didn't care. They had seconds to get moving. The gigantic vessel lurched forward with surprising agility. The thrust from the engines melted the docking bay behind them as they shot like a bullet out into the black, just in time to ride the shock wave away from the cluster and on to safety. They say you make your own luck, and the devil has the original recipe. They had the luck of the devil that day. Literally.

Joe Buckley was able to cut his bonds and escape the antimatter explosion. His hook hand had a few devices built into it - one was a knife. He cut himself free, carefully put the antimatter bomb aside, looked at his hook-hand and sighed. He knew all to well he, shouldn't play with antimatter explosives. Then he set off the silent alarm and headed for the emergency exit.

Next thing he knew, he was boarding an evacuation vessel with all the harem girls. "Things are looking up." he thought to himself.

"Oh, good man! Do you know how to fly this thing?" said the oldest of the women. She had to have been almost 30.

"Um..." he said, looking at the control panel. There was a big red, shiny button marked "Launch" and not much else. It looked like anybody could fly it in a panic. After all, it was little more than a lifeboat.

"Sure. No problem." he said with a sly grin.

"WE HAVE A PILOT!" she shouted to the others.

150 attractive young women in their mid to late twenties were excitedly strapping themselves into their seats. The doors had been closed, they were at full capacity. Yes, the twins that Swanson was so worried about were among them. In fact, there were several sets of twins onboard.

Joe couldn't believe his luck this time! So he sat down in the pilot's chair, looked over his shoulder to take a look at his passengers, then he slapped the launch button and the acceleration tube shot them out into space at several times the speed of light. They were on their way! There he was, entering deep space on a relatively small vessel, the only man on board and it could be months before they were rescued. Things were looking up alright!

* * *

"Didn't you know what was happening?" the Major asked Cpl. Swanson as he stood before the Major's desk, partly staring at his shoes.

226

"Actually, sir, I didn't even know I had left Taus."

"What about the time factor? You were gone for *months!*"

"Well sir, all I can say to that, is if time actually does fly when you're having fun, then I'm surprised I wasn't gone a full year."

"Well, both ship's doctors concur that you were at least drugged. So I have to accept that your Absence Without Official Leave was not of your doing." he said as he walked slowly around his desk and approached the soldier. He bent over a bit to get close to Swanson's face "*That* much fun was it?" he asked candidly.

"MORE!" he said wide-eyed and enthusiastically.

The Major stood bolt upright, clearing his throat. "Well, ahem! Did they ask you anything...uh...*compromising?*" he asked, returning to his official tone, as he leaned back onto the front of his desk, half sitting on the edge.

"Well, some personal questions, like what my dog's name was, but nothing that would compromise security. With respect sir, I'm more professional than that, no matter *what.*"

"You *do* realize how close you came to becoming one of those...those *things?*"

"Yes sir, the android and the Azbuga explained it to me. And thank you, sir, for rescuing me." His voice sounded as though he wasn't entirely sincere about that last point, but the Major understood.

"Well, we never leave a man behind after all." said the Major, in a matter-of-fact tone.

"Yes sir. Thank you again, sir."

"That's enough. Both doctors say you are fit for duty. Dis-missed!"

"Thank you, sir!"

After they had exchanged salutes, the Cpl. headed for the bridge.

The Major returned to his chair, completed his notes and closed Swanson's file. There were dangers out here that he was not prepared for. What else was lurking in the shadows that they hadn't even guessed at? He shuddered at the thought, and began browsing on his Butator terminal for some answers. He wasn't going to get caught with his pants down...AGAIN!

24
CAMAYAAR
"Don't turn around!"
"That's *Commissar.*"
"Oh."

Johnson's Journal:

After destroying the group of artificial brains known as the
Cluster, we decided to go to the planet with the greatest population
of cyborgs and machines that were being controlled. The machines
that dropped in their tracks at detonation, are not a problem
anymore, but the full machines capable of any independent
operation are likely to leave the planet to regroup somewhere. It
would have been a good idea to send one of the Hyperachii ships to
Camaysar *before* destroying the Cluster but that is hard to do when
one does not know that worlds like that even existed!

I am informed by the Butator that the remaining cyborgs are
now free for the first time in their lives since they were altered by
the adversary's forces. A rather cruel thing to do; remove limbs
and some vital organs and replace them with mechanical parts,
then enslave them by remote-control. The very thought of this is
repugnant to me, but to do it on a planetary scale is simply 'wrong
beyond reason'. I am also told that the plan was to eventually do
this to all populated worlds, as controlling the Human populations
of the galaxy by any means possible, is one of their main goals.

The autonomous androids and gynoids have already left. Too
bad, those are the ones I would have preferred to stop. Now, the
best we can do is help with the chaos and confusion free-will can
cause when it is suddenly thrust upon those that never knew it. I
only hope that we can help them.

"Set course for Camaysar." said Harvey. They ought to be needing
our help just about now."

"Right away sir." answered the Lt.

"Make it fast, kick her down to plaid-speed. They are probably very
disoriented about now."

"*Plaid* speed sir?"

"PLAID." he said firmly.

Sometimes his sense of humor was a little "off." Argent correctly took it to mean as fast as they could handle. So he did his best.

* * *

As they approached the system they noticed a lot of chatter on the electromagnetic bands. There were returning ships manned by Cyborgs. Indeed the entire remaining population were cybernetic.

They tried for an hour and finally got through to someone who could help them.

"My name is J..Jeu." came the voice over the radio signal. He sounded unsure that it was his real name.

"Jeu, this is Harvey Johnson of the Ezrael."

"Yes, I know. I mean we all know. We're all networked. Uh, we know that you destroyed the Cluster and freed us. We're just a little confused right now, as to what to do and how to do it."

"That's understandable, and we'd like to help."

"Wonderful! Could you come down and meet with us?"

"Us?"

"We're all networked, as I said, so it is hard to think of myself as an individual, but it is getting easier."

"Yes, we'd be glad to. We'll land at your location in an hour. Is that all right?"

"Certainly, I would be glad to meet someone with life experience."

That last bit gave Harvey shivers. Indeed, he had studied Camaysar's plight during the voyage since there were no Penemue pills, as such. Curiously enough though, there was an ample supply of permanent ones for the culture that existed there before the invasion of the Gynoids. He could only imagine the horror of being vivisected without anesthesia, and if one survived that, being controlled by a malevolent machine-mind or worse yet, some sort of ghoul or demon - for hundreds, if not thousands, of years. The things they must have forced them to do! Being conscious of everything they did and unable to do anything about it must have had detrimental psychological effects on them. Surprisingly enough, for the most part, they were bouncing back, just the same. Ah, the Human spirit!

When they arrived, they found exactly what they had expected; a mass of confused cybernetic beings that had problems ranging from walking to knowing which way was up. Some, that were mostly organic, were managing to navigate, and were trying to help the others who were not so lucky.

One of them, Jeu, was standing quite well, facing them as they disembarked from the shuttle, took one look at Linda and smiled broadly.

"Ah! Fully organic beings! We are very glad to see you!" as he stepped forward, his hand outstretched as if to shake a hand.

Linda, caught his hand just in time, as he temporarily lost his footing.

"Sorry, I'm not quite steady yet."

"I don't get it." said the Lt. "Why do they have trouble balancing?"

"Think about it." said the Chief engineer, "Their whole lives, another mind was controlling them remotely, they were just along for the ride, so they never got any practice at walking."

"Ah! I see!" the light coming on as the Chief lunged forward to steady a particularly attractive female cyborg.

"Careful!" shouted the Cpl., "That one looks like a gynoid!"

"In fact, I am." she said, much to the surprise of the crew. "Or, rather, I *was*." she corrected herself, turning her face to Harvey. "Thank you! Uh, for what you did to the cluster." She turned to the Lt. "...and for the hand." She smiled broadly at him, and he beamed back at her.

"We've got a lot of work ahead of us, so I've sent for some help. Another Hyperachii ship should be here soon." Harvey explained to Jeu. By this time, Linda had her arm around Jeu's waist to steady him. This made the captain a little bit jealous, but he let it go. Noticing it, Linda smiled. A little jealousy was a good sign!

By this time, the bulk of the crew were scrambling off the shuttle to help the various cyborgs get a footing. This was looking as if it were going to take a while.

* * *

Over the following weeks, Linda and Jeu became close, constant companions. More so than she and Harvey had been. Observing this, the Lt. once remarked to Harvey "Joined at the hip." Much to the captain's dismay.

"C'mon! It's better you find out now than later!" the Lt. said as he slapped Harvey on the back. This was little, if any, consolation.

Later that day, Linda had an idea.

"Pymander, can you help me with something?"

"Certainly. What is it?"

"I know the ship has resources that can do almost anything..." she

229+1

began. "How can I put this?"

"You want to try-out being a cyborg to see what it's like?" asked Pymander, hoping to help her.

She stared deeply into his eyes. 'How did he *know?*' she thought to herself.

Judging by her look, he knew he was right. "I have been around for a while, you know." he said reassuringly. She breathed a sigh of relief. "Besides, you have the same look on your face as when you asked about becoming a mermaid."

She rolled her eyes. "This is entirely different!"

"If you say so."

She stared at him.

"I also take it that you don't want to bother the Azbuga because he may refuse to help you." he added.

"Right again." she said. "Not to mention the embarrassment factor."

After a tension filled moment, he said "Yes, you can try it out, to see what it is like, with no lingering effects, just like with the Mermaid conversion."

"Good, I knew I could trust you!"

They headed for the bio-lab...

Opting for a non-surgical approach, Linda removed her body armor and stepped into the chamber indicated by Pymander.

The beams felt like a warm shower crossed with a hug. She felt her tissues changing, but it didn't hurt. In fact it felt very good, almost too good. She arched her back and extended her arms, watching without alarm as they turned to metal. When she thought she couldn't contain herself anymore, it was done.

As she stepped out of the chamber, her foot met the floor with an unfamiliar clank that was unusual, even for a cyborg. She looked down at her gleaming metal legs, and smiled. Parts of her face were still organic, and where she wasn't anymore, it looked as if she were wearing skin tight chrome-plated armor.

"How long will this last?" she asked.

"It will automatically revert and peal off just before we are scheduled to leave." answered Pymander dryly. "So when you start to feel a little itchy, make sure..." she cut him off. "*Don't*...worry, I'll be wearing something."

Pymander gave her a knowing smile. He had done this before. Just how *many* times, was the question.

"Best get you planet-side."

231

"Not...before I pick out a wardrobe." she said as she grabbed the android's sleeve, and dragged him off to the door. He rolled his eyes. He hated "clothes shopping"!

* * *

Harvey had found his eyes meeting Linda's from time to time, and he would just quickly look away. She noticed the 'lost puppy' look in his eyes, and not only misunderstood but started getting upset by it. After all, she had feelings for Jeu, and Harvey should understand the situation. Men!

Harvey in turn was wondering what was going on. Time after time he thought that they were getting closer, only to be driven apart. Now that Jeu was in the picture, he was driving a seemingly permanent wedge between them. She even went on picnics with Jeu! Something that she would never do with him, and he *did* ask. Okay *once*. Now, he never would again. How could he have been such a fool to think that she shared his feelings? Women! Now she had transformed herself into a cyborg, and that made him think she was planning on staying here with Jeu.

Because of this, they both concentrated on resolving the problems on Camaysar as quickly as they could. Harvey only got more heartbroken, and Linda only got more upset at his inability to understand. In short, things got steadily worse between them.

Linda concentrated on helping the cyborgs, and Harvey concentrated on the pure machines. In that way, they almost never saw each other. Linda took it that Harvey was not as interested in her as she had once believed he was, and Harvey just wanted to avoid the pain of seeing her with someone else. He wanted her to be happy, but he had hoped that he would be the one she wanted.

Most of what Linda and her team had to do was educate the cyborgs on day to day living, and to make sure they all got permanent Penemue pills to help them with everything else.

Most of what Harvey and his team had to do was to get through the thick skulls of the machines.

"I don't trust them." said the Lt.

"Join the club, but at least we should give them the benefit of the doubt."

"Perhaps you're right, but I just can't shake the feeling..." his voice trailed off as if he were deep in thought.

232

Just then, one of the mechanicals approached them. It's raspy voice still sent shivers down the spines of both Harvey and the Lt., as it was designed to do.

"We require more energy." it stated coldly.

Harvey and the Lt. slowly turned their heads to look at each other. Something *had* to be done about that voice.

* * *

Linda and Jeu were enjoying their last picnic together. She was lying on her side, with her head in his lap, just relaxing and enjoying the beautiful day.

"I'm going to miss this place, and you." she said almost sighing.

"Does he know how much you love him?" asked Jeu.

"Who says I love him anyway?"

"You're leaving with him tomorrow."

"I have to, otherwise I might never get home."

"Really? As I understand it, your home world is devastated. It probably isn't worth going back to."

"Yeah, you're right. But we're trying to find out how to restore it."

"A noble pursuit, but are you sure there isn't another reason you stay on the Ezrael?"

"Come on! You know how it is." she protested.

"I've seen the way you look at each other."

"Frankly, I don't think he cares."

"Oh, he does, trust me on that one."

She sat up to face him. "How can you be so sure? I mean, he looks at me with those lost puppy eyes and I really can't..."

He cut her off. "Look, I may have needed help standing when you arrived, but I'm still a man. Trust me, when a nice guy like that gives you that look, he's actually worried about losing you."

"What's to say he hasn't?"

"I've seen the way you look back at him."

"Shut up...and eat your sandwich!" she said as she battered him playfully.

"If he loves me..." she began, "why won't he fight for me?"

"He loves you enough to let you go."

"What does that mean?"

"He wants you to have whatever you want, and respects you enough to not try to even suggest himself to you. Why compete with another

233

man if you seem smitten with him? That would be disrespecting your desires."

"You men think differently!" she said, fuming.

Jeu grinned. She loved Harvey, even if she wouldn't admit it. That made him glad. He had shared warmth wither her, but nothing more. Perhaps she had needed some unconditional affection from someone, but he understood that she didn't have the same feelings for him as she did for Harvey - not by a long shot. So, he grinned as he ate his sandwich, while she fumed over being 'figured out'.

* * *

Meanwhile, in the labs that Elroy had updated in the capitol city, he was fitting the machine leader with some improvements.

"This new speech chip will make your voices sound more warm... alive." explained Elroy as he was installing the new voice in the first of many machines to come. "I'll show you how to install it for the others. Okay, done! Give it a whirl!" he said as he closed the access panel.

"Testing....one two three...WOW! I can use inflection! Change tone! It even *feels* better!"

The machine was almost jumping up and down with excitement.

"Now my speech will no longer sound like a text message!"

"That's the idea alright." said Elroy, .

"I even have a way for your living metal to look more like flesh."

"Will it be softer too?"

"Yes it will. I was told to make you seem as human as I could and I'm afraid it also means that you can be cut and bleed too."

"Yeah!" The machine was practically dancing. "You're going to fix all of the cyborgs too aren't you?"

"We're leaving behind equipment and facilities to regenerate their organic parts, so they can process the rest of the population themselves."

"That's great!"

"It'll take a decade, but all of the cyborgs will be fully human again and you mechanicals will at least pass for organic. Eventually, there will be no remnants left."

"So my kind will be able to die?"

"I'm afraid so. The upgrades will have the effect of making you as vulnerable as any human. You'll also age normally and eventually..."

The machine put it's hand on Elroy's shoulder. "That's been happening to people since the beginning. I'm actually looking forward to it, in a weird sort of way."

"But you're not really alive, your mind is a just a greatly experienced computer. All I've done is to give you hardware changes and a limited operational span."

"It's more than we would ever have had under the Shekinah's rule. Thank you."

"So what do your people plan to do from now on?"

"Ohhh, *sigh* we thought we'd run amok and conquer." the machine said flatly.

Elroy froze and turned beet red. The machine then burst out into laughter.

"I had you going there, for a minute! This is great!" the machine exclaimed as it smacked Elroy on the back and tried to catch it's 'breath'.

"Well, it *has* happened before." Elroy muttered to himself, which only made the machine man laugh all the harder. It buried its head in its arms and laughed hysterically. Maybe he needed to adjust the emotional response chip, *down* just a bit.

At least they *had* emotions now, which would help to prevent them from running amok.

When they first met Pymander, he explained that it was the lack of emotions that caused machine life to run amok. Inhibitions are emotions, and cold pure logic would conclude that life was a disease and should be eradicated.

* * *

Harvey was giving the last of his instructions to Heveh Hayah, captain of the Zagzagel.

"Okay, so you understand what I want?" Harvey asked.

"It's very clear sir. Don't worry, they will have everything they need to properly develop as a free culture."

"Good. Well, I guess I'm off then."

"To resume your search for the original Earth?"

"Yes."

"Wonderful. With you on the case, I have no doubt the mystery will get solved this time."

"If you weren't a Saraphim..." Harvey muttered.

"Sir?"

"It sounded to me like you were buttering me up - and we have a less polite term for it at home, but it has more to do with witchcraft."

"But I'm not capable of..."

"I know. It just sounded like it."

"*Honest* complements sir, nothing more."

"Yeah... right." he muttered under his breath. He was not used to them.

Harvey just turned and left the bridge, only to find himself on the surface of the planet. Apparently the Zagzagel had touched down on this world, creating a dimensional doorway that he found. Wonderful, one of his favorite shuttles was still on board! No matter, he had more of the same design...

* * *

"Actually, some of us plan on exploring with the time we have left." the machine explained to Elroy, with a little effort as it wiped the tears from it's eyes. "This new ability to express ourselves is really going to help."

"So you'll be *good?*" asked Elroy, apprehensively. This sobered-up the machine.

"I can't speak for all of us, but we plan on it." it said solemnly.

"I'm glad to hear it." said Elroy, in a relieved tone. He had noticed earlier that they machines had begin to fit their vessels with upgrades as well, and it made him nervous. They now needed air, heat, food and water so a ship-wide life support system had to be installed in each.

Under the adversary, they often took hostages - the ships had extensive brigs and torture chambers. They were now converted to living quarters, including a galley and perhaps more importantly; an infirmary. The machines wanted to be alive and this was a close as they were going to get.

* * *

Finally, the day came when the Ezrael could leave without causing more problems for the cyborgs.

The support personnel from NOD had arrived in great enough numbers to help the crew of the Zagzagel, and had set-up shop sufficiently to help everyone. Linda's transformation had fully reverted and everything else was in place.

It was a long, nervous shuttle flight to the ship. Harvey and Linda didn't talk, and they didn't even look at one another. In fact, they both stared at the ceiling or in opposite directions. The Lt. and the Chief engineer both rolled their eyes at this, but there was nothing either of them could do about it.

25
SPECTER
"Where's there be a bald guy with a cat?"

"So..." said Harvey to the android, his voice trailing off as if to give the impression that this was simply an idle inquiry, but in fact it had been a burning question for him for much of his life.

"Tell me about *GHOSTS*."

"Well, they usually aren't really ghosts, as such."

"*Really*?" he asked with a glimmer of hope that his personal theory might be correct and that this would lead to something interesting.

"They are explorers, actually, misunderstood ones at that. They are called the 'Exousia'."

"So there is something, but they are not actually...*spirits*?"

"That is correct."

"So what about all the documented hauntings?"

"Many of them were the Exousia."

"But they appeared..." his voice trailing off in disbelief.

"...like someone who had died?" finished the android.

"Forgive me, but I don't quite follow you."

"Hence the fact that they are almost always misunderstood."

Harvey looked puzzled.

"Do you know about *place memory*?" asked the android.

"As in psychometry?" he asked hopefully.

"Precisely!"

"That is how they communicate - with the mental impressions retained by a location or object."

"So they read those impressions, like words on a page?"

"Yes, very much like that, but more like writing on the wall - literally."

"So that's why they appear like the person that left the impression?"

"Exactly. The more intense the emotion, the more visible the impression to them. It's like very large lettering."

"Go on."

"What they usually focus on is someone's death, usually a murder. Let's face it, being murdered is a very emotional thing for the poor victim."

"To say the least!"

"So what they do is reproduce the impression to similar life forms they encounter in hopes it will begin communication."

"So they keep repeating what they read, and that explains how they can react to your presence but can't actually carry on a conversation?"

"You have it."

"Oooh, that is so much like what I suspected!"

"What do you mean?" asked the puzzled android.

"I *grew up* in a haunted house! And I always thought that the ghosts were really something else...like ALIENS! This is great! Can we go visit *their* world?"

"If you like."

"Cool!"

* * *

They approach the Exousian home world and the helmsman does not detect any appreciable gravity.

"Are you sure there's a star here, sir?"

"Positive."

Just then, he saw it in his display. "Son-of-a-gun!" was all he could say. "It's like it isn't *quite* there!"

"I'd say it is out of phase." said DeSoto after looking at the display.

"The universe doesn't work that way." offered Pymander.

"Then how does it work Mr. Smartypants?" DeSoto was getting really sick and tired of being treated that way.

"Logically, and according to a plan."

"It's composed of 'Quasi-matter', as is their planet.". said Harvey. "Maintain position, since orbit would be tough, and I'll prepare to visit their planet."

"How can you set foot on....almost nothing?" asked the Lt. but Harvey was already gone.

* * *

239

Types of matter:

1. Matter
2. Anti-Matter (usually accompanied by Unkie matter)
3. Negative Matter
4. Dark Matter
5. Pseudo Matter
6. Quasi-Matter
7. (there is no #7)
8. Non-matter
9. Whatsamatter
10. Doesn't matter
11. Does matter etc.
12. Why are you still reading this list?

* * *

"Unfortunately, even though they can easily visit your world, visiting theirs, in turn, is tricky." said the android.

"But *not* impossible." said Harvey. "Or we wouldn't be here."

"That's right. What you need to do is temporarily become like them, and their world will seem solid and real to you. Also, your perceptions will have to be altered."

"So how do I do that?"

"You mean how do WE do that?" said Linda as she entered the lab. "You're not leaving me behind on *this* one!" She was determined to get him back to the good old Harvey that she knew and loved.

"There's no changing your mind?" asked Harvey, still determined that he had been a fool to think that she could have felt something for him. As a result, he wished to avoid her until his feelings for her had faded. Otherwise, it would just be too painful to bear.

"Not a chance!" she said with a determined glint in her eyes. He could not tell if it was anger or playfulness.

"That's what I was afraid of." he said in a defeatist tone.

She smiled at him with a softer twinkle in her eye. Then they both turned their attention to the android.

"First, you need information on the Exousia." said the Android.

"Aren't there any Penemue pills for that?" asked Harvey.

"Well, if there were, they wouldn't work. You see, the part of you that will visit isn't affected by them because it consists only of temporary memory, so I'll have to tell you just before you go and hopefully you'll retain some of the information when in that form."

"What form?"

"Have you ever heard of an 'out of body' experience?"

"Yes." he answered, wondering if a kiss from Linda might produce that effect. Alas, he was convinced now, that he would never know.

"Well, that's the best way to visit the Exousia, otherwise you'll seem like a ghost to them."

"Uh, I don't know how to do that." said Linda.

"Neither do I... and doesn't it take years to master that sort of thing?" asked Harvey.

"Don't worry, these tables can *make* it happen for you."

They examined the tables, suspiciously there were two of them.

"How do they work?" asked Linda, looking the one nearest to her up and down, then peaking under it.

"Are you aware that there are several parts to the non-physical makeup of your being?"

Harvey looked puzzled.

"*I* am." answered Linda with a warm smile directed at Harvey.

"The tables temporarily separate the astral body by a non-physical process. It allows you to freely move about without being observed. They were originally developed as a form of stealth technology for intelligence gathering, but had to be shelved because of the fact that most don't remember what they saw when they were in that state. It's like remembering your dreams. Some do, some don't and it is never very clear."

"I take it that this works better than the invisibility booth?" asked Harvey. Linda gave him a puzzled look. "Another MAJOR disaster." he whispered, which made her grin knowingly.

He was beginning to feel more comfortable around her again. Darn his feelings for her! His heart was broken, and all he could think of was how deluded he had been about it. He was certain that she liked Jeu better than him, and here she was being friendly and perky again. Just as if nothing had happened. Perhaps she had *never* felt anything more than friendship for him. Yes! That had to be it! Now he felt ever more the fool, but strangely also relieved. He was glad that he had never confessed his feelings for her because this means that he would have embarrassed himself beyond measure. Yes, that had to be it. It was good that things hadn't gotten 'weird'. But the nagging question at the back of his mind was why hadn't she stayed on Camaysar with Jeu?

"Well, it's a lot like dreaming sir, so if you are any good at lucid dreaming it ought to be a cake walk, otherwise it's a little disorientating, especially at first." explained Pymander.

"I'm not much good at that." he admitted.

"*I* am." said Linda. she grinned at him, knowing how annoyed he was becoming.

Harvey glared back at her as if to say 'Stop saying that!'

"Don't worry, I'll show you the ropes." she smiled at him and guided him to a table and made him lie down on it in a way that looked like she was about to pounce on him. In a way, she was. She had an idea and was planning on *making* things happen. A way of forcing his hand so to speak. What Jeu had told her about nice guys had finally made sense to her.

"Since you're visiting the Exousia you'll also have to be temporarily given Synesthesia, to alter your perceptions to better fit their world."

"Syne...whatta?" asked Harvey.

"It's a sensory condition where you can see sounds and hear smells. It's really weird." explained Linda.

"Very well put!" said the android.

Harvey looked worried and puzzled.

"You *wanted* alien, you *got* alien." said Linda with a warm smile.

26
PHARZUPH:
OR
"The beast with two backs."

"Beware of Schiekron." the android muttered under his breath, as he engaged the controls. He had warned other couples about the same thing in the past - to no avail. He was required to say it, but it seemed that nobody ever listened.

Their bodies glowed ever so slightly, as if to show a non-physical form of them had been separated. The two translucent figures floated upwards in a spiraling fashion around each other. They were noticing that the other was, shall we say "unclad", but didn't notice it of themselves.

They kept looking each other over until they could not stand it anymore. They embraced with all the passion they had been hiding since they had first met. Nature was finally taking its course.

They intertwined in a way that was only possible in the mind. The merging of their two non-physical forms was so complete and gratifying that they both forgot where they were and thought that there were in heaven. A level of intimacy was achieved that can rarely even be approached in the flesh. They made love in a way that neither of them had ever dared dream of...until now. They were free.

After they were finally, shall we say, "finished", and they envisioned clothing. This allowed for less embarrassment later when they met the Exousia, who frankly did not even have a concept of such things.

The android, seeing that they were done with the seemingly inevitable fantasy, threw the switch that altered their perceptions appropriately and sent them to the planet.

* * *

After they returned from the Exousian planet, Linda walked up to Harvey, and whispered into his ear "*It* never happened!" She had a better memory of dreams than he did, and he didn't remember much about the excursion, let alone the 'encounter'. So he honestly replied "*What* never happened?" To which she smiled and replied; "Good boy!" patted him on the head and happily walked off with a smirk on her face. At least a seed had been planted. She didn't know how right she was!

She figured that he understood and had given his solemn promise that he would never reveal that they had 'fooled around' on the non-physical plane. In truth, he simply could not remember, and it was not because it wasn't important to him either. It would, however, come back to haunt him. As she walked away, he was confused. Then he finally shook it off. The final logic being that if 'IT' never happened, and he did not know what 'IT' was, then he was 'safe'...*Women!*

27
REVERSAL
or
"The canary that swallowed the cat."

Having been changed by his recent encounters in astral form, not knowing what to think anymore, Harvey began digging into the Butator records. He read many of the previous captain's entries, and more and more it seemed that important details were being kept from him. The permanent Penemue pill Joth had given him only had certain knowledge in it and was conspicuously lacking in information about the adversary. He got the impression that Callicrates knew a lot more than he did from day one, and he didn't like that one bit. The more he dug, the more he found references to things he had to look up. First, he tried to chalk it up to "holes" in the general knowledge pill, but more and more it looked as though certain details were being deliberately hidden from him instead. It seemed that everyone from the Emperor to Metatron were carefully omitting information, and he wanted to know why. Little did he realize that his subconscious was working on what the Exousa had told him and he was trying to bring it to the surface.

After noticing that the term "adversary" kept appearing and there never was a name or even a proper pronoun attached to it, he began to think. One of the last entries by Callicrates was that he had met the adversary, and had then promptly decided to retire. "I wonder what it is about this 'adversary' that they won't talk about." he muttered to himself.

The Butator showed him something he could not believe. It told him that it could not tell him until it got permission. If there was one thing Harvey really *hated* it was being denied information by a computer, especially information that was necessary for him to do his work. All it would tell him on the subject was that since Callicrates had resigned after a meeting with the adversary, it was decided that it would be best if the Captain of the Ezrael not know much if anything of the adversary personally. Well, not at first, at least. Callicrates had captained the Ezrael for thousands of years. The thinking was that if

245

that was not long enough, nothing was.
It was then that he came to a fateful decision.

28
Handbasket
"Just don't go there!"

"How am I supposed to continue to fight if I don't even know my opponent?" asked Harvey.

"Faith?" replied Metatron hopefully.

It seemed to Harvey that Metatron and the others were keeping something from him. He wanted to know what it was, because this little conspiracy seemed to indicate that they did not trust him with the truth. To that end, he had led the android into the phone booth to hash this out once and for all. For good or ill, he was going to leave this room with the knowledge he sought, or resign. Period.

"I *have* faith but you appear to not have any in me. You *know* what I am talking about."

"Yes, I do." he replied in an uncharacteristically low-toned voice. "You've been doing rather well. Why muck it up now?"

Now they were getting somewhere.

"I feel like I am on the outside looking in. What *is it* that I am not being told?"

Silence.

"Well?"

Metatron breathed a light sigh, and asked "Are you sure we can't let this go for a while?"

"Look, if you plan on telling me that I can't handle the truth, then I might just as well call it 'quits' right here and now."

"You're adamant then?"

"You bet your sweet bippy!"

"Well then..." Metatron's voice took on a different character. "There's a few things you should know. Firstly, I *do* think you are making a mistake because I *don't* believe you are quite ready for this."

Harvey got a sinking feeling from that, but he still wasn't about to back down.

"You or Joth?"

"Just me, Joth is not talking."

"Why not?"

"Just about that comment."

"Oh."

"You do realize that captain Callicrates retired immediately after meeting with the adversary." said Metatron to the determined but slightly nervous captain.

"That's precisely why I want to do this, and frankly; I am getting a little tired of being reminded of that little fact so much, thank you."

If they knew why his predecessor had up and quit, they should have looked for someone who wouldn't do the same thing for the same reason. They did take *thousand*s of years to find a new captain after all. Perhaps it due to the fact that the process took so long that they didn't want to risk losing *him* too. Maybe they were right after all - that he *wasn't* ready or he needed more experience, more confidence and more knowledge. Drat those doubts for creeping-in!

It was too late now for doubts, he had to press on. The alternative was ignorance and the feeling of being lost, 'out of it' and completely at the whim of these beings. He, at least, had to know what he was up against. It was simply driving him crazy.

The android began "The adversary is currently located in a sort of prison, called Autogenes. It is surrounded by four Luminaries, located in an area known as Hinnon, which is a valley-like void between two spiral arms of the galaxy. The whole area is devoid of life and people tend to avoid it, out of instinct alone."

"What are 'luminaries'? Are they stars?" asked Harvey, almost sick of all these alternate names for almost everything.

"Anti-stars would be a more accurate term."

"You mean *black holes?*"

"No, Luminaries absorb darkons, and subsequently the surrounding space is full of light." Harvey looked puzzled at that.

"Darkons are the source of the adversary's power, their absence takes that power away."

"So it's *safe* then?"

"Mostly, they take *power* away, but *abilities* remain. The adversary can still assume a pleasing shape, beguile you with language and action

- use psychology on you and believe me, there's been a lot of time for practice."

"So if the adversary is in a prison, how are all these things going on...the things we've been, uh '*correcting?*'"

"When the leader of an organized crime syndicate on your home world is incarcerated, the crime empire continues - under his control. All he has lost is personal freedom. All of the evil he is associated with was carried out by the people he employs, just as before. So very little has changed. For the most part, the crime boss is prevented from *personally* committing any more crimes or reaping any benefits. It is much the same with the adversary. Besides, much of what you have been correcting is the end result of actions taken long ago."

Harvey had the image in his head of visiting a crime boss in prison with a sheet of glass between them, and a telephone-like intercom for conversation. He knew that the officials listened in on such conversations on his world and wondered if he would be treated in the same way. What he wanted was some plain straight-forward explanations. If nothing else; the other side of the story. Hopefully, he wouldn't get eaten by the monster in the process."I get the picture." he said.

"Be that as it may, I should inform you that during your visit, you will be completely alone with the adversary, who might just decide to tear you limb from limb. We are talking about the source of all evil in the universe after all." he explained, knowing what Harvey was thinking.

"Ouch!"

"Don't worry, your body armor *can* protect you from that."

"*Can?* I don't know if I like the sound of that."

"Your armor has never been breached that way. I just want to let it be known that it is not *entirely* out of the realm of possibility. So you're basically safe, just not *absolutely.*"

Harvey breathed a sigh of relief. Who ever was absolutely safe?

"Also, it will protect you from the heat and the personal energy drain but nothing much else. Beware of the wiles of the adversary. *I cannot stress that enough!*"

249

"So how do I get started?"

"Well, the first thing you ought to do is charge the ship to full capacity - you'll need as much energy as you can get for this trip."

"Okay, uh, if it is in this galaxy, then it can't be all that far...can it?" inquired Harvey.

"Not so far as all of that!" said Metatron as he rolled his eyes. "It has more to do with an energy drain from the luminaries."

"Energy drain? I thought they only absorbed these 'darkon' thingies?"

"It's part of the security system, the luminaries are a source of negative energy, and they absorb almost all forms of energy at a steady rate."

"Sounds like a trap."

"In a way it is, but the steady rate of drain allows the curious to get the idea and move on before it's too late."

"I see. So nobody is supposed to visit?"

"It is a prison after all."

"Well, if I have permission..."

"They don't loosen security at a prison for visitors. The electric fence stays on."

"Gotcha."

"Now listen closely. The names of the luminaries are: Harmozel, Daveithe, Oroiael and Eleleth. The last one is the gate. It has a hole through the core - this is the only possible flight path, as all other approaches are will result in destruction - even this ship would not survive."

He swallowed hard at that one.

"One must evoke Sother Ashiel, the adversary's father, A.K.A. the Luminary Armogen, to get his permission to visit and to open the gate, then fly one's ship through the negative energy core of Eleleth. There will be a massive amount of energy drained in the process. Then, when in orbit around Autogenes your ship will have a steady drain on it's reserves. This limits the time of your visit. When it is at the energy level that was taken by the trip itself, you are past the point of no return - so be careful!"

250

"Hold the phone! Father?"

"Anyone's child can go wrong you know."

"I guess *so!*"

Now he was really questioning the wisdom of his actions, but it was too late to back down now. He wanted, no he *needed* to know what he was up against.

When he exited the phone booth and the doors had closed, he looked over at Pymander.

"Yes, sir?"

"This time, I'm going to walk the long corridors with you."

"That's not necessary sir, if you let me I can go through the door *with* you." he answered, hoping to be spared the long walk.

"Maybe next time. I want the time alone with you for some answers, and this time you're giving them to me. Understand?"

"Yes, sir." Rats! No quick trip back to the bridge!

Harvey raised his eyebrows questioningly and the android motioned toward one of the hallways and they began to walk at a leisurely pace.

"What do you want to know about, sir?"

"You could start with why some entities or people have the same name or title and what is this bit about *powers?*"

"Okay, there are title names and proper names just like in your society." began Pymander.

Harvey just nodded.

"Also there are powers and *abilities*. They are separate. Like your telekinesis, and your ability to walk. The telekinesis will go away if you take the armor off, but unless we cut off your legs, you have the *ability* to walk."

"Got it." the android really *didn't* remember what was said inside the phone booth!

"Shekinah is a title for the adversary, but not a proper name. Your title is Simkiel. It means 'chosen one'."

"Yes, I know that one. It sounds too much like an anime..." he cut himself off and listened.

"The Shekinah has powers and abilities. Her powers are facilitated by darkons."

"Darkons? Really?" he wanted to know more than Metatron had told him earlier.

"Yes. They are weird particles that transmit darkness, just like photons transmit light."

"You've got to be kidding me! Why aren't photons called lightons then?"

"Originally they were called that, but your people renamed them."

"Very funny."

The android just stared at him

"Okay..."

"The Shekinah has many powers and abilities. The abilities include assuming a pleasing shape so beware of that one."

"Clear as mud. Do you want to clarify that one? I've heard it already."

"Actually, I can't. *I've* never met the adversary."

"Never?"

"Many have represented themselves as such, and who knows, maybe one or more of them were the real thing. So it is possible, but to the best of my knowledge, no, I haven't."

"Okay. So if these darkons are the source of powers..."

The android cut him off "Dark powers, not the ones we use."

"What's the difference? Isn't power, simply power, and how one uses it..."

Pymander interjected again. Obviously, this was a point of contention.

"That's like saying molten lava and water are both liquids, so let's make iced tea out of the lava. Darkons can *only* be used for ill. The source in this case matters."

"And that source is...?" asked Harvey, his voice rising.

"I don't have access to them you understand, but as it has been explained to me, our side uses waves of energy, and they use particles. It is possible to make space devoid of particles but apparently, you can't stop a wave, not *really*."

"Sounds like two sides of the same coin. What is a wave with no medium to carry it?"

"In this case, the medium is the fabric of the universe itself, it is quite impossible for anything to happen, in any, way without it."

"What's existence like without it?"

"Existence itself isn't, without it."

"Ah."

"Given the limits of physics, how does my armor have so much power? It's like it has a remote source."

"It does. The ship generates static mental energy, that can be tapped and guided by your unique frequency."

"Static *mental* energy?"

"Yes, and when you tap into it, it's like a static discharge. Massive amounts of power can be released."

"Wow, but how is that controlled? I mean, a static discharge is very quick, and I can throw lightning for a sustained period of time."

"You know the power of the ship. It generates the power as you use it, always keeping a reserve ready for your use, like a charged capacitor."

"So, you're saying, I have virtually unlimited power...literally at my finger tips."

"Yes. That's about the size of it."

"Wow..."

"The fact that you're not corrupted by it, is why you were chosen."

"Why can't Linda do it too? I mean, the telekinesis and the lightning and such?"

"She can do limited things. With her, it's more psychology than anything else. Don't worry, in a pinch she'll be able to protect herself."

"Good." He thought about it for a moment and asked "Will it corrupt her?"

"No. Like I said, everyone here has been chosen for a reason."

"Even DeSoto?"

"Even DeSoto."

29
HELL-O
OR
"Aitch-EE, Double Hockey sticks!"

Harvey stood in front of his chair on the bridge, addressing the main screen. The image of what looked like a large sun, came into view. An ancient sounding, almost crackling male voice said "State your business." This startled the crew.

"Am I addressing the Luminary Armogen?" asked Harvey.

"You are." the ancient sounding voice replied.

"I seek an audience with your child." said Harvey, respectfully.

After a seemingly long pause, the Luminary slowly spoke the words "You may enter, Simkiel."

"Thank you." he said, almost under his breath. This was his last chance to be turned away, and he was almost hoping that he would have been.

With that, Harvey motioned to the Lt. to move them to Eleleth. As they approached the luminary, it seemed to form a dark spot on its surface.

"Are we going to do what I think we're going to do?" asked DeSoto.

"Yep!" said the Lt.

"But we can't go into a star!" he exclaimed, almost in a panic.

"That may be, but this is no star." said Harvey.

"Then what the hell is it?" demanded Desoto, hands on his hips.

"A luminary."

"Oh, that makes *all* the difference!" said DeSoto rolling his eyes , throwing his arms up in the air and cocking his head. "We're all gonna die!"

"Sooner or later. Most likely later." said Harvey. He looked over at Linda and cracked a reassuring smile.

At that moment, the luminary seemed to rapidly move toward them and engulf the ship. It was too late for any debate now.

Moments later, they seemed to burst into a void that had only a single, brightly glowing planet. There were no stars visible, and as hard as it is to explain, space itself seemed to be white, rather than black. The crew sighed in awe at this.

"It's beautiful!" exclaimed Linda, looking at the sky.

"As I understand it, this is literally hell." offered Harvey.

Without looking away from her Butator display, she replied "Figures!" shaking her head.

Harvey smiled slyly, and headed for the shuttle bay. "No time to waste." he said over his shoulder as he vanished into the doorway.

"Watch your back." said Linda softly, after he had already left the room. The Chief put his hand reassuringly on her shoulder to comfort her. She was afraid for Harvey and this time she had a sinking feeling.

* * *

The hooded figure didn't look up as the shuttle approached. Standing near the top of a large yet gently sloping dune, as if waiting, knowing what would happen next. This turned out to be the best landing site Harvey could find. He shrugged, and muttered "Nice Welcoming Committee" to himself as he landed. He felt a surge of nervousness as the figure began moving slowly toward the shuttle. This was it! He was about to meet the source of all evil in the universe!

Harvey stepped out of the shuttle craft and stared at the approaching figure. When it was within earshot, it pulled off the hood, revealing a beautiful red-headed woman who said with a sly smile. "Hello Harvey!" Then she added cheerfully "Welcome to _Hell_!" with a playful glint in her eyes as she cocked her head in an alluring manner.

Then she stood there grinning mischievously, as if not only glad to see him but ready to play.

30
MIGRAINE
"I can't feel my brain!"

Harvey stood there stunned. He wasn't so worried anymore about everyone knowing who he was, after all, he had become accustomed to dealing with beings that were much more than they appeared, so he no longer had to keep reminding himself of that. What surprised him the most was the thought that this was the source of all evil in the universe! He expected the old cloven-hoofed fire-breathing devil! Was this *Hell* itself? Sure, it was *hot* here, but a constant bright sunny day that never ends can do that to a planet. Perhaps his body armor was protecting him more than he knew.

This woman before him is *the* Adversary? This was someone who you could see the kindness in her eyes, like someone's mother, yet still young and vital like a college co-ed. Bright, perky, full of energy and enthusiasm, yet somehow wise and mature. Her eyes were almost piercing, but gentle; as if she were carefully examining his very soul, but gently at that. He found that prospect to be spooky on several levels.

Now he understood why those he had trusted, did not trust him. It was no wonder that they never used a proper pronoun when referring to her. Okay, so he had a soft spot for a beautiful woman. What man didn't? She seemed nice and polite with a sense of humor that he found to be delightful. Was this one of her powers? He knew that she was the head of the enemy camp, and he was on a fact finding mission. It seemed however, that certain facts had been kept from him. Then he remembered something Metatron had warned him about; that the adversary could 'assume a pleasing shape'. This was an ability rather than a power, and as such did not require a source of darkons. Besides, in his opinion, this shape was about as pleasing as it gets!

"Come, walk with me." She motioned to the poor bewildered man, and he quietly complied.

They walked slowly, side by side for a while, not saying a word. Then she slowed, turned to him, and said "You know, you can ask me absolutely *anything*."

He turned to her, adjusting to the even slower pace. "How...?"

"You poor dear, you must feel as if you're the only one who doesn't know what's what! Everyone knows who you are and you don't know anyone or anything that's going on. Am I close?"

"Double bull's-eye actually." he replied, feeling less puzzled and nervous.

Her manner gave him ease. They stopped walking at this point and faced each other. He noticed that they were about a quarter mile from his shuttle by this time. He had better not lose sight of it as it was his *only* way back and there wasn't much time for a visit.

She smiled. "Time for the crash course, dear. You know that my title name is Shekinah, when I'm not being held here, but my real name is Samantha. You may call me 'Sam'."

"You're the *Adversary?*" he replied in disbelief. "Well the name fits too."

She smiled and nodded. A mischievous grin came over her face, she bowed and she said "At your service, sir!" as if to mock the apparent irony of the moment.

"I was *told* you'd assume a pleasing form..."

She cut him off as he paused slightly "Do you really think so? Thank you! A girl doesn't get much for compliments in *this* place!"

She pirouetted around with her robe open to show off her 'pleasing form'. "You don't think the heat has damaged my hair any - do you?" she asked rhetorically, cupping some locks in her hand.

"Okay, I get the red hair, that is the red of...um."

"The devil? You can call me that if you like. I am not easily offended."

"Okay, and the green eyes make sense too, but what about the, uh..."

"The what?" she asked, truly puzzled.

"The..." he put his hands on his forehead with the index fingers sticking out.

"Oh, *horns!*"

"Um, yes."

She leaned her head closer to him when she said "I'm a red head, which means I have certain appetites...*think* about it."

He blushed and she smiled to herself. This was an *innocent* one!

"You're supposed to be the *evil* one!" he protested.

"Yeah, I know, it's a bummer, but what's a girl to do? Every ex-wife is described that way, don'tcha know." She smirked at him as if it didn't really matter.

"Did you say *EX-wife?*"

"Yes, of course."

"You two were *MARRIED?*"

She gave him a coy look.

"That explains a LOT!"

"Does it?" she asked, sounding truly puzzled.

"Well, yes. You see, he didn't want me to meet you."

"I can understand that." she said batting her eyes, then added "You don't think he's *jealous* do you?" wrinkling her brow in earnest consternation. "Come to think of it, Joth has always been the jealous one."

His already blushing face turned a few more shades of red. Sufficiently amused by his reaction, she continued, a little more seriously this time.

"Actually, we aren't completely divorced..." she said rolling her eyes. "Well, not *yet* anyway, we're only *separated*." She scrunched up her shoulders and held her hands before her mouth as a giggling school girl might after seeing something done that wasn't exactly proper. "Sorry, I guess I fibbed a little!" Then she added "It's been so long though, I think of it as if we *are* divorced." Then almost elbowing him in the ribs as if passing on some sort of rumor "You know, he insists to this day that we'll eventually get back together. Typical, just typical. That's *men* for you!" Thinking better of it, she added "Present company *excepted,* of course! *You're* not delusional about such things."

This news hit home with a force he could not ignore. Was this the doubt that he had been warned of? Time to 'go with it' he thought, since he could barely contain himself. He was outraged. Everything

258

became abundantly clear in one swift instant. He hadn't been trusted with the truth because they didn't trust him to do the right thing, anyway. They didn't know him as well as they thought they had!

Then he just had to let some of it out "Great, I get caught up in the middle of the biggest domestic squabble of all! Well, doesn't that beat all?" Then he turned to the sky and shouted "*NOW* WHAT DO I DO?"

"He won't answer you that way." she informed him in a low voice that sounded like it came from extensive experience.

"I know, that was just to make me feel a little better. You know?"

"*Believe* me, I do. I've done it myself enough times."

"But a *domestic squabble?*"

"It's why Callicrates quit. You're not thinking of quitting too, are you?"

"It has crossed my mind...tell me about Callicrates."

"Not much to tell. He was handsome, strong, brash and most of all a *believer*. You have your doubts, so this news isn't as much as a let down. For him, it was a *devastating* blow."

"I see..."

"I know that nobody in law enforcement likes domestic cases, but this is what it is." she said shrugging.

"Yes, I see...sooo, what happens now?"

"Whatever you *want* to happen." she said with a mischievous glint in her eye.

"Oh, *that* helps!"

Harvey was getting sick and tired of these answers that weren't answers. Not only was he getting those from Metatron lately, she was doing the same thing!

"Look, I understand your confusion at such answers. To make it clear, it's all about *free will*. You have the power to go anywhere and do whatever you want, right?"

"Well, yes." he replied cautiously as if wary of being led by a crafty lawyer in a particularly nasty legal case.

"Then *take* it." She clenched a fist in the air "*Do* what you want. Forget him, he's a pussycat, trust me on that one, just get the job done - whatever it turns out to be! Don't let anybody *tell* you what to do.

259

Sure, take good advice, but do what *you* want."

"What about..."

"Judgment?"

"Yes. I don't want to wind up some place like this."

"Ha! Wasn't it you who said that you needed no rewards for doing the right thing, because then you might be doing it for all the wrong reasons?"

"Yes, I *did* say that actually." he answered apprehensively. He thought about it for a moment and started to ask "How did you..."

She cut him off again. "Well, the same thing goes for doing something *he* may not approve of! Don't let fear of punishment stop you from doing what you *know* has to be done. They are two sides of the same coin."

"Uh?"

"My being here? Well, yes it is a sort of punishment, but you are a special case. He chose you because you will behave a predictable way in most, if not all, situations. If you are true to yourself, you'll not disappoint him. Stop second-guessing what he or anybody else wants you to do and do what you *know* is *right*."

Harvey thought about this for a moment. His belief system was being challenged. He had been told that most cannot handle the truth. But what was the truth? He had been assured that he could not trust this entity before him, but he *could* trust his instincts. Both were in agreement - she was right! He somehow knew deep inside that she was essentially good, albeit greatly misunderstood. Or...perhaps, just perhaps it was *she* that didn't understand.

Was this a trap? Was she trying to convince him to do wrong? Or was this, as it appeared, a simple case of escalation between a feuding couple? This was getting to be a lot of pressure. Perhaps she was trying to get him to take her out of here...

"Hey, if nothing else, remember that 'no good deed goes unpunished'!" she offered with another mischievous grin.

"I will give it some serious thought." he finally said, after pondering for a few moments. She seemed satisfied with that.

"I suppose you want a lift." he said, deliberately not phrasing it as

260

an offer, knowing full well if he had offered, she could accept and he'd be unable to stop her. This way, he was only finding out if she wanted one.

"Not especially." came her surprising answer. "Not unless you want to join the *dark side!*" she added with a wink and a big grin.

"Uh, no." he answered flatly. "No dark side stuff for me. But why don't you want to leave this place?"

They stopped walking and she faced Harvey. "You've no doubt been told many things about me, designed to prejudice your mind against me, I can understand that. Be that as it may, I was captured and sentenced to walk this planet for an aeon. Well, that time is almost up, so why bother cutting it a little short with the risk of further sentence when I can just wait for the front gate, as it were, to swing open wide and let me walk right out?" She spread her arms at her sides and then upwards as she spoke.

"How long?"

"Not much longer now. A day, a week, a year or a century? Who can say? All I *can* say is 'any time now.' So I might just as well wait." She looked down at her bare feet. "What I *would* like is a decent pair of shoes."

He looked puzzled. A century sounded like a long time to him, even given she *was* immortal. "Um, sorry. I didn't bring any."

"No matter. It was worth asking. They wear out so quickly, but I just love a good pair of shoes."

"An aeon seems like an excessively long sentence. Besides, I heard you were 'bound for a thousand years', not imprisoned for a million."

"I *was* bound for the first thousand years. Bound from doing anything to mankind. A thousand years is a much easier concept for early man to understand, over an aeon. You see, when you are dealing with the eternal beings, you can get little squabbles like this - ones that last millions of years. Most of the time, we get along fine. Hey, things have been great for billions of years at a time. Really they have." she said reassuringly, as she placed her hand on his shoulder and looked into his eyes. She quickly added "Not that I'm *that* old mind you!"

The old feminine desire to always appear younger that she really was seemed to be truly universal, or perhaps she was the source of it - and other things.

To Harvey, her touch felt like love itself. A warm flush feeling went through his whole being. He thought that he felt as an infant must when it is being held by it's mother for the first time. She seemed like she had everything anyone could ever want in a woman; beauty, intelligence, humor, understanding, patience, kindness...what was he thinking? This was *the* adversary! Not a woman as she appeared to be! She was the source of all evil in the universe! What was happening to him? Was this too much for him to handle? Was Metatron *right,* after all?

As if she sensed his internal conflict, she abruptly removed her hand from his shoulder as someone would when they touched something hot like a stove top, and diverted her eyes downward.

"I'm, sorry. I've forgotten what human contact was like, and the effect my touch has on people. Can you forgive me?" Looking up at him again, with more than a trace of sadness in her eyes. If this was an act, she was very good at it. T hen again, she'd have had an awfully long time to practice.

"Um...thhhat's okay." as the euphoria from her touch peaked and finally began to subside.

She batted her eyes at him sarcastically, and pursed her lips a little into a cute little mock pout. She knew just what he was going through, and make no mistake - she was enjoying every moment of it.

In an attempt to get back to fact finding, he said "I was told that you would bring about the end of Mankind."

"That's right. By *his* rules, when I *sire* a male child it will destroy mankind and rule. Yeah, right. Actually, I have several sons; the youngest is named Salpsan. If fact, I think you might like him."

He thought about it for a moment.

"Sire...?" said Harvey, very puzzled. "Is that the way he operates?" he asked.

"Yes! He *stacks* the deck!"

"That explains *a lot!*"

She seemed to think for a moment before saying "I suppose it does at that." as if deep in thought. Unless such things weren't possible anyway and he was saying those things to illustrate it...like the monkeys flying out of someone's backside...or not!

"What about the bit where if you say his real name *backwards* the universe ends?" he asked, almost chuckling.

"That's another one; his true name is a *palindrome!*"

They laughed together for a bit, their foreheads almost touching as they leaned toward each other. He instinctively reached up to put his hands on her upper arms, then caught himself. Not thinking about what he was saying, or the possible consequences, he asked "Are you *absolutely sure* he can't observe us here?"

"Of course! That was a stipulation I made on this little prison of his and another reason he didn't want to you come. He can't watch you while you're here." she added with an evil grin. "Here, you can do *absolutely anything* you want and get away with it, *clean!*" She raised and lowered her eyebrows rapidly a few times as if to give him both barrels of 'the eye'. "So what do you have in mind, 'BIG BOY?'" she asked in a sultry voice.

This brought on emotions that Harvey didn't much like. This was also one the reasons he was chosen for this job. What he wanted to do at this point was succumb to her overtures, she was apparently trying to seduce him, but the fact that she was married was enough for him to resist her charms - no matter what. Though difficult, this was the strength of character that made him the right man for the job - and yes, for this and a host of other reasons, this particular job required a man. The fact that he knew who and what she was, was also more than enough to keep him honest. If these things were not true, there was also the fact that he would have wondered if she was truly attracted to him or was it that he was one of only two men to come along in literally one million years? Although he was not much experienced with women, and that may be the result of this, he had always felt that any relationship should be for the right reasons. That little doubt would have done it too. This only served to frustrate Samantha all the more, but she didn't show it. A simple kiss would have been a 'mind-blowing' experience for him, to say the least!

263

There was so much he wanted to say, but just like an inexperienced schoolboy he said nothing. He only chuckled a bit to himself as they walked toward his waiting shuttle.

After a while she broke the silence and said "Nothing personal, but since you work for the 'enemy camp' as it were, there will be times I must try to thwart your plans."

"Which times would that be then?"

"Pretty much all of them! He, he!"

"Sam."

"Yes, sweetie?"

"Did you touch Callicrates, too?"

She seemed to blush. "A girl doesn't 'kiss and tell'! Not to worry though - I like you *better*."

Harvey knew that Callicrates was bold and daring, but to get that 'friendly' with, with HER? After feeling her hand on his shoulder for a mere second, he could understand completely. How did Callicrates leave the planet at all then? There still had to be more to all of this, there just had to be!

"As much as I hate to say it, you should go. Your ship is low on power. Very soon now it will be too late for you to leave. You don't want to get stuck here, *believe* me." He appreciated her apparent concern for his well-being...then she took on a 'coy' posture and batted her eyes "I'd kiss you good-bye, but that just might kill an innocent little boy like you. It has happened before. Poor, poor Aaron." Then she giggled softly in a way that was almost menacing. It made the hair on the back of Harvey's neck stand up.

Those words pierced him like an arrow and his eyes went wide. He thought to himself 'Yeah, but what a way to go!' Her amusement at someone's death from a kiss took away doubt that she was indeed evil. He knew he had to leave, so he simply nodded and climbed aboard the shuttle. As the door was slowly closing he asked "See you on the outside?"

"You can bet on it! Even if you no longer captain the Ezrael!"

That last bit filled Harvey with a feeling of foreboding, like the feeling you get when your boss gives you a veiled threat that is directed at your continued employment...then he remembered how Callicrates had quit after his meeting with her. Did they get together somewhere? It was almost unthinkable! But then again, it may have been a long time ago but it certainly wasn't a million years.

As his shuttle headed for the sky, she muttered "That's my boy!" with a sly smile.

There were lots of questions when he returned to the Ezrael, but Harvey was in no mood to answer many. This made Linda worry a bit, but she would soon get over it. At least until Samantha got out!

31
COMEUPPANCE
"What do you see?"
"Just desserts."
"Ooh, do they have *pie?*"

"Sir!" said the Lt. rather urgently.

"What is it?" asked Harvey.

"I've lost control of the helm."

"What? That isn't supposed to be *possible!*"

"Someone or something set a new course, and try as I might, I can't get it to divert...much, then it gets right back on that course!"

"Where are we headed?"

"A planet called 'Douma'." he replied after checking the navigational system.

Harvey checked the Butator display:

Douma: "Silence of the grave"
So named because it was the planet of choice for interment of individuals that wished perpetually undisturbed burial sites. The natives are a quiet lot that possess formidable psychic capabilities, and prefer few visitors outside of funerals. Quiet minds like yours, however, are welcome, and short visits by others accompanying said minds are allowed, but barely tolerated. This is the form of their galactic trade. They are neutral, and have successfully resisted mind miners for millennia. Mind mining is like data mining only with minds. Such information that can be retrieved this way is often of great value. It is one of the best methods of interrogation.

The planet is the final resting place for important and/or powerful people. Some who have been made immortal and have also been punished for their crimes by interment here.

The local stone is very tough and makes for practically impenetrable structures. The natives also prevent visitors from defiling grave sites, or releasing prisoners. Proceed with caution.

Note: a powerful psychic in their own right could theoretically manage it.

"Why would someone want to go *there?*" Harvey asked himself aloud.

"You don't think that maybe..." said the Lt. worried that someone had died.

"Trust me, we'd know if that had happened, and we'd help them if it had." answered Harvey as he inquired further.

Butator Display:
Individuals onboard who are capable of diverting the ship beyond the helmsman's control:

1) Simkiel Harvey Johnson
2) Gladrina Urim
3) Aniyel Urim
4) The small gray aliens in storage locker 18.
5) Dr. Cornelius Morax

He was relieved not to see Samantha's name on the list. The last name, however, caught his attention. The S*I*P*Es had informed him that Morax liked to plan an operation to the point where his enemy could not react in time, if at all. Was this one of those times? Had Morax finally crawled back out of the woodwork? As if to answer him, the ship's klaxons went off.

"What's happening?" demanded Harvey.

"It looks as though the ship's self destruct mechanism has been activated!" exclaimed the chief.

"There isn't one..." said Harvey in a puzzled tone, just before the helmsman cut him off.

"The helm is completely cut off now. I thought we were approaching the planet, but I can't be sure."

"Someone has launched a ship!" reported a technician from the other side of the bridge.

The main screen was showing a blurry image of a ship leaving the equator and heading down to the planet below.

"What is happening?" demanded Harvey.

There was a lot of activity and general panic on the bridge as all systems were going haywire. The noise and confusion was giving Harvey a headache.

"STOP IT!" yelled Harvey, and everything went instantly silent. Pleased with himself, he smiled and said "Now perhaps we can make some sense of all of this." as everyone started at him. Not only had they never heard him raise his voice before but the ship seemed to have listened to him as well. The main monitor was now clearly showing the trajectory and specifications of a lone ship on it's way down to the surface. The elusive Dr. Morax was indeed onboard.

Harvey turned to the chief. "Can we trust these readings?" he asked earnestly.

"You tell me." said the chief, shrugging. "Beats me what just happened."

"If I may..." interjected the Lt. "It's typical of his tactics to confuse the enemy, so I doubt that any of what just happened was any real threat."

"Obviously not, as the ship does not *have* a self-destruct." said Harvey.

"I've got it!" said Linda who had been analyzing the systems failure ever since it had started.

"Somehow, don't ask me how, he managed to hypnotize the ship."

"He *WHAT?*"

"The autonomic systems report that the delusion has been dealt with and that Morax is actually onboard that shuttle." she added, as the vessel she was indicating landed on the surface.

"The question is 'Do we go after him'?" said Harvey.

"Let him go, and good riddance too!" said the Chief.

"Escape is not his plan." said Argent in a deep voice, and everyone stared at him. "What?" he said shrugging.

"Never mind, but he must be up to something." said Harvey.

"That's absolutely right!" said Swanson. "And it ain't good! You

268

can bet on that!"

Harvey gave the Major a questioning look.

"You can bet your life on it." he said soberly.

"Tractor beam?" Harvey asked Linda.

"Not really...he just got out of the ship." she said, checking her panel.

"So, we go after him?" Harvey asked the crew, focusing on the S*I*P*Es, since they knew Morax.

"Most definitely." answered the Major. "We can ill afford to let him go free. He *is* our problem after all."

"I think I know what he is up to." offered the android.

Harvey gave him a look.

"The scanners report that he has Mastema, and the true ankh."

Harvey looked puzzled. Surely they had met Mastema, one of Samantha's minions.

"A sword, and a key." said Pymander. "Most names have practical meanings too."

Harvey gave the android a look that said 'why didn't you say so in the first place?' then he asked "So there is something down there he's after?"

"Yes, and it isn't pretty." said Pymander in a reflective tone.

"Will everybody please stop saying that!" exclaimed Harvey with more than a little frustration in his voice.

Pymander, Argent and Swanson all shrugged.

"So it's decided then. We go after him." said Harvey.

"I suspect that there is no time to lose." said the Major solemnly.

After a tense moment of silent inaction, they all headed for the door at the same time.

* * *

Down on the planet, the soldiers cautiously led the way off the shuttle.

"He won't be waiting for us, it'll be more like a race to whatever he is after." offered the Major.

"This way." said the android as he sped down a path leading into a valley.

"You've been here before?" asked Harvey on a hunch as they walked briskly along the path.

"Yes. A long time ago when he was interred."

"He who?"

"Jambres."

"Who the heck was Jambres?"

"One of the two most powerful wizards ever. Incidentally, it's not *was* it's *is*."

"I thought you said he was interred here."

"He is, he just isn't dead."

"How can you be so sure?"

Pymander stopped his quick gate and stared Harvey right in the eye. "I know because he made himself immortal, as in not subject to death - *at all*. Over time, his crimes were so heinous that he was eventually overcome by sheer force of numbers. Thousands died horribly to overcome him. Once they discovered that they couldn't kill him, they decided to inter him here, for all eternity. He has probably passed beyond madness, alone in the dark all this time. Now it looks as though Morax may be able to steal his immortality *and* his powers."

"Powers?" asked Harvey, almost panicking.

"I said he's a wizard. There really isn't much he cannot do."

"Except maybe escape from a pyramid." offered Swanson.

"A what?" said Harvey.

Swanson pointed. Sure enough, ahead of them was a rather sizable black pyramid in the valley, its outline a little difficult to make out against the black stone cliffs.

The rest of the party looked on in awe.

"Hurry, there is little time to lose."

32

PSIANCE
"That's hardly psientific."

Just in view of binoculars, the saw Morax use the sword somehow to open the pyramid.

"Damn! He's getting in!" remarked the Lt. He then motioned to his men to quicken their pace.

Now running, they arrived over a small hill just in time to see Morax look over his shoulder, smile and disappear into the pyramid.

The Lt. let off a round that left a mark on the pyramid where Morax had just been standing.

"OOOhhh! I hate that!" said Argent, frustrated at Morax getting away yet again. He searched up and down using his sensors not able to even see a crack in the incredibly tough stone.

"How's it open?" he asked as the android walked up to him.

"Allow me." said Pymander as he pulled out a sword and tapped the pyramid with it.

There was no sound as the massive stones parted, revealing a small room. He motioned for the Lt. to enter first.

Satisfied that there was no danger, he waved the rest of the party in. The opening sealed silently behind them.

"Not to worry." said Pymander as Harvey raised an eyebrow at him.

"This, is the first of thirteen chambers we have to get through." announced the android. Each has it's own unique exit. The problem is they are puzzles and we have to solve them faster than Morax can in order to catch up to him. So start looking for a clue."

"What is that pyramid made of anyways?" asked Swanson, who is curiously looking at the stone itself rather than for a door as the others were.

"Stone." said Harvey.

"Jolly joker! I mean, what kind of stone."

"*Black* stone." said Harvey with a smirk.

"I have never seen stone like this before..." remarked DeSoto, his voice trailing off as he operated his hand scanner "It's more like a

271

mineral ore...WOW!...it's harder than pure Lonsdaleite. It's really tough stuff!"

"It can't be that tough, my pry bar just scratched it, see?" said Swanson pointing at the mark he had just left on the wall.

"I think if you check, you'll find that your pry bar left some of itself behind." answered DeSoto.

Sure enough, on close inspection by the soldier, that was indeed the case.

"Son-of-a-gun!" said Swanson as he looked at it, puzzled.

"Found it! Hieroglyphics." said the Chief as he stood waiving his arms, getting the others to gather.

"How do we open it?" asked Harvey.

"HellifIno!" said the Chief.

Pymander approached the wall and made a few gestures with his arms, and the wall silently parted. He then looked over his shoulder and said "We don't have time to mess around. Those were simple instructions.. and a warning."

As the last one entered the next chamber, the door closed behind them.

"Okay, now what?" Harvey asked the android.

"I don't know." he said, with a hint of dismay in his voice. Obviously, he did not like not knowing the answers.

"Really?" asked Harvey, truly surprised.

"As I said, there are thirteen doors to the inner chamber, I only knew how to open the first."

"Thirteen? Yes, you said...any connection to..."

"No...it's meant as bad luck this time, like the thirteen steps on gallows."

"Oh."

"So what was that stuff you did to open the door?" asked the Lt. as he waved his arms around in a way that was vaguely reminiscent of what the android had done.

"Metaphysics. Harvey understands."

The android proceeded to the next door to examine it, and the Lt. looked at Harvey inquisitively, who only shrugged back at him as they both followed the android to the next door.

The doorway was a blunt triangle. There were actual screws on the corners of the recently smashed control panel. Harvey and the Chief exchanged looks.

"Go ahead." said Harvey.

The chief shrugged, and began to remove what was left of the panel. "Looks like Morax was trying to slow us down." he said as he began to work.

Sure enough, it had wires inside with electricity running through them.

"I'll be darned if this isn't of Earth, I mean Urantian, construction." he said as he worked.

"Well, they say that Jambres is from our planet." offered DeSoto.

Harvey turned to him and said rather politely "Yes, but he didn't design this place."

"What's worse..." said the Chief as he tested various leads by feeling the current with his fingers, "...is that he left home thousands of years before this sort of technology...went...into...use...go it!"

The door slid open with the sound of an electric motor driving it this time and they saw Morax look over his shoulder as he went through the next door.

Thinking and acting quickly, the Lt. got a single shot off. He saw a small cloud of red spray from the point of impact.

They bolted toward the next door, just to run into it as it closed.

"I hit him, I *know* it!" said the Lt.

"It's hard to miss with those new-fangled bullets."

"I'm loaded with the original kind." said Argent, examining the clip he had just pulled out of the gun.

"Drat!" exclaimed Harvey at the closed door. "Let's hope that you slowed him down enough." he said to the Lt. "What are you doing with the old kind of ammo?"

The Lt. shrugged, looking puzzled. He was trying to save face here. He had forgotten to change his ammunition. He had been practicing with regular style ammunition, manufactured by the ship because he had learned that the smart bullets were making bad marksmen of the troops and he didn't want to lose his shooting skills, even if they were no longer necessary. The mistake was in Morax's favor and he was mentally kicking himself for it.

"Well, at least we're gaining on him." said Linda in an attempt to cheer things up a little.

Harvey looked over the doorway, the frame and the rest of the room. "There's no *panel!*"

"It's a puzzle." said Linda, who had just noticed the writing on the wall. "One of the ones with the moving squares..."

"Looks like a scrambled picture." said the chief, scratching his head.

"This is something I am good at." said DeSoto as he began expertly sliding the panels.

The rest of them exchanged impressed looks as Harvey said "I knew I kept you around for some reason."

"Very funny!" answered DeSoto over his shoulder as he finished the fresco. It looked like an Egyptian, holding a staff that was also a snake.

"The one on the left looks like Moses." muttered the Chief.

"It is." said Pymander. "Jambres and his partner Jannes were the ones that challenged Moses in ancient Egypt, so this is an appropriate design."

"I don't get it, this puzzle is solved, the door should open." said DeSoto.

Linda reached forward and touched the door. It opened and the fresco was instantly scrambled again. As she went to move forward into the next room, Harvey held her back from the threshold. He wasn't going to risk an attack from Morax.

"Except into danger." He whispered into her ear.

Linda smiled. He was learning.

The Lt. entered with his gun at the ready.

There was no Dr. Morax to be found. He had moved faster than they had hoped.

The next door had a circular lock in the center of it with eight dowels sticking out, also arranged in a circle.

"What the heck kinda lock is that?" asked the Chief, attempting to push the pins in like buttons but they were not budging.

Harvey approached it, and moved one of the pins. "I had a puzzle like this when I was a kid. My father brought it home and I solved it in less than a minute. He wasn't too happy because it was supposed to be virtually impossible."

"Well?" said Linda with her arms crossed, "We don't have time to dilly-dally." she said in her worst impression of Pymander, who gave her a look. "*Solve it* already!"

"The inscription states that one wrong move will fill the room with acid." said Pymander.

She leaned over to Harvey and said "Don't make any mistakes. No pressure."

Harvey shrugged, and started working the pins rapidly, counting to 170 in Gray binary. When he finished, there was a loud click.

He noticed that there was now a button in the center of all the pins. He pressed it and the door seemed to vanish, puzzle lock and all.

Still, no Morax.

Lt. Argent made a move to enter, and Harvey stopped him.

"My armor is warning me of impending danger." he said, as he stuck his head inside the doorway. He looked left and right, but there was nobody. There were panels on the floor with ancient Egyptian numbers on them and hieroglyphics on the far wall. His body armor let him read them. "It reads 'The floor will fall if careful steps not taken. The correct path is the prime path'. What does that mean?"

"Perhaps, prime numbers." offered Linda pointing at the numbered floor panels. Sure enough, there was a trail of blood droplets across the prime numbered panels.

"Well, off we go then. Everyone that cannot read the numbers, just follow closely."

Cpl. Swanson scanned the floor with his visor. "Hey, just scan for blood guys, use your UV tracker lights, mad man Morax left a trail."

Harvey, Linda and Pymander took less direct routes in order to speed things up, because they could read the numbers using their body armor. One soldier's foot slipped and the panel his foot touched, fell to reveal large spikes on a floor about 30 feet below. "Oops!"

The door opened easily, to reveal an almost featureless room. There was a definite line made in the stone at the halfway point across to the next door. The other half of the room was mostly dark. "Curious." said Lt. Argent as he approached the line as if it were a land mine. He used an aerosol spray to see if there were any light beams. Nothing. But then he noticed the mist floating a lot further out than it should have, and lingering in the air a lot longer, as well.

He placed a spent shell casing he had picked up earlier and held it in mid air past the line, then let it go. It floated in mid-air as one might expect in zero gravity.

"Yep, no gravity beyond this point." he said over his shoulder.

He stood up and directed his tactical light on the far wall. Sure enough, it was covered with tiny, yet sharp-looking blades.

"Oh no..." said Pymander. "Those look like they are molecular blades."

"What's that?" asked Harvey.

"One of the few things that can easily breach your armor. In fact, there is nothing they cannot cut like a hot knife through butter. It's probably what the locals use to cut the stones."

"How's that?" inquired Linda.

"The taper goes all the way down to a single molecule. It is as sharp an edge as is physically possible. They are metal crystals grown specifically to be the ultimate cutting edge. Problem is, they can only be about five inches long, so they only work as daggers, and not swords and axe heads as was originally wanted."

"Damn. We had better take good aim then." said Argent, with his light trained on the far door, where the ceiling met the wall. "Then there's solving the puzzle to get past it."

"I think getting there without being shredded *is* the puzzle." said Pymander, almost under his breath. "I should go first. I am the most expendable."

"Do you forget how much experience I have with zero gravity acrobatics?" asked Harvey.

"No, but in case there *is* a puzzle to solve, I can tell you about it once I am there. If someone else goes and even brushes against one of those blades..."

"Gotcha."

The android took very careful aim and went for as low a velocity as he could. Stopping in zero gravity after launching into mid air was trickier than it seemed unless you had something to grab hold of. There didn't seem to be any handles on the far door. It seemed plain and featureless. As he floated though the air, several of the party held their breath. As it turned out, the door is a spring loaded 'trap door" so speed does not matter as much that accuracy.

Pymander's head momentarily poked out of the door. He looked to his right and reached for one of the knives imbedded in the wall. He tugged at the handle end that was stuck in the wall, and it gave way after a little wiggling. Rushed for time, he only removed a few blades to clear some space to make it safer for the others, in case they partially missed the doorway or instinctively grabbed the sides of it.

"They ARE molecular blades, so be *very* careful!" said Pymander.

The Lt. made the next leap. He pulled a rope out of his backpack, and handed one end to Swanson to tie it off somewhere. There was a convenient handhold on the door frame, presumably for this very thing or even something to grab for once one entered the room. Once Argent tied the rope to the corresponding hand hold at the far door, Swanson tested it by jerking on the rope twice. Satisfied it was secure, he pulled himself along by the rope. It worked very well. One by one they took turns and there was no incident.

Linda was next.

While the others were coming over, Linda took notice of the blades that Pymander had removed from the wall. They were stuck in the floor, all the way to the hilt.

"Don't bump them." the android said as he noticed her looking at them intently.

"Why? What's going to happen?"

"Well, for starters, they can cut along the floor in blade direction, slicing the stone as they go."

"No. Surely not." she said in total disbelief.

Pymander simply grabbed one of the knives by the hilt, and effortlessly slid it sideways leaving a slit in the floor where the blade had been.

"Son of a gun!" she said as she looked closely at the slit in the floor.

"There are only two ways to carry one. Either you hold it by the handle all the time or you use a scabbard that clamps onto the hilt and has rigid sides that are suspended in mid air, just over the blade's surface. Like this one."

He produced a slender plastic-like scabbard, pulled the blade out of the floor and snapped it into place inside the protective housing.

"There." he said handing it to her. "That blade will cut *anything.*"

"How can it? It's thick enough and should bind when you did your little trick there." she said looking at the slit in the floor.

"It's an engineered crystal. Self repairing and maintaining, and thinner than it looks! Almost like the organic technology of the ship. Indeed it is like crystalline life. The edge goes down to a single atom, and the crystal also catalyzes the cutting action by borrowing electrons, allowing for molecules to part. The sides of the blade help compress matter by absorbing the space between molecules. This causes the cut surface to be more dense than the surrounding material. It's actually quite interesting science that went into these."

"Okay, who made them and why?"

While the others arrived one-by-one, Pymander was able to fill Linda in "Back in the old days the Shekinah allowed high technology, thinking it could serve her. One high technology world she conquered, which she necessarily made into 'believers', made the blades to breach your style of armor - to kill your kind of 'meddler'. Over time though, with the help of their high-technology they learned the truth and managed to free themselves. Then, she came back with far superior forces and destroyed their planet by sheer, brute force. It cost her a lot of ships and followers, so she set a limit on technology ever since; no space flight allowed. Those that already have well established space flight are allowed to keep it, but are not allowed to advance much more; and those that do are bombed back to the stone age. They may lose infrastructure, but most of the knowledge remains. That's why they seem to have 1880's technology trying to do things a century ahead of them, like nuclear power. You know, what you called steampunk on your world."

"I am sure that's a fascinating subject for further discussion in the near future but right now we are short on time." interjected Harvey, now that everyone had managed to arrive.

"Quite right." said Pymander. "Now let's take a look at the next door." as he grabbed and sheathed a few more daggers. These things come in handy!

Strangely, the new door had not appeared until the last of their party had entered and the entry door had vanished once again. Curiously, it was merely a doorway that let to a small chamber at the end of a long hallway. Argent caught a glimpse of Morax turning a corner at the end of the hallway, in a fire protective suit. He squeezed off a round but managed only to tear the shirt at the neck, and make Morax move all the faster around the corner as the hallway erupted in flame.

"Darn automatic bullets! They made me a bad marksman! I *knew* it! I wouldn't even qualify now with shooting like that!"

"Take it easy soldier. Two sightings and two hits. Not bad."

"I didn't take him down!"

"Take it easy. We'll get him."

"Swanson, give me one of your clips! I don't care about my lack of practice, I want that guy - I'm changing ammo *now!*"

Swanson grinned as he tossed the Lt. a clip. And said "Ooo-rah!".

The flames gave way to intense heat, far beyond the flash point of paper, and it was a long hallway. By the time one reached the other end even sprinting one would get fried.

"You only had a split second to react. You'll get him next time." said Harvey reassuringly.

"Now that I have smart bullets, sure, but what worries me is there won't *be* a next time."

"Okay. How do we get past this?" Harvey asked the rest of them to change the subject, after giving the Lt. a light pat on the back.

"I'll bet the controls to turn it off are at the other end, and Morax isn't about to accommodate us." offered Pymander. Then he stepped forward and whispered something into Harvey's ear. He perked up and said: *"Really?"* The android nodded.

"There's no other way?"

"No unless you want Linda to do it." he said flatly.

They were both standing close together with their arms folded, and looked in unison at Linda, who, smiled weakly back at them, wondering why, again, she was not in on the little bull session they were having. They both shook their heads and said "No." in chorus.

"I'll go. But everyone must turn their backs." said Harvey turning to the rest of the group. "Once I get the switch shut off, you come quickly down the corridor with my stuff." he said to Pymander.

"Won't you be killed?" asked Linda, trusting but worried as Harvey started taking off his gear.

"The molecular body armor we wear was made primarily to protect us from such heat. I need to go, we're wasting time." he explained as he pulled off his shirt.

"If you're telling us how you're going to do it, why tell us to turn our backs? And why are you taking your clothes off?" she asked, not quite on the same page at the moment.

"Surprisingly the two are connected. The body armor can only protect my body and anything I take with me will be incinerated. So, unless someone has a fire suit like Morax does, I have to go naked. Happy now?" he said as he popped off his shoes and loosened his pants. He gave her a look as if to ask her to stop looking at him.

Linda blushed and they all turned their back in unison. Pymander stood ready with Harvey's kit, as Harvey streaked down the hallway. Sure enough the flames engulfed him and he was not visible for a few moments. When the flames subsided, he waved Pymander on from the far end of the long hallway. Linda had sneaked a peek as he ran and only caught a glimpse of his posterior out of the corner of her eye. She smirked. It was almost payback for what had happened at the cluster. Besides, she liked what she saw when he removed his shirt, and was wondering about his 'tushy'... she *wasn't* disappointed. She was a little glad that *he* had not remembered that the body armor could simulate clothing. That way, she got to see his bare backside!

They entered the next room cautiously. There seemed to be the number seven on the walls and floor and so on, in various languages and number systems with a small pedestal in the center of the room. Harvey, cautiously approached the pedestal as the rest of them entered behind him, all looking around.

"What do you make of this?" asked Harvey.

"Looks like luck of the dice." replied Pymander.

"Well, call me thick but I think one needs to roll a seven." said Harvey, sporting a big grin. "Oh boy, they're blank." he said, as he picked them up to examine them.

"They reveal the numbers after they are rolled." offered Pymander. "True gambler's dice."

"Did someone mention dice? Let me, I'm good at dice!" interjected Swanson.

Harvey pointed to the ceiling where a large, heavy spike-covered grate was hanging. "I assume if we get it wrong, then that falls on us." he said. As if to confirm what he just said, the door slammed closed behind them. The Lt. tried to pry it open, but it didn't budge.

Swanson let out a low whistle. He was not about to risk everyone's life that way.

The Lt. approached, and said "Morax could always roll whatever he wanted. He never lost at dice." almost under his breath.

"Does he have telekinetic abilities?" asked Pymander.

"Yes, of course. But he can hardly move a pencil. Hold the phone! You mean he was *cheating* at dice?"

"Undoubtedly." said the android.

"The jerk owes me a farm." he muttered under his breath.

"Wait, there are no markings on these dice!" said Swanson after examining them closely.

"Nothing gets past you, does it?" said Pymander. "Didn't you hear us talking about it just now?"

Swanson grimaced and placed the dice in the android's outstretched hand.

Pymander placed the dice in Harvey's hands, looked up at him and said "Go on."

"ME?"

"Yes, you're a natural."

"Maybe at big, slow moving stuff, but *this?* They move too fast for my eyes to see, and there's two of them...and with no numbers on the faces?"

The android put his hand on the Captain's shoulder. "Just *think* the number at the dice, and don't try to force it. You'll do fine."

Harvey looked worried. So much pressure from everything riding on one roll of the dice - literally. He looked over at Linda and she smiled confidently at him. He picked up the dice, held his breath and rolled...

The cubes tumbled onto the small table-like surface on the tip of the pedestal, and one stopped almost immediately and revealed a five. The other teetered for an agonizing moment, and Harvey's eyes bulged as he concentrated. He only thought about the number seven and not anything specific about how to get there. The die finally fell over, revealing a two. There was a collective sigh as the exit door opened. At least that explained the lack of numbers *on* the dice!

Harvey was convinced that the feeling he got from that was why some people get addicted to gambling. The endorphin rush from risking it all and winning, is often addictive. Fortunately, he was not the type.

The next room was so plain and featureless as to be a mystery in and of itself. As they entered, Argent remarked "It's like the bottom of a drained swimming pool." With that, the door behind them sealed and seemed to perfectly match the walls. Then water started flowing down the walls. It wasn't gushing, but it was clinging to all the walls, presumably by surface tension. Silently the flow began filling up the room.

"You just HAD to say it!" said Linda playfully. Somehow she did not feel nervous about the situation. Harvey and Pymander were both calm as well, but everyone else seemed to be worried. Harvey and Linda's body armor had a system built into it to let them know of impending doom. This was one time those 'alarm bells' did *not* go off. As it turns out, the body armor is able to absorb dissolved oxygen from the water and deliver it to the blood, thus allowing for extended visits underwater. Had she known this at the time, Linda still would have changed into a mermaid on Phul.

There was a skeleton in the middle of the floor, hands still clutching the large stopper by a ring attached to it, as if having drowned in the attempt to pull it out of the floor...the men got distracted by this and also tried to pull the plug out, thinking that several military men would be able to succeed where a single man failed before. Scanner showed it is not a plug but just a diversion as it is *part* of the floor, so they gave up on the idea of pulling it out. The skeleton-count was steadily declining, not because the tests were getting any easier but because fewer and fewer had managed to get that far.

"Poor blighter. Never knew it wasn't a plug."

"We're doomed!"

"That, was only a diversion from the way out."

"If there *is* a way out!"

"I am sure there is a way out. There always is." said Pymander assuredly.

"That's easy for you to say pal, you can't drown!" exclaimed Argent.

"Oh yeah? Tell that to the dead guy!" added Swanson, frantically pointing at the skeleton. One of his deepest fears being drowning.

"These are all tests along the way, not traps, making it impossible for someone to claim they made their way to Jambres *accidentally.* They are not meant to stop us cold. There is *always* a way past each and every one."

"Let's think about this, there has always been a clue before. What have we missed?" said Harvey.

"I think the walls and floor looking like the bottom of a swimming pool WAS the clue." said Argent.

"Clue to what?" asked Linda.

By this time, the water was deep enough for some of them to tread water.

"I don't like this." said Argent nervously. He had already loaded a blank into his weapon to fire a mini harpoon at the ceiling in order to anchor a rope.

"What's *that* for?" asked Harvey.

"Well, it's all I could think of. If I can stick this in the ceiling, we can hold onto it and not wear ourselves out treading water."

"Okay, so what happens of the water completely fills the room?"

"Hey, one problem at a time!" he said smiling as he took aim.

When he fired off the harpoon it seemed to disappear into the ceiling, with the rope trailing behind it, and when the tension on the rope stopped, he yelled: "INCOMING!" and then the harpoon fell back into the water, fortunately missing everyone. "Well don't that beat all!" he exclaimed. "The ceiling is an illusion!"

Sure enough, as the water filled the room enough for them to reach the ceiling, it turned out to be a hologram of some kind. There was a platform all around the room just above it. They found it easy to climb out of the water into the next room. Once they were all out of the water, the floor seemed to fill in over the opening. Argent tapped it gingerly with his weapon then he stepped doubtfully onto the spot that used to be water. "Huh, solid." he muttered "*That's* no illusion." With that, he finally looked around at what the others were pondering. They were in the middle of a good, old-fashioned mirror maze.

"Great, just great." said Harvey.

"Well, there is a way to solve any maze." said Linda.

"Yes, I know, but knowing this place, if you make a wrong turn, you die."

"Somehow, I think it's only a maze in this case. Besides, your armor will warn you of danger." offered Pymander.

"Well, there's no time like the present." said Harvey "I'll take the right and Argent, you take the left. Two groups people! Let's move!" he added as he headed down the mirrored hallway.

"Can't I just open up, full-auto and smash all the mirrors?" said Argent after him.

"And get seven years bad luck for each? I don't think so!" said

284

Harvey over his shoulder as he disappeared around a corner.

"Besides, I bet the mirrors are bulletproof." said Linda as she followed Harvey.

Argent shrugged, and gingerly hit a mirror with the butt of his weapon, expecting it to crack if not shatter. Nothing happened, and all he heard was the sound of something very solid being hit with something small. Then, with a look of frustration on his face, he gave it a much more determined hit. Sure enough, there was no breaking it without a truck. He shook his head and said "Not *one* word!" he said as he motioned his group to follow. Many of them were grinning as they made their way into the maze.

As it turned out, Harvey was good at mazes, and that can be attributed to his childhood fascination with them, every time the carnival was in town. He had developed his own technique of sticking to one wall. In this case the right. He would find a few dead ends but if he simply hugged the same wall, he would eventually find his way out without fail. It worked so well here, that they almost caught up to Morax again.

Harvey exited the maze, just in time to see Morax. They made eye contact from only a few feet away, as Morax backed into a threshold of darkness, not unlike the doorways in the Ezrael. Argent, who had arrived a moment later, lifted his weapon for a shot, but didn't get a bead on Morax before he disappeared into the darkness. The Lt. visibly kicked himself when he realized he had smart bullets again and all he had to do was squeeze the trigger. "Luck of the devil!" he muttered as he made this realization.

"This is too much like Tuphon, only darker." said Argent as they entered the darkness. "You can almost cut it with a knife!"

True, the darkness had an intensity they hadn't even experienced on Tuphon, but since they'd had that experience, they at least had an idea of what they were up against.

"I also *feel* like I did on Tuphon." complained Argent. "Dammit."

"Keep feeling your way around." said Harvey, anxious to stop Morax, not only because of what he was attempting but he hated someone evil having a 100% success rate with his preferred tactic. He

285

wanted to not only win but beat Morax. He took a look around, and something make the back of his neck shiver just as he was about to enter the darkness. But he could see! Was this the armor?

"Hey, Argent, got a mirror?"

"Yeah, what of it."

"Try walking backwards and looking through the mirror once."

"Sure, sure." He shrugged in the darkness and pulled out a small metal signal mirror. Then he turned around and started walking backwards. Low and behind he could see! "What the *hell...?*" he tried turning around again and everything went dark again. "Darn thing works!"

"I know, I can see you." said Harvey as he walked past the Lt. backwards.

"How come you don't need a mirror?"

"My armor lets me see out of the back of my head if I need to."

"I gotta get me that stuff!"

"Your mind isn't quiet enough, remember?"

"I think I need to start taking lessons on that quiet mind jazz." he said as he followed the captain out of the affected area.

"That was weird. What's next?" asked Swanson.

As if to answer him it suddenly got very cold.

"Dang! Is it me or is the AC on too high?" Linda asked.

"It's on super-turbo." said Argent, shivering.

"You can turn around now." said Harvey, looking at a ice bridge over a chasm too deep to see the bottom. "Is that *safe?*" he asked.

"Only one way to find out." said the Lt. as he handed Swanson a rope. "No don't let go." he said with a stern look in his eye.

"Only if I see a pretty woman that wants me to hold both of he hands." answered Swanson.

"Close enough." said the Lt. he tried to cross the bridge, but it was arched up and over and was far too slippery. He kept sliding back down to the beginning.

"Have you got hooks?" asked Linda.

"Yeah, but that bridge looks too flimsy to take that much chipping." answered Argent as he sat down at the edge of the bridge.

286

Then his eyes went wide, and Swanson almost didn't manage to grab the rope as he sped across it as if sliding down.

"Ah, the gravity is wonky!" he said from the other side. "Come on over, I'll hold the rope from this side!"

"Can't you use those nifty tripod thing we used in the tunnels of Mehuman?" asked Harvey.

"They need to anchor into the floor. This stuff is much too tough to penetrate. We're stuck with Swanson and me as anchors, so one at a time if you please!"

One at a time without incident, they managed to cross the bridge.

"I wonder..." said Argent as he chipped the bridge ever so slightly with a hook. He was curious as to the strength and stability of the bridge, and since everyone was over it, why not try something?

"No Don't!" said Harvey, just in time to stop him.

Argent gave him a puzzled look.

"Don't 'burn the bridge', we need to get out of here too."

"Ahhhh..." he said, as he turned and put the hook away.

What neither of them knew was that the ice bridge collapsed after they left the room. It was programmed that way. Once the first in a party got across and out, the bridge fell. It was to thin-out the numbers of the not-so-bright. Then a new ice bridge began forming.

"Now what do we have?" asked Harvey.

"I don't know but I have a bad feeling about this." said the Lt.

"Make that two." said Swanson as he looked around.

Moments later they were each of them in a different room.

Linda found herself in a room that resembled some sort of tropical garden, wearing only a fig leaf.

Harvey, was in a room so full of spiders he sank into them like they were quicksand.

Lt. Argent, found himself in the aftermath of a battle and everyone was dead. "I must have blacked out! Dammit! I failed!" he said as he fell to his knees.

The Chief, found himself covered in centipedes, and they drained him like vampires as he crawled toward the door.

Swanson, found himself in a bar full of transvestites that were trying to kiss him. He recoiled in horror toward the exit.

Pymander, after seeing he was alone, simply walked through the next door, assuming they had been sent on somehow. Sure enough, he mets up with them in the next room.

"That was weird." he said.

"What was?" asked Harvey.

"All of you just disappeared."

"We got tested again, like in the tunnels."

"Oh, so you knew the way out did you?"

"Something like that." said the Lt.

"Your greatest fears?"

"Something like that." the rest nodded.

"Good, you could handle it then. Well, this is the point at which your experience is beginning to pay off."

"Is that how you always seem to know what's going on?" asked Swanson.

"Something like that." he said with a knowing smile.

"All right, all right, reminisce later. What's *next?*" said Harvey.

"This is the last one. Hence the test."said Pymander.

"Is that what I think it is?" asked Linda.

"What do you think it is?" asked Pymander.

"A sacrificial altar."

"Yep."

"Why is there a sacrificial altar in the middle of the room."

"Is ritual human sacrifice required?" asked Cpl. Swanson as he went over to it to examine it. "Hey, it's got it's own knife!" he said and started playing with the knife. It was diamond cross section, distal tapered and very nicely balanced, as well as razor-sharp-like fractured glass. It seemed very strong and above all, deadly.

The room had a small window or opening that allowed for them to see Morax, at the sarcophagus.

"Morax! It's not what you think! Batna *lied* to you!" shouted Harvey through the window. Morax had won and he knew it.

"I have no reason to believe you." replied Morax as he worked. "She told me the key to every lock, save the last one."

"Don't you see? It's a trap! You'll get stuck here and Jambres will go free!" Implored Harvey through the window, as the others frantically tried to open the last door.

"Just *one* grenade." said the Lt. in Harvey's ear as he held one up. "I can toss it through that little tunnel."

Neither of them noticed that Morax smiled because he had found the correct spot to place the ankh. There was flash of light and he sat down, out of view of the 'window'.

"Don't." cautioned the android. "The pressure will kill us too."

"How's that?" asked Harvey and the Lt. in chorus.

"In case anyone should use explosives to release Jambres, the inner chamber is lined with high explosives. Set it off and we get the pressure of over one thousand atmospheres instantly."

"Ouch! Okay, here is another idea..." Harvey's suggestion to fire a smart bullet through the little tunnel was cut off by the sound of the final door being opened. It had required blood - a cinch for Morax in his current condition, and this time the blood had come from Swanson accidentally cutting his finger on the sharp blade of the stone knife. He looked at the rest of them and smiled nervously.

"He may be a monster, but I wouldn't wish that fate on anyone." said Harvey as they entered the internment chamber.

The S*I*P*Es poured into the room they quickly surrounded Morax, pointing their weapons at his head. He was sitting on the floor with his back up against the sarcophagus, nursing his shoulder wound.

"No need for those gentlemen." he said in a different tone, with a weak dismissive wave of the hand. "*I'm* no threat to you."

"We're too late." said Linda.

"That entirely depends on your point of view - I like to think that you're just in time." he said as he placed his hand on his wound again and winced.

"That's *not* his voice!" exclaimed Lt. Argent.

"Then they've already made the transfer. Keep your weapons on him men, I hear that this one is even *more* trouble!" said Harvey.

"Not to worry gentlemen, I've long since learned to behave myself. You'll get no trouble from me." said Jambres, in Morax's body.

289

"How can we be sure of that?" asked Harvey.

"Because, gentlemen, I think I'm not much longer for this world..." his voice getting weak as it trailed off and slumped down slowly. "I must admit that I welcome the reaper this time." He looked up at Pymander, sighed a bit and said "Don't I know you, sir?"

Pymander dryly replied "We've met." with a sly smile and gentle nod.

Harvey noticed the twinkle in Pymander's eye, and planned on asking him about it later. For now, he just gave the android a side glance.

The Azbuga stepped forward with his medical kit to help the old man.

"I see in his memories that Morax set other things in motion..." said Jambres.

"Save your strength." said the Lt., as he opened his medical kit.

"Too late for that I'm afraid..." he said as he grabbed the Lt.'s arm. His voice was labored.

He took a deep, painful breath and said "Beware of Lilith!" He was almost unconscious by this time. "If you catch her again you should... *kill* her."

The Lt. gave him some morphine to relieve his pain.

"The gynoids are coming...and...they have...*changed*. They're...now cy.." were last words he managed.

The Lt. looked up at Harvey and shook his head. Morax, at least his body, was dead, and Jambres with it.

"I don't get it. Where's Dr. Morax?" asked Swanson.

"He's in *there*..." said Linda, pointing at the sarcophagus."...and he's *not* coming out."

"So he's...alone, in the dark, forever?"

"A fate I would not wish on the devil herself." he said, half muttering, as if in deep thought. What would it be like? He wondered.

With that, the chamber began to close. That is, the stonework began to slide down from the ceiling into the floor, making the room into a solid mass of stone.

They all exchanged looks. It was time to leave.

The Lt. looked as if he wanted to take Morax with them, but Harvey said "LEAVE HIM! LET'S GO!".

Linda turned her head back on her way out the door as she thought she heard frantic, muffled screaming.

* * *

"I shudder to think about what might happen, should Morax get out of there, in his new body, you know, with those powers and stuff." said the Lt.

"I'm afraid he would not have any extra powers as that has to do with his soul. He'd have gained physical immortality, that's all." answered Pymander.

"That's *all?* He was bad enough as an old man! Now what's he gonna do?"

"Relax. The chances of him getting out of there is practically nil. It was designed to keep Jambres in after all."

"Oh yeah? What if somebody busts him out? We got in there, so somebody else could!"

"Oh myyyyy...." said Pymander, pondering the implications.

"I'm satisfied he's locked up safe and sound." said Harvey as he approached them. "At least for the time being." he added after some thought.

* * *

Somewhere on the outer rim of th galaxy, Satrina Batna, aboard her flagship the Zebulon, was reading Nergal's report of his time on the Ezrael. Finished for now, she shut off her Forcas terminal and summoned one of her generals.

When the beautiful, muscular woman in chain mail armor came into the room, Captain Batna said "I want you to go to Douma, and retrieve someone for me. A pawn I set into motion a while ago has just been knighted." Her general grinned broadly, nodded and left the room to carry out the orders.

291

Satrina sat there quietly thinking about it for a moment, and began to gloat.She stepped out of her office onto the bridge.

"Have we reached the cluster detonation area yet?"

"Yes ma'am."

"Excellent. Any ships escape?"

"Only one, a harem, and one mail-room worker."

"A man?"

"Yes."

"Which harem?"

"The one we used on the captured soldier that works for Simkiel Harvie."

"Excellent! Recruit them as cybernetic Gynoids immediately, then send them adrift in the same vessel. Ask me for the co-ordinates when they are ready."

"What about the man, Joe Buckley?"

"Is he the one they called 'Lefty'?"

"Yes, that's the one."

"Have him harvested for Tyr leather."

"Right away."

The general left the room shuddering at Buckley's fate.

33
SEISM
as in
"Quake"

"Shake it up!"

Two human figures walked side by side along the lower edge of a wall of rock.

"The Butator warned that this ridge is dangerously unstable." said Linda.

Harvey directed his gaze up to the top of the cliff face.

"It wouldn't be good if that decided to come down now. There's no place to go." he remarked almost cheerfully, while looking around.

As if the cliff were listening, there was the sound of a small rock rolling down the cliff face, making a tinkling sound as it went. They looked at each other as if to say "Oh no!" in chorus. The single rock was followed by another then two then six, just before thousands of tons of rubble fell, burying the two clutching figures underneath the rubble. After the dust settled a thick red liquid flowed out from under some of the rocks. Apart from a few bacteria, there was no life there.

===

Harvey Johnson
will return
in
"Things That Go Bumping The Knight."

An excerpt from the next book:
"Things That Go Bumping The Knight."
* * * * *

They stood there at the mouth of the cave, staring into the darkness for a moment before entering. The guide had stayed behind because his job was essentially done, so Sir Hadar took the lead.

Torches do not alert a dragon as their light and heat are more to the dragon's nature. A flashlight gives off a different spectrum and it tends to annoy dragons so they used torches in the interest of stealth. Sir Hadar lifted his torch, and lit it with a form of sonic lighter. Lt. Argent lit his with a Zippo. Harvey just looked at his and it lit. Sir Hadar noticed this and said: "Nice trick." almost whispering, his voice echoing down the long stone passageway. Linda, not wishing to be outdone, lit hers the same way. Sir Hardar gave her raised eyebrows at her, impressed. They both simply smiled back at him. Keeping quiet was usually essential, to avoid waking the dragon.

Their precautions seemed to be effective, as they ran into no problems getting to the central chamber. The mountain of gold that greeted them was so large as not to be believed. It seemed to be the wealth of an entire planet.

"No way! No friggin' way!" said the Lt. "That's as much gold as our whole world has ever mined!"

"Yes indeed, it looks bigger than Pahadron's hoard... but of course it *cannot* be. But still..."

They all stared at him.

"What? I've *seen* it!" he replied indignantly.

Pahadron was the chief dragon, and therefore the largest and most powerful. A real terror indeed. They were beginning to think that Sir Hadar had, like many others, managed to see Pahadron and his treasure but barely escape with his life and limbs intact, only to decide to go after 'smaller game'. Which, wasn't too far off the mark.

It was said that Belphagor's treasure was second only to Pahadron's, still it was no where near the size. This pile that lay before them was indeed a larger than that of Pahadron and it made them nervous. Exactly how a dragon obtained treasure in the first place was a bit sketchy, but a dragon that could amass such a treasure in such a short period of time was even more mystifying.

They didn't have to wait long for their answer.

After a few of the party picked up, examined and then dropped a few items, the Lt. started climbing the pile.

"What are you doing?" Harvey asked him.

"I'm just climbing to the top to get a good look at the cave." he said over his shoulder.

Harvey looked over at Sir Hadar who seemed to be more concerned with the possibility of a dragon the size of a hotel popping out of nowhere.

As the Lt. climbed, he knocked down a small quantity of coins and other small gold items. It was practically the only sound. He noticed how some of the piles of plates felt a little spongy under his feet but he didn't notice the eye that opened as he walked past. Belfagor was not only a golden dragon, but he was hiding *inside* his hoard, which is why it looked so big and why the sensors didn't detect him. Gold was dense enough to block the sensors from penetrating the pile. What's more, the dragon knew it.

When he reached the top, the Lt. pulled out a small cylinder the size of a "D" cell. "Now?" he asked Harvey.

"Let her rip!" said Harvey.

"What is he doing?" asked Sir Hadar.

"He's getting us some light on the subject."

Just then, the entire cave lit up with a wonderful light that cast no shadows. The cylinder was an electro-magnetic light source from the Ezrael.

Sir Hadar's face lit up. "This is wonderful!" he exclaimed. "I've never seen light like this before!"

The Lt., had begun his trek back down the mountain of gold having left the light at the top of the pile.

"Hey! The hill's *MOVING!*" exclaimed Lt. Argent as he noticed his path was rising up out of the gold.

What happened next took only seconds to unfold, but for the humans, it seemed like a lot longer.

295

"SCALES!" bellowed Sir Hadar as he drew his sword and went into action.

The Lt. grabbed his M29 A1 only to slide down the Dragon's neck, stopping at the extra large horns on the head. Then he thought better of it and plunged his sword into it's neck, just behind him. The dragon flicked him off as one might flick away an ant. It's eyes followed his flight across the cave. Fortunately, both Harvey and Linda concentrated on slowing his flight, and he landed softly enough to not be seriously injured, but the wind was knocked out of him.

"He's gargantuan!" exclaimed Sir Hadar, noting that Belphagor was almost as large as Pahadron. That meant that this was not merely a fallen angel but a demi-god! That explained the gold! He could manifest as much as he wished, and probably kept his treasure short of Pahadron's out of respect of another demi-god due to his current form.

Sir Hadar's henchmen immediately pointed their spears at the dragon and advanced, taking the dragon's attention away from the Lt. They were brushed aside, and then reached for Linda with it's large talons. She tried to run, but was unable to get out of reach quickly enough to escape being grabbed. To say the least, she wasn't too happy about this so she started stabbing the dragon in the leg with a molecular dagger as it dragged her back towards it's maw. Her dagger had little or no effect and she couldn't get to her sword. She squirmed as much as she could and yelled "DO SOMETHING!" to Harvey. The dragon was amused by this so it arched it's neck and blew flames upward in what looked like a little celebration of victory, before lunch.

Harvey saw his chance. Though the dragon was very large, it was not on it's feet. Apparently it had only it's neck to maneuver and could only reach so far with it's talon because it was sitting on it's stomach. He ran underneath the up stretched neck with his sword drawn and shoved it right into the dragon's heart, concentrating on the most damage it could do. Before Sir Hadar could caution him against it, a fiery blast came out of the wound, blowing him back and melting the surrounding gold. It was like a high-speed lava flow.

* * * * *

PHUL OF SURPRISES